Spirit Bird Journey

Sarah Milledge Nelson

 **RKLOG Press**
5878 S. Dry Creek Court
Littleton CO 80121-1709

This book is a work of fiction. Names, characters, places, and incidents are products of the author's imagination or are used fictitiously.

> RKLOG Press
> 5878 S. Dry Creek Court
> Littleton, CO 80121

Library of Congress Cataloging in Publication Data

Nelson, Sarah Milledge
    Spirit Bird Journey
    Fiction
        1. Fiction
        2. Korea – Fiction
        3. Archaeology – Fiction

Library of Congress Catalog Card Number: 99-96124

ISBN: 0-9675798-0-5

RKLOG Press trade paperback printing, first edition.

Cover by Kristin Doughty

Printed in the U.S.A. by Eastwood Printing, Denver, Colorado.

*For the strong, swift, wise and
beautiful women of the Nelson clan:
Tracy, Cindy, Carrie, Erika and Morgan*

Flyingbird's Travels

Dragon River Village

Sacred Lake X

Jade Village X

Expedition from Bird Mountain Village

Tigertail, Big Bear,
Flyingbird

Three Rocks Village

X Bird Mountain Village
Flyingbird, Tigertail, Big Bear
and Children

X Rock Shrine
Village

X
Shell Island Village

X Acorn Village

The Prehistoric Characters in
Spirit Bird Journey

The Golden Clan of Bird Mountain Village

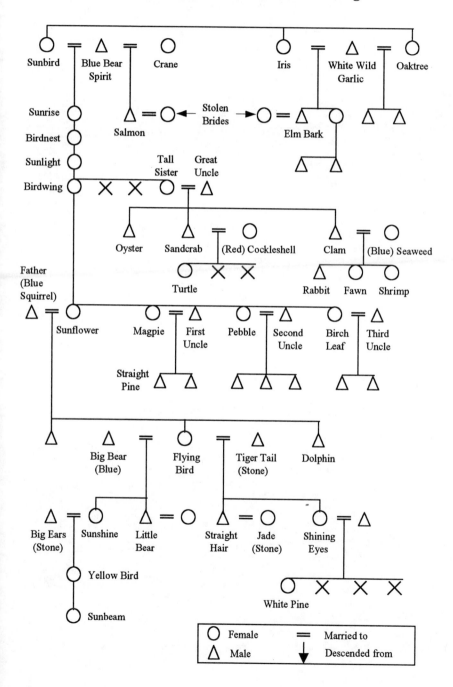

1

The cymbals abruptly stopped clanging, leaving a metallic aftertaste in my ear. I watched Elaine end her dance with a graceful turn. She untied the bow that held her costume together and in the same motion slipped out of it and handed it to the shaman's helper, bowing slightly and touching her outstretched right arm with the fingers of her left hand. Later I learned that's the polite Korean way to give people things. At the time I was just absorbing gestures.

As I sat cross-legged on the floor, I had to squint to keep my eyes open at all. Not that I wasn't interested in the ceremonies, but I hadn't slept for a day and a half. In this moment between dances, I looked around at the women here, and felt again the shock of faces like mine that I felt in the airport. At home, the only Asian faces I saw were in my mirror, and on my sister. Ed's blue eyes and sandy hair would be out of place here. It might teach him something about differences! I tried to think about something else. Unhealthy to dwell on him. I came to Korea to forget him.

To quash thoughts of Ed, I deliberately looked around the room, taking in the "orchestra" of drums and gongs, and the way the pale colors of the musicians' dresses set off the bright red of a large hourglass drum. The three musicians were women, who sat on a mat chatting idly. Along the side of the room, a table covered with plates of neatly stacked fruits and bowls of flowers stood in front of a wall of poster-like paintings. Elaine told me this was the altar. I was working on the concept.

The ceremony seemed to be over. I didn't understand it, but it was colorful and like nothing I'd ever seen. Three robed shamans danced themselves into trances, one at a time, like acts in a play. One did something with rolled-up flags, another gathered up what I supposed were blessings from the air, and put them into the skirt of the woman who was the center of activity. The third drank something from a brass bowl, and spat out the door. The *mudang* in charge of the ceremony was called Yol-i's Mother in her everyday life, but here she was addressed as *manshin*, meaning ten-thousand spirits.

After the *kut* each of the village women danced, one at a time. Several of them leapt about with abandon when Yol-i's Mother put robes on them. Their dances were laughingly critiqued by the other women. In my semi-stuporous state, I saw the *kut* as both serious and fun, a spiritual

1

occasion, but social, too. The women were enjoying the whole affair, including the patient. She must have believed in it. Maybe they all believed to some extent.

Yol-i's Mother gestured toward me.

"It's your turn now," Elaine nudged my bottom with her socked foot, "The *manshin* wants you to dance next."

"I only came to watch." I closed my eyes and tried to be invisible. "Leave me alone, Elaine. I'm still groggy from jet lag. I can barely keep my eyes open just sitting here. Next time? Don't you think there's been enough audience participation?"

The toe prodded again.

"You can't refuse, Clara, it isn't polite. Where's your anthropological spirit? I didn't bring you here to decorate the floor. You know we can't offend the *manshin* . . ."

I'll look a fool, I thought, grudgingly getting up. Give the locals a laugh at the awkward foreigner's expense. As I pushed myself to a stand, the *manshin* gave me a sharp look through narrowed eyes, tossed the blue robe to a helper, and rummaged through an old wooden chest that folded down from the front. With the robe over her arm, she bowed to the altar and rubbed her palms back and forth.

"This one suits you better," Elaine translated for her, as the *manshin* beckoned to me.

I was held back by a premonition of myself forever changed, but the shaman invitingly held out a robe of shimmering yellow-gold. I slipped into the sleeves, and she tied the ribbon with an expert hand. Unlike the crisp synthetic texture of the blue robe Elaine wore, this one was soft. It was an old robe, made of fine silk, but worn where the bow had been tied many times. Tiny triangles in various colors were embroidered on the edge of the collar and sleeves, and a pattern of flying cranes was woven into the fabric itself, like a brocade.

I sensed that the *manshin* had honored me by choosing this robe, although I didn't know why. A flash of recollection, as if I had been in a place like this before, came and quickly vanished. The room again looked as unfamiliar as it had when I first stepped up to the wooden floor. But I was suddenly wide awake. The dance became a homecoming to a Korea I never knew, or couldn't remember. I caught my upside-down reflection in the brass cymbals, and saw that the yellow-gold costume was becoming to my dark hair. Ed always called me "Jade Princess," which I took for irony, but now I felt like a princess. While I admired myself, the manshin placed a light headdress over my hair - a peaked yellow cap that matched the robe.

The drums began a slow rhythm. TONK, tonk, tonk, ta KUNK. I raised my arms tentatively and tried to copy the movements of the other dancers. At least I could begin with the slow and stately movements, even if I couldn't manage the jumping frenzy when the cymbals get fast at the end. Holding my arms shoulder high with elbows slightly bent, I shuffled my feet and made a turn.

The percussion beat continued, TONK, tonk, tonk, ta KUNK, but the room changed, and so did I. My feet became bird claws, gripping a wide wooden beam. I looked down on a dimly lit scene, which came into focus as my eyes adjusted. The room had an oval floor, dug down a foot or two into the sandy soil. It was well swept, bare except for a pile of dark brown furs. Two pottery jars covered with gourd bowls stood in a corner beside a bundle of twigs. In the center of the room, river cobbles outlined a square hearth where a small fire sent up red sparks.

At each end of the hut a crotched stick held the roof beam where I perched. Thick braided ropes with pendant tassels swagged from the beam, and a similar rope hung across the doorway. The other roof and wall supports leaned on the central beam, leaving high spaces at each end of the ridgepole for light and ventilation. A bundle wrapped in bark cloth lay next to me on the roof beam.

I noticed movement below, and peered at four women in black and white robes, lit by the flickering fire. Then I saw that these four surrounded another woman in a plain brown wrap-around, who gripped a large pole planted in the floor behind the hearth. A gray-haired granny thumped a small drum with her hand and chanted, while the others joined in after each line with a vigorous shout of "Ho!"

When the central figure of the tableau released a long drawn-out "H-o-o-o-o," mingling with the cry of a newborn infant, the chanting stopped. The drummer picked up the baby while another woman cut the umbilical cord with a shiny black knife. She washed the infant in briny water from a large pottery jar, wrapped her in a rabbit-skin blanket, and held her up to the mother.

"Congratulations, Sunflower, it's a girl! A *girl*!" said the older woman.

"Praise to the Hearth Spirit, a girl at last!" the other birth helpers whispered. Sunflower smiled.

The women attended to Sunflower. One washed Sunflower with water from the large jar, and others untied a bright yellow sash from the new mother's waist, and rewrapped it to hold moss and crumpled elm bark.

After helping Sunflower into a fresh black and white robe, they settled her into a thick pile of furs.

A woman picked up the afterbirth with a pair of sticks and dropped it into a small jar, scooped up and added the bloody sand, and replaced the gourd on top. Another woman sprinkled new sand near the hearth, and evened out the floor with a twig broom. The birth hut was tidy again.

The old woman looked up at me, and pointed with her chin.

"A powerful omen! The golden bird on the roof beam beside our family spirit is the baby's spirit guide, who came exactly at her birth. It's a wondrous sign, never seen before. It promises her a bright future but suggest there may be trouble in her life. We should name her for this event .- Flyingbird of the Golden clan. The bird will help her become strong and swift and wise and beautiful."

I was flattered to have a namesake, and would have smiled if my beak had let me. The women's faces, turned toward me, showed wide blue tattoos around their mouths, making their lips look huge. Their white ankle-length robes were appliqued with wide black curving designs. The young ones wore sunflowers in their brown wavy hair, but the oldest had fastened her hair at the nape of her neck with a carved bone in the shape of a bird.

After a slight bow to me rubbing their palms back and forth, they went back to the hearth, where each birth helper planted a stick in front of the fire. The sticks had curly shavings cut down from the top but still attached to the stick, each with a different design. They reminded me of stylized poodles. The women again rubbed their palms.

The older woman spoke.

"Hear us, Hearth Spirit, as we present to you Golden Flyingbird, first born daughter of Golden Sunflower, granddaughter of Golden Birdwing, whose other ancestors in this village were Golden Sunlight, Golden Birdnest, Golden Sunrise, and Golden Sunbird. Her mother's sisters, Golden Magpie, Golden Pebble, and Golden Birchleaf, are here to present the child to you. Flyingbird was born in the presence of her familiar spirit, a golden crested bird, and you, guardian of the Golden Clan, must also know her and help her."

Birdwing stood on her tiptoes and reached for the bundle beside me on the ridgepole. I felt her warm breath. She untied the cord, and unwrapped several layers of cloth, until at last a carved bone figure gleamed in the firelight. Each woman in turn took the figure in both hands, bowed toward the row of sticks, and asked for blessings for the child, while Sunflower held the solemn infant toward the fire. When Birdwing lifted the bone figure toward me, I stretched down to get a

4

better look. To my archaeological eye it seemed to be made from a long bone of a mammal, probably from a deer, maybe *Cervus nippon*. It was decorated only on one end, the other end whittled to a point. The carved end resembled a head, with daisy-petal-like bumps surrounding a crude face, with only circles for eyes and a mouth, and below that circles representing breasts.

One by one the sisters spoke to me.

"Golden Bird of Wisdom, keep this child safe. Help her to become wise in the ways of our people. Let her learn our stories easily and remember them well. Give her the courage to seek, and the persistence to find."

"Give her all those blessings and more," I added. "Let her have both love and independence, both adventure and security." My voice sounded only like a chirp to me, but to my surprise the women seemed to understand.

Rustling noises drew my attention outside through an opening in the eaves, where I saw other people gathered, waiting for the news. Birdwing took the bone figure to the door and announced the birth of Golden Flyingbird. The villagers repeated to each other in soft voices, "A girl! A daughter! To carry on the lineage! The village is saved! Give praise to the Hearth Spirit and Grandmother Moon."

A young man with a wavy brown beard and long thick hair stepped forward from the group, and Birdwing beckoned him into the birth hut.

"Greet your daughter, Blue Squirrel!" said Birdwing formally but with a big smile, exaggerated by her blue tattoo.

"What a beautiful child." Squirrel hugged Sunflower and pressed his cheek by hers. "You did well. The whole village is pleased."

Squirrel held out a translucent stone, almost gold. "I've brought you a crystal of topaz," he said to his newborn daughter. "It was lying near the path to the forest. It's golden, like your clan, so I knew the spirits left it there for you this morning. I don't understand the meaning of its location, but that will become clear in good time. In the meantime its powers will protect you. From this day, my little daughter, you will begin learning to be a wise leader."

Flyingbird's eyes followed the crystal, and her small fists waved in the air. Birdwing knotted a cord around the topaz crystal and fastened the cord around the baby's neck, to keep its crystal power near her heart.

The bone figure, pointed end down, was added to the row of shaved sticks. The group in the birth hut began to sing, while Birdwing picked up the drum again and beat out the irregular rhythm.

The sharp sound of the cymbals crashed into my attention and then stopped. I was back in the *mudang's* house beside the colorful altar, so different from the muted tones of the birth hut. My senses were heightened, making the altar seem to shimmer. In front of me brass bowls on pedestals held neatly arrayed cakes and candies, dyed with pinks and greens. Wine, rice, dried fish, and a cooked pig's head lay on the altar, surrounded by large paper flowers in primary colors. Pasted above the altar, bright paintings of various spirits blinded me with an avalanche of color.

"Back to 'reality,'" I thought.

Out of breath, I let the shaman's helper take the costume, and tried to dismiss from my mind the small thatched cottage with its new baby. It was only a vision, conjured by my jet lag. The *mudang* looked at me closely, but asked no questions. The village women clapped and laughed - "a wonderful performance!" - "not a bit like a foreigner" - "the girl is really Korean after all!"

After Elaine jotted her final notes, we said good-bye to Yol-i's Mother.

"Come to my next *kut*," she said to Elaine. "I'll call to tell you the time and place - and be sure to bring your new friend. She doesn't know who she is yet, but I will help her get to know her bones. She has a gift."

2

Elaine and I caught a bus back to Seoul, and found an empty booth in the dining room of International House for supper. She was the luck of the draw for a roommate, and I guess we made an unlikely pair, but we liked each other right away. She's two decades or so older than I, at least 50 pounds heavier, and my opposite in coloring. I've always been quiet and serious - a "good-girl" type, according to my sister. Elaine's a brash bushy-haired blonde, and she says and does whatever she wants to. I've never known anyone as free from conventions. She considers life a high adventure. She dragged me off to the *kut* when I'd barely put my bags down in the room, telling me I'd adjust to the time change better if I didn't sleep until bedtime, to get on Korean time right away.

I looked in despair at the menu with its unfamiliar letters made up of circles and straight lines. Pretty, but not a hope of reading it. "What's good for a confused stomach that thinks it's breakfast time?" I asked Elaine, not willing to admit that I couldn't read the menu.

"Try the *bibimpap* - it's just rice and veggies, with a raw egg. It's good."

"Goot for you, too," said a new voice with a slight German accent. "I saw you come in this morning. Do you spik English? May I join you?"

"Clara, this is Liesl, our resident art historian by training and Jungian dabbler on the side." Elaine made room on her side of the booth, and patted the seat beside her. "Slide in," she directed Liesl.

"Hi, Liesl, nice to meet you. Do join us."

Liesl's eyebrows rose.

"When I saw you I was afraid I'd have to expose my bad Korean," Liesl confessed to me, as she took up our invitation. "You speak English very well. Are you the archaeology student who's rooming with Elaine?"

I was annoyed, but tried to hide it.

"Guilty to the archaeology charge. But English is the only language I speak, so I hope I speak it well! I wish I knew even a little Korean. Today at the *kut* I learned *anyonghaseo*, which seems to mean hello, and *anyonghikasipsio*, a long-winded good-bye."

"Hey, pretty good!" Elaine complimented me. "I thought you were too tired to remember anything."

"I never thought about it before, but now it feels strange to be Korean born and not know a word of the language. Not to mention having to explain that my first language is English." I rolled my eyes to show I was kidding, and was rewarded with a laugh.

"Elaine's Korean is impressively fluent," Liesl told me. "Maybe she'll give us lessons. All I know is Chinese, which helps with reading Korean characters, but not with speaking. How does it happen you never learned the language at all? Didn't your parents speak Korean to you?"

"No, I'm adopted. My parents are of English descent. My Mom traces some of her ancestors to Plymouth Rock. She even belongs to the Mayflower Society. I've never thought much about Korea before now. I was told it was the land of my birth, of course, but Korea was nothing to me but the name of a far-away place."

"Can't you remember Korea from before you were adopted?"

"No. I don't know exactly how old I was, but I could barely walk when I was adopted. I have a recurrent dream that could be a memory, but there's not much to it. There's a lattice window in the dream, and people quarreling. Maybe it's just as well that I didn't remember. My sister Heidi came from Vietnam when she was three, and she had a hard time at first. I was eight then, and I was the only one she responded to, so I taught her English, and how to be American."

"Weren't you curious about where you came from?"

"We both just wanted to be one of the kids, to belong to the group, to be part of our family. Learning about our countries of birth was the last thing either of us wanted. Looking different was bad enough! Kids teased us and called us `slant eyes' but I'd tell Heidi not to cry - we had lots of friends, we didn't need the mean kids. Mostly we were accepted in the town we live in - liberal types, you know, with assorted odd-looking adopted children. One kid in my kindergarten class told me he could always tell adopted children, because they turn brown!"

"Only your eyes make you look Asian. You must curl your hair," Elaine scrutinized me without mercy. My mother would have thought her very rude.

"No, it has a natural wave. And my hair isn't really black, although it's very dark brown. I've wondered about that. Heidi's hair hangs like a thick curtain, black as ebony."

"I've seen lots of Koreans with brown wavy hair. Anyway, since you're small and dark-haired, you can melt right into the Korean crowd. I'm envious. No matter how well I master the language, I'll stand out as a foreigner. You'll always have that problem too, Liesl."

Liesl's long lank hair seemed silvery in the dim light. The two tall blondes exchanged a smile. They didn't really mind looking foreign. It was my turn to envy.

"Why did they name you and your sister after characters in a Swiss story? Do you know it?" asked Liesl.

"Every little girl in America must have read *Heidi,*" I answered with a knowing grin.

"Since I'm Swiss I'll have to adopt you myself!" said Liesl, making me feel accepted, but I went on to explain about the names.

"I was named after my grandmother - my mother's mother. There's a tradition going back many generations. This cameo ring" I waved my right hand - "has belonged to six Claras in a row. I think calling my sister Heidi was an afterthought, to go with Clara. It's trendy and cute, and suits her. The name Clara's a bit stuffy, but I like it. I'm serious, and it fits me. Still, I've wondered if I'd be a different person if I'd been called something like Melissa or Wendy. Do you think names influence people's personalities?"

"Of course. Don't you think I'm the personification of the Lily Maid of Astolat?" Elaine grinned, indicating her copious figure. "What was your Korean name?"

"I never thought to ask. Maybe my parents don't know."

The idea of having had a Korean name and not knowing what it was seemed worse than not knowing the language. Total strangers were asking me things I'd never thought about. Creepy. I'd taken too much for granted. Now everything seemed to be coming into question.

"How did you get to come here to study without learning Korean first? I learned Korean when I was here with the Peace Corps, and Liesl spent years and years grappling with Chinese, and because of that she can read the same characters in Korean. Didn't you have some background or at least a briefing or *something*? The Korean culture is full of pitfalls." Elaine sounded horrified.

"It's only a quirk of fate that I'm here. A Korean-American Club advertised a fellowship for Korean adoptees, as a chance to learn something about their native land. It seemed like a good chance to study Korean archaeology, so I put in a proposal. I thought Korean archaeology would be as interesting as any other, and I needed a thesis topic. A `window of opportunity' for a poor graduate student," I added lightly. I didn't tell them I was running away from Ed because my Asian face was unacceptable to his parents.

"Quite a few so-called Overseas Koreans stay here at I-House," said Liesl. "My roommate, Michiko, for example. She lives in Japan and speaks only Japanese, but her parents are Korean. She and I don't have any language in common, so I don't know much about her. We just nod and point and smile at each other. But I think she's unhappy being in Korea. She cries a lot."

9

I thought I could understand Michiko. There *was* something unsettling about knowing so little of the place where I was going to study for a year - and where I was born. I hadn't let myself think about it before. Worst of all, people would look at me and assume I *did* know. Maybe Michiko had the same problem.

"What did you think of the *kut*?" I asked Elaine, changing the subject.

"Your dance was astonishing," she answered, and then explained to Liesl. "They asked Clara to dance last at the *mudang's* house, and she seemed to go into a trance. That's very unusual without training."

"Did you see anything?" Liesl asked, with too much eagerness for my taste.

"I must've read too many books about East Asia," I began carefully, hoping not to make too much of my odd experience, which unnerved me more than I wanted to admit. I tried to strike a distant and professional note. "I saw the birth of a baby girl, and a very nice naming ritual complete with fetishes, which took place in a prehistoric style of hut. My subconscious must have been putting it all together for me. Noise and the cadence of the music, not to mention the stimulation of the dance movement, and then jet lag - - -"

"These experiences can't be rationalized," Liesl said, dismissing my explanations. "Some unresolved problem is bothering you, one that your conscious mind can't work on. You'll work it through, but don't fret it. Did it seem like you were in the hut a long time?"

"The birth and ceremony took about half an hour, I guess."

"You danced for barely six minutes," Elaine referred to her notes. "You made some impressively high jumps."

"I jumped?"

"Marvelously!"

This news gave me the shivers. I was actually jumping around in a frenzy when I thought I was standing still, holding onto the roof beam with my claws, far off somewhere in time and space?

"They named the baby after me," I said, looking down at my *bibimpap* with a little smile to show it wasn't important.

"They called her Clara?"

"No," I laughed, "Flyingbird of the Golden Clan, Golden Flyingbird. They didn't see me as human, but as a golden bird, who appeared just when the baby was born. I hope she does grow up strong and swift and wise and beautiful."

"Clara, you're psychic! You've tuned in on an ancient ritual!" said Elaine, slapping her palms together.

The exclamation points in her voice were unwelcome intrusions. The vision or trance or whatever it was seemed real, yes. But of course it was just a trick of the mind caused by jet lag. I must have reconstructed a prehistoric scene out of what I'd read - part archaeology, part Ainu. Blue mouths indeed!

"I don't believe in time travel, or previous lives, or any of that spooky stuff. I'm a scientist," I insisted.

"Don't confuse Clara with your talk of the real past. It clearly is a message from her psyche," Liesl told Elaine firmly. She patted my arm. "You have interesting dreams. I'd like to hear more about them."

"Later," I yawned. "Now I need some sleep."

In spite of Elaine's recipe for avoiding jet lag, I woke up the next morning at 5:00 o'clock and lay staring at the ceiling, keeping quiet in order not to bother my roommate. Traffic noise had already begun, beeping and grinding city sounds. Then a rooster crowed. City mixed with country. Contradictions. I'm really in Korea, I thought. I succeeded in running away. The scenes before I left replayed themselves in my head.

I didn't tell anyone but my graduate advisors that I was applying for the fellowship, so when I won it I had some explaining to do at home.

"Letter for you, Clara, from some Korean-American Club," my Mom said as I walked into the house one day. "What do you suppose they want?"

She had on her painting smock, and a streak of viridian green colored a clump of her pale hair on one side, sticking out untidily in an unintended echo of punk.

I ripped open the letter and scanned it. "Listen to this, Mom! I get to go to Korea for a year, to study archaeology at Taehan University. The Korean-American Club will pay for travel, food, lodging - everything! I'll live at International House in Seoul, and I get to go on a dig. *Everything* is arranged."

I looked up and caught a concerned expression on Mom's face, like she was trying to be thrilled for me, but not managing. The little line between her eyebrows had deepened.

"I didn't know you wanted to go to Korea," she said, tensed up as if she were perched by Humpty Dumpty, terrified she might jostle him. "Are you looking for your roots? Do you want to find your . . . your birth mother?"

11

The question of my birth mother had never come up between us - and in fact had never interested me at all. I had never fantasized another family, nor considered that another mother, a "real" mother, was out there somewhere. It didn't take much insight to see that it bothered Mom, though.

"You're my only mother," I assured her. "And if I found a Korean mother I couldn't talk to her. But it would be interesting to see Korea, and learn about it, since I was born there."

I'm terrified of emotional scenes, and I always do the cowardly thing. All my life I've had a repeating nightmare of two adults, shouting and shouting at each other in high-pitched voices. The dream is always exactly the same. It takes place in a small room. I can see nothing but a lattice pattern, with light coming through it, but I hear the voices. I think I could close my eyes and draw that pattern even now. The shouting has something to do with me, and I wake up shaking, my heart pounding.

Maybe that's why I prefer my emotional life placid, and I can't stand up to anger. When I'm angry I cry, which embarrasses me, so I run away. I wasn't angry now, though, just sorry Mom misinterpreted my motives. But I wasn't going to tell her about Ed. She'd make me face up to him, and I just couldn't. More running away from scenes. I seized on the notion that I needed a Korean identity.

"I'm curious about Korea, that's all. *This* is my home and family. There isn't another one, and I don't need another one."

I gave her a hug, avoiding the paint, which looked wet. "Will you tell Daddy, or shall I?"

"You tell him. He'll be so proud of you."

He was proud of me for getting the fellowship, but concerned about how I would get along. I've always been "Daddy's little girl." I was small for my age all along, and I'm still not very tall. I guess it's hard for him to let me grow up. Even when I got to high school he wouldn't let me go to bowling alleys and skating rinks. If Daddy knew I'd been to bed with Ed he'd have a heart attack.

"You're such a picky eater, how will you find enough to eat?" Dad teased me. "Do you know what it's like in Korea? They eat dogs and snakes."

"Then I should have been a boy. `Rats and snails and puppy dogs tails . . .' I quoted. How can we Koreans produce any girls if we eat that diet?"

12

"We Koreans" rang in my head in the silence. I had never said, nor thought, "we Koreans" before.

Mom and Dad exchanged a look of concern. Now both my parents were upset, but trying to be understanding of my supposed need to find out about Korea.

"When I was stationed in Japan, I went to Korea once," Dad reminisced. "It was such a poor country, even more than ten years after the Korean War. Just to go there for a few days we had to have shots for cholera, malaria, yellow fever - I don't remember what else."

"Korea's not like *M.A.S.H.* anymore, Daddy," I insisted. "The people at the Korean-American Club tell me it's clean and modern and full of high-rises. But - I didn't know you'd been to Korea. Why didn't you ever mention it?"

Dad studied his fingernails. He doesn't speak before he organizes his thoughts.

"I didn't like the place, and I didn't want to hurt your feelings. I didn't see much of the country - but I didn't come away with a good impression. I mostly remember being shocked at children with runny noses, some without a stitch of clothing, playing in the bare dirt. And little girls who looked about four or five years old, hauling babies strapped onto their backs. There were no neat flowerbeds like in Japan. And the smells! Pew! Sorry, Clara. When we adopted you, I knew we were taking you away from all that, and giving you a good home. Maybe Korea *is* better now. That was before you were born, after all."

I knew he didn't mean it that way, but I felt attacked by my father's dislike of Korea, and wounded further by the fact that he had never told me.

"I've seen beautiful pictures of Korea," I said defiantly. "I'll be just fine over there."

I bolted from the room so they wouldn't see the tears coming.

Saying good-bye to Ed was worse. I was afraid if I saw him I'd change my mind, so I waited to call him just before I left. I had tightened up my story of needing to find my roots, and polished it to a high sheen. Ed bought it too well.

"You never would have thought of going to Korea if my mother hadn't called you Oriental," he said, with deadly aim. "But running off to Asia isn't necessary. Read books. Meet Koreans. Prepare yourself for a trip later. We'll go together on a voyage of discovery."

I made a little squeak of protest. I needed to do my own discovering.

"Listen, Jade Princess, you have no idea what you're getting into. Don't you read the papers? The students are rioting, labor unions are striking, there's political unrest. You can't speak a word of the language, and you know nothing of the customs. This isn't a good time to go. Can't you wait?"

"I'll never have this chance again. I'm leaving next Thursday, and I'll be gone a year. We should both feel free to see other people. Maybe you can find a girl without 'Oriental' eyes, and please your parents."

"Clara, be reasonable," Ed pleaded. "You have a mirror. You and I both know that no matter what you feel like inside, you have an Asian face. I think it's beautiful. It will just take my parents awhile to get to know you."

I hung up the phone and walked away from the rings that started right away. Of course I know my face is Korean, but somehow that never seemed important before I met Ed's parents. I didn't want to talk about it. To anybody.

Stubbornness is one of my less attractive traits. With everyone urging me not to do it, I was certainly going to go to Korea. But I began to wonder what I had gotten myself into. What if I couldn't eat the food? What if I didn't like Korea? A whole year . . . .

Ed called Mom to find out when my plane left, and came to Logan airport to see me off. But Mom and Dad and Heidi were there too, so I flew off without further discussions with Ed, except of the most trivial sort.

In the short time I had to prepare, I read everything I could get my hands on about the archaeology and anthropology of Korea. I read about villages with thatched roofs, about *mudang's* ceremonies called *kuts*, about the Confucian ethic. I read that men are more important than women. I read about the Ainu, a "Stone Age" people of northern Japan, who tattoo their mouths blue and worship bears. But all these pieces of information were so much flotsam, unconnected in the sea of my ignorance about Korea. Now it was time to get out of bed and face the real thing.

3

Seoul is full of universities - it must have more than any city in the world. So it was a lucky coincidence that I was headed for the same university as Liesl. She took me under her wing, suggesting we meet in the lobby of I-House at 8:00 in the morning, to ride the bus together. Liesl had been in Korea for a mere three weeks, but she had already mastered riding the buses - no mean feat for a non-Korean speaker. There are so many buses, and such crowds. I found it daunting. You have to cross the street, find the right bus stop, push your way onto the bus when it comes, offer a ticket marked "*hakseng*," meaning student, and ride the bus to the end of the line. Then you have to change to another bus that goes into the campus. Coming back, you have to know the right bus stop on campus and which bus to board, and most important of all, where to get off. The stops are as much as ten blocks apart, making a hefty walk back if you stay on the bus too long. Liesl's European background made her an experienced bus rider, but I, who always drove everywhere back home, had to learn the skills.

The bus was full, and neither of us got a seat, but we did find floor space by a window. Liesl became my guide. She'd read up on Korea thoroughly, and knew all about the landmarks she pointed out along the way.

"See that little building with the tile roof? Inside there's an old bell from the Choson Kingdom, when high walls surrounded Seoul." She told me the date, and I realized with shock that it was 100 years before Columbus discovered America! "The bell," she explained, "announced the opening and closing of the city gates. It rang every night at dusk, when the city gates were locked. Since upper-class women weren't allowed to mix with strange men, all men had to go inside when the bell rang to give the women a chance to go out walking." (How oppressive, I thought.) The impressive structure with upturned eaves is South Gate, which was the main gate to the old city. Back in behind it there's a street market where you can get great bargains, but watch out for seconds."

I began to tune out this flow of information, which I wouldn't remember in detail anyway. I was more interested in looking at people - women with babies wrapped onto their backs with blankets, boys riding sturdy bicycles carrying twelve-foot stacks of boxes, taxi drivers dodging expertly in and out of the traffic. I saw a sight that made me laugh, and nudged Liesl.

"Imagine carrying chickens on a motorcycle!"

The chicken crates were stacked four wide and six high, and chicken heads stuck out of a couple of them, but the motorcyclist whipped through traffic as if he had no load at all.

"Koreans can be very ingenious with transport - once I even saw a full-grown pig being taken to market on a bicycle!"

"How was that done?" I giggled at the thought.

"I'm told they get the pig drunk on crude rice wine, and then tie up its snout and legs. The pig rides on the back fender, all trussed up. It doesn't look comfortable, but I suppose it's happy."

The rest of my year in Korea I looked for pigs on bicycles, but I never saw one.

Seoul is a huge city with wide streets, tall buildings, and most people wearing western clothing, but the strangeness dominated my perceptions. You'd never mistake it for Boston! I noticed the women street vendors in the same graceful clothing worn by women at the *kut* - a long skirt topped by a very short jacket with long sleeves, tied with a ribbon of the same material across the left breast, all in pastels. This was neither the grubby Korea of my father's memory nor the Korea of the slick brochures. I felt warmed by what I saw, the hominess of it. I am Korean. I am one of these. For the first time, it wasn't a scary thought.

Liesl directed me to the archaeology department, where I presented my letters of introduction. After a short wait, I was ushered into a large, high-ceilinged room with a pair of stiff armchairs placed squarely on each side of a low table. A handsome graying man greeted me in Korean.

"Annyonghasimnikka," I responded. "That's about all the Korean I know."

"Well, Miss Alden, you must find that quite a nuisance. I'll arrange for you to have a tutor, to overcome your handicap as quickly as possible. I am Professor Lee Dong-won, Chairman of the Department of Art and Archaeology."

"Professor Dong-won, I'm pleased to meet you," I said extending my hand and smiling up at him.

"We do shake hands with foreigners, although we mostly bow to each other," said the professor, giving my hand a limp touch, then demonstrating the bow. "But surely you know that in Asia the family name comes first? I am Professor Lee."

"Ah, Professor Lee, I'm sorry." I lowered my eyes in embarrassment. "I'm afraid I don't know anything about Korean customs. Please correct me when I make a mistake."

"Correcting your mistakes would be most unKorean! It might injure your *kibun* - that means something like your mood, or soul. Westerners sometimes call it "face," but that misses the meaning. One must listen for hints, and try to catch the meaning behind the words."

I've never been good at reading the hinted subtext, the oblique message. I hoped this warning might alert me to the subtleties. He seemed to be warning me that messages were intended. But worse, I'm inclined to blurt out my thoughts before I know I have them. I foresaw a hard year ahead. I forced my attention back to Professor Lee.

"You'll find the university structure here is different than in the United States. We don't have archaeology with anthropology as you do. But I am being rude. Please sit down. Would you like a cup of coffee? Do you have an archaeological project in mind, or would you like to join one of our expeditions? You are so small and delicate, perhaps you would prefer to stay in the lab?"

"I can handle a shovel as well as anyone," I smiled, suppressing my irritation. It was the familiar put-down, based on my size if not my sex. "I've participated in excavations in Arizona and Mexico. I'm especially interested in the origins of agriculture. If there are early pottery sites being excavated, that would be my preference."

I didn't know if it was polite to accept or refuse the coffee, so I ignored that question, although I craved caffeine in this unfamiliar situation. Anyway, it seemed to have been left behind in the conversation. I cancelled the notion I had on the bus about belonging here. I didn't know the first thing.

"Our early ceramic sites don't represent plant or animal domesticators, but perhaps you would like to research the Chulmun period anyway. Chulmun is a kind of incised pottery, sometimes called Comb-ware in English. The presence of pottery doesn't mean that there is also agriculture," added Professor Lee in response to my raised eyebrows.

"We have located a new site on the east coast which looks as if it may be quite interesting. Probably the people were mostly fishermen. We've just received permission from the government to excavate it."

I wanted to ask about getting permits, and other such nitty-gritty details, but Professor Lee waved in a gangly young man perhaps a few years older than I, and introduced him as Oh Ki-dok, his graduate student assistant. I stood up, and offered him my hand. The young man bowed with his hands rigidly at his sides, but when he saw my outstretched hand, he quickly reached for it, just as I pulled my hand back and tried to copy his bow. We seemed to be doing some jolly little dance routine. The corners of my mouth quivered, but I didn't dare laugh.

Eyes on the ground, Oh Ki-dok muttered something that sounded like, "First time I meet you."

It struck me as an odd remark, but perhaps I heard him wrong.

The coffee mysteriously appeared on a tray in the hands of a silent secretary, and Mr.Oh sat down gratefully and attended to adding sugar. I sat in the chair across from him, and Professor Lee took the seat beside his student.

"Tell Miss Alden about your project," Professor Lee prompted.

"Uh . . . we find . . . we have finded . . . we found . . . yes, we found . . . v-e-ery interesting site on east . . . east side Korea. Site show on surface m-a-a-any kind pottery. Maybe site has more than one revel."

"Revel?" I asked.

"Rayer," tried Oh Ki-dok, gesturing flat stacked areas with his hands.

"Oh, level, layer," I said, embarrassed again.

"Perhaps can solve problem early neorithic," Mr. Oh doggedly continued.

"What problem, exactly? Are you speaking of chronological change, questions of subsistence base, settlement patterns, social organization?" now it was my turn to prompt. "Do you call it neolithic because there's pottery, or is there evidence of plant domestication?"

I had to learn this lingo in grad school, in order to be taken seriously. It was especially important for me, since I'm small, female, and considered pretty, or at least exotic. But I didn't get the expected response of a tirade about the neolithic. Oh Ki-dok merely smiled a broad smile. Later I learned it was a smile of embarrassment for my bad manners, but then I thought he was making fun of me.

"Of course no curtivated prants, it is a fishing virrage. But if pottery present we call time period neorithic."

There was a pause while I mentally substituted "l"s for "r"s, and I suppose Oh Ki-dok was rehearsing another English sentence in his head.

"We must solve chronorogy probrem first," Mr. Oh pronounced, emphasizing each word equally. Then he lapsed into silence, either exhausted by the effort of speaking English, or unhappy with my rapid-fire questions.

After we knew each other better, he told me he was dismayed when he met me. For one, thing, he found me confusing. He thought I was

Chinese or something - he didn't guess Korean! I wasn't anything like his idea of an American student. He'd been expecting to meet a male of the large, hearty, bearded kind, like Indiana Jones. He had looked forward to relaxing over beers with a helpful foreigner. He knew he would meet Clara Alden, but had no way of knowing that Clara is a girl's name. What a disappointment!

"Did you make a surface collection? What's the extent of the site?" I interrupted his reverie with yet more questions, eager to know more about the archaeology.

"I will show you." Ki-dok stood up.

I realized I was still holding the nicely wrapped bottle of scotch I had bought on the airplane, after learning from my seatmate that presents were customary in Korea when meeting important people. Especially when asking for favors. I wasn't sure who to give it to, but opted for the older man.

"This is for you," I said to Professor Lee with a smile, handing it to him with my right hand and touching my right arm with my left fingers, as I had seen Elaine do. I hoped the gesture was right in this context. I felt like a baby, with so many things to learn.

Professor Lee accepted the gift gravely without making any move to open it, and excused us with a nod.

I followed Ki-dok into the museum store-rooms. Rows of colorful plastic bins lined the shelves. Each bin was labeled with roman letters and arabic numbers, using a system that was unfamiliar to me. Ki-dok showed me the bits of broken pottery and stone tools which had been collected from the surface of the site, each with its location precisely noted. A map included the grids and their numbers, and I figured out that it was the key to the labeling system, letters for north-south and numbers for east-west.

The extent of the surface scatter - stone chips and broken pieces of pottery called potsherds, or just sherds - was about 40 meters long and 15 meters wide. Another area of sherds and chips had been found on the next hill. A test pit, Ki-dok explained more fluently as he gained more confidence in his little-used English, uncovered a burned post in a dwelling ("dwerring" gave me a moment's pause) which gave a radiocarbon date of about 6200 B.C. The date was surprisingly early. Another unexpected finding was the pottery, which was not the typical Chulmun "comb-ware" of the other early villages. Instead the pottery was well made and sophisticated, with impressed or pinched patterns around the rims. A fragment of a strap handle contrasted with the handleless jars found elsewhere. The site was a major discovery, which

19

might change the understanding of early Korean prehistory. We moved to the stone tools.

"Do you know what this is?" asked Mr. Oh.

He handed me a polished cylindrical stone object that was about as thick as a pencil. One end had a groove around it near the rounded top, the other had a flat slanted side.

"What is it?" I asked, like a proper acolyte.

"It's half of a composite fishhook, made of this stone piece and something else," he explained. "The other half was made of some perishable material, maybe bone or wood, and was joined rike this with twine," and he demonstrated the V shape of the entire object.

"That makes a very large hook," I observed. "What size fish bones have you found?"

"No bones were preserved at the site. It is a pity."

"What's this?" I picked up another polished stone tool that was shaped like a toy top, complete with a groove around the upper edge.

"A weight of some kind. We not know exactry. How do you think about it?"

I didn't have a clue. It must have taken many hours to grind the sides down into that point, with each side ground flat, but the tip showed no obvious sign of use.

Several dozen artifacts had been found on the surface and in the test trench. I decided to make an appointment to come back and study them in more detail.

"Do you have an excavation plan?"

"We'll cut a T-shaped trench through the site, and widen it out when we come across house floors or other features."

"How about a random sample? We could grid the site, and select some of the squares, say, twenty percent, with a random number table to select the sample to excavate."

Oh Ki-dok smiled even wider than before. "Why?"

I wondered again if I was being teased, but I answered seriously, because this was a topic I'd had drilled into me.

"With a random sample, you can estimate the total assemblage at the site with a statistically quantifiable margin of error. If you just dig a hole in the ground and widen it when you find something, you'll never know how representative of the whole site your finds are."

"You could miss many dwerring floors with your method."

"And with your method, too! Look, didn't you tell me there are two concentrations of artifacts? Could we use your method on one locality, and mine on the other? Then we can compare the results."

Mr. Oh promised to discuss the matter with Professor Lee. As we came out of the laboratory, Professor Lee was passing by.

"How soon does the excavation season begin? I'd like to prepare myself by spending several days with these collections," I suggested. "And I'd feel better if I could speak at least a little Korean."

"How about your friend Kim Dong-su? Would he make a good Korean tutor for Miss Alden?" Professor Lee asked Oh Ki-dok.

"Yes, fine," and Ki-dok bowed to his professor. But he told me later he had mixed feelings about his handsome friend Dong-su spending time alone with me. His protective male instincts were already aroused. It turned out he was right to worry.

I fell asleep early, tired from my long day and still jet-lagged. Yesterday and today scrambled together. In my mind I heard the rhythm of the cymbals, and saw the sherds and stone tools as parts of a puzzle with many pieces missing. They tumbled around in my head, refusing any analysis. Flyingbird returned to my thoughts, too. She had an auspicious beginning. What kind of life would she live? Then I laughed at myself for thinking of her as real. But I saw her again just the same.

4

You know how you sometimes know you're dreaming, but don't wake up? This dream was like that. I felt myself flying, and looked down to see a rocky coast. Two children had their brown heads together, looking down into a tide pool. Flying closer, I saw they'd found a starfish. The boy put his hand into the water and pulled it back several times.

"Is this what you want?" said the little girl, putting her hand into the water and pulling on the starfish, which held firmly to the rock.

"It doesn't want to be picked up," said the boy.

"O-o-o-o-o, it feels hard and fuzzy," the girl said, swishing her fingers in the sea to take the sensation away. "Aren't you glad we came here, Straight Pine? It's more fun than the sands beside our village. Look at all the sea lions, so close to shore!"

"We shouldn't have come so far from the village, Flyingbird. Your curiosity will get us into trouble." Flyingbird, it seemed, was already famous for wanting to know everything, small as she was.

They left the starfish and drifted to a tide pool farther out. Flyingbird found a small green rock with a hole through it.

"I'm saving this for Sunflower," she said. "Isn't it pretty, Straight Pine?"

"Why don't you keep it for yourself, Flyingbird? The Sea Goddess must've left it for you."

"Because I thought of giving it to my mother first, so that must be what the Sea Goddess wants me to do. Where can I put it? I wish I had a basket to keep it in." She clutched the rock in her small hand.

The children's bare brown bodies glistened with seawater, leaving crusty salt behind as it dried. Picking their way across the rocks away from shore, they found a tide pool with tiny swimming fish, then climbed a large rock that stood higher above the water.

The tide began to splash against the rocks as it turned to come in again. Fascinated, the children lay on their bellies on the big rock, watching the hypnotic water swirling and eddying. They looked out to sea, and saw that the group of sea lions was leaving them.

"Oh, look!" Flyingbird pointed with her chin, "don't they look silly with their noses just sticking up out of the water."

"Speak softly," Straight Pine corrected automatically. And then - "Uh oh! The tide's coming in!"

Straight Pine, charged with looking after his younger cousin, saw it was time to worry. They had wandered far from shore. He was old enough to swim back, but Flyingbird didn't have enough strength. Already the sea covering the starfish pool was over Flyingbird's head. Soon their rock would be covered, too.

"It's your nosiness that got us stranded here! You're always poking into everything."

The older children thought Flyingbird was a pest, with her persistent looking and asking. Now her curiosity had them stranded on a rock. Straight Pine squinted toward the shore.

I thought the children might be in trouble, but I was just a bird. Flapping my wings, I conjured up no magic powers. Some Spirit Bird! Following Straight Pine's gaze, I saw that a dugout boat was moored on shore, but I couldn't think of a way to get the boat out to the rock. Without the boat, the children would probably drown.

Straight Pine was still looking wistfully at the boat.

"Wait here," he told his cousin. "I'm going to get that boat."

But as Straight Pine slid down the rock, he lost his balance and slipped, hitting his left arm on an irregular outcrop. He shrieked as his arm snapped.

"You can't swim with that arm," said Flyingbird. "It's all crooked."

Straight Pine tried not to cry, but added a few salty drops to the sea.

I was really alarmed now. The village elders had put me in charge of this child at her birth, and I was failing her. Was this a test? But why would they let her wander out of their sight, I thought indignantly. Children should be watched better! I was never allowed such freedom!

Circling around helplessly, I noticed a rope coiled in the boat, attached to the prow. I flew down and tugged at it with my beak. I gagged on the rope; it was too thick for a beak to hold, but gradually I pulled the boat into the water. In despair I saw that with each wave, the boat washed back up on the beach, as the water bubbled and eddied. And with each wave the children had less rock to sit on. What *could* a small bird do?

The sea lions continued to bob in the waves, moving slowly out to sea. I didn't know how to get their attention, but they were my only hope. I flew out and perched on the top of the rock.

"Look at the pretty yellow bird!" said Flyingbird, who didn't know enough to be afraid.

I targeted the nearest sea lion, and flew down near its nose. The creature dived under the water as I came near, but it surfaced nearer the rock, which by now was nearly under water. The sea lion looked at the children curiously.

I flew behind the sea lion, urging it toward the rock. Given the choice between the children and this aggressive bird, the sea lion chose the children, and climbed up on the rock. The water rose even higher.

Flyingbird understood what they should do.

"Hang onto the sea lion with your good arm," she called to Straight Pine, and she put her left arm around the sea lion's neck so her cousin could use his good right arm. Burdened with these strange little creatures, the sea lion sat on the rock and kept its nose above water. The children clung to the sea lion and did the same.

I flew as high as I could, looking for the village. I spotted it not far to the north, and flew as fast as my wings allowed to a group of adults who were emptying nets filled with fish. In the boat were a top-shaped stone attached to a cord and composite fishhooks, like the ones I saw in the Taehan University lab, and I wanted to look closer, but there wasn't time. Instead I flew right in among the fishers and flapped my wings.

"It's Flyingbird's Spirit Bird!" said Sunflower. "Something's wrong."

I flew to the mast, trying to indicate that they should come in the boat.

"Quick, let's follow the bird," Sunflower urged. "Flyingbird's wanderings must've got her into trouble again."

I led them to the rock where the children clung to the sea lion. Sunflower and Squirrel followed in the boat, rowing at top speed.

The water completely covered the rock, but the sea lion stayed with Flyingbird and Straight Pine, keeping their faces above water level as the waves rolled in. Sunflower pulled the children into the boat one by one, and the sea lion swam lazily away, unburdened.

"My arm really hurts," said Straight Pine, sniffing and shivering a little, and Sunflower saw that it was broken, although the bone hadn't come through the skin.

"Birdnest will straighten it and make it feel better as soon as we're home," Sunflower comforted him.

"I brought you a pretty rock from the Sea Goddess," said Flyingbird, unclenching her chubby hand and offering the green rock to her mother. "See, it already has a hole for a string."

"I'll wear it in thanks for your rescue. But I wish you had less wanderlust. It's a good thing you have a protector. But I warn you, when the Sea Goddess is ready, she will take you, whether we are watching you or not."

I woke up, feeling relieved but shaken. I hadn't really rescued Flyingbird, but I did bring her help. What an odd dream. Why should I feel so responsible for that child? Her parents obviously didn't, letting her go so far from the village. I was indignant about their lack of attention to her. Besides that, my shoulder blades ached from so much unaccustomed flying.

"I dreamed about Flyingbird," I told Liesl and Elaine at breakfast, since Liesl had said she was interested in my dreams.

They demanded the details, and I told them everything I could remember.

"You can tell it's time travel," said Elaine to Liesl. "She saw those stone tools and simple boats. She couldn't make that up."

"It's her subconscious," Liesl insisted. "Flyingbird represents some wild part of Clara that's never been expressed. After all, she's Korean, and Koreans are volatile people. But Clara's been taught to be WASPy and repressed."

"I am *not* repressed," I said firmly. "It's just a dream made up of things I already know. Quit looking for deeper meanings. And please don't talk to each other about me as if I weren't here."

5

Kim Dong-su was a good teacher, and I an apt pupil, if I do say so myself. Sometimes he laughed at me when I couldn't make the sounds properly, but it was good natured teasing, and I'm sure my words sounded as funny to him as Oh Kidok's "rayer" and "revel" did to me.

Some of the Korean letters were difficult for my ear to distinguish. "L"s and "r"s are considered to be the same sound, causing some trouble saying my name - Clara Alden sounded like "Kara Aruden" most of the time. I heard about a place where some Americans lived that seemed to be called "Liverside Virrage" which I thought was a reference to hepatitis before I understood about the l/r convergence.

On the other hand, a whole set of letters: b/p, d/t, g/k, and j/ch, have *three* contrasting sounds, rather than the two in English. My pronunciation was often amusing to native speakers, and I was always afraid I was saying something dreadful after Elaine told me that the word for Mr. is almost the same as the word for sex. I worked every day on retraining my ears to hear the differences, and my mouth to say them, but it was hard.

"You can't use the excuse that your mouth is formed wrong," Kim Dong-su scolded me. "It was made for this language."

"I'll have to blame my unaccustomed ears."

The writing system was easy, though. Anybody can learn to read and write the Korean alphabet in half an hour, it's so simple and logical. Pretty soon I was sounding out the street signs. Some would make me laugh when I figured them out and realized they were Koreanized English words. On the corner was a sign that said *duh-rah-i kuh-ri-ning* - dry cleaning! And I found *ah-i-suh kuh-ri-muh* on a menu, which turned out to be ice cream, of course. One of my favorites is *syo-ping sen-toh*, a place where you can buy almost anything. I also enjoyed *Y-shirsu* in a department store, but I had to look at the object under the sign to understand. There in a pile were men's dress shirts, "white shirts." Why not? If there are already T-shirts in English, then Y-shirts make as much sense.

Across the back street from I-House there's a sign that I was sure must represent Koreanized English words, because of the consonant clusters, but I just couldn't figure them out. "*Hel-suh Suh-pa*" the sign read. "Hell's Super?" I wondered. What could that be? Expensive cars were often parked there, and men in business suits went in and out briskly while their drivers lounged about outside smoking cigarettes.

One day I remembered to ask my tutor, a little timidly, since I thought it might be a house of ill repute. The answer, supplied by Dong-su when he could stop laughing, was less sinister. Health Spa! the light dawned. Korean has no "th" sound.

Within a few weeks Kim Dong-su decided that I was ready to learn Chinese characters. He brought a newspaper to show me that, although most of the street signs are written in *hangul*, the Korean alphabet, the newspapers use Chinese characters for Chinese-derived Korean words. I had not a clue as to how to say them, but my tutor declared that I should learn to write the characters at the same time as I learned their meaning and pronunciation. My lesson began with the numerals.

"Here's the number ten, pronounced `ship'. Can you write this?" asked Kim Dong-Su, making a horizontal line and crossing it with a vertical stroke.

The character looked like a large plus sign.

"Easy," I bragged, crossing a vertical line with a horizontal one.

"Wrong."

"It looks just like yours. How can it be wrong?" I thought he was kidding me.

"Because you made the strokes in the wrong order," smirked my teacher. "Foreigners never get it right. Stroke order is very important."

He took my hand and demonstrated how it should be done. His hand was warm, and he had a pleasant touch. I wondered what else I might learn from him besides Chinese characters. I had mixed feelings, but the prospect was fun to consider.

6

Over breakfast one morning, Elaine and Liesl were discussing Korean men.

"They can be very sweet," said Elaine. "My best Korean lover was a charmer. We went all over the peninsula meeting *mudangs*, watching *kuts*, and staying in *yogwans*. That was before all the tourist facilities were built for the Olympics, and the *yogwans* were quite primitive, with no electricity, only outhouses and a central well for washing. People might have been scandalized that we stayed in the same room, but mostly they just stared at me, like a freak from the circus. I learned a lot about the Korean culture from Don Kim - *and* he was fun in bed. You can't beat that combination."

Liesl had another point of view. "They're all grown-up babies, who can't do anything for themselves. They're used to being waited on by some woman or another. First their mothers and sisters, then their wives. `Yobo,' they say in my lesson book, `polish my shoes.' The book translates *yobo* as `honey,' but that's not accurate. It's the same as `yoboseo' that you say on the telephone - it means something like 'you there'! Korean men might be all right for a fling, but can you imagine being married to one? They're trained to be insufferably arrogant."

"Well, my lover Don was different. He was lyrical about my blonde mane, wrote poetry about my ample breasts. He made me feel special. I didn't fall for him, but I loved every minute of it anyway. Great make-believe."

"Kim!" I broke in. "That's the family name of my tutor. Do you suppose he's a relative?"

Elaine and Liesl laughed together.

"Nearly a third of Koreans are named Kim," Elaine explained.

"And many of the rest are named Lee or Pak," added Liesl. "In a distant way all Kims are probably related - but in a very distant way."

"What happened to your Korean romeo?" I asked Elaine.

"He went abroad to study, and that was the end of the romance. We didn't write because he's married, although I get a postcard from him now and then. He'll look for me when he gets back. I'll be glad to see him again." Elaine smiled a far-away smile.

She was still thinking about the subject when we went to bed. In the dark, she brought it up. "You didn't have much to say about sex."

"You make it sound like an athletic event."

"Are you a virgin?"

"No, I had a nice steady lover in college."

"Was he the first one?"

"Yes. Well . . . No. Not if you count the college professor who seduced me - or maybe raped me is more accurate, since I wasn't entirely willing."

"The usual story? Adoring girl student, handsome professor? Girl doesn't know how to resist an authority figure?"

"Pretty much, except he wasn't handsome. Kind of paunchy and balding. I admired his beautiful mind."

"What did you do about it?"

"I cried, and dropped his course. If I saw him on campus I hid behind a tree, or took a different path to avoid meeting him. Would you have reported him?"

"You should have filed a grievance, so he wouldn't hit on other students. You were probably number two-hundred and forty-two in a long series of conquests, each one feeling used and afraid. But would I have reported him? Honey, in my day they would have just laughed and said `what a guy' - and then thrown *me* out of school for being a delinquent."

"Maybe things haven't changed as much as you think," I suggested sleepily, and turned toward the wall. "G'night."

But Elaine wasn't through asking. "How about the lover? Is he fun in bed? Tell me about him."

"More fun than the professor, for sure. Ed was just a pal at first. After my earlier experience I was terrified of men. But he didn't give me a line, just treated me like a friend. The first time he kissed me, he said, `Your nose is cold.' Unromantic, huh? So after that I trusted him, and one thing led to another. Want to tell me about your ex-husband?"

Elaine snored softly in response.

7

Liesl and I sat in our usual booth at I-House, talking over the day's accomplishments and problems as we waited for Elaine to join us for dinner. Liesl missed her "boyfriend," as she called him, and told me tales about him to assuage her loneliness. She couldn't understand Elaine's attitude toward her ex-husband. Elaine had no bitterness toward him, but little fondness either. Their two sons were in college, and Elaine gloried in having this chance to live her own life, to explore new places, to make her own mistakes.

"When my ex asked me a question," Elaine said, "I never knew whether he wanted information or just to show off what *he* knew."

"We've all known men like that," Liesl observed. "And even a some women."

We shifted to discussing Elaine's bouncy personality, and wondered if her husband was as stiff and stuffy as she portrayed him, and if so, how she could have stuck with him as long as she did.

"Probably out having *his* fling, or a mid-life crisis," was Liesl's opinion.

"I forgot to tell you, I met your Korean tutor yesterday," added Liesl, apparently following a train of thought about flings. "It turns out he's a friend of my advisor. We all had lunch together in the faculty dining room. Did you know he got his doctorate in France? His French is as good as his English. But I think he's quite a ladies' man. We'd call him a 'sonny boy'. Watch out!"

"He seems quite nice, to me," I protested. "Funny, and clever, and rather sweet." I wondered if Liesl was jealous.

"Mail call," sang Elaine, materializing near us in the dimly lit dining hall. I was glad we weren't still talking about her.

She handed two letters to me and one to Liesl.

I opened the letter from my parents and scanned it quickly, planning to read it in detail later.

"Nothing much new at home," I reported. "Mom and Dad have decided to come visit me in the spring, and then they'll see some of the rest of Asia. It'll be fun to show them around."

"What about the other letter? Who is R. Edward Howland, and why haven't we heard of him before? His handwriting is an aristocratic scrawl, and his return address is Cambridge, MA, confirming the red shield with Veritas in the corner of the envelope. A Harvard man. Do I smell the "boyfriend"? Do you want privacy to read it?"

I ran my substantial eyebrows together and squinched up my eyes,

I ran my substantial eyebrows together and squinched up my eyes, indicating, I hoped, great pain. "I was working hard on not thinking about him at all."

Elaine is persistent, and she pried out of me the fact that Ed was my college lover, and I had assumed we would marry someday. But there was no reason to hurry, and we both had graduate plans. Ed went to Harvard Law and I started graduate study in archaeology. We lived in different cities, but we still saw each other often, although we were both busy.

Finally, I told them the story. "Ed's parents had been pressing to meet me, the girl who had enchanted their only son, as he said. Ed kept putting them off. One day Mrs. Howland phoned me with an invitation to join them for dinner at a fancy restaurant in Boston. We had a pleasant chat, and I was looking forward to meeting Ed's parents. But Ed was nervous."

Here I disgraced myself by getting misty eyed. Why was this event so hard to talk about? I was over it. Liesl made noises indicating I should continue, so I pulled myself together.

"I should have read the signals, that there was a problem. But I didn't. At dinner, things were clearly going wrong, but I couldn't figure out why. I didn't belch, or even use the wrong fork. My mother always harped on table manners. But Mrs. Howland was exceedingly frosty from the first minute she saw me, and Dr. Howland quickly sank into silence, and just stared at his plate."

My eyes overflowed.

"Sorry, I never learned to be an inscrutable oriental," I tried to make a joke, wiping my eyes on my napkin.

"Afterwards Ed called and apologized, and said he should have warned them that I was Asian. Asian! That was a real shocker. I mean, I never thought of myself as Asian, or anything but American. I had to face it that Ed's parents took one look at me and knew I wasn't good enough for their son. I suppose they didn't want slant-eyed grandchildren. What an identity crisis! You know how some African-Americans disparage others as "oreos" - black on the outside but white in the middle? So what was I, a banana?"

Elaine patted my arm while I paused to blow my nose. This time I found a tissue.

"I decided the best thing was to break up with Ed. The opportunity arose to come to Korea, and I pounced on it. As I said, I've been staying too busy to think of Ed. I hope he marries another Mayflower descendant and they spend all their time comparing family trees."

"It isn't Ed's fault that his mother is prejudiced," Liesl pointed out.

"If he thought it would be a problem, which he clearly did, why didn't he warn them - and me?"

"Maybe he thought that when his parents met you, their bias would melt away in the glow of your warm personality," suggested Elaine, perhaps with irony.

"He said something like that," I admitted. "But I couldn't believe he would expose me to such a big shock without trying to protect me at all. Asian! I knew nothing about Asia, nor how to be an Asian - nor what it meant to be Asian. So now I'm learning."

"By the way," I said, tired of the subject, "I'll be gone for a few weeks. The Taehan University crew's going to excavate a neolithic site on the east coast, and I get to go. They'll even let me try a random sample on part of the site. I guess Professor Lee thinks that area isn't important or he wouldn't let me do it."

"What about your Korean lessons?" teased Liesl. "Won't you miss your handsome tutor?"

"He's coming too, and I'll have my next lesson on the bus. At least *his* parents shouldn't mind my Korean looks."

Liesl and Elaine raised their eyebrows at each other. The look said that I was a silly romantic. I realized I'd revealed my growing interest in Kim Dong-su. He's so-o-o handsome and suave - and so different from Ed. Ed's more like a pal than a lover. Kim Dong-su gives me goose bumps. But it would certainly shock my parents if I fell in love with a Korean man.

8

The rain poured down as I surfaced from the subway at the bus terminal. I looked in dismay at the rain, and then at the terminal. The place was huge! How will I ever find Mr. Oh and the students, I wondered. Why didn't I think to ask directions ahead of time? I framed a Korean question in my mind, and hoped it was understandable. Looking around for someone to ask, I was relieved to see the broad smile and friendly face of my tutor.

"Miss Alden! Over here!"

Mr. Kim steered me by the elbow toward the bus to Kangnung. The gesture surprised and amused me. I thought it must be an imitation of western movies, or perhaps something he picked up in Europe, because I hadn't seen any other Korean man touch the woman he was with at all. Usually the women walk three paces behind. Not that I minded his touch. I didn't miss Ed, but I missed being touched.

We climbed on the bus and found our seats. The bus was nearly full, but none of the archaeologists were on board.

"Where are Mr. Oh and the other students?"

"They got a university van at the last minute and went ahead. Mr. Oh couldn't reach you, so I volunteered to meet you here and escort you on the bus. I am honored to have so many hours alone with you. Do you mind being alone with me?"

I glanced significantly around the full bus.

"We're hardly alone."

"When you are with me, I only have eyes for you."

I wondered if Mr. Kim learned his English from old sheet music. But I was flattered all the same, which was the intended effect, I'm sure.

Then a disturbing thought crossed my mind. Could this be a set-up? I didn't buy the tickets, and didn't know where we were going. I was completely in Kim Dong-su's clutches, if that was what he had in mind. Maybe what I was thinking showed on my face. Anyway, Mr. Kim began to instruct me in the names of things, all business, and I was reassured.

The bus was soon out of Seoul, and into the countryside. Maple leaves were beginning to turn color, and the downpour had left the countryside washed and shining under the late September sky. Sunflowers and cosmos bloomed cheerfully along the roadsides. Mr. Kim pointed out various features of the landscape, both natural and cultural, and taught me their names in Korean.

Small houses clustered into villages. The rice paddies terraced down, one level after another, catching the run-off from small streams. Groups of small mounds, which I learned were graves, covered high hillsides. Mr. Kim told me that people are buried where the auspices are good - which usually turns out to be on hillsides.

"It's handy that the graves don't occupy valuable crop land," I observed.

"Blue dragon, white tiger," Mr. Kim said, as if that explained something.

"Huh?"

"The best place to be buried has a dragon and a tiger. The blue dragon is the stream, and the white tiger is the hill. People believe their ancestors' spirits will make them prosperous if they are buried correctly and their graves cared for."

Sometimes ideology has a practical side, I thought. It's better to bury people on the hill slopes, not using the prime agricultural land.

It was harvest time, and men and women could be seen in the fields harvesting the golden ripe rice with metal sickles. The reapers didn't bend at the knees, but bent over double like croquet wickets. When the rice plants had been cut off neatly at the base of the stalks, the fields looked like day-old whiskers. The unharvested fields were full of cloth scarecrows, flapping in the breeze.

Mr. Kim was pleased when I noted the beauty of the countryside, but I kept to myself what I thought about the human-built environment. It was often shabby, scruffy even. Hard-packed dirt surrounded the houses and shops near the road, and piles of building materials or other debris were scattered around. The contrast was disquieting. Was I born in a place like that? I must've been from a poor family, I reasoned, or they wouldn't have given me away. Would I have grown up playing in that dirt? Or maybe the family was rich but already had too many girls, but no boys yet. Did I have sisters here?

"See those trees with the big yellow fruit? What do you think they are?" Mr. Kim quizzed me.

"They look like enormous yellow apples. What are they?"

"They're called *bae*. Foreigners call them pear-apples, because they're crisp and juicy and yellow like pears, but shaped like apples. They're delicious. Wait til you try one!"

Gradually the road gained elevation, around curves and through the forest. I had to open the window for air, but the view from the top of the pass, falling steeply down to the East Sea, was worth the queasiness. Glimpses of the gray-green sea could be seen through the gnarled pines on the way down, as the bus twisted down the U-turns. A thin mist added to the feeling of an Asian painting come alive.

A teeming bus station, full of pushing and shoving humanity, broke the spell. Our trip required a change of bus, and I was glad to have my tutor along to steer me and negotiate the tickets. I find Korean crowds disorderly and unnerving. I'm easy to push, so I rarely get my turn. Mr. Kim shoved bravely into the swarm and stood his ground until he got our tickets.

We rode north along the coast, with the rocky shore appearing and disappearing from view. At last we alighted at a small town. Walking away from the main street for a block or so, we came to a small *yogwan*, a Korean inn. Mr. Kim spoke to the woman running the place so rapidly that I didn't understand a word, then put both our backpacks into a bare room. Looking in, I saw chests along one wall, but otherwise the room had only a shiny paper floor and a light fixture in the ceiling.

"Oh Ki-dok and the students haven't arrived yet. They must've had trouble with the van along the way. Shall we rest in our room or walk to the site?" asked Dong-su with a broad smile.

I thought I detected an invitational edge to his voice, and the smile made me nervous. What did he mean, "our" room? What Korean custom had I stumbled upon now? I remembered what Elaine had said about her travels with Don Kim.

"I need a walk after that long bus ride," I said, putting off a confrontation about the room. "Do you know the way to the archaeological site?"

"Yes, I came along when the surface collection was made. It's about five kilometers away. Is that too far to walk? We could take a taxi."

"Of course not. Let's run, and I'll beat you there."

I ran off in front of him, making it a challenge, but he caught up easily, laughing. Was I wrong to worry about his intentions? Why should I care?

We came to the beach as daylight was fading. The place looked dimly familiar, like a person you used to know grown older. A grove of gnarled pines stood behind a fishing village, each trunk a work of abstract art. On the beach, fishnets with stones for weights were spread out to dry. Dogs barked, and the air smelled of fish and salt and tar. The smell brought an image that might have been Flyingbird, racing across the beach, but the vision turned out to be a real, local village girl.

The beach itself was fenced off, and soldiers patrolled it. A rocky islet just off shore was rigged out as a lookout post. One soldier carefully raked the sand on the beach, erasing his footsteps as he backed toward the road.

"What on earth is he doing?"

"We're not far from North Korea here. It would be easy for them to launch an invasion in boats at night, or to infiltrate spies along the coast.

If anyone should land unnoticed, when the sand is raked, the soldiers would see footprints in the morning, and send out a general alert."

"Is that likely? It seems so peaceful here."

"The government believes they can't be too careful."

We walked away from the shore. The archaeological site is a hundred meters or so back from the sea, next to an ancient fresh water lake. Sand dunes have covered it, but the two sections of the site were on distinctly separate ridges. I walked all around "my" area, thinking about how to lay out the grid.

In the fading light we picked up potsherds and stone tools, replacing each one carefully after examining it.

"Look, this is Classic Chulmun!" I handed Mr. Kim a sherd, showing off what I'd learned in the museum. These sherds had deeply incised marks in a design of nested Vs.

Mr. Kim held my hand with the sherd in it, then tilted my chin up with his other hand and kissed me. My residual loyalty to Ed told me to pull away; but my body, so rigidly kept from wanting anyone for so long, responded anyway. I backed away, uncertain. How did you negotiate a love affair in Korea? What would people think?

"I thought you liked me. I'm sorry."

"Of course I like you. But we haven't even gotten to first names yet. I've never kissed anyone who called me Miss Alden," I joked, to cover feeling flustered.

"People in Korea don't use their given names as much as you do. May I call you Clara? It's a beautiful name." He said my name without any trace of accent.

"Everyone does. I've never had a nickname. What shall I call you? Do your friends call you Dong-su?"

"Yes. Please call me Dong-su," he said with a solemn face. "Now that we call our names, may I kiss you?"

"We're crossing our cultural signals here. Names are only the first step. It must be confusing to you that I look Korean, but inside I'm an ordinary American girl. I'm sorry."

"No use both being sorry. Let's walk back while we still have a little light."

A waxing moon rose large and misshapen out of the sea, promising us enough light to walk by.

Dong-su steered me lightly by the elbow in a proprietary way. This time the gesture annoyed me and I pulled my arm away.

The students had arrived by the time we got back, and were already cooking a dinner of noodles on a hotplate in the *yogwan*. I joined the two girls in the crew and tried to practice my Korean. They giggled. I asked them their names. They giggled. Giving up, I went to talk to Mr. Oh about the artifacts on the site.

Later, I was relieved to find that my backpack had been moved to a room with the two girl students. I wasn't ready for a foreign entanglement.

"Looks like we're roommates," I said in English.

"Good, let's try speak English," said one of them. "O.K.?"

Everybody's English is better than my Korean, I thought, discouraged. But I tried to be a good sport.

"O.K. I'm Clara Alden. Please call me Clara."

"Yes, Miss Aruden."

They introduced themselves as Pak Sun-hi and Lee Hwang-ok. It was quite a while before I learned anything else about them.

9

During the first week at the dig my main task was to make a contour map of the surface of the second area, where I was planning my random sample. First I established a reference point on high ground outside the artifact scatter. Everything would be measured from that point. My crew and I mapped the contours of the ground surface at one-meter intervals. I labored over the map, trying to be very precise.

Next the entire site was gridded with strings two meters apart, set to the points of the compass. Each two-meter square was surface-collected, and the artifacts put into cloth bags labeled with the designation of the square. Dong-su had little to say to me, except for correcting my Korean, and went back to Seoul after one day of this tedious work.

Evenings we washed the artifacts collected during the day and wrote permanent numbers on each one, mulling over similarities to pottery at other sites. It was easy to see that most of the sherds on my hill were different from the first test pit on the other hill - there were more pinched designs and many fewer pieces with impressed designs.

When Saturday came, so did Kim Dong-su. He had his usual big smile, but kept a respectful distance, except for calling me Clara.

"Time for your language lesson, mixed with a little sightseeing. Have you heard of Soraksan, Clara?"

"Everyone here has told me about it. I've heard that it's very beautiful, especially in the fall. Is it far away?" I asked eagerly. I'm a born sight-seer. My Dad says I like sights, sites, and cites.

"Not too far. I drove my car, so I could have the pleasure of taking you there. We can't see all of it - the park is huge - but we'll have time to hike around enough to get the flavor of it. It's a national park, so you'll see real Korean wilderness."

Sorak Mountain was indeed a lovely place. Hotels, restaurants, and souvenir shops clustered together where cars were left at the edge of the park, but inside the grounds nature reigned. Only ancient temples, on crags or hillsides, represented human works, and even they blended in or were disguised by the forest, where deep red and orange maple leaves seemed to shine against the dark pines.

We wandered around without a particular plan, up one path and down another. Dong-su was companionable, but walked with a space between us. I relaxed.

A large map showed the way to a Buddhist temple, and we set off toward it through an ancient forest.

"The forests have been protected here," Dong-su told me.   "Even during the Korean War, when firewood was so scarce, people wouldn't cut the trees on the temple grounds. That's why such big trees grow here.   Around any temple it's like a nature preserve - they're the numinous places in Korea, full of nature spirits. Can you feel them?"

"No, but I can appreciate the beauty."

"You're resisting the spirits, but they'll get to you."

I shrugged. Highly unlikely, but I wasn't going to say so.

At the entrance to the temple, I was surprised to see mats and large red drums for rent - the same kind of double-ended hourglass-shaped drum I'd seen at the *mudang's kut*. They were obviously hot items, with a mob clustered around to rent them. The temple grounds were full of revelers.   Family groups had brought picnics, and crowds of school children followed their teachers. People danced in circles, flinging their arms high.   Some groups were giddy - from drinking *makkolli* - home-made rice wine, Dong-su said.   Some sang, accompanied by musical instruments, especially flutes and drums.

"Isn't this a sacred place?" I asked.   "Isn't all this merriment sacrilegious?"

"Temples are sacred but not solemn.   Restrained and formal behavior in church is a western idea. Here we know that dancing, singing and drinking are ways to honor the gods. It says so in the oldest Korean writings.   Even the ancient Chinese historians wrote that Koreans loved to sing and dance. If it has been going on for millennia, can it be wrong?"

"Women have been suppressed for millennia, but that's wrong," I snapped.   "Antiquity is no guarantee of justice or beauty."

Dong-su only smiled and nodded.

The temple was composed of a bunch of wooden buildings, seemingly helter-skelter up the hillside.   A drum tower and a bell tower framed the entrance, although neither the bell nor the drum had survived the centuries.   The buildings were rectangular, with wooden columns holding up the roof. Each roof was elaborately constructed, and painted on every beam and post in now-faded colors of aqua and coral. Here and there, carved wooden dragons peered down over the roof beams, looking more playful than fearsome.   Some rooms contained altars displaying Buddhas of various sizes and materials, sitting in rows, a sensory whirl.

"I want you to see something special, "Dong-su told me, leading me into a small room.   He pointed to a painting of an old man with a long white beard, riding a tiger.

"Isn't that wonderful? I always look for the Old Man of the Mountain"

The painting was done naively in poster paints, but the lines were so full of tension that the old man seemed alive.   The tiger wore a silly smile, and the man's thin white beard jutted out in comical wisps. Even the pine tree was painted with vitality, as if the bark might flake off in your hand.

"I can see why you like it. I wouldn't be surprised if he spoke to us."

Dong-su explained that the painting represented the Mountain Spirit with his tiger helper, and was pre-Buddhist. I thought the painting must be out of place in a Buddhist temple, but Dong-su said that Buddhism didn't try to obliterate prior gods, incorporating them into the belief system instead. A row of painted plaster Buddhas on the altar in front of the Mountain Spirit emphasized his point.

"Sometimes I'd like to believe in the Mountain Spirit," said Dong-su softly, almost to himself. "I wonder what he would think of modern Korea - of all the dams and factories that have reduced his territory. Of polluted rivers and dirty air. Of ancient customs put aside. He must be very sad."

"Do you wish you had lived in Korea in ancient times?" I asked him, thinking of Flyingbird. "Based on nothing but stones and sherds, it's hard to imagine how it might have been. Difficult and dangerous, don't you suppose?"

"I think it was simple, without competing cultures. Everybody knew who they were, and knew their place in society."

"Surely it's better to have a chance to be anything you can be than to have a 'place,'" I objected.

"That's another way to look at it, " said Dong-su.

I felt ashamed, not for my values, but for blurting them out judgmentally. But Dong-su hadn't taken offense. I was touched that Dong-su showed me the Mountain Spirit and his tiger, even though I didn't entirely comprehend it.

We wandered back by a group of people wearing their traditional clothing. The women were especially appealing in their pastel *hanbok* - they were a flock of butterflies dancing a round dance.

"Come join us!" someone called from the group, and we went closer.

A man with a white towel wrapped around his head poured some *makkolli* from a pottery jar into a brass bowl, and offered it to us, laughing and making it a challenge. The stuff tasted sour and harsh, but I swallowed it, and wiped the dribbles off my chin with my sleeve.

The red drum beat out a rhythm, and people made a circle. I stood back bashfully. It seemed wrong to intrude. But Dong-su pulled me into the group, and I copied the dancing style as well as I could. Soon we were laughing and shouting along with our hosts, hopping and flinging our arms around. The *makkoli*, or the drum, sent me back to Flyingbird.

40

C.10

DONK daki daki, DONK daki daki, Donk da KUNK. The drumming summoned everyone to the central dance ground. A group of five naked children, looking for seashells at the edge of the beach, responded too.

"I'll race you back, Flyingbird," challenged a boy slightly bigger than she.

"No fair, you have a head start."

But Flyingbird ran with energy toward the dance ground, arriving in a dead heat with her cousin, Straight Pine. I saw that his arm had healed straight, and he used it easily. The children ran to their mothers, who slipped garments over their heads and rubbed their hands with sand to clean them, in time for all of them to join the ceremony.

Twenty-four people of Bird Mountain Village stood in a semi-circle, holding tall, carved sticks in their right hands, while Birdwing beat the ancient wooden drum stretched with reindeer hide. They gathered in an open space, marked by a tall pole topped by a wooden bird, cleverly whittled from the natural branching of a small tree. I found myself on top of the pole, with an excellent view of the village. The gathering place opened toward the sandy shore where the ceaseless music of the sea murmured an obbligato to the villagers' daily lives, toward the source of both their livelihood and their disasters. As the red sun began to reflect on the shining waves, the villagers shuffled their feet and sang the daily incantation for safe passage through the day.

Let me tell you what I learned of these people, and about their village.

Birdwing was the leader of Bird Mountain Village, occupied by the Golden clan. She was the person whose drum called everyone together, the person who knew the stories, the person who could foretell the turning of the seasons. She lived with Grandfather in the house on the south side of the dance ground.

Across the dance ground, anchoring the north side of the arc of houses, lived Tall Sister with her husband Great Uncle and their two teenaged sons, Clam and Sandcrab. Their oldest son, Oyster, was married and lived with the White clan in Three Rocks Village, only a day's boat trip to the north.

Between the houses of Birdwing and Tall Sister were the homes of Birdwing's four daughters: Sunflower, Magpie, Pebble, and Birchleaf. Each had found a husband to bring into Bird Mountain Village. Flyingbird called these men Father, Red Uncle, White Uncle, and Black Uncle. Father was Blue Uncle to all the children but his own. The colors

41

named their birth clans - the men were outsiders in this village, where all the women and children belonged to the Golden clan.

Although Flyingbird's mother Sunflower was the oldest of Birdwing's daughters, Flyingbird was nearly the youngest of the village children. After her, there were only Pebble's son, and Dolphin, Flyingbird's baby brother. Her two brothers and seven boy cousins would have to leave the village when they married. Flyingbird was the only girl, the only heir - the one who would learn the village songs and stories and become the leader of the village. All the adults knew they mustn't spoil her - but her big brown eyes framed by thick wavy hair were almost irresistible. It was hard not to dote on the only girl in the whole village.

Each house was entered by a low door. From the doorway it was a step down into a single room. In the center of the house a fire was kept burning at all times, for that was the abode of the Hearth Spirit. This fire goddess ruled over them all, and kept each household from harm. Flat river cobbles were set on edge in a square to mark the boundary between the sacred hearth and the rest of the house. A framework of poles held up the roof beam, and a thick layer of thatch kept out the summer's heat and the winter's cold. Smoke could escape through openings on either end of the roof beam, and high on the west side, the sacred window looked out toward the mountains.

Outside the sacred window, several yards away, each family kept a row of offering sticks. The animal skulls among them were decorated with sacred wood shavings, so that each animal would report to its kin that it was well treated by the villagers. More game would come, and the spirits of the animals would not desert the village. In the place of honor on the right, each family had at least one bear skull, with wood shavings and offering sticks protruding from the eye sockets.

The bear cage, empty now, stood to the south of Birdwing's house. It was elevated above the ground, and so made a pair with the elevated storage hut on the north side of the village. Only the women were allowed to enter the storage hut, as the owners of the village and guardians of the food supply.

A path on the north branched into four parts. The first led to the latrine area on the beach, where the tidy sea cleaned it twice a day. The second led to the dumping area for plant material, the third to the animal bone pile, and the fourth to the fishbone disposal pile. Mixing these heaps would offend the spirits, so they were kept ritually separate. Each place was sacred, and each had its prayer sticks.

If you followed the path from the south side of the village, you would soon find yourself in the forest. Pine, walnut, oak, cherry, and apple trees gave the villagers their bounty in season. Each tree was kept carefully clear of underbrush, and when new trees sprouted, they were gently dug up and moved to the edge of the village and given offerings to help them grow.

On this sacred side of the village, one small side trail went to the birth hut, and another turning back to the north led to the cemetery, where wooden grave posts marked the first founders and later people who had lived and died in Bird Mountain Village. Their spirits were happy there, especially on feast days, when millet porridge and wine were sprinkled on their graves.

As the main path began to climb the mountain, it was no longer straight, but zigzagged around boulders and avoided the mountain streams where they cascaded too steeply down the mountainside. This was dangerous territory, not because of spirits, but because here the hunters set their traps with poisoned arrows along the numerous deer trails. The children were never allowed to take this path without an adult.

When Birdwing stilled her drum after their brief song to welcome the sun, she sat down on a mat and waved her hands inward, indicating that everyone else should bring their mats and sit with her. The villagers sat cross-legged in a circle and waited for her to speak.

"Perhaps we have offended the gods," she began. "Flyingbird has now seen ten summers, and still she is our only girl, the only person who can carry on the lineage. Even after she brings a husband here and has children, this will become a very lonesome village as our sons move away and we older people go to the spirit land. We don't want to have the kind of trouble our ancestors did."

She called Flyingbird to her side. "Remind us of our past."

Picking up the stick and concentrating on it, Flyingbird became her ancestor, Golden Sunbird, and sang in a sweet voice.

"I lived in a house by a wide rushing stream.
Every day I embroidered uneventfully."

"So true, all true," sang Birdwing, and most of the others joined in.

"We were ten sisters, only two with husbands.
I was the fourth. Too many girls, said third sister,
and she offered to me and sisters six, seven and eight
a boat and two strong men to help us row
to establish a new village and populate it well."

"So true, all true," came the refrain.

"We left the northern streams by the Seven Stars,
down the river to the sea, and kept the land on our right side,
our sacred right side, until we found the sandy beach
we found the sweetwater lake, we found the welcoming birds,
and we built our houses here.
Birds swarmed on a hill behind the village.
We called our new home Bird Mountain Village.

The names from the Golden clan
were Golden Sunbird, Crane, Iris, and Oaktree,
the men were Bearspirit of the Blue clan and
Wildgarlic of the White.

Some of the Golden clan still live where the great salmon
come up the river every year, still live on the northern streams
by the Seven Stars to this very day. To find the way back,
row toward the Seven Stars for many days,
past the spit of land that is shaped like an otter,
past the three bare rocks, splashed night and day by the sea.
past the Blue clan at the mouth of Dragon River
that issues forth from the lake at the center of the earth,
Turn left into the next river there you will find
a large and prosperous village with many houses and many boats.
When you arrive, sing them this song, and sing the morning prayer,
They will know you are their long lost sisters."

"Word perfect!" said Birdwing, pleased.   "Now take your great-
grandmother Birdnest's stick and sing her story. See how well you
remember the last two verses you learned yesterday."

Flyingbird took a moment to set aside the persona of Sunbird, so that
she could let in the spirit of Birdnest. When she was ready, she held
Birdnest's singing staff firmly, and stood squarely beside it.

"I was born in Bird Mountain Village, the daughter of Golden Sunrise
and the granddaughter of Golden Sunbird, the first village leader.
We lived together, six houses altogether,
and we did our embroidery uneventfully.
"One day Golden Sunbird called us together
saying, `Golden Birdnest is my only granddaughter.
Where are her sisters, her girl cousins?
What will become of Bird Mountain Village?'

"My brothers Elmbark and Salmon took a boat to steal

44

girls from other places. We would teach them the secrets
of the Golden clan to carry on our lineage.
The men went far away, and stole one girl from the Blue clan
at the mouth of the Dragon River,
and another from the Black clan who live where the earth shakes.
We had our women, but now the sea would not give us any food.
The animal spirits were angry too, and would not feed us.

"Elmbark and Salmon went to the mountain and caught a bear cub.
We brought him up respectfully and well and we gave him
a splendid feast. He went back to his ancestors
with many gifts, and told them the humans
were sorry. We promised never to steal girls again.
So prosperity returned, and we all embroidered uneventfully.

The notes of the song tapered off, and respectful silence followed for
a few moments.

"So you see why it's important to remember the old ways," said
Birdwing. "We have promised not to offend the spirits by stealing girls
again. The oath of Elmbark and Salmon is still binding on us today.
What shall we do?"

Tall Sister raised both hands, palms outward, to indicate her wish to
speak. At a nod from Birdwing, she made her suggestion. "Suppose we
look for a village with too many girls and ask for two of them. Perhaps
Clam and Sandcrab could bring wives to Bird Mountain Village, and
their wives could become sisters to Flyingbird."

"They would have to be polite and industrious. They would have to
learn our customs well," warned Pebble. "Perhaps we can find such
women, but it will be difficult."

"Tall Sister speaks well," said Grandfather, ignoring Pebble. "We
should pay visits to all our kinfolk along the rocky shore, and discover
the true nature of each village. Surely there's a crowded village among
them which could supply our need."

"We'll have to catch a bear to welcome the brides," said Magpie.
"It's the right season of the year to find a bear cub. Shouldn't we have a
bear to raise before setting forth on such a serious journey?"

"Then someone will have to stay with the cub, and we can't all go,"
objected Birchleaf with a tight mouth.   "There'll be plenty of time to
catch a bear cub afterward."

The pros and cons of these possibilities were discussed until the entire
group settled on a plan. They decided that they should catch the cub now,
before all the bears left their dens. This meant that only a small group

could go on the journey. Six adults were needed on the oars. Birdwing, as the village leader, had to go, although she wasn't expected to row. Tall Sister, Great Uncle, Clam and Sandcrab should go to help choose the brides - or rather, to hope the girls would choose to come back with them. Father had relatives in the Blue clan far to the north at the mouth of the Dragon River, and he knew the winds and currents, as well as being a strong oarsman. White Uncle was selected as the sixth rower, for his brother was married into a village far to the south, said to have many daughters.

After lengthy discussion of the dangers, the adults decided that Flyingbird could go too, for the brides would become her sisters, and it was important for her to get along with them for the future harmony of the village. The rest of the villagers would stay home and tend the bear cub, but they would have first choice of the gifts brought back. Birchleaf was promised a chance to travel the next time. She pouted anyway.

The preparation plan was as follows. Grandfather, Red Uncle, and Clam were selected to go to the mountains to find a bear. White Uncle, Black Uncle, Father, and Sandcrab would build a new boat big enough to hold eight people and everything they would need for the journey. Tall Sister was in charge of constructing the sail. The older boys would make ropes, oars, and a new depth marker for the boat. All the women would make new ceremonial clothes, as well as extra decorated baskets to give as gifts to their relatives among the Blue, Black, Red, and White clans.

When the arrangements were decided, Birdwing dismissed the meeting. Flyingbird waited until the adults arose, as it was polite for a child to do. Her glance darted around since she couldn't, and fell upon me perched on the Bird Mountain Village tribal pole. Flyingbird nudged her cousin Straight Pine, and pointed to me with her chin. Soon the eyes of all the children were on me, which directed the focus of the adults my way as well.

"It's Flyingbird's spirit helper! The yellow bird has come! She hasn't been seen since she saved Flyingbird and Straight Pine from the tide when they were little. Now we know we've chosen the right plan," Grandfather rubbed his palms back and forth, to thank the spirits.

"Thank You for attending this meeting at Bird Mountain Village," Birdwing addressed me, also rubbing her hands together respectfully. "On behalf of the Golden clan, I welcome You. Now we must all get busy with our tasks. Please excuse us, and make Yourself at home."

I watched as Flyingbird beckoned toward herself with both hands in the gesture of welcome, and then ran into her house, reappearing with two gourd bowls, each full of gruel. She poured a bit from one bowl at the foot of my pole, and gave the other to Birdwing with her right hand, pulling up the long sleeve of her robe with her left hand at the same time.

46

They ate in silence. I flew down to try the gruel and found it tasty, flavored with garlic and onion, with flakes of something red that might have been cockscomb, which I saw growing nearby.

"Grandmother Birdwing, I'm ready to learn today's lesson. I'll try to do especially well, with my spirit helper here."

"Very well. You had every word correct of the songs you sang, so perhaps I should begin teaching you another. Each word is sacred."

"What happened to the girls your uncles stole?" Flyingbird asked Birdwing when the lesson was over. "You and Tall Sister are the only village elders."

"Questions, always questions. You'll learn everything in good time," grumbled Birdwing. But she did explain.

"Prosperity returned, and my mother Sunlight had four daughters of her own. Then Great Uncle Elmbark's wife wanted to take her daughters back to her own people. Her only son had already married a girl from Three Rocks Village to the north. We made them a boat and blessed it, but Elmbark died before they were ready to leave. He lies in our spirit yard. Taking his death as a signal from the spirits to hurry, Salmon and his wife and daughters loaded their boat, helped Elmbark's wife and daughters with theirs, and both families went back to their original villages. Salmon stayed with the small people of the Black clan catching fish for them to make up for stealing their daughter. He lived there until he died, and his spirit is there still. The women promised not to reveal our secrets. They took their own song staffs back with them, and that's why we don't sing of them and their lives."

"But you said your mother had four daughters. There's you and Tall Sister. Who are the others?"

"The Sea Goddess took two of my sisters away one day when they were fishing. We were sad, but Tall Sister and I were strong and healthy, and we each found husbands from villages up the coast. I was blessed with four daughters of my own, so Tall Sister's three sons didn't seem like such a calamity - until this generation, when we have only you."

"You're not old enough yet to be told the secrets, or to learn how to reach the spirits. Let's get to work on the new clothes."

Birdwing and Flyingbird joined the other women, working in the sunshine on simple looms, the warp threads kept taut with hanging stones.

The day was crisply pleasant. Azaleas were beginning to bloom at the edge of the woods. It was late in the season to catch a bear cub, and getting dangerous - most of the bears would be awake already, and hungrily looking for food. In order not to think bad thoughts and spoil the hunt, the weavers sang a weaving song, making up new verses in turn. Flyingbird admired the blue mouths of her mother and aunts, and wondered how soon they would begin her tattoo. It would be fun to have some other girls around to be her sisters. And the trip! Flyingbird hugged herself with the excitement of finding out, at last, what was out beyond the sparkling sea.

Birdwing thought of the Bear Spirits and hoped they would intervene again, but it wouldn't be wise to say so aloud. Instead, she took up her needle to embroider.

"After your first mouth tattoo, I'll teach you how to see far, into the past and into the future, as I am going to do now. I want to know how the hunters are doing."

Birdwing held the needle horizontally between the thumb and index fingers of both hands and stared at it, into it.

11

"Are you all right?" Kim Dong-su was looking anxiously at me as the drums stopped and the dancers mingled. I blinked Bird Mountain Village out of my eyes.

"Maybe the *makkolli* was too strong for me. I think we'd better go back to our *yogwan* now. It's a pretty long drive."

"You need some dinner first. Let me treat you to a real old-fashioned Korean meal."

At the suggestion of food, I discovered I was starving. A Korean meal sounded perfect. Dong-su knew which inn served Korean banquet dishes.

"You choose the food. I'll try anything." I abdicated all responsibility. "Anything but dog or snake, that is," I amended, remembering what my father had said.

"Dog is considered a delicacy, but you have to go to special restaurants to eat it. Snakes are used for a kind of medicine; we don't eat them much. Maybe you're thinking of eels."

"Could we skip the eels, too?" Maybe my father was right!

We sat on floor cushions at a low table - not quite in the ancient way, where each person would have had an individual table, but close enough. At first I tried to kneel the way Japanese women do, but my feet went to sleep in a few minutes, so I switched to sitting cross-legged like Dong-su, glad I had on jeans.

Dong-su ordered a series of traditional dishes. The waiter brought more than a dozen small bowls, with foods of various tastes, colors, and textures. I tried to follow Dong-su for the proper manners, as we plunged our chopsticks into the small bowls. The crisp and salty squares of seaweed were delightfully crunchy, contrasting pleasantly with the batter-fried squash and a spinach-like green vegetable.

"Try the *kimchi*," urged Dong-su. "Most foreigners don't like it, but a real Korean eats it at every meal - the hotter the better. Find out if you're a real Korean."

I had avoided *kimchi* so far, sure I wouldn't like it, even though Elaine was always urging it on me. But after blanching at dog and eel, I thought I should try at least one strange thing. As I lifted a leaf of cabbage spiced with red pepper and garlic with my chopsticks, the aroma stirred a memory - too indistinct to capture and hold, but very strong, even compelling. It was a memory of being held snugly, and being fed. Was the lattice from my nightmare there, too? No, this wasn't a visual memory. The feeling floated away.

"It's delicious," I agreed. "I guess I'm not a foreigner after all."

"You are the most intriguing mix of foreign and not foreign. You're learning to love your Korean roots, aren't you?"

I happily admitted it, keeping my reservations to myself this time.

"There's so much to learn. Thanks for showing me the temple today, and your favorite painting. You certainly know a lot about your country." I smiled into Dong-su's eyes, and immediately realized it was a mistake. His return smile was more than friendly.

"You could have another Korean experience. We could spend the night here in a Korean style room. Who knows what else you might learn? I'm a good teacher." Dong-su's voice was soft, and his eyes begged.

What would it be like to make love to a smooth Asian body instead of hairy Ed, I wondered, but then I squashed the dangerous thought. I couldn't deny my attraction to Dong-su, and obviously, he knew it. With an effort, I summoned up enough common sense to overcome the temptation. I just didn't know what difficulties I'd be getting into.

"I have to worry about my image," I said, a little flippantly, trying to hide my desire. "I'm a scientist, an archaeologist. Who would take me seriously if I had an affair with you? Anyway, my roommates will miss me. We definitely must go back."

I put my napkin on the table and stood up.

"Sure, I'll deliver you safely to the *yogwan*. You have to try some pear-apples first, though. Remember, we saw the trees from the bus. They're in season now. And you should at least see one of the elegant old-style rooms this hotel has. We'll have some dessert and ginseng tea, and then go back."

Dong-su made arrangements with the waiter, and I followed uneasily down a corridor to a room with a low table set up with china bowls and silver chopsticks, and cushions on the floor. Several antique chests lined the walls, their wood polished to a high gloss. I couldn't resist touching their satiny surface. I decided that I'd been silly to worry about the private room. Without a bed, what could happen?

The waiter coughed at the doorway, and then brought in the *bae* - pear-apples - peeled, cut up and skewered on toothpicks, and served on a black lacquer tray. He also brought small handleless cups and a teapot, and disappeared.

"Sit here," Dong-su patted a cushion, and then took the cushion beside me. "We have to eat the *bae* before the tea - the tastes don't mix well. But see what you think of our famous pear-apples."

The crisp, juicy fruit was halfway between a pear and an apple, but better than either.

"Delicious. Even tastier than I expected." The juice ran down my chin, and I gave it a swipe as I reached for another piece.

"Tell me about your family, and life in America. How is it different from here?"

So I told him a bit about Mom and her painting, about Daddy the lawyer, and about Heidi, who wants to be a ballerina.

"Do you think you belong there, or here?"

"What an odd question - I don't speak Korean even as well as a three-year-old child, and I don't understand your customs. How could I belong here? I just happen to have Asian features. Otherwise I'm true-blue American."

"True-blue?"

"It means the real thing all the way through."

"But why blue?"

"Maybe it has something to do with red, white, and blue, the colors of the flag - or maybe with blue-blood, I don't know. Maybe because it rhymes. It's just an expression. I've never thought about it."

"What's blue blood? Ours is red."

"It means noble by birth, like people who came over on the Mayflower think they are." This was a Boston joke.

"What's noble about that? I thought they were prisoners, or rejects of some kind."

"Well, they were rejected for their religious beliefs - and certainly weren't nobility in England. Nobody pays much attention to it, unless you happen to be one of them, although WASPs - White Anglo-Saxon Protestants - pretty much ran the country until recently. I just used the Mayflower descendants as an example of what blue blood means."

"You know what we call it?"

"No. What?"

"True Bone. We think breeding is in the bone, not in the blood."

"Are you True Bone?"

"My ancestors were Kims of the royal family of Kaya. There's an ancient book with the names of all the generations inscribed."

"How ancient?"

"My father says it goes back seventeen hundred years."

I was awed. "That makes Mayflower descendents real Johnny-come-latelys! But to get back to your question of belonging, how did you feel in France? Did you belong?"

"I felt very much at home there. I liked the people, and they were very welcoming to me. I would have liked to stay longer, but when I finished my degree, my visa ran out. I'm glad I came home, though - otherwise I wouldn't have met you."

"Your experience in France is different, I think," I objected, ignoring his flattery. "My roommate at I-House feels at home in Korea, too. She speaks Korean well, and she knows how to behave. But when she makes

51

mistakes, she's forgiven - she's still a foreigner, after all, and can't be expected to know all the customs. It's not the same with me. People *expect* me to act like a Korean, and when I don't, they think I'm being rude on purpose, and they're insulted. I feel like I've let them down, without knowing what I've done. And no one will tell me!"

"Eventually you'll learn. We call it *nunchi*, eye discernment. I've seen you developing it already. You're beginning to think before you speak, as Koreans do."

He poured the ginseng tea into the small cups.

"Do you know about ginseng? In Korean we say *insam*. That means man-shaped, and the root often does resemble a man - with all his parts, if you know what I mean. The more manlike they are, the better the plants are for you. They say that if you have some every day of your life, you'll live forever."

"Isn't ginseng supposed to be an aphrodisiac?" I asked warily.

"You've heard that, have you? Well, you don't need to worry. It only works if you want it to. It just helps you to make up your mind."

"Does it still grow wild in the woods?"

"It's pretty rare in the wild. Most of what's sold is grown commercially, under shaded roofs. It takes at least five years to grow a proper root, so it's expensive to grow. But the best plants are those that grow deep in the forest. The person who chances to find a full grown plant with a well-shaped root can make a fortune."

I looked into my cup, at the tea-colored beverage with small seeds floating in it.

"Are those lemon seeds?"

"No, taste one. Haven't you ever had pine nuts?"

"Never. Another first."

I liked the flavor of the pine nuts, but I thought the ginseng tasted like dirt. Still, I was thirsty, so I drank it. We talked of comparative cultures, and finished the whole pot.

Dong-su put his arm around me companionably.

"It's pretty late. Still want to go back to the *yogwan*?"

I didn't. Was it the ginseng? I leaned my head on his shoulder. A brief soft tempting kiss pushed me farther in the direction of staying.

"What would people say? That Clara Alden is a bad girl? That she doesn't know how to act like a proper Korean?"

"This is very proper, and very Korean. We can stay in this room, and no one need ever know we were here together."

The bedding turned out to be in the chests along the wall, and soon we had a soft and cozy nest on the floor. We made love slowly and thoroughly. He did have some things to teach me. He called them Buddhist poses, but I think he was joking.

I woke up early, tasting the garlic from the kimchi. As I looked around the room, it dissolved into another place. I was on the bird pole again at Bird Mountain Village.

12

Perched on the village pole, I could hear a distant rhythm - ta ta ta DONK ta KUNK. The sound came from the mountain path, and I looked expectantly toward the forest. From my high perch I caught a glimpse of the returning bear hunters. Grandfather beat the drum, Red Uncle carried a parcel of deer meat wrapped in its own skin, and Clam came last, with a bear cub not much bigger than a human baby sitting serenely on his shoulder.

Soon the entire village heard the drum's announcement of the hunters' successful return. By the time the procession rounded the last turn into the village, the rest of the inhabitants had assembled into a respectful line, ready to welcome the bear cub in the traditional way, waving both hands toward themselves. The bear cub waved too, making the gesture solemnly and politely. Flyingbird laughed with delight.

The cub wasn't old enough to be weaned. According to custom, a nursing mother shared her milk. Sunflower had the only baby, so she took the cub to suckle along with her infant son. When Flyingbird realized that the bear would live in their house, she couldn't keep still. She ran around in circles and did cartwheels.

"My brother bear, my brother bear," she sang.

"Your sister bear," her mother corrected, having had a chance to inspect the cub. "The bears have honored us by sending a she-bear." The small bundle of fur snuggled up and nursed, gurgling and slurping.

That evening by the fire the hunters told the story of capturing the cub. It was late in the spring, but the hunters were lucky. The first day the bear seekers climbed the mountain, where Grandfather and Red Uncle set spring traps with poisoned arrows. The next day a deer was caught. Grandfather skinned it leaving the hide all in one piece, and Red Uncle cut up the meat into chunks. Clam wrapped the meat in the skin, to make it easier to carry.

Taking the deer meat with them, Grandfather found a cave he had visited many times. Some years bears used the cave and some years they didn't. The hunters groped into the dark cave quietly, leaving the deer meat at the entrance. Feeling along the rock wall, Clam put his hand into a pile of fur that moved. A she-bear and her two cubs were just waking up!

"Bears!" Clam whispered, startled. He reached into the furry mass and plucked one cub. Red Uncle went back to the entrance for a large chunk of deer meat, which he tossed to the mother bear.

"Think of your other baby!" said Grandfather softly. "We will take good care of this one, and send it back with gifts and blessings when it's grown."

The hunting party snatched up the rest of the meat and hurried down the mountain.

The bear cub settled happily into its new surroundings. Sunflower said she nursed more gently than Dolphin, who was beginning to teethe. The cub grew as fast as a mushroom, and soon was eating everything the villagers ate. Each morning Flyingbird took her to the waste area. All the children played with her while the sun was up, but at night she slept on the mat beside Flyingbird. Sister Bear, as Flyingbird called her, loved to imitate, and the children taught her the gesture of welcome and the gesture of thanks. The bear was given the run of the house, and explored every corner. She took things out of boxes, and turned them around and over in her paws.

"She's just as curious as you are, Flyingbird," her mother said with a smile, "but don't encourage her explorations too much. The first time she gets into trouble she'll have to be put into the bear cage."

And sure enough, it was curiosity that started the trouble.

Next to the sleeping platform, birchbark chests stored extra mats and ritual clothing. One day Flyingbird saw the cub looking at an embroidered robe. Sister Bear seemed to be studying the details, as she turned it around and looked at it from different angles.

"If you like it so much, I'll make a you your own robe," Flyingbird promised.

Flyingbird rummaged through one of the chests where cloth was kept, and found a practice piece she'd woven from nettle fibers. It wasn't too bad for a first try. She went outside to draw various designs in the sand. Looking at her creations, she selected a curving design with the birdwing pattern that belonged to the village, a bear's ear as Sister Bear's emblem, and enclosed the whole in a radiant sun, the symbol of the extended Golden clan. She cut the designs from black cloth, and sewed them on the white cloth with tiny stitches. It took Flyingbird several days to make the robe, sitting and sewing with the grown up women. When the robe was finished, the women admired it, and praised Fyingbird for her handicraft.

The bear looked very fine wearing her new robe. Flyingbird put on her own ceremonial robe and carried the cub around to all the houses, introducing her as Sister Bear. Sister Bear acknowledged her new status by making the village beckoning gesture. Everyone smiled about this except Birchleaf. Birchleaf had no children, and she was impatient with all of them. Flyingbird particularly annoyed her, with her curiosity, her incessant talking, and her perpetual motion.

55

"It isn't right to give the bear a name, and dress her like a human," she huffed to Birdwing. "The Bear Spirits will be offended. Something terrible will come of it, mark my words."

Birdwing ignored Birchleaf at first, thinking she'd soon find something else to complain about. Instead, Birchleaf began grumbling to Black Uncle. It was easier for him to agree with his wife than to try to talk her out of her bad humor. Birchleaf worked on Pebble to convince her that Flyingbird was offending the spirits, and soon both Pebble and White Uncle agreed that dressing the bear was wrong.

Birdwing continued to ignore the mutterings, because confrontations weren't good for village harmony. An unforeseen event forced her to deal with it.

One night, when the moon was full and should have been radiating its luminous light, a shadow crept across it, darkening the sky. Uneasiness fell upon Bird Mountain Village. Out of the silence, Birchleaf began to scream, "It's Flyingbird's fault, it's Flyingbird's fault. And yours," she pointed at Birdwing. "You shouldn't have let Flyingbird treat the bear cub like a human."

Birdwing said nothing. She brought out the sun-up drum, and thumped it with her hand, at first slowly and then faster and faster, and gradually brought back the whole moon. But the villagers were still unsettled, even with the moon back. Birchleaf and Pebble insisted on having a meeting then and there.

Everyone in the village, including the children and the bear, brought their mats to the meeting circle. Birdwing brought a packet of cloth, covered with embroidery. When each person was settled cross-legged on a mat, Birdwing drew out of the packet six divining sticks made of split yarrow stalks, each with a flat side and a curving side. She gathered them in both hands and held them for a moment, then threw them with force to the ground. As she studied them with concentration, the villagers, adults and children, sat very still, to allow the spirits to send their message.

After a long silence while she studied them, Birdwing picked up the sticks and handed them to her left.

"Birchleaf, they point to you. It's your privilege to ask the first question, and throw the sticks for an answer."

Birchleaf held the six sticks in both hands briefly, wasting no time in contemplation. "Are the bear spirits offended?" she asked, and tossed the sticks up, letting them fall to the ground between her hands.

The sticks fell with all the flat sides up. Flyingbird drew in her breath. It didn't take an interpreter to know that the answer was "yes!"

Flyingbird and Sister Bear both sat rigidly, and the other children looked anxious. Straight Pine closed his eyes. This was serious trouble. It looked like Birchleaf was right.

Birchleaf passed the sticks to Black Uncle, on her left, with a triumphant smirk. He took his turn with the sticks.

"Do the bear spirits object to the children playing with the cub?" he asked.

All the round sides were up, clearly "no." Birchleaf sniffed. Flyingbird let out her breath. That was better, but the session wasn't over yet.

Red Uncle took his turn. "Should the bear cub go back to the forest?"

The sticks fell three up and three down, meaning yes and no, the answer was too complex to respond yes or no.

There was muttering around the circle. What could that mean?

Pebble threw the sticks next, asking whether the bear should wear human clothes. Five round sides and one flat indicated that the spirits didn't like it much, but it wasn't a punishable offense. Pebble nodded grimly and passed the sticks to White Uncle.

He considered his question for a moment. "Should Flyingbird spend so much time with the bear?"

This time there were four flat and two round - the spirits didn't care strongly, but tended to agree that it was okay for Flyingbird to spend time with the cub.

Magpie passed the sticks on without asking a question. She was on Flyingbird's side, but was afraid she might harm the case with the wrong question.

"Is the bear happy in Bird Mountain Village?" Great Uncle asked before his toss, and got five flats and one round. The bear cub was happy with nearly everything.

The children weren't allowed to touch the sacred sticks, for they carried too much power. Great Uncle passed them over Flyingbird and Straight Pine to Father.

"Are the Bear Spirits offended by something the adults do?" Father asked as he threw the sticks. Six flat sides said yes. The complaining faction was offended by both the question and the result.

Sunflower took the sticks, and laid them carefully across her palms. She paused, and considered a moment before asking, "Do the Bear Spirits object to Birchleaf's complaining?"

This was a dangerous question, because it might cause a division in the group, especially if the answer wasn't clear. But the sticks were all flat - a very plain yes. Birchleaf made her mouth tight and narrow. Sunflower always made her seem in the wrong, and it wasn't fair.

Tall Sister reached for the sticks across Clam and Sandcrab. She hadn't taken sides.

"Will this bear cause trouble in Bird Mountain Village?"

All the flat sides turned up again. There was trouble ahead. Big trouble. Why hadn't someone asked this question earlier, so there would be throws left to find out what kind of trouble? Only Grandfather and Birdwing were left to ask the necessary questions.

"Will sickness come because of the bear?" asked Grandfather. The answer was six round sides, definitely no. If not sickness, then what kind of trouble?

Before Grandfather could pick up the sticks and hand them across Sister Bear to Birdwing, the cub leaned over and scooped up the divining sticks with both paws. She put her head back and hooted, a long, slow, eerie howl, and dropped the sticks on the ground in front of her. Everyone drew in their breath and held it fearfully. This time the sticks fell with all the flat sides up. Yes, they said. But yes, what? What had the bear asked? The villagers sat wide-eyed in silence, looking to Birdwing for an interpretation of this strange event.

In the stillness, Sister Bear picked up the sticks and handed them politely to Birdwing.

Birdwing framed her question carefully.

"Is this a very special bear?" she asked. "Is it all right to call her by a human name, and let her play with the children as if she were a child? Is that what the Bear Spirits want?"

No one objected to her multiple questions.

All eyes were on the sticks as they fell. Five were flat, yes. The one round one meant "not quite."

"The divination tells us," Birdwing summed up, as she put the divining sticks away, "that Flyingbird must not dress Sister Bear in human clothes. Otherwise, it is acceptable to treat her like a relative, as Flyingbird does, and Birchleaf must stop complaining about it. The spirits want us all to consider the bear cub to be Flyingbird's sister, and a member of the Golden clan.

"We came out of that all right," Flyingbird whispered to Sister Bear after the meeting broke up. "But how did you learn that trick?"

Sister Bear didn't answer. She nuzzled Flyingbird, and they curled up together on Flyingbird's sleeping platform. But, as messenger of the spirit world, I understood what Sister Bear said. She asked if she would ever go back to the forest.

When the moon was new, marking the proper day to fell a tree for the boat, the log cutting party assembled. Flyingbird asked permission to go along, and I flew with them, curious to learn how a large tree could be chopped down without metal tools. Grandfather brought a stone axe, newly sharpened, lashed to a wooden handle with a cord made of gut. We went deep into the forest until Grandfather pointed to a large tree, marked with prayer sticks. Grandfather had reserved this tree for a boat several seasons earlier, but it hadn't been used because it had grown so tall. The prayer sticks with their shaved curls were still standing erect.

"The tree has agreed to become a boat. It will carry us safely across the waves, in good weather and bad," said Grandfather. "See how the sticks stand tall."

After thanking the tree for its sacrifice, Grandfather cut it down with his axe. Chips flew, but it took many blows to cut it down, while the helpers sang a wood-cutting song to the tree so it would give in to the axe easily. When the tree finally toppled, Grandfather took twelve strides and marked off the other end of the boat. After he chopped off the top of the tree, everyone helped remove the limbs. Flyingbird and Straight Pine set out the prayer sticks for the treetop and greeted it by rubbing their hands together. It took all six of them to bring the large log back to the village, and even carrying it lengthwise, some small trees had to be sacrificed to bring the log out of the thick forest. "This is the forest primeval," I quoted to myself.

Grandfather supervised the boat building. The cavity of the boat was made with fire - embers given by the Hearth Spirit. As the wood burned it was scraped away with a thick but pointed stone tool, and more embers applied. The process was slow and tedious, and the assigned workers did it by turns, two at a time. It took many days to hollow out the log to its full depth. The sides were pushed out by heating water with stones from the fire, and inserting longer and longer planks to keep the sides apart. We've lost that kind of patience in the modern world, I thought, watching the process.

The final shaping of the boat's interior had to be done with great care so that it would be deep enough to sit in while the hull remained thick and sturdy. Next the boat was fitted with seats, resting on ledges that Grandfather had directed to be left in the wood in exactly the right places. The seats helped to keep the sides of the boat apart, as well as providing places for rowers and passengers to sit, on each side of the boat. The prow and stern were whittled to their proper square-ended shapes with knives of obsidian, newly sharpened by removing tiny flakes with pressure from an antler tool. Notches were carved along the sides of the boat to rest the six pairs of oars and keep them from slipping.

Grandfather fixed the mast firmly into a notch amidships. A rough cabin took shape on the stern, and a high platform to stack the baskets of gifts and provisions was lashed on the prow, so nothing would wash overboard.

The boat lay proudly on the beach, and the other villagers left their tasks to admire it. But it wasn't quite finished. One more step was needed. After further prayers for a safe journey, Grandfather carved eyes into the sides of the prow so that the boat could see properly, and in the middle of each side carved a bird above a mountain, so that anyone who came across the boat would know it belonged to Bird Mountain Village. Straight Pine rubbed white clay into the incised designs to make them stand out, so the carvings could be seen from far away.

In the meantime, Sister Bear played. Ever since she threw the divining sticks, she'd become the jester of the village, and was accepted as one of the children. Everyone laughed at her tricks except Birchleaf, who avoided her. One of Sister Bear's favorite pastimes was paddling in the water by the shore. Sister Bear clowned by floating on her back, with all four legs sticking out of the water. She also liked to slide on the rocks when they were wet with seawater, and splash into the ocean. Sometimes she scooped up a fish with her paw, and offered it to the nearest person. If they threw it back, she'd catch it and eat it herself. When Flyingbird gave her treats, she stood on her hind legs and put her paws together in a clumsy salute. Sister Bear learned the shuffling dance step that the villagers did each morning to greet the new day. She stood in the line beside Flyingbird, attached to a rope. But she never tried to run away.

"She's not a bear, she's a person!" Flyingbird said to Sunflower.

"No, Flyingbird, she's a spirit, a gift from the bears, and someday we'll give her presents to take back to the other Bear Spirits. The Spirits said it was all right to treat her like a person, but you have to remember that she isn't one of us. When we send her back to her family, she'll tell them how well we've treated her, so that more bears will come. But that day is a long way off. First she has to grow up. I love the bear cub, too, and we should enjoy her while we can."

Everyone in the village knew how to make pots, but Magpie's were the most beautiful. Flyingbird began to make pots along with her, for she needed to know all the skills of the village as its future leader. You could never tell when the spirits would take someone back, so an apprentice was needed for all special skills. Flyingbird, as the only girl, had to learn all the women's skills, and know about the men's tasks as well. Magpie showed her a place at the edge of the fresh water lake where reeds grew. Under the reeds the earth was gray and slippery, and it smelled like the air just before a summer rain.

"This earth makes the best pots. It's naturally smooth, free of rocks and other particles, and it's very sticky. If you don't add sand, though, it will crack when you give it to the Hearth Spirit," Magpie instructed.

Flyingbird added sand to her clay, as Magpie told her, and pounded it to get all the air pockets out. When Magpie said it was ready, she made a flat base, and pressed it into a large leaf which could be turned without touching the pot. Then she made coils, pinching each round together and forming the coils into a round neckless jar. She flattened a coil and broke it in half to make two strap handles, one on each shoulder, and smoothed them with wet fingers into the body of the pot, so the joins didn't show. Magpie made ten pots - eight jars and two bowls. Flyingbird made two rather small ones, adding loop handles to the neck of a tiny jar. The pots were set aside to dry for several hours.

Later in the day, before the pots were completely dry, Magpie showed Flyingbird how to decorate them. Using carved sticks, she pressed the designs in rows. Magpie's signature was a circle within a circle. Flyingbird asked Red Uncle to carve a design that made a rosette each time she pushed the stick into the soft clay. After they were decorated, Magpie set out six sticks beside them. Each day at sun-up she took one away, until they were ready for the Hearth Spirit to make them hard.

On the proper day, Magpie started a fire with an ember from Birdwing's hearth. Next she planted prayer sticks, and when the fire blazed and began to make glowing coals, she set the pots upside down into the fire to cook. Rubbing their hands, palms together, Flyingbird and Magpie asked the Hearth Spirit to harden the pots evenly, and not break them. These vessels had to carry fresh water and other provisions for the journey along the coast, in case Grandmother Wind pushed them far out in the salty sea.

Flyingbird and I followed Pebble as she gathered tall reeds to make the fine, soft baskets that were used to hold dry food. After digging up roots of a large lily plant with long pointed leaves, she cut them into chunks, and tossed the root chunks into a large open bowl. She added water and half of the reeds. The rest she soaked in plain water, then spread them on a mat to dry. Several days later, the lily root had dyed part of them a soft, shining yellow color, the rest were bleached oyster white by the sun. As the yellow reeds dried, Pebble searched for the round black reeds that grew on the edges of the pond. The finished baskets of various sizes were works of art to my eye. Patterns of yellow edged in black on the stark white background made eye-pleasing contrasts.

Some baskets were small, and would be used to contain treasures like shell earrings, shell bracelets, and special amulets left by the spirits for the finder. Some baskets were larger; they were for knives, scrapers and other tools. The largest were for grains. Pebble wove basket hats, too, and in the very best and finest ones she included bird feathers. I dropped a few yellow feathers for Flyingbird's hat, and Pebble thanked me by rubbing her hands, and nodding to me.

Sunflower and Birchleaf made new clothes for everyone. They made a foray into the forest to locate an elm which had been marked by prayer sticks. After stripping off some of the bark, the inner bark was gathered, soaked and then hung to dry. In a few days it came apart in fine threads. Next, they wove fine white robes on plain looms, the same ones they used for mats and belts. I marveled at the skill it took to make the supple, shiny cloth. The shape of each robe was a simple rectangle, with a slit to slip it over the head, and a sash to tie it around the waist

When the twenty-four robes were completed, each woman took out her bone embroidery needles. They chatted and sang together as they decorated the robes with bold curving designs in black, made with applique of black cloth. Every robe was different, but each had stylized birds and suns, and each was recognizable as the style of Bird Mountain Village.

When the robes were finished, Tall Sister organized the production of the sail. She used the strong inner bark from the mulberry tree, which had to be carefully peeled off and cut into strips to be sewn together with hempen thread. The sail needed to be firm enough to hold the breath of Grandmother Wind, but it had to be flexible, too, so it could be rolled up easily when Grandmother Wind was angry and blew too hard

Straight Pine organized the boys to make new ropes and oars. A boat needs lots of lines: fishing lines, mooring lines, ropes for the sails. They worked in pairs on the ropes, one holding the end, the other braiding. Straight Pine made the depth marker himself, for he was the one with the patience to grind it to a point. He searched the beach for a heavy, solid rock of the right size. There was nothing on the beach, so he walked to the river where the stones are well rounded. He picked up many pebbles before he found one with one end thinner than the other to start with, which made his work much easier.

Taking his selected pebble back to the village, Straight Pine first chipped it into the approximate shape he wanted. He prepared a striking platform and then struck the pebble with a rounded piece of granite. When he was satisfied with the general shape, he rubbed and rubbed the stone on a coarse sandstone grinding slab. One side at a time became flat, each angling in toward the point, until the implement took on the shape of a thin top. Finally, Straight Pine carved a groove around the upper end, to keep the cord wound through it from slipping. Finally he attached one of the new long cords, and made a knot in the cord every arm's length. With this tool they would measure the depth of the sea on their journey. It was dangerous where the sea was more than twenty arms deep, and they went there only briefly, for the large fish. To go a long distance they stayed closer to shore, in shallow water.

The bear cub grew faster than a human child, and soon was as big as Flyingbird.   Sister Bear was really too big for Flyingbird to control. She could have run away when they went down to the water, but she never did.   The girl and the bear floated lazily on their backs, or raced each other on the sand.   Flyingbird could win easily when Sister Bear tried to run on her hind legs, but on all fours the bear could outrun any human.   Sometimes Flyingbird would throw a clump of seaweed to Sister Bear, and they'd play catch, which ended with a tumble on the sand. Sister Bear was usually gentle as they tussled on the beach, but one day she cuffed Flyingbird by mistake, leaving long shallow claw marks.

"The time has come to put that bear into her own house," announced Sunflower, putting willow bark on the scratches.   Flyingbird pleaded that Sister Bear didn't mean to hurt her, but Sunflower called for a meeting, and everyone agreed it was time to cage Sister Bear.

The bear cage was reconstructed so that it would be strong, but with wide gaps between the logs to allow the bear to be seen by everyone, and to take part in village life.   The bear could be taken in and out by removing a single vertical log.   Flyingbird had tears in her eyes when Sister Bear was led up the notched ladder, but she didn't want the bear to feel unhappy in the cage.

"This is your house now, Sister Bear. I'll come here every morning to take you to the latrine area, and we can play on the beach. But I'll miss your warm fur by my side at night."

"Sister Bear will go to sleep for the winter anyway," said Sunflower. "Look how plump she's getting.   And you'll leave soon on your journey."

The bear's rich glossy coat showed that she was well fed, and she didn't seem to mind the cage.

The villagers had plenty to eat and extra to share.   Extra provisions, gathered up over the spring and summer, were kept in a raised storehouse.   When the berries were ripe, after the villagers ate their fill, the rest were dried and stored in baskets in the storehouse.   The millet grains that grew on the flat land near the river were beaten into baskets as they ripened, and the grains were put away for winter, too.   The stalks were dried for thatch.   Several kinds of turnip and potato-like roots were collected, and the tops of some had been put back into the ground as thanks to the root spirits, asking them to send more roots the next year.

Some of each fish catch was split open to the head and hung on sticks to dry. The sticks were fitted into notches near the top of the storehouse. Mushrooms were collected, dried, and put in covered baskets. Azalea petals for the wine, other flowers and leaves for color and taste, and wild onions and garlic for soup flavoring went into other baskets. Deer meat was cut into strips and dried. Root crops were preserved in jars holding brine and flavored with garlic, onion, and small shrimps, with red cockscomb flowers added for color. It was delicious with millet gruel.

Finally, the storehouse was full except for the space reserved for acorn cakes. The clan would have to wait a week or so for the acorn harvest, and then everything would be ready for the trip to go looking for brides for Clam and Sandcrab. While White Uncle and Pebble went fishing, everyone else was busy with their handicrafts, sitting cross-legged on their mats in the shade of the pines. Red Uncle, Black Uncle, and Father were making fishhooks out of stone and bone. Red Uncle made the stone cylinders, Father ground the bone shanks to a fine point, and Black Uncle lashed them together as the pieces were completed.

In the midst of this activity, a visitors' boat was sighted. A fan-shaped shell was carved on each side of the unfamiliar craft, telling its village name. White Uncle and Pebble's boat escorted the strangers to shore. Work was abandoned, and everyone scurried to the shore to greet the two boats. Visitors didn't appear often.

"This is my brother, White Playful Seal," White Uncle introduced his relative. "Rowing with him are his wife, Red Apple, and her sisters Red Seaweed and Red Sunset. They've come from Shell Island Village to invite us to their Bear Festival. The Sea Goddess guided them here."

Red Uncle gave the women a special greeting, rubbing noses with them, since they were his clan, although not from his village. Pebble brought dry robes for the visitors while the children rinsed their salty ones in the freshwater lake. Sunflower speared some of the new fish catch on green willow sticks, and put them above a bed of coals. When they began their feast, the women of Bird Mountain Village were pleased that their guests followed the proper etiquette, putting all the fish bones in a pile to be taken afterward to the proper dumping ground. White Uncle had to explain to them that the spirits in Bird Mountain Village expected this treatment, for it was not the custom among the Red clan.

When guests and villagers had eaten their fill, Birdwing ladled wine out of a decorated jar which stood in the place of honor under the spirit window. Each woman brought her own family's gourd bowls, decorated with red and black lacquer and painted in curving designs. The visitors had their own bowls, too, wooden ones with intricate designs carved into the sides rather than painted on the surface. A short carved stick with a unique design was held across the bowl. Each person dipped her stick into the wine, and sprinkled a few drops into the fire.

"The Hearth Spirit will be tipsy tonight," chuckled Grandfather. "She loves a party."

13

I fell asleep again, so deeply that Dong-su had to shake me awake. Breakfast was like the dinner the night before - another feast with lots of little dishes, which we ate in our room. I nibbled pear-apples and seaweed, which seemed more like breakfast than the other choices set out before me, but Dong-su sampled all the bowls, even the *kimchi*. He must have a cast-iron stomach.

We decided to have another hike in Soraksan. This time the path we chose led us up a steep slope to the top of a crag, with a view of jagged mountains in all directions. Morning mist added an unreal dimension to the scene, detaching the mountain tops and making them float above the valleys. A bird with long wings glided into the view. In this atmosphere I was almost willing to believe in dreams of Spirit Birds.

Dong-su and I giggled a lot on the way back to the *yogwan*, and I was sorry to see this lovely weekend come to a close. Dong-su went to talk to Ki-dok in his room, so I took my pack to my room. When I entered, I was surprised to see Elaine and Liesl there.

"You don't mind if we cozy up with you, I hope? Makes the *won* go farther, and the girls said it would be okay if we slept here too."

The room was big enough, though barely, for five quilts on the floor.

"Sure. I've been missing our daily chats. But what are you doing here? Did you come to help with the dig?"

"Elaine wanted to tape the women's round dance that's ritually performed only once a year by the lunar calendar," explained Liesl. "So we had to come now. My work is to photgraph Buddhist temples on Soraksan. We're here for a week, if you can stand it."

"The ceremony sounds interesting. Can I come, too?"

"You missed it while you were out carousing last night. Didn't you notice the full moon? Those women were having a great time. Elaine has it all on tapes; maybe you can see it later. The local gossip is that your `sonny boy' came and whisked you away in his chariot. I hope you had fun. " Liesl batted her lashes and smirked.

"Soraksan was nice. We had a couple of hikes in the mountains, and a delicious traditional Korean feast." I left out the other details, but they must have showed on my face.

"So," Elaine cleared her throat. "What's your informed opinion about Korean men now?"

"Ssh!" I giggled. "The walls have ears. Dong-su's still here, talking to Oh Ki-dok. Let's go out front so you can meet him before he leaves, if you'd like."

But Dong-su's car was pulling away as we stepped outside. He gave a wave without turning around, and was gone. I felt abandoned. At least he could have said good-bye after seducing me. I wondered if there were some cultural meaning I missed, or if that was just Dong-su's way.

"Dong-su had to leave in a hurry," Ki-dok explained. "He had a phone call to get right back to Seoul."

"What could be so urgent?" asked Elaine.

"He didn't say. But he did ask me to tell Miss Alden he'll be back next weekend."

14 🛠

After I assigned numbers to the squares in my grid, I wrote the number of each square on a separate piece of paper. To choose the random sample, we made a ceremony of drawing the slips of paper out of a prehistoric pot which Hwang-ok had pieced together over several evenings. Each member of the crew in turn drew out a numbered slip, until we had the numbers of eight two-meter squares. The test squares selected chanced to fall into one group of three squares and one of four, with the final square off by itself. I decided to excavate them in clusters, and began with the group of four squares nearest to Locality A, where Ki-dok was excavating.

The two girl students were assigned to my excavation team, as well as two of the guys. I split them into two teams, each with a guy and a girl. The girls giggled and the boys made faces. "It would be better for Sun-hi and me to dig together," Hwang-ok whispered in my ear. "The boys don't like to dig with us."

"You're just as competent as they are, what difference does it make?"

"Maybe none in America, but big difference in Korea."

I sighed and reassigned them.

Everything had to be just right, so I told them to trowel from the surface. Troweling takes longer than shoveling, but it improves data recovery. I made them screen every bucketful too, in case any small items had been missed. They got so good at troweling that only very small stone chips were found in the screens. We saved every scrap, for whatever information it would afford.

The crew dug for several days before anything of much interest emerged from the ground. Keeping the edges of the pits straight was hard in the sandy soil, which seemed to slump inward as fast as the side walls were cleaned up, but I was strict with my crew, and they learned the importance of straight walls. The square went down to one meter deep, and then almost two. The Korean students were too polite to grumble where I could hear them, but I felt their dissatisfaction anyway. I wasn't too pleased myself, and began to wonder if random sampling could be inappropriate here.

At last artifacts were found in greater and greater numbers. The students left each object in place until the whole level was cleared. Every square was drawn and photographed, both the floor plan and the sides, and each artifact was located in three dimensions before it was removed. This information, plus a unique designation of letters and numbers, went into my laptop computer, to be augmented later with measurements and other observations on the artifacts.

This is a labor-intensive way to excavate, but it's important. There were hundreds of potsherds, and many were different from those in Ki-dok's squares! Instead of stamped designs there were pinched-up ridges in triangular designs. The two areas had similar stone tools, but more of the stone in our squares was obsidian. These distributions were puzzling.

In Ki-dok's area, hearths and then house floors were discovered. Most of the floors were quite similar - four or five meters in length and width, with a central square hearth surrounded by river cobbles. They were all dug below the surface of the ground at the time they were built. One floor, just like the others but much smaller, was found at the far end of the trench, some twenty meters from the cluster of dwellings already excavated.

"This floor is too small for a house," Ki-dok mused. Do you think it's a storage building?"

"With a hearth in it? Don't you suppose it's a special purpose building?"

"Like what?" challenged Ki-dok.

"Like a birth hut," I said. "Or a menstrual hut."

He didn't know the English word, and in spite of my anthropological training I had a hard time telling him. It seemed he didn't know the basic facts. I'm not sure he believed me.

"Let's look at another odd house in the long trench," he suggested. "Maybe you have some ideas about that one, too."

We strolled over to the other end of his dig.

"Maybe we made a mistake," said Ki-dok, "but it looks like there are two hearths in the same house. What do you think?"

The two square hearths, about a meter apart, did seem to belong to one house. I troweled the side wall to look at freshly exposed earth for evidence of overlap, but didn't find any. The outline of the floor was continuous, and longer than the usual floor. The hearths were at exactly the same level, too.

"I think you're right that it's a twin-hearthed dwelling," I concluded. "Have you ever seen another one?"

"In the far northeast they excavated a house floor with five hearths, but that's the only other one I know of. Naturally, I haven't seen it - I'm not allowed into North Korea. Why would a house have more than one hearth?"

"Maybe an extended family lived there - brothers and their wives and children, for instance, or the basic family at one hearth and the grandparents at the other. In English they're called extended families."

"That makes sense. Some farm families still live in extended families."

15

Elaine and Liesl enjoyed their explorations of the east coast, but neither one had finished what they set out to do. They decided to stay longer.

"Come with us to Sorak for the weekend," Liesl invited me.

"Sorry, previous engagement. Dong-su is coming and we're going to the beach at Yangyang. I have to keep up my language lessons, you know." I smiled smugly.

"Finally I get to meet the elusive tutor," said Elaine.

But it didn't turn out that way. Liesl and Elaine had planned to leave for Sorak early. They dawdled and missed one bus, but when it was time for the next one they couldn't wait any longer. Ki-dok kept getting phone calls, and acting mysterious. Dong-su turned up almost as soon as they left.

The coast at Yangyang is perfect for swimming, with a long sloping beach of crunchy hot sand and cool refreshing water. It was past the tourist season, so Dong-su and I had no trouble renting a cottage right on the ocean.

We had a swim, and afterwards enjoyed each other's bodies. Dong-su admired my small breasts, and I rubbed oil on his lithe form. The day was totally decadent, and I loved every minute of it. I hadn't had much time for goofing off, which made this even more fun. The night wasn't too bad, either.

On the way back, Dong-su stopped a few miles before the *yogwan* to make a phone call. I pointed out that he could do it just as well when we got there, but he mumbled something and made his call.

"O.K.," he said cheerily, "We can proceed."

He didn't seem to want to linger and chat with the crew as he usually did. He was just getting into his car when the bus from Sorak pulled up, and Elaine and Liesl stepped down from it. Elaine spotted him instantly.

"Don!" screeched Elaine, running over to Dong-su. "When did you get back from France? I knew you'd find me! But how did you trace me here?"

Dong-su smiled a large smile that looked pasted on. He moved to stand facing Elaine with his back toward me, and said something to her softly. She laughed.

"But why are you here?"

Dong-su put a brave face on it. "I came to give Clara Alden her Korean lesson. Do you know her?"

Elaine and I both figured it out in a flash. Kim may be a common name, but her Mr. Kim and mine were one and the same.

"Go!" she screamed at Dong-su. "Get out of my life, get out of my dreams. Prefer a scrawny, insecure, goody-goody! Have you written her poetry, too? Did you admire *her* 'full breasts,' and *her* 'halo of fair hair around her face'?"

Dong-su continued to wear his embarrassed grin, saying nothing. My heart was pounding. I turned to flee, as I always run from confrontations, but the entire population of the *yogwan* blocked the door, staring open-mouthed at this spontaneous entertainment. I hoped they didn't understand English, at least, although the general scenario must have been comprehensible in pantomime.

Ki-dok put himself between Elaine and Dong-su.

"Kim Dong-su has to leave now," he said to Elaine as if Dong-su were a deaf mute. "He'll be in touch with you later. And he says good-bye to you, too, Clara," he added as Dong-su got in his car and drove away.

Elaine turned away from me, but I thought I should try to patch things up. She needed to be consoled for the loss of her Don Kim (why had he called himself "Don" to her, I wondered), but I wasn't at all sure what to say. Liesl and Elaine walked down toward the beach, and I caught up with them.

"I'm sorry, but it wasn't my fault," I said. "How could I know that your Don Kim was Dong-su? You told me that Korea is full of Kims. And maybe you shouldn't blame him, either. How long had it been since you saw him?"

"Seven years. People change. That's what Liesl said, too. But it makes it harder that it's you, of all people, that he's romancing."

I should have let well enough alone, but - "Anyway, he's too young for you," I blurted out. Dong-su is nearer my age than Elaine's, after all.

"Maybe you should find another roommate when you come back to I-House," said Elaine with an edge to her voice. "You're probably too young for me, too."

I couldn't think what to say, so I turned back toward the *yogwan*. Should Elaine's prior romance with Dong-su make any difference to me? It seemed that Dong-su had broken off with Elaine. Should I break off with him out of loyalty to Elaine? I didn't think so. Finders keepers.

16 ◥

After Elaine and Liesl left, the dig got back to normal.

"What do you make of this pinched design pottery?" I asked Oh Ki-dok one evening. "Have you ever seen anything else like it, or is it found only here?"

Turning it around to catch the light in various ways, Kidok pondered.

"It is something like pottery found at some of the southern coastal sites," he said at last. "We have some in the university collections, but I don't think you saw them. Would you like to go see the southeast coast this weekend? Dong-su is busy and sends his regrets," he added, when I hesitated.

If I couldn't be playing with Dong-su, of course I wanted to see other sites, and so it was arranged. It didn't occur to me to wonder what Dong-su was busy at, or why he hadn't called. I guess I was too involved in the archaeology to fret about him.

Ki-dok drove the van. We planned to stay at Kyongju, so I could spend some of time seeing the spectacular Three Kingdoms tomb excavations and the artifacts at the museum. Even I, poorly versed as I am in Korean history, had heard of the sheet gold crowns and dazzling jewelry from the tombs in and near this ancient capital of the Silla kingdom. I was thrilled at the prospect of seeing them.

First we went to see the Neolithic site. It's on an island on the south side of Pusan harbor, but the island was joined to the city by a bridge years ago, and it doesn't seem remote at all. The city has grown up around the old shell mound. As Ki-dok and I walked through the vegetable patch that covered the site, I was surprised at how abundant the surface artifacts still were. I noticed a pinched design sherd like the ones in my squares, as Ki-dok said I might.

To get a better view, we climbed the steep hill behind the site. In the far distance the hills of Tsushima, the nearest of the Japanese islands, were dimly visible. It must have been easy to navigate across to Japan even in prehistoric times, I thought. On a clear day the sailors would never have been out of sight of land.

"The southern coast of Korea is a drowned plain, and the islands are the tops of former hills," explained Oh Ki-dok, shifting into teaching mode. "The sea level rose in oceans world-wide as the glaciers melted at the end of the Ice Ages. About 20,000 years ago, when sea level was more than 100 meters lower than the present, Japan was joined to Korea by land, and the islands you can see were high hills. By 8000 years ago, the sea had reached its present level, and all these islands made more coast-line and more niches for various sea and shore creatures. People moved toward the abundance of food."

"Do you think there are drowned villages under the sea?"

"Hard to say. Any submerged sites will only be found by accident, because they are under too much silt to be seen. The shell mound we visited was occupied from about 5000 to 1000 BC, beginning at the time when the sea had risen as high as it was going to. A few fragments of Jomon pottery from Japan were found there, though, showing that Kyushu was not cut off from Korea in terms of trade or contact. The radiocarbon chronology on both sides of the Tsushima Strait matches nicely."

"How large was the Neolithic village here?" I asked.

"No house floors were found, so we don't know. The site included a large pile of shells and other garbage. I think you call that a 'shell midden'. The shell helped preserve fish and animal bones, so we know what they ate. Analysis of the bones shows that they hunted deep-sea fish and marine mammals almost from the beginning. No wood or other perishable material has been found in any Korean Neolithic site, but boats would have been needed. We can only guess what kind of boats they made. Dugout canoes have been found in both Japan and China, though. It's reasonable to suppose they were used here, too."

The wind stirred up the salt air and whipped my hair across my eyes. I wondered what it would have been like to live here, and depend on the sea for food.

In Kyongju, Ki-dok took me around to several of the sights, including a huge excavated burial mound that visitors can go inside and look at replicas of the burial and the grave goods. I found it breath-taking to walk inside the mound and imagine the burial ritual.

Next we saw the remains of Half Moon fortress, where the rulers of the Silla dynasty lived. It reminded me of Iron Age hill forts in Europe. Our final sight-of the day was another late tomb, which had twelve plaques of zodiac animals around it. Ki-dok told me that they are believed to govern the people born in their year, in the same way as our twelve signs of the months.

"How do you know which is your animal, and what it means?" I asked.

"It's complicated," he said, meaning he didn't want to talk about it.

"What's your animal sign?" I persisted.

"Chicken," he answered, clipping the word and shutting his mouth firmly afterward.

I wondered what my sign would be, but the set of his jaw told me the topic was closed.

At the museum in Kyongju, we admired the bronze bells and stone pagodas in the garden, and then went inside. Ki-dok introduced me to the director, a Mr. Chung, who showed us through the exhibits. I was amazed how much gold was found in the tombs of the early kingdom of Silla, and I felt the power of the gold crowns and belts. I could imagine a bedazzled populace obeying any edicts of any ruler who wore these shining masterpieces.

Mr. Chung took us into the basement where the collections are kept. We had the obligatory refreshments, and then he showed us the artifacts from the island site we visited in Pusan, and let us look through the stored boxes. As Ki-dok had promised, there were lots of sherds with raised line designs, but perfectly plain ones also came from the site we had just seen. There was also Classic Chulmun, thicker than the pots I examined in Seoul, but with the same design motifs. Kidok told me they're later than the raised-design vessels, from higher levels of the site.

Ki-dok picked out a sherd with a very elaborate design.

"This one came from Japan. It stands out clearly from the other sherds."

I took the piece of pottery and looked at it carefully. The main design had been made by pushing cord into wet clay.

"We guess there was trade across to Kyushu, because we found these sherds from there. There's also obsidian, which isn't found in southern Korea, but it does occur naturally in the Japanese islands."

Net sinkers, composite fishhooks, rectangular obsidian saws with sharp serrated edges, shell bracelets, and pointed bone tools were also in the collection. I was attracted to a beautifully polished bone needle, and picked it up to examine more closely. It was long and slender, and had an eye in one end that had been drilled from both sides. I held it in both hands, and turned it around.

ℭ.17

Bird Mountain Village came into focus through the eye of the needle. At first I was only aware of activity. The bustling seemed to center around gathering up baskets and piling them on the dance ground.

The visitors from Shell Island Village were still there, and I soon learned that everyone was headed for the forest to collect acorns for winter storage. Nut gathering looked like a festive occasion, with contests to see who could fill their basket first, and who could fill the most baskets. I was astonished at the size of the acorn harvest, which filled fifty baskets. I didn't have to spend long wondering what would be done with so many acorns.

The drudgery followed the harvest - cracking the nuts and grinding the nutmeat to flour on sandstone slabs. Adults took turns at this repetitive chore, so no individual was overburdened. Or so it seemed to me, but I wasn't doing the work. When the flour was ground finely enough, it was dumped in a large pot and covered with water for three sun-ups. The water was poured off through fine, flat baskets, and the acorn meal spread out to dry in the sun. When it was dry Birchleaf and Pebble mixed the acorn meal with honey and berries, and patted the batter into cakes for the storeroom. A hole was made in the middle of each cake for a pole to go through, for easy storage. Everyone had a taste of the acorn cakes before they were stored, and Flyingbird broke off a bit for me. Delicious! At least for a bird - I'm not sure how my human palate would have responded.

Everything was prepared for the journey. The new boat was loaded with presents, provisions, and water. Flyingbird said goodbye to everyone staying behind, with special hugs for Sunflower, and a treat for Sister Bear.

"What about my Spirit Bird?" asked Flyingbird. "Shouldn't she come too to protect me - and all of us?"

Sunflower watched Flyingbird give Sister Bear a sad good-bye hug. It seemed too much to leave her Spirit Bird behind, too. She snatched up a basket and with a few twists, turned it into something that looked too much like a birdcage for comfort. Was she thinking that if bears could be put in cages, perhaps it would be all right to make a cage for a Spirit Bird? Sunflower lured me with sesame seed, and I walked into the basket trap, not out of greed, but because I was eager to go on this adventure with Flyingbird. I hated feeling confined, though. Sunflower couldn't know that I would have flown along anyway.

"Be sure you give the bird plenty of food and water," said Sunflower, handing Flyingbird my basket cage and entrusting me to her care. "Here's a jar of sesame seeds for treats. Your Spirit Bird seems to like them."

Birdwing and Flyingbird climbed into the middle seats, where their job was to raise and lower the square sail. They also had to take care of the fire bowl, which held embers from Birdwing's hearth, so their own Hearth Spirit would protect them from all the dangers of traveling. Three rowers sat single file in front of Birdwing and Flyingbird and three behind.

After rowing all day, the people from the two boats camped on a small sandy beach. A fire, made with embers from the bowl, was soon blazing, as they sang to it,

"Sparks arise!
Oh Fire Goddess
Send up Your flame."

The rising sparks assured them that all was well so far. Freshly caught fish were skewered on sticks, and deliciously roasted over the small fire. After supper, Flyingbird was designated to give the bones back to the Sea Goddess, with thanks for Her bounty. Then each person wrapped up in their mat, and slept under the stars. Birdwing showed Flyingbird the Seven Stars, far in the northern sky. The path of light through the sky was made of sparks from all the Hearth Spirits, Birdwing said. Every time a fire was lit, a bit more light was added to the sky.

Five camps were made on the journey south. At every stop more pines grew along the shore, and bamboo in tall spiky shoots. As the sun was getting low on the sixth day, Playful Seal signaled from the front boat that Shell Island Village was in sight. Lookouts came out to greet our boats, and many helpful hands beached them.

Flyingbird greeted each person the way Birdwing had taught her women should do, grasping right hands over left hands. The men stroked their beards, and everyone rotated their hands inward. It was a warm welcome, indeed.

Visitors and villagers sat in a circle, and each person recited her genealogy. There were eight houses at Shell Island Village, placed halfway up the hill, well away from the shore and safe from the typhoons that raged across the island every year. The village pole was streaked with red dye from cherry juice, to signify that this was a village of the Red clan. A carving in the shape of a turtle topped the pole. After the greetings, hosts and visitors feasted, then talked and sang until the starry sky was bright.

When our group was divided up to sleep in different houses, Flyingbird was assigned to Red Maple's house, and she took me along. Maple was especially blessed, with five daughters. None were married yet, but the two oldest both had husbands already promised from the Black clan of Three Springs Village, in the Land Across Where the Earth Shakes. The young men were cousins. They would arrive in time for the Bear Festival, and then they would settle in Shell Island Village. The youngest daughter was too young to be in the running as a wife for Clam or Sandcrab, but the middle two, Pearl and Cockleshell, had not yet chosen husbands. If one of them liked Sandcrab or Clam, she might agree to join the Golden clan at Bird Mountain Village, since there were so many girls here. Perhaps they both would come, and the Golden clan's search would be over.

It was only two days before the new moon, so preparations were nearly finished. Ceremonies could be carried out only under the waxing moon, for the waning moon was unlucky. Cockleshell and Pearl invited Flyingbird to go diving for oysters, one of the last things to be done before the Bear Festival.

"Will you teach me how?" asked Flyingbird. "Our shellfish are near the surface so we just bend over and pick them up with only our ankles in the water. But we don't have oysters. What are they like?"

"We'll show you," said Cockleshell. "Here's a basket, some sandals, and a stone pick to pry the oysters with. Today we're going to the oyster bed on the south side of the island."

The girls walked around the island edge, wearing tightly woven straw sandals to protect their feet from the sharp rocks. Flyingbird had never had anything on her feet before, and the sandals made her feel clumsy. At the proper spot Pearl and Cockleshell slipped out of their robes and waded into the water with their sandals on.

"You do know how to swim, don't you?" asked Pearl.

Flyingbird nodded.

"Then follow me."

Pearl waded out for twenty yards or so on the rocky sea floor, until she came to an abrupt drop-off. Cockleshell and Pearl dived down, each carrying her basket and stone tool. Flyingbird followed, surprised to see so many forms of sea life that were different from her native shore, only six days away by boat.

Cockleshell pointed to the oyster beds and showed Flyingbird how to pry the shells loose and drop them into the bottle-shaped baskets. Flyingbird had to surface for air by the time she pried off the first one, but Pearl and Cockleshell were still working on the ocean floor.

After an hour of going up and down for breath, Pearl and Cockleshell had full baskets. Pearl put a few more oysters in Flyingbird's basket, and then took her own basket up. Cockleshell stayed to help fill Flyingbird's basket. The baskets were heavy enough under water, but they felt like boulders on land. On shore, Cockleshell showed Flyingbird how to attach a wide flat band to her basket, to wear across her forehead. This device steadied the baskets and distributed the weight. The girls went back to Shell Island Village in single file, carrying their three full baskets of oysters.

As the girls sat in the dance clearing, prying open the oysters for the evening meal, Sandcrab and Clam joined them and offered to help. Sandcrab volunteered to take the oyster shells to the proper dumping ground, but he was shocked to learn that in this village the garbage wasn't separated, but just placed in one enormous dump by the sea.

"In our village, we have different disposal piles for different kinds of spirits," he explained.

"How silly!" said Pearl, with a twitch of her lip. "Seems a waste of time to me."

"Other places, other customs," Cockleshell reminded Pearl. "Perhaps Sandcrab will tell us more about the way they do things in Bird Mountain Village."

Sandcrab's ears turned red, but he managed to tell about the village spirits, and about Sister Bear.

While he was talking, Flyingbird found a small translucent ball in one of her oysters.

"What's this?" She held the object up for inspection.

"Oh," said Pearl, "that must have been from one of the oysters I put in your basket. They were on top. Let me see it."

Flyingbird handed it over, and Pearl looked it over.

"This is a precious one. We call it a pearl, like my name," she explained."

Pearl dropped the pearl into her treasure basket.

"It belongs to Flyingbird," said Cockleshell disapprovingly. "You know the rule."

"Even if it was mine, I give it to you now," Flyingbird put in quickly. There was no use getting into a squabble with one of their hosts over such a worthless thing.

Cockleshell found a pearl in one of the oysters she was shucking.

"What a lucky day! Look at this pearl!"

This one was rounder, bigger, and shinier than the one Pearl found.

She passed it around and everyone admired it. Flyingbird couldn't decide if all those colors were in the pearl or reflected from it, but the effect was quite magical.

"It has a spirit inside," she said as she let the pearl roll on her palm. "A rainbow spirit."

"It's for you, Flyingbird. You're our guest. The spirits sent this pearl for you."

Flyingbird refused it, but still Cockleshell insisted.

"I'll drill a hole through it for you, if you like, so you can wear it on a cord around your neck."

"Thanks. Could you show me how to drill a hole in a pearl?"

After all the oysters were opened, Cockleshell demonstrated the bow drill for Flyingbird.

"You place the pearl on this board, finding the right sized hole to wedge it into so that the pearl can't turn. Then put the tip of the drill down exactly where you want the hole. Wrap the bowstring around the drill. Then move the bow up and down rapidly, and it will spin the drill." Cockleshell demonstrated on the ground first, to show how it worked.

"A little sand will help the drill cut faster," Cockleshell explained, sprinkling very fine sand into the cavity already forming in the pearl.

When the hole was drilled halfway through, Cockleshell turned the pearl over to drill the other side. Flyingbird made a knot in the cord that held her topaz crystal, and added the pearl. She was delighted with her new finery. Now she had two treasures. Birdwing had told her that someday she would have six, and then she would become the leader of the village.

The next day several of the adults went fishing with nets, and came back with many kinds of fish for the feast. A wriggling turtle was tangled in the net, so Cockleshell and Flyingbird pulled his flipper from the net and set him on the ground.

"He'll be good in the soup," said Flyingbird

"This is our village totem," answered Pearl stiffly. "Didn't you see the turtle on our pole? We don't eat turtle in Shell Island Village. It would make us sick."

She picked up the turtle and returned him to the sea, waving a ceremonious farewell as the turtle splashed into the water. Pearl turned and gave Flyingbird a self-righteous glance, but Flyingbird wasn't looking.

Maple asked the girls to gather seaweed for soup. They waded out to the kelp beds, and gathered the large, flat, rubbery leaves. When they brought them back, Maple cut the seaweed into pieces with a slate knife on a flat sandstone slab, and threw the pieces into a pot of water on the fire. Being trained to observe such things, I noticed that the wide-mouthed cooking pot had pinched designs around the rim, instead of being impressed like those of Bird Mountain Village. Flyingbird fed me a bit of the raw seaweed, which smelled salty, and tasted like the sea. Maple kept adding various small sea creatures as the soup bubbled on the fire.

Pearl and Cockleshell started a rock-tossing game with Clam and Sandcrab. The game is played with partners, so Flyingbird drifted off, carrying my cage. We explored the village, eventually arriving at the bear cage, where she stopped to talk to the bear. This bear was bigger than Sister Bear, and its coat a deeper brown. It looked depressed, leaning against the bars of the cage.

"Don't look so sad, bear. Soon we'll have a ceremony just for you," she told it earnestly. "We'll and dance and sing and feast. I hope you'll enjoy it."

She put her hand in to the cage and scratched the bear's nose, and the bear licked her hand in appreciation. I felt queasy. Somehow I doubted if the bear was going to enjoy the festival.

One of Pearl's cousins, Red Sea Urchin, brought fish for the bear and scratched him behind the ears. Sea Urchin looked at Flyingbird, but didn't say anything.

"Does your bear do tricks?" asked Flyingbird, always ready to talk. "Ours can play catch, and she lets us ride on her back. She has good manners, too."

Sea Urchin didn't answer right away. Finally he said, "This is a good bear, but no one has taught him tricks. I'm the one who feeds him, though, so I guess he's my bear in a way. The hunters had to go very far into the mountains to find a cave with a bear. Father says there were lots of bears near his village when he was a boy, but they're getting scarce now. This is our first bear sacrifice in many harvest seasons."

"I haven't been to a Bear Festival in my whole life," Flyingbird said. "I can hardly wait!"

As the day for the Bear Festival dawned, everyone arose to the sound of the drum for the sun-up ceremony. After a simple meal, the visitors joined the villagers to gather in a circle to watch as the bear came out of his cage. Red Maple beat the drum. Four people held ropes which were fastened around the bear's neck and chest. The rope holders were the strongest people in the village. Flyingbird stood in a line with the village children, and they danced back and forth, rubbing their hands to the bear as a spirit.

The bear was brought near the dancers, and then halted. Each man of the village shot an arrow into the bear from close range. The bear, who had been treated with kindness up to now, didn't know what to do. First he roared with pain, and then he rampaged, just trying to get away. The rope holders pulled him in different directions, struggling to keep control. When the bear finally became weak from loss of blood, two logs were brought and the bear was strangled between the logs.

Flyingbird, was sick and terrified in sympathy. It was horrible, but her family was cheering! She turned away, retching and retching. The adults were too busy to notice.

Grabbing my cage, she went down to the beach to cry alone. Sea Urchin was there too, sobbing, but Flyingbird didn't want to talk to him. Couldn't he have stopped this? It was his village! And his bear! She found a boulder to hide behind.

"Spirit Bird," she asked me when she felt calmer, "how could they hurt the bear? How could they kill him? I can't believe the Bear Spirits approve of such cruelty!"

I couldn't find any way to comfort Flyingbird, but I chirped sympathetically. I was quite upset myself. I'd read about bear sacrifices, but I hadn't empathized with the bear in all the abstract anthropological prose. Now that I'd seen it, I was definitely on the side of the underbear. But what could Flyingbird and I do? I feared this was in store for Sister Bear, too. Maybe, I hoped, different villages had different customs about the bear ceremony.

Flyingbird stayed on the beach as long as she dared, but she had to go back to the ceremony. To stay away any longer would have been appalling manners. She put my basket down on the edge of the empty bear cage, where I could observe, and stood behind some tall adults so she wouldn't have to see the butchered bear.

Maple, as senior woman, was skinning the bear. She laid out its head, still attached to the pelt, with the fur stretched out like a bear rug. An altar was erected in front of the bear's mouth, and freshly cut prayer sticks were arrayed in front of it. Each adult in turn stood in front of the bear's head and gave it lengthy instructions to take back to its spirit kin. Some of the men cut up the meat and set it to cook in large pots as a kind of stew with mushrooms and wild tubers. Some wild onion, wild garlic, and mugwort were added for flavoring. The bones would be boiled the next day, for the nutritious marrow.

Then it was time to entertain the bear. The head and pelt were treated with great respect. Dancing, singing, and story telling for the pleasure of the bear were followed by an enormous feast with bear meat. The paws were a special delicacy, offered to the four most senior women, who accepted them and then shared bites with everyone else. Afterwards everyone drank millet wine and offered drops of it to the bear head with their wands.

Flyingbird tried to be polite, and the dancing and story-telling did distract her. But she was still upset and couldn't eat a bite. I was glad birds don't eat meat. I couldn't have eaten bear meat either.

"How could you kill the bear?" Flyingbird asked Maple at bedtime. "Didn't you raise him from a cub? Didn't you love him, and play with him like one of your own children? How could you do it?"

Maple explained that this was not cruel, but a kindness to the bear, which was longing to have its spirit return to the land of the bears.

"The bear *enjoys* the festival. Didn't you see how we poured out millet wine, and gave the bear gifts of beautiful prayer sticks? Look how elaborate and well-carved the prayer sticks are. The bear will take its gifts back to the Bear Country, and will arrange a big feast for its relatives there. In return the bear leaves us its meat for us to enjoy, and its pelt to keep us warm. Don't be silly."

Flyingbird wasn't comforted by this explanation. She felt a shiver of foreboding. What was it Sunflower said about sending Sister Bear with gifts to the spirit world?

"I saw you throwing up," Pearl said as they slid into their sleeping mats, her mouth still greasy with bear meat. "When you're a leader you'll have to skin the bear yourself. How will you manage that? What kind of a leader will you be, if you vomit over a mere bear?"

Flyingbird's answer was a shiver of revulsion. I didn't think she would ever be able to skin a bear. Would she have the power to change the customs, or would something terrible happen to her?

In three days the bear meat was all eaten, and the bear head was added to the row of animal skulls behind the houses. Over the next few winters, it too would become just a skull. It was time for the inhabitants of Bird Mountain Village to continue their journey.

"What do you think?" Birdwing asked Sandcrab and Clam. "Did either of you find a girl to take back to Bird Mountain Village?"

"What did you elders think of Cockleshell?" asked Sandcrab. "May I bring her back if she will come?"

"Splendid," said Birdwing, for the adults had observed the budding romance and discussed it already. "We like Cockleshell, and we think she'll fit well into Bird Mountain Village. How about you, Clam? What did you think of Pearl?"

"Maybe I can find a bride somewhere else. Pearl doesn't seem to get along well with Flyingbird."

"She's too self-centered to care about the welfare of our village," said Flyingbird. "But Cockleshell is sweet and lots of fun, and I would like having her for a sister. Besides, I think she fell in love with Sandcrab at first sight."

Sandcrab blushed.

When Sandcrab asked her, Cockleshell smiled broadly and her eyes shone.

"I knew the spirits had sent you for me, and I'm glad to live with you for life, even in your village instead of mine. I'll be happy to learn the secrets of the Golden clan and be a sister to Flyingbird, if it means being with you."

The visitors from the Black clan were consulted about the possibility of finding another girl in one of the villages in the Land Across Where the Earth Shakes.

"My village has no extra girls," said Black Pine. "But I've heard that Acorn Village has many daughters. The trouble is, Acorn Village is hard to find. That shore is packed with villages, and it's hard for me to tell you how to reach the right one. But I could lead you there in my boat. Maybe my new bride Red Snake would like to come along and see the village too."

Agreeing to this plan, the visitors from Bird Mountain Village loaded up their boat. They presented more gifts, and received seaweed, dried oysters, and clams to take along for snacks in addition to other presents. Decorated lacquer gourds were a specialty of Shell Island Village, and a stack of gourd bowls took the place of Birchleaf's baskets in the storage area on the boat.

Cockleshell brought one of her pots with the pinched design along with her, full of her treasures. She had a string of 22 pearls, 12 shell bracelets, and a large cockle shell with three holes punched in it, representing eyes and a mouth, much like a mask. Cockleshell gave her mother and sisters many warm hugs and promised to visit often. But she stayed by Sandcrab's side. Even though she had to leave the village of her birth, she had chosen happily.

Pine knew how to catch the currents and make the boats ride them toward the Land Across where the Black clan lived. We never camped in a lonely spot, since every cove held a fishing village. Each night we were welcomed with dancing and feasting, but no group had an extra daughter.

On the sixth day, the two boats rowed up to the beach of Acorn Village. The people of the village welcomed us, but when they learned of our mission, they explained that during the waning moon two girls had been taken by the Sea Goddess when Grandmother Wind turned their boat over, so they had no extra daughters after all.

"The Sea Goddess is greedy," said Birdwing. "I'm sure you're lonesome for your lost daughters. But my drowned sisters now have friends to play with. We can hope that they all swim with the Big Turtle under the sea."

We were invited to stay for several days. Acorn Village was the place where Birdwing's great uncle had stolen his bride and later returned with her and their daughters. The story of the stolen brides was told in this village too. The leader leaned on the songsticks and sang the familiar story.

The Bird Mountain villagers decided to stay for three days and to gather provisions for the long trip home. We would go return the way we came, stopping off briefly at home before going farther north. Because the current and winds would be against us, there might be no time for fishing.

I wondered if I would be let out of my cage at last. As interesting as this adventure was, I was getting anxious to go back to Kyongju. Too much time was passing.

While I watched for a chance to escape, I had a good look at Acorn Village. The houses were arrayed in a U-shape around a central dance ground. Not far from the center of the village, a circle of stones was laid out, with one tall stone erect in the middle, looking suspiciously phallic. Special ceremonies for boys were held around it, I heard someone say.

The villagers had tattoos all over their bodies, not just around their mouths, and men were tattooed as well as women. Strangest of all, people knocked out two teeth when they got married, to show commitment. Flyingbird could hardly keep from staring at their mouths, they looked so odd with their missing teeth.

Unusual pottery was made in Acorn Village, too. It had conical bases, and was decorated all over the surface. Designs on the jars were made by rolling knotted cords onto the wet surface, and then smoothing away part of it the corded pattern, to leave zoned designs.

Sandcrab and Clam were invited by the village boys on a day's outing to a sacred spot. Flyingbird was shocked to learn that she and Cockleshell would be left out of the adventure. Her curiosity thwarted, she appealed to Father. The Acorn Village adults were surprised that the girls wanted to go, for they believed that girls naturally stayed close to home. They agreed, though, that there were no rules against it, so the girls were included after all. Flyingbird carried me along in a basket on her back.

Black Arrow, the oldest boy, led the way, following a narrow track into the mountains. Flyingbird worried aloud about spring traps with poisoned arrows, which surprised the Acorn Village children. Animals near the village were rare since it had grown so large, and the shore villages were so close together. They depended more on the sea for their food than the land.

The sacred place had steaming earth, and bubbling pools of warm water. Arrow clapped his hands to get the spirits' attention, instead of rubbing his palms in the Bird Mountain Village way.

"We come here to worship," said Arrow, facing the pools.

Reaching into the folds of his robe, he brought out a strangely shaped clay object, and set it down by one of the pools with its feet stuck into the ground. The object looked like a clay doll, a grotesque figurine with shell-like eyes and bumps sticking out all around its head. It was clearly female, for it had two arms and legs, and female breasts. The fat legs and body were incised all over with curving designs, and the whole figure was painted with red pigment.

Sandcrab and Clam cut some nearby willow branches and shaved prayer sticks in the way of the Golden people, and stuck them in the ground alongside the clay figurine. Arrow stared at them with the same intensity as they had gaped at his clay statuette.

"There's a song our old people know," said Arrow, with his head tilted back, "that sings of carved spirits. So that's what they look like. I wonder if the Black clan made carved sticks many generations ago. We're more up-to-date now, though, making clay representations of the spirits. That's the way of our people Where the Land Shakes."

Taking no offence, the Bird Mountian Village children tossed off their robes and sloshed about in the warm pools. Afterwards they climbed nearby trees and picked apples and walnuts for a snack. I watched as they played a game, tossing wrinkled apples at a line drawn on the ground, to see who could come the closest.

When we returned from the outing, we found the adults discussing the next leg of the journey. The children fetched their mats and sat down cross-legged in the circle, and Flyingbird brought me in my cage.

"We don't dare go any farther in this direction," Birdwing was saying. "Wild tribes who don't speak as we do live across the next water. We couldn't teach their daughters anything, even if they have extra girls."

"We should turn back. The Blue clan by the mouth of the Dragon River is our last hope to find a bride for Clam to bring to Bird Mountain Village unless we go very far toward the Seven Stars," said Tall Sister. "We know that the White clan of Three Rocks Village doesn't have daughters to spare. They have only three girls themselves."

"I have seven sisters in Dragon River Village," said Father. "Passing fishermen have told me over the years that they each bore several girls. Even if there is only a very young girl, surely someone will want to come home with Clam. See how strong he is, how handsome, how his beard is beginning to grow thickly down his cheeks and chin."

Clam smiled modestly, looking at his toes.

The visitors from the Golden clan gave the last of Pebble's yellow and white baskets to their hosts in Acorn Village and received obsidian lumps in return. The black glassy stone was known to come from only a few places, all of them hard to reach, so this stone was a treasure. From these nodules they could make many sharp blades for precise woodcarving, as well as to tattoo the blue lines around the women's mouths.

Pine and Snake were given one of the fancy Acorn Village pots, full of honey, to take back to Shell Island as a marriage present. They said good-bye, and angled their boat down to catch the current going northwest.

The Bird Mountain Village boat set out in a different direction. Heading more north than west, the boat picked up the coast to the north of Shell Island Village. In six days of hard rowing the villagers were home again. Those left behind were glad to see them safely back, and delighted to welcome Cockleshell. But they were sorry to learn that the trip hadn't been entirely successful.

I hoped I would be set free, for I felt I had stayed away from my archaeology project much too long. I twittered demandingly, but no one paid any attention, not even Flyingbird. Finally, I pecked at the basket with my beak, until I was able to escape. I soared high into the sky, stretching my wings.

18

"That must be a very interesting needle," said Ki-dok, startling me back to the here and now.

I looked up, shaking Bird Mountain Village and Flyingbird from my thoughts. "My mind was captured for awhile. I'm sorry."

I peeked at my watch and was relieved to see that the day and date hadn't changed. In fact, only a few seconds had passed. I hadn't been daydreaming as long as I feared.

Over dinner, Ki-dok started to speak, then hestitated and cleared his throat, so I would understand that he was working up to some difficult topic. He drew air noisily over his back teeth, and sighed. I waited, as I had learned to do. Finally he asked me what I had been thinking about as I stared at the needle.

"Your thoughts were far away. Was it Kim Dong-su? He tells me he enjoyed spending time with you at Soraksan and Yangyang."

I tried to suppress the rush of pleasure it gave me just from hearing his name, but I wondered what Dong-su might have told or implied. *Enjoyed?* Had he bragged to his friend? Did he think of me as a conquest? I decided not to admit anything, even indirectly.

"We did have fun," I said brightly. "We visited a fascinating Buddhist temple, and afterwards we joined the picnic of some people from a nearby village. I learned some Korean words from them."

"So Dong-su told me. . . . But I must say . . . . Well . . . Do you know what your crew is saying?"

"What are they saying?" I asked, not wanting to know, but knowing I was going to hear it anyway.

"They are saying that you have fallen in love with a married man. It's OK to have an affair, but you shouldn't get so involved. Would it be all right in America?"

"What are you talking about? . . . . A married man? . . . . Who? . . . Are you telling me Dong-su is *married?*"

A tenseness crept into my voice in spite of my attempt at iron self control. I was prepared to deal with Elaine, but a wife? And then I remembered that Elaine had said her friend Don Kim had a wife. The very same. I should have figured it out for myself, but I'd been concentrating on Elaine. Besides, I hadn't seen Dong-su since the Big Scene at the *yogwan.*

"His wife is pretty, and very compliant. But it was an arranged marriage. He is rebellious. And he might be a little in love with you. You are so direct, so sure of yourself. He can't help himself."

I was flattered to be described as self-assured. It wasn't the way I felt.

"My Swiss friend calls him a `Sonny Boy.' I think she means he's smooth, and has many girlfriends. Do you agree?"

"I never heard the expression Sonny Boy. But he is my friend, and we are both very modern. I think if you love him, and he loves you, then everything is all right. Don't you?"

I put my elbows on the table and rested my chin in my hands.

"I think people should be honest with each other. He didn't tell me he was married, so it *isn't* all right. I do find him attractive," (maybe I shouldn't admit that, I thought a shade too late), "but love? I guess not. I enjoy his company. He's fun to be with and a good tutor," I added, wanting to be fair.

"I will be honest with you," blurted Ki-dok, changing the subject. "I am not married. But my father has found me a very plain girl. I do not want to marry her. Will you talk to my parents and tell them?"

My eyes opened as wide as they would go. It sounded medieval.

"Your father would tell you who to marry?"

"It is the old custom. And by the old custom a son must obey his parents. But someone else could tell them that I am unhappy, and it could make a difference."

"You tell them! Get Dong-su to do it! Or some other friend. How can I interfere?" I managed to say, after opening and closing my mouth several times without making a sound. "They're *your* customs, and I'm a foreigner." I didn't like this at all.

"It would not be proper for me to say anything. But my parents would listen to you. You are Korean born, but very modern. You are not very old, but being foreign, you carry some weight. Besides, no one else will do it. Will you try?"

I was sure this was big trouble, but Ki-dok had gone out of his way to be helpful to me, and I felt beholden to him. Besides, Elaine told me that direct refusals are impolite - injuring to one's *kibun*, a difficult concept thought of in the west as "face."

"I'll think about it," I temporized.

"Did you know that Dong-su used to be Elaine's lover?" I introduced a new complication into the conversation.

Ki-dok gave me a fish-faced stare.

"I didn't think *you* knew it!"

"So you did know. You could have told me. For that matter, you could have told me sooner that he's married!"

Oh Ki-dok sucked wet air across his molars again. "That would have been ve-e-ery difficult," he explained. "Dong-su and I are classmates."

I didn't get it. "So - ?" I prompted.

"It is a special relationship. Classmates are honor-bound to each other."

"Why don't you ask *him* to speak to your father, then?"

"He is too young. But the point is, I have to help Dong-su with his - um - arrangements. It is awkward for Dong-su to be your, um-um-um . . tutor when your roommate is his old girlfriend. He has enough trouble getting away from his wife. You see the problem. So we decided I should tell you about his marriage, so you will not be angry when he has to disappear suddenly."

"I am angry. Very angry. Tell him I don't want to see him again."

"Let's have some beer, and be friends. It will improve your *kibun*."

I'm afraid I drank too much. The next thing I knew I was back in Bird Mountain Village. These dreams were beginning to take over my life.

19

I returned to discover that Cockleshell adjusted easily to her new home. She moved in with Tall Sister and Great Uncle to become their daughter, waiting to learn the secrets before she could build a house with Sandcrab. They examined the gifts from the other villages, and divided them by households. Pebble tried making a few pots with pinched designs, to copy Cockleshell's jar.

Flyingbird had only a short time to play with Sister Bear, who was getting very plump, almost ready for her winter sleep.

"Don't worry about the next Bear Festival," Flyingbird told Sister Bear privately. "I'll find a way to protect you."

Sister Bear nuzzled her neck, as if to say, I trust you.

Birdwing decided to stay in the village rather than continue on the next leg of the journey to find a bride for Clam. Sandcrab and Cockleshell stayed, too. This made room in the boat for Pebble, Birchleaf and Black Uncle, which pleased them very much, especially Birchleaf. The new traveling group loaded up with more baskets of presents and provisions, and prepared to hurry onward in their quest. I let Sunflower trap me in a new bird basket. It seemed like the safest way to travel, and easier on the shoulder muscles than so many miles of flying.

A stop in Three Rocks Village of the White clan confirmed what was already suspected - there were no extra girls there, but Oyster was delighted to see his relatives. He offered the finest hospitality, but the Bird Mountain Villagers could only stay over night. The days were getting short, and the distance remaining to be covered was long.

Five more days they rowed on. Without much wind in the sails it was slow, hard work. Finally the blue mountains loomed up, and gradually we could make out a sandy beach, with houses in a line along the ridge above. Someone from Dragon River Village spotted our boat bobbing in the waves, and several people jumped in a small fishing boat and came out to greet us, escorting our boat to shore.

"Blue Squirrel!" called out an elderly woman as Father hopped out of the boat. The woman's mouth tattoo was so elaborate it went from ear to ear, announcing that she was a particularly important person.

"Mother!" said Father with tears in his eyes, embracing the old woman and pressing noses.

I hadn't heard Father called by his given name Squirrel since Flyingbird's birth. I'd almost forgotten what it was, because men are usually called by their clan names. But Squirrel was such an apt name for the man who played with Flyingbird and gave her treats, that I opened my beak in a birdish smile.

On the shore the people of both villages greeted each other formally. Each person told her name, and shook crossed hands with every member of Dragon River Village. Father's mother was Blue Tortoise, leader of Dragon River Village of the Blue clan. With twenty houses, this village was more than twice the size of Shell Island Village. Keeping so many people living in harmony was a hard job, but Tortoise used humor and suggestion to smooth over small daily problems as they arose. Larger disagreements called for ingenuity, and sometimes even required calling in the spirits to have their say with yarrow sticks, in order to persuade the unwilling to conform.

Villagers and visitors gathered in Tortoise's extra long house after a feast of fish, venison, millet, and mushrooms. Tortoise once had three husbands, each with a hearth of his own, but only the youngest was still living. Squirrel's father had died in the mountains in a hunting accident many years before. Besides the three hearths for the three men, a special hearth was placed on each end of the house, one for brewing millet wine and one for baking acorn cakes. The winter was colder in Dragon River Village than farther south, so cold that some activities were better done inside, where they added to the warmth of the house.

To make the visitors welcome, everyone sat in one oval around all the hearths, instead of separating into the subgroups of Tortoise's family. Squirrel had grown up in this house, and told stories from the past, as the memories flooded back. His own father had lived at the central hearth, as the first husband. During the long, dark winters, they used to play games with string on their fingers, and a stick-tossing game with four lengths of yarrow.

Blue Tortoise entertained us. She sang of the founding of Dragon River Village, in times so long ago there were giants. She sang of a hero who came from Whitehead Mountain, where a huge lake in the sky gives birth to Dragon River. The hero returned to the lake to become a spirit, and dwells there still.

The next day one boatload went out fishing, while the rest stayed on the beach, sitting on mats and talking. Clam played string games with one of Tortoise's granddaughters, Blue Seaweed. Clam admired Seaweed's slender fingers, and her friendly face. When Clam shyly told her about the shortage of girls in Bird Mountain Village, Seaweed agreed to think about possibly moving there, and to ask her mother and Tortoise. Out of so many sisters, Seaweed was stuck in the middle. Maybe it would be nice to go with gentle Clam, and be one of just a few girls, instead of many.

"I'd love to see Whitehead Mountain again, with its lake of spirits, since we're so close," said Father to Tortoise. "Flyingbird should see it, too. She might never have another chance to go there, but as the future leader it's important for her to bathe in its waters. Do you think there's time for the trip before the snows come?"

Tortoise considered. She took out her bone needle and held it in both hands. After gazing at it for some time, she put it down and stared out to sea. I began to understand that bone needles have the magic of far seeing.

20

"You're far away again," said Ki-dok. "Please cheer up. I shouldn't have told you about Dong-su's marriage."

I searched for some other topic of conversation.

"We have a long evening with nothing much to do. There's plenty of time to tell me about the zodiac animals that circled the tomb we went to."

"Let me ask Mr. Chung to join us. He knows more about it than I do. He's over there at a table by himself."

Mr. Chung was a genial man, his face running to jowls. He brought his beer and joined us, seeming to take up more than half our table.

"So you want to know about the animals that govern the years. It's a long story." He leaned back and folded his hands across his belly. "The concept came from China, a long time ago. There are twelve animals, beginning with the horse, which is the animal of the south. Going around in order clockwise, there's the goat or sheep, then monkey, chicken, dog, and pig. The chicken is in the west. The north animal is the rat, followed by ox, tiger, rabbit (east), dragon and snake. The animals belong to years, as well as directions. This is the Year of the Horse, and all children born from last lunar New Year to the next are influenced by the characteristics of the horse."

"What characteristics?"

"Independence, elegance, popularity."

"So what am I?" I told him my birth year, and he worked it out on his fingers.

"You're a goat, or sheep, if you prefer. In the Chinese zodiac sheep and goat are the same thing."

"Yuck. I want to be a dragon or a tiger."

"Nobody gets to choose his own symbol." Mr. Chung frowned slightly. "Nature takes care of that. But dragon and tiger years aren't good for girls, anyway. The sheep is gentle, compassionate, and timid."

It was even worse than I thought.

"The twelve years just go round and round, then?"

"Yes, but they also join with the ten earthly branches. The combinations have all been used up in five cycles, or sixty years. So we consider sixty years a full life, and celebrate it with a big birthday party. The *hwangap*."

"It's even more complicated than that," added Ki-dok. "The first year in the sixty year cycle isn't just a horse year, it's the Year of the White Horse. It's an exceedingly lucky year for boys, but girls born that year have a hard time finding husbands - they're too dominant."

93

"I'll drink to that," I said. "And then I must retire. It's past my bed-time. This gentle, timid sheep can't stay up too late." They didn't catch my intended irony. Ki-dok and Mr. Chung stayed at the table, apparently prepared to drink all night.

I closed my eyes in my room, and saw horses and goats and chickens and the rest, circling in a never-ending procession. It was dizzying, so I let my mind slip back to Dragon River Village, and the far-seeing needle of Blue Tortoise.

21

Tortoise put down her needle.

"You can only visit the sacred mountain if you go tomorrow. The snow will begin falling after Grandmother Moon shows her whole face again. Until then the trail will be clear. But I am warned of a different danger, although its shape is dim. Take Flyingbird, and have her bring the Spirit Bird in the basket cage. As soon as you've bathed in the lake and gathered the black stone, the bird must be set free, high in the mountains. Be sure not to linger, and don't try to bring the bird back in the basket. That's how you can avoid the danger, whatever it is"

The prospect of being freed cheered me, but I would have been glad to fly along in the first place, instead of being jounced in a backpack.

A party of six set out, selected because six is a sacred number, and the destination a sacred place. The hiking party was made up of Father, Flyingbird, and Clam, along with Father's favorite sister Blue Oak and her children Bigbear and Seaweed. The baskets on their backs carried provisions for two weeks, since there wouldn't be time to set deer traps, and it was growing too late for other kinds of forest food, especially in the high, snowy mountains. Flyingbird carried my cage on top of her basket backpack, and I enjoyed the scenery. The path to Whitehead Mountain was overgrown, and often steep. Nobody lived in the deep woods along the track. Dark conifers stood out against the blue sky, and a sharp pine smell pervaded the air. Now and then a maple tree added a bright red accent, and the yellow larches seemed to be everywhere. Water rushed and roared down steep side canyons. It was a treat for all senses.

Father and Oak talked and talked, catching up on family and friends. Clam and Seaweed walked together, not talking much, but casting each other shy looks. Flyingbird took off running up the path. "Can't catch me!" she called to Big Bear. "Just watch me!" he said striding after her. I thought Flyingbird could have run faster, but she let Bigbear catch her, and they laughed and started the game again. I poked my head all the way out of the cage to feel the wind rushing by.

The river runs through a gorge, so we had to climb a ridge. When we reached the river again, the going was easier in the river valley. After six days of climbing, two pointed rocks, home to the spirits of the obsidian quarry, could be seen in the distance. "The Rabbit Ears," Father pointed out. "We'll leave our things here and go to the lake."

We circled around the Rabbit Ears to approach the top of the mountain from the direction of the Seven Stars. Around a bend, Flyingbird stopped and stared. I peeked around her head to see what caught her attention. A huge waterfall thundered down the mountainside, spread out across the rock with changing patterns like living lace. I never imagined so much water could pour from the top of a mountain, and I couldn't imagine where it came from. Along the river, I could see steam rising from small pools.

"The pools are heated by the Mountain Spirit," Father explained. "They were put here for us to purify ourselves before we approach the sacred lake."

Father stuck prayer sticks into the mud beside the pools, and asked for the spirits' permission to bathe in them. Outer robes were laid aside, although it was chilly in the mountain air. As she waded into a pool, Flyingbird held her nose against the smell of the water, but sighed as the warmth soothed her tired legs. They splashed, and rested, and dressed again.

The path to the right of the waterfall led us steeply up to the rim of the crater. I was awed by the sight of a vast lake of shimmering blue, contrasting with the dark purple and violet sides of the crater that contained it. The lake was so big it was hard to take in all at once. It seemed like an ocean in the middle of a mountain. Passing puffs of cloud duplicated themselves in the lake. Snows had already touched the slopes above the caldera. The total effect was so vivid it almost hurt my eyes. For a moment we were a group turned to stone.

The trail continued down to the lake, and they trooped down silently in single file.

Father and Oak placed prayer sticks before the hikers bathed in the lake. They came out soon with chattering teeth, for the lake was as icy as the pools below had been warm.

Over a small rise on another path, we arrived at the obsidian quarry. A high black glassy cliff stood before us, guarded by the Rabbit Ears. We had made a wide circuit of the top of the mountain. More prayer sticks were planted before Father showed Flyingbird how to select a good place to chip off a block of stone. Black glassy flakes glittered all over the ground, and it was necessary to step carefully to avoid the sharp edges of the shatter.

Bigbear picked up a large flake, and expertly chipped a small knife.

"I made this for you," he said to Flyingbird. "I want you to think of me after you go back to your village."

I had a peek at the knife as it exchanged hands. It was almost oblong, was very sharp on the cutting edge and blunt on the back. Flyingbird smiled as she accepted it.

96

"I'm sure it will be useful. It's beautiful craftsmanship."

She picked a yellow leaf to wrap the knife, and added it to her treasure basket with the topaz crystal and the pearl. I wondered if this counted as her third amulet, of the six she needed to collect before she became the village leader.

When their packs were full of obsidian chunks, the little group set off quickly down the mountain, mindful that Tortoise had told them not to linger. I was still in the cage in the pack on Flyingbird's back, on top of the black stone she carried, and the remainder of her provisions. No one thought to let me go.

Clouds gathered from nowhere as we started down the path, and soon we were wrapped in a cottony mist. I saw the turn to the river path, but Father kept going straight, and everyone followed. Suddenly, my feathers ruffled, and I sensed some peril. I tried to scream, which only sounded like agitated birdsong.

"What is it?" said Flyingbird to me.

I sang some more, as energetically as possible.

"Wait!" she called to the people ahead. "My Spirit Bird is trying to tell us something. She's been quiet the whole time, but now she's talking fast and loud."

"I don't know what the chirping means, but let's stop anyway," said Father. "We just passed a grove of trees where we could rest for the night."

Glad to stop, they ate cold food, made a small fire, and lay down close to it wrapped in their sleeping mats. Flyingbird gave me some seeds to eat and water in my little gourd.

In the morning the sun lit up a cloudless sky. Not ten paces farther on we could see the edge of a sheer cliff, a drop-off that would have been sure death, at least for Father in the lead, if we had continued in the dark.

After the sun-up ritual, they gathered on their mats in the customary circle.

"The Spirit Bird saved us," Flyingbird pointed out. "Why do you still look worried?"

"There's still a problem. I've never seen this cliff before. I didn't know it was here. Where are we, Oak?"

"I've never been here either. We're lost. We can't go ahead. Can we find our way back?"

Sitting cross-legged in the circle, Flyingbird waited until everyone else had spoken. Then she suggested, "If we let my Spirit Bird fly, she can show us the way."

Father belatedly remembered what Tortoise said about releasing me right after they collected the black stone. Everyone agreed to let me go, and Flyingbird opened the basket cage. I soared high, glad for a chance to stretch my wings after the long confinement.

Never had I seen such a magnificent view. The volcanic peak flaunted its ragged edges in magentas and purples against the brilliant sky. I wanted to stay aloft playing in updrafts, but, mindful of my duty, I flew down lower and searched until I caught sight of an overgrown path leading down through a cleft in the cliff face. I flew even closer, and discovered that it joined the river trail after a steep descent.

Returning to the hikers, I directed them to the trail by perching on branches each time until everyone caught up. It was hard to see the beginning of the path from the top of the cliff, and at first Father hesitated. But I didn't change my position until they understood, and Father started down, and the rest followed.

22

Back at the dig, the weather grew unpleasant, but the work went on. The crews bundled up against the wind, and suddenly the most popular place to be was down in the pits.

In the second cluster of squares we found animal bones! They were just food refuse, but I was excited because bones are rare in Korean sites. The two-meter square was full of fish bones, large and small, from one end to the other. There was no telling the extent of the pile. A local fisherman identified the bones as those of seabream, mackerel, plaice, cod, pollack, and - most surprising to me - whale.

Two squares to the west and two to the south, we came across bones again, but here all the bones belonged to land animals. They seemed to be mostly deer and pig, but there were some dog bones, and even chicken bones which Ki-dok said hadn't been found before in the Korean Neolithic. There were also a few bones of rabbits, wolves, weasels, bears, and tigers, our faunal analyst told us later.

Kidok and I were thrilled, but the students were not so thrilled. They found it a lot of trouble to clean the dirt around all those bones without removing them. The bone piles were also hard to draw, even with the ten-centimeter grid of strings placed over the two-meter square. To me, this data on the eating habits of the prehistoric people was as priceless as it was unexpected, and had to be treated with the care of precious jewels. After they were drawn and photographed, the bones were carefully collected and labeled for more precise identification, and for further study. These bone piles seem to be on the same level, but they're so different there must be time elapsed between them" Ki-dok mused, looking into the pits. "One group fished and the other hunted."

"Could the inhabitants have disposed of bones in different places?" I asked.

"Why would they do that?"

"Superstition about mixing the bones?"

"Farfetched. And not testable."

I didn't respond.

Another curious fact was that there were no skulls among the mammal bones. Sorting through the bones confirmed that most other skeletal parts were represented in the bone pile. I wondered if we would find the skulls in some other context. I wanted to suggest trenching behind the houses, but overcame the temptation. After all, I was the one who had insisted on a random sample. If they trenched and skulls *weren't* there, I'd feel very silly. And if they were there, how would I explain why I suspected it? Better to keep quiet!

When Professor Lee paid a visit to the dig, he wasn't half as thrilled as we were about the bones, but his imagination was caught by a shell that had been found in the lowest level of Kidok's trench, near a small round house. Three holes had been punched out of a fan-shaped shell in a triangular pattern. They kind of looked like eyes and a mouth.

"You've found a mask! This is very important," he said, clasping his hands behind his back and shifting into lecture mode. "It represents the beginnings of art, and maybe the beginnings of ceremony and ritual. This is something to tell the reporters who come around when other news is slow."

Ki-dok and I didn't know what to make of the shell. Once the likeness to a face was pointed out, you could see it, but I was pretty skeptical.

"Couldn't those holes have been punched by accident?" I asked. "It doesn't look very artistic to me."

Professor Lee turned and stalked away without a word, hands still joined behind him, with Ki-dok following after. I watched them go in disbelief. What was that about?

Hwang-ok enlightened me later in private.

"It's very rude to contradict the professor," she explained. "Especially in front of other people. And when those people are his students - it is double rude. He may forgive you after a while. If a real foreigner had done that, he wouldn't have been so upset. Foreigners are barbarians anyway; they can't help it. But you - he looks on you as one of us. You should know better."

"Well, I will from now on. But how was I supposed to know it, if nobody told me. I was just acting like an American. Those lessons aren't in your genes, you know!"

"Not in your genes, but in your bones. *I've* always known it!"

"You just don't remember learning the basic rules of your culture. And you'd have to learn American manners if you lived there."

"Are there American manners? Americans seem so rude."

"Of course there are manners! They're just different from yours!"

Hwang-ok flicked her eyes up at me and then studied the corner of the room. Somehow I didn't think I had convinced her.

One student had brought a guitar, and we sat around singing one evening - mostly American popular songs. I asked about Korean folksongs. At first they were bashful, but then the students sang a few old songs for me. The one I liked best was Arirang - a haunting tune that made me think of Bird Mountain Village.

23

Perched again on the bird pole at Bird Mountain Village, I looked down and saw only the village women sitting cross-legged on their mats. There was not a sign of the men and boys, not even Dolphin, Sunflower's toddler. Birdwing beat the drum, sitting in a line with with Tall Sister, Sunflower, Magpie, Birchleaf, and Pebble, dressed in their ceremonial robes of black and white. Flyingbird, Red Cockleshell, and Blue Seaweed sat facing them, decked out in freshly made black and white robes. A tiny fire flickered on the sand between the two rows of women. Each girl had a large sunflower braided into her wavy brown hair. A new moon had just risen.

"These girls are here to learn to be women of the Golden clan," Birdwing told the Hearth Spirit. "You have known Flyingbird since her birth. Her familiar spirit, the golden bird, has come to witness the ceremony as well, showing that she has forgiven us at last for trapping her in a basket. We also bring you Cockleshell from the Red clan and Seaweed from the Blue clan, who wish to become Tall Sister's daughters and marry her sons, to help carry on the line of Bird Mountain Village. Please accept them all, and care for them well."

The pine wood snapped and crackled. Sparks flew upward.

"Thank you, Hearth Grandmother. Now we can proceed."

Each of the six women gave one length of processed elm bark to each girl, so that each had six strands. The elm bark had been dyed a soft yellow with lily root. Birdwing showed them how to make a six-stranded braid by knotting the ends of the strands together, and holding the knot between their toes.

When the girls had learned the braiding technique, Birdwing gave them thin black reed fibers to weave patterns into the braid. Birdwing drew the patterns in the sand for the girls to copy into their braids. They all had to include reminders of the foremothers of Bird Mountain Village - the symbols of Sunbird, Sunrise, Birdnest, and Sunlight. Next Flyingbird braided in Birdwing's and Sunflower's signs, while Cockleshell and Seaweed used Tall Sister's symbol, to finish the lineage of their new family. As the final design, each girl was instructed to include her own pattern, the one carved into the top of her singing stick. Flyingbird's symbol was a bird with outstretched wings, its talons tucked back carrying a sun disk. It was hard to simplify this complex design enough to produce it in the six-stranded braid. Flyingbird worked it out by sketching it in the sand several times until she was satisfied.

As the three girls braided their belts, the women took turns reciting the secrets. The girls learned that their new golden belts, signifying their membership in the Golden clan, had to be worn constantly. If any man from another clan saw a girl's belt, he had to become her husband, so they should be careful to keep the belt well concealed until the proper time. It was forbidden by the Hearth Spirit for any woman to marry a man whose mother wore the same color belt as her own, even if he came from a distant village.

The girls learned how Grandmother Moon had given them the gift of the tides in their own bodies. Once a month, the sign of blood would come to them. At that time, they should rewrap the golden belt to pass between their legs and hold moss and crumpled elm bark, which would catch the flow. The used moss should be buried behind the cemetery, in a small plot sacred to Grandmother Moon. The older women took the girls into Birdwing's house and showed them how to wrap their new belts. An inner robe was worn to cover the belt, now that they could no longer run around naked, and the ceremonial robe was worn on top of that.

"Men were given to us by the Hearth Spirit to help us fish and plant," explained Birdwing. "They were also created to give us pleasure. If they are treated gently, you will find that they will warm your innermost parts, and it will bring you great joy."

She taught them how to help the male spirit rise, so it could give them pleasure, and how to make a special drink to prevent babies from coming too close together.

Out in the dance ground, Birdwing lit a new fire with embers from her own hearth. She prayed to the Hearth Spirit and Grandmother Moon, and then rubbed her hands toward me.

"Spirit Bird, you saved my granddaughter once from the Sea Goddess, and again at Whitehead Mountain when everyone was lost. I'm grateful for your attention to your duty, but I must ask for more. Keep Flyingbird safe. Let her husband be loyal and her birthings be easy. For now she will become a woman, and new dangers await her."

Birdwing beckoned Flyingbird to her mat, and Flyingbird knelt beside her. She held Flyingbird's chin firmly in her left hand, and with her right hand dipped a small obsidian knife into a pot of seawater. Slowly and precisely she made six groups of six incisions above Flyingbird's upper lip. Blood ran into Flyingbird's mouth and down her chin. Her tears stung the cuts, but she kept rigidly still until the cutting was finished. Ashes from the fire were rubbed into the cuts, which would give her tattoo a rich blue color when it healed. Cockleshell and Seaweed were decorated in the same way, but with fewer cuts.

Later that day, the men returned, and everyone gathered to discuss the coming Bear Festival. Twelve sun-ups before the ceremony, they would send boats to invite the people of each village where they had kin - Shell Island Village of the Red clan, Dragon River Village of the Blue clan, Acorn Village of the Black clan, and Three Rocks Village of the White clan, where Tall Sister's son Oyster lived. Twelve sticks were sent to each village head woman, who discarded one stick each day, so that the guests would arrive at the appointed time. Flyingbird looked forward to seeing all her relatives, but most of all to being with Blue Bigbear, with his merry laugh and teasing ways.

Having so many visitors meant that special sleeping places had to be arranged. A temporary shelter was built on the dance ground. The storehouse was crammed to the rafters with food - nuts, fruits, grains, dried fish, dried seaweed - and the spring traps were set for deer.

"This big bear will feed us for a week!" Grandfather grinned, nodding at Sister Bear's cage.

Flyingbird's eyes grew wide, but she couldn't speak with her lip so swollen. Would they actually kill and eat Sister Bear? They couldn't! She looked pleadingly at Birdwing and Sunflower. They both avoided her eyes.

"There will be three young men at the festival who would like to build a house with you," Sunflower changed the subject. "Red Sea Urchin, Black Arrow, and Blue Bigbear will all come with hope in their hearts. You should be thinking about which one to choose."

Flyingbird remembered Sea Urchin, who let his bear be killed, and Arrow who seemed so arrogant. Neither of them appealed to her. But the thought of Bigbear brought happiness and a warm glow to her cheeks. Her choice was already made.

When the swelling of their lips went down, Flyingbird, Cockleshell and Seaweed admired each other's faces.

"Let's go to the Looking Pool" Flyingbird suggested. "The Wind Grandmother isn't playing today and ruffling the lake, so we should be able to see our faces well."

They took the path to the fresh water lake, formed behind a sand dune. Reeds grew into two sides of the lake, and the stream disturbed the water where it entered on the west, but the south side was deep, and the water there was still and clear. The girls leaned over the pool carefully, not even breathing so as not to disturb the water. The Looking Pool showed them three pretty girls, each with her mouth widened by a blue band above her upper lip.

24

"I loved your singing," I said to my roommates as we settled into our quilts on the floor.

"Can I ask you something?" said Sun-hi in a soft, little-girl voice. She was delicate and willowy, but taller than I by several inches, and her coy manner irked me.

"Anything at all."

"How do you know when you are in love?"

"You want to be with a person all the time - you'll know."

"My family is Christian, and my parents will let me make a love marriage. But I'm afraid. What if I don't recognize love?"

Hwang-ok said she thought it was silly to worry about love.

"Find a nice boy with a rich father. Then chase him without mercy. That's how to have a happy life." An impish smile lit up her face.

"Don't listen to Hwang-ok," said Sun-hi. "She's teasing. She's had the same boyfriend since Middle School. He does have a rich father, but she'd marry him if he was poor. But I think it must have been easier in the old days when your parents picked out your husband. I like the boys on this dig as friends, but I wouldn't want to marry any of them. When will I ever find a husband? Are you ever going to marry?"

"Maybe not," I said. "I'm a difficult cross-cultural case. I'm Korean-American, or maybe American-Korean - too independent for a Korean man but too Asian-looking for an American. I think I'll be a single scholar. Maybe I'll just take lovers."

The shock registered on Sun-hi's face.

"What about children? You'll need sons to look after you in your old age!"

Before I could answer, Hwang-ok voiced a different opinion.

"Your life is just like a movie! Why marry? I'd like to follow your footsteps and study in America. Can you help me get into your university?"

I told Hwang-ok I'd help her fill out the forms, but I doubted if I had any clout with the admissions committee.

Changing times are hard on these young women, I realized. I wasn't the only one trying to find a place in a complex world.

25

It was quiet in Bird Mountain Village after the boats had left with the invitations. One day, when most of the people who stayed behind went fishing, only Birdwing and Flyingbird were left in the village. Birdwing took the opportunity to give Flyingbird her first lesson in reaching the spirit world, while I watched from the village pole.

"There are six ways you can reach the spirits when you need them. Remember them carefully. They are needle, drum, song, amulets, garlic, and dance. Repeat that after me."

"Needle, drum, song, amulets, garlic, and dance," said Flyingbird, ticking them off on her fingers.

"If you want to see what's happening in another place, you must look into the needle. Any needle will work, but if you find one that sends you clear, sharp images, you should put that one aside in your treasure basket and use it for far-seeing only, and never dull the tip by other uses.

"To get the spirits' attention for small matters, or to thank them for a favor, beat the spirit rhythm on the drum. You know the rhythm that calls them - we use it every morning at the sun-up ceremony. Drum music is irresistible to the spirits, so be careful not to use the drum when you don't want them to come.

"For more complicated problems, or to consult the spirits, you must sing the appropriate song for the spirit you want to contact. These are the simple six-line songs that you learned when you were very young. Grandmother Moon, Grandmother Wind, the Sea Goddess, the Hearth Spirit, and even the spirits of rivers, rocks, and trees - each one has her own song.

"When a serious problem arises, and the solution is not clear, go to a quiet place, take out your amulets, and rub them slowly, one at a time. Each amulet will help you think about a particular person or place. It may remind you of something you've forgotten, or perhaps the feel of the amulets helps you find an answer. The various shapes and textures will stir your mind.

"Healing is yet another matter. In order to be able to heal, you must find a bulb of wild garlic at the edge of the woods. Chew the garlic, and wait for the spirits to lead you to the plant that will cure the illness. You may have to try different parts of the plant - root, stem, leaves and so forth, but I'll show which parts to use of the plants I know.

"With any of these methods, the spirits always send you back. But to dance yourself to the tree of life in the spirit world is dangerous. It should never be tried without an important reason. Since my grandmother Birdnest taught me how, I've only had three occasions to dance to the spirit world, all before you were born. Once was when my uncles stole women, once when my sisters drowned, and then when we needed a girl child, and the spirits sent you.

Flyingbird sat still and kept her round eyes on her grandmother.

"I planned to teach you when the need arose, but thanks to the Hearth Spirit we haven't had a serious calamity in a long time. Now you're almost grown, and I don't know when I may be taken to the spirit world forever. I must teach you now, while everyone's gone, and your Spirit Bird is here. Here's how I can show you and get back safely. First I will teach you the way to bring someone back. Then I'll dance, and depend on you to bring me back. After that, you will try it, and I'll keep you on my sacred thread and draw you back when the time comes. Are you willing?"

Flyingbird nodded, but I saw her hands tremble.

"What is the spirit world like? How will I know when I've reached it?"

"When you see an immense tree it is the tree of life. The spirits will show you whatever else they want you to notice."

The first task was to make a container for Flyingbird's amulets. Birdwing had saved the ears from a fawn, and tanned them with the rest of the hide. Now she brought them out for Flyingbird.

"You must sew these deer ears together with yellow elm bark cord. Leave an opening at the base of the ears, here, where the leather is rounded. Punch evenly spaced holes near the edge with your awl, and thread a braid of elm bark through the holes, in and out. Put your sacred amulets inside, draw the braid tight, and fasten the pouch to your belt. You draw your power from your amulets. This keeps your power close to you, ready to be used when you need it."

I watched as Flyingbird completed the pouch, then placed in it the topaz crystal given to her by Father at her birth, her pearl from Cockleshell, and the small knife Bigbear made for her from Whitehead Mountain obsidian. She wrapped each object in a soft piece of birch bark to keep them from scratching each other. Birdwing gave her a divining needle to add, shiny with years of use. Now Flyingbird had four special amulets. Birdwing reminded her that when she had collected six, the sacred number, she would be ready to be the village leader. Flyingbird fastened the pouch to the end of her golden belt.

"I'm ready, Grandmother Birdwing."

Next Birdwing demonstrated how to bring someone back from the spirit world by pulling on the lobes of both ears at the same time, stroking down, and down, and down,

In the evening, when the sparks from the Hearth Spirit were rising to the Spirit Path in the Sky, Birdwing drummed the villagers to the dance ground.

"I am going to the spirit world, and if it is safe, then I will return and Flyingbird will go. You all know it is not right to dance just for practice, but I must be sure Flyingbird does the proper steps. Does anyone have a message I should take, or a request, to make this a meaningful trip?"

"Could you ask for the safe journey of the boats from the other villages?" asked Cockleshell. "Perhaps you could ask the Storm God to stay at home, and not come to the Bear Festival."

"How about asking the Birth Goddess to send us girl babies?" added Seaweed. "To secure the village for a long time to come."

"Good suggestions," said Birdwing, very pleased with her new granddaughters.

Flyingbird began to beat the drum, DONK, daki daki, DONK, daki daki. Birdwing held her arms high with her wrists down. Her feet scarcely leaving the ground, she moved in a circle. After ten minutes or so, sweat broke out on her face, and her eyes looked inward.

"Trouble," she muttered. "Trouble ahead. Flyingbird causing trouble."

Hearing her name, Flyingbird went to Birdwing and pulled on her ear lobes. Birdwing came out of the trance, and sank exhausted onto the mat.

"The spirits want to talk to you, Flyingbird."

After catching her breath, Birdwing began the drumbeats anew. Flyingbird raised her arms and shuffled her feet in a circle. I saw her vision with her - a huge tree, with branches reaching out horizontally to cover the world. A fire burned near its base.

"What do you want, child? I can see that you are troubled," said a voice from the fire.

"Hearth Spirit, they're going to kill Sister Bear. Can that be the right thing to do? I love her as much as anyone. She is just like a person. She is my sister. My mother suckled her along with my baby brother, Dolphin. I would rather have them kill and eat me than her. What can I do?" Tears ran down Flyingbird's cheeks.

"You have understood that Sister Bear is not an ordinary bear. The mother bear gave her up without a fight, because Sister Bear has a special purpose. Are you brave enough to save her?"

"How can I do it? Please tell me how."

"You will see the way when the time comes."

"Thank you," said Flyingbird. She looked up and saw Birdwing.

"A beautiful dance," complimented Birdwing. "The spirits sent you back safely and easily, so perhaps there won't be trouble after all."

26 ◤

At the dig, the weather turned chillier, and sleety rains began to fall.
I was disappointed to have to stop digging, and just plain bored. We
stayed for three more days, hoping for a let-up, playing cards and string-
finger games at the *yogwan*. When then bad weather continued, it was
obvious even to us die-hards that the digging season was over - the
ground had gotten soaked, and there was no way to continue to excavate
with precision. We lined the pits with plastic sheeting and covered them
with sand so we could start up in the spring where we left off. When the
van was packed with bones, artifacts and equipment, we had a soggy,
slippery drive back to Seoul.

Elaine wasn't mad at me about Dong-su any more When I told her
about his marriage, she raised her eyebrows and said, "I told you already.
So?"
"So that's the end of it."
"Didn't you enjoy your weekends with him? Isn't he a fabulous
lover?"
It made me uncomfortable to discuss Dong-su's prowess with Elaine,
and I needed to suppress the tingle this conversation was giving me.
"It's all over for me," I said, folding my hands for emphasis. "He'll
have to find another partner to philander with."
I thought I caught a ghost of a smile on Elaine's lips. "Suit yourself,"
she shrugged.

I slipped back into the routine at I-House. Two more letters from Ed
had arrived. I put them, unopened, with his other letter. The temptation
to read them was avoided by keeping busy. I spent many hours
memorizing Chinese characters, a task that requires repetition and
concentration. I practiced spoken Korean, chatting with anyone who was
willing.

At the lab I studied the artifacts from my grid squares, then created a
computer code for the important traits of each class of artifact, and
entered the codes into a computer software program called MINIARK
that I had brought with me. The software was giving me fits. Something
caused the program to reject some of my categories, and the codes
wouldn't line up right, but I couldn't figure out what I was doing wrong.
"What are you doing day after day with that monster machine?"
Elaine spoke disrespectfully of my nice if not state-of-the-art portable
computer.

"It's this soft-ware package called MINIARK . .," I began to explain, but Elaine interrupted with a hoot.

"Menarche? Are you serious? Is this a rite of passage? That's a great feminist name for computer software. Who named it?"

"I doubt if the writer of the software ever thought of the construction you put on it." I spelled it for her. "It probably stands for MINImum ARKaeology, or something like that," I laughed.

I'd never thought much about the name of the program. But its character changed for me with this new interpretation, and I could master it now - or mistress it?

Dong-su called to ask me to meet him in the Toksu Palace park for my Korean lesson. I figured he didn't want to risk seeing Elaine at I-House. With some misgivings, because the surroundings were too pretty for what I needed to say, I agreed to meet him there.

"And how is my charming American pupil?" Dong-su asked with his usual broad smile. "I see you're wearing a most becoming golden yellow sweater - my favorite color."

I couldn't repress an answering smile, but I wasn't going to be diverted from my purpose.

"We need to talk. Do you think it's OK to sit here on the palace steps?"

We settled in where Yi dynasty kings used to greet their ministers.

"Oh Ki-dok tells me you're married - is that true?" I came straight to the point.

"According to Korean custom, that is true. My parents chose the daughter of their friends, and she is a good Korean wife. But when I agreed to marry her, I had not yet met you. How could I know that you would come into my life? Now I am miserable."

He raised his eyebrows in the middle, looking sad and appealing.

"A Korean would have led up to that slowly, by the way, not just blurt it out." Dong-su could never resist giving lessons. "Even English has an expression for it - you should bash around the bush, isn't it? My *kibun* is injured by your abruptness."

I refused to be diverted into a discussion of my own behavior.

"Your misery isn't my problem. Don't you think you should have told me you're married, instead of just pursuing me?"

"Well, but - I thought - "

"You thought what?" I'd never known Dong-su to be at a loss for words in any language.

"American girls - - Everyone says - - "

"Well, what?"

"Isn't free love all right in your country? I thought, well, I hoped that we could . . . you know."

"That we could just have a love affair, and your marriage wouldn't matter?"

"You could express that more delicately."

"Is that fair to your wife?"

"She doesn't care. Why would she care? That's a strange American attitude. In Korea men are allowed their adventures. Everyone knows men can't be monogamous."

"Well *I* care. I don't want to be anyone's `adventure.' Anyway, I wouldn't want to go behind the back of another woman. Now that I know, any more adventures are out of the question."

"But you looked me straight in the face like a lover from the very beginning. You smile at me all the time. Haven't we had a good time?" asked Dong-su in a soft and seductive voice. "How could you put my wife ahead of me? You don't even know her!"

"In my moral code, women count for something. You're off-limits because you have a wife, and that's that. Do you want to continue the lessons?"

"Of course. If I cannot have you, at least I can be near you," Dong-su mooned.

I suspected that this whole performance was insincere, and that an adventure was indeed what I amounted to for him. I wished I hadn't fallen for his smooth talk earlier. Whatever "Sonny Boy" may exactly mean in German, I thought I took Liesl's general meaning!

"When I need to talk about the Neolithic period, do I call it *shin-sok-ki-shi-dae*?" I changed the subject.

Elaine had collected various *mudang* paraphernalia, and she was looking for an antique Korean blanket chest to store them in. I went with her to Insadong, the downtown antique area where the old tile-roofed one-story buildings had been left among the skyscrapers of modern Seoul. It's charming, but all the chests seemed touristy and overpriced.

"I hear that a new area for antique dealers has opened," said Liesl one day at lunch. "It's four blocks long, one shop after another. I think I'll go and see if there's any Buddhist art for sale. You might find your chest there, Elaine. Who wants to come with me?"

We both did. The three of us studied the subway map and planned our approach to the antique section. The shops turned out to be several blocks from the subway stop, and by the time we got there I was glad I'd worn my running shoes, even though people stared at my feet.

The stores had much more merchandise than those in Insadong, but also more cramped. We walked through tiny rooms, where chests of all sorts were piled up to the ceiling, leaving only narrow aisles to walk through. Some shops had Yi dynasty artifacts and even pieces as early as the Koryo dynasty from a thousand years ago, with bits of earth clinging to them as if they had been recently stolen from tombs. I hoped tomb-robbing was illegal, because the pillaging of graves spoils the context and destroys much valuable information. I made a mental note to ask Ki-dok or Professor Lee about the antiquities laws in Korea.

Wonderful things, ordinary things, broken things, artistic things greeted our eyes. Spread through the shops were antique farmers' tools, cooking pots, clothing - practically a museum of old Korea. Liesl's eye was caught by a pair of brightly painted wooden chickens, with wings on hinges. The shop owner said they had been saved from a dismantled funeral cart. They were amusing and beguiling. Elaine and I urged her to buy them.

Another store had buttons and beads from bygone costumes. Elaine showed me a pair of amber buttons. They were an irregular teardrop shape, each pierced with a tiny hole that had been drilled from both sides. I was tempted to have them made into earrings. The rich golden color of the amber attracted me. Examining them closely, I noticed that each button had a small trapped insect in it - an ant in one, and a spider in the other. I bargained them down to a price I could afford, and stuffed the small package into my jeans pocket.

In the meantime, Elaine must have looked at every blanket chest in the four blocks of stores. Finally, as Liesl and I were running out of patience, she narrowed her choice down to two. One was ornamented with heavy iron latches, the other was more delicate, with carved cloud patterns and curved dragon feet.

As Elaine studied the details and tried to decide between them, I poked around in odd corners of the store. High on a chest in the back was a wooden bird, more refined and graceful than the folk-art chickens Liesl bought, but probably made to serve the same function. The bird had outstretched wings, also hinged to flap. It was clearly in flight. The neck and beak stretched forward, and its legs were tucked straight back, the claws holding a red sun disk. The bird was painted a golden yellow, with details emphasized by thin black lines.

"*Olmaeyo*, how much?" I asked the shop-keeper, turning the bird several ways to admire its craftsmanship.

The price named was far more than I could afford. "I'll have to think about it," I said with disappointment.

"How much you willing to pay?" asked the proprietor.

"Less than half of that," I replied, breaking off the bargaining with regret.

Elaine chose at last, the chest with the iron decorations. Negotiations for having it sent to I-House took more time.

"You want *delivery*?" said the proprietor. He sucked his back teeth audibly. "Ve-e-ery difficult."

Elaine offered to pay extra, and finally it was arranged. Then she looked at her watch.

"Damn! I'll be late for Yoli's Mother's *kut*! Guess I'd better take a taxi. Want to come?"

It was a general invitation, declined by Liesl, but accepted by me - a ride in a taxi wherever it was going sounded better than walking back to the subway. Shopping was much more tiring than archaeology, I decided.

"*Oso-osipsio*," said Yol-i's Mother when we arrived at her front door. "Please come in."

We slipped off our shoes and stepped up to the *maru*, the polished wood floor room where the ceremony would be held. An altar was arrayed with fruits and rice in pedestaled metal bowls. Above the altar hung pictures of various spirits of the *mudang*'s pantheon. The General was there, and the Three Spirits in peaked caps, as well as the spirits of the Seven Stars.

"This *kut* is for healing," the *manshin* explained to us. "It's a stubborn case. This poor man keeps having one illness after another. I think the spirit of the first wife of the sick man is causing his problems. She died many years ago, but she is still jealous of the new wife. If she shows up, I'll have to send her far away. She's very troublesome."

The patient lay on a mat near the altar, wearing his traditional white clothing. His present wife and daughter by his first wife sat nearby. Other on-lookers were behind them - friends, family, and neighbors. Elaine took up a position where she could have a good view, and I sat beside her, cross-legged on the floor, leaning back as unobtrusively as possible against the wall.

"I don't know how you can sit like that, Clara." Elaine had squirmed into a kind of side-saddle position, which she shifted frequently. "I wasn't made for anything but chairs."

"This is comfortable for me, but I can't sit like a Korean," I answered, gesturing toward the village women.

Some women squatted with their feet flat on the floor, their legs apart, bottoms not touching the floor, and their skirts pulled into their laps. Others sat with one knee up, and the other leg behind it. There seemed to be no time limit for these postures; they could sit like that all day. You must have to practice from childhood.

Several of the lesser *mudangs* danced first. One, in the guise of the General, demanded money from the patient and his family. As the family peeled off hundred-*won* notes, the dancer tucked them around various parts of her costume - the chinstrap of her hat, her belt, her sleeves. She flourished two metal knives with heart-shaped jangles hanging from the blade. The knives set up quite a racket as the *mudang* whirled around shaking them. Next she grabbed two dried fish from the altar, and swung them about. Finally, she took a mouthful of rice wine from a brass bowl, and spat it out of the house.

"She's getting rid of evil spirits," whispered Elaine.

The second dancer was dressed all in white, with a multi-colored sash across one shoulder and tied at her waist on the opposite side. She danced herself into a trance, and then stood on the rim of a large *onggi* vessel, the clay pots in which *kimchi* is preserved, and chanted. I found this part less than engrossing, and took out my amber beads to admire. I rubbed the dust off them, and they sparkled as they caught the light. I decided they were a great purchase and tried not to regret the wooden bird I couldn't afford.

Yol-i's Mother danced last, taking the role of the dead wife. She scolded the sick man and his present wife for their lack of attention, and made the village women laughs with her imitation of the former wife.

Then she changed to a different robe, and chased the evil spirit out, running out into the yard to send it far away, too far to return.

Neighbors and friends danced next as well. When it was my turn to dance, I slipped the yellow robe over my jeans and sweater, and tied the ribbon. My thick white socks looked a lot like the homemade cotton socks of the village women. I raised my arms to the drumbeats.

113

28 ☙

As I flew in I saw the Dragon River Village boat arriving for the Bear festival. Bigbear hopped off the boat and I saw his eyes searching for Flyingbird. He greeted his elders in suitable slow ceremony when it was his turn, but then he bounded away to greet Flyingbird and meet her brothers, cousins, and new sisters. I was interested to note that he greeted Seaweed with crossed hands, as is done for another clan rather than with the palm only, as members of the same clan greet each other. Seaweed had truly become a member of the Golden clan, even to her siblings.

The next day Big Bear suggested a fishing trip to Flyingbird. "We passed a school of large fish, not too far away. Shall we catch some for dinner?"

"Sure! I'll pack our water and provisions. You go borrow the net and depth marker from Father."

Blue Squirrel gave Bigbear the fishing things, but looked uneasy. "Be good to my daughter," he said to Bigbear. He pointed his chin toward me, indicating that I should go along.

The small fishing boat danced over the waves. Out into the current, the breeze picked up, so Flyingbird hoisted the small square sail, and watched the shore slip by. Dark mountains rose on their left. Far out to the right, the sea became dark as well. Above and below was the azure of the sea and sky. Seabirds dipped and splashed, catching fish. I followed them at a discreet distance. I wasn't sure if this was my business or not, even if Father thought I should go.

After an hour, a sandy beach came into view.

"Shall we pull in over there for lunch?" Flyingbird pointed with her chin.

They pulled the boat well onto the shore, then raced on the stony shingle, with Flyingbird in the lead. I perched on the mast, but they were having too much fun to notice me. Bigbear put on a burst of speed and caught up enough to trip Flyingbird, sending them both down in a tangle into the sand, laughing.

"My robe is full of itchy sand. I'll have to go into the sea and wash it." Flyingbird stood up and shook her robe.

"We could wash our robes and put them in the bushes to dry, and then go swimming like we did at Dragon River," Bigbear suggested.

Flyingbird thought of her new restrictions.

"I can't do that anymore. Then I was a child who could go naked. Now I'm grown up. And I think you are grown up, too," she ran her hand across his beard.

Bigbear reached up for Flyingbird's hand and pulled her down beside him. "We're both grown up. I want to hold you in a grown up way. Don't you?"

Flyingbird looked at Bigbear thoughtfully. I guessed from her expression that she was considering what Birdwing had told her about men. She liked Bigbear much better than Sea Urchin or Arrow. With Bigbear, she could build a new house, and maybe have some daughters. Even a little son, who could be called Littlebear. Bigbear was strong, and good at fishing. She looked at him, shining.

"Yes, I do. But first I have to show you my secret, and tell you what it means. If I do that, then you will be my husband. You know I'll become the village leader. Is that all right with you?"

They walked into a clump of trees holding hands.

I looked out to sea, and kept watch on the weather.

Flyingbird asked Sunflower and Father, and then Birdwing and Grandfather, what they thought of Bigbear, although I knew it was too late to ask. Happily, they all approved of the marriage, and so it was agreed that Bigbear would stay in Bird Mountain Village and build a house with Flyingbird after the Bear Festival.

Flyingbird skipped to the bear cage to tell Sister Bear.

"I'm going to build a house with Bigbear. You know him. He brought you fish yesterday and scratched your nose. You're still important to me," she explained. "And the spirits don't want you to be sacrificed. Please don't worry. We'll find a way."

Each day when she took Sister Bear to the seashore, Flyingbird felt the weight of the coming Bear Festival. "I'm happy and scared, Spirit Bird," she told me. "Happiness over a new life with Bigbear, and fear for Sister Bear. What can I do? I can't shield Sister Bear from the arrows, and I can't talk Birdwing out of the bear sacrifice. All our kin are expecting bear meat."

I didn't have any answers, but I knew I'd be needed soon - otherwise I wouldn't have been called here.

When boats from all the invited villages were lined up in rows along the shore, more than a hundred people had gathered. Dancing, singing, and story telling lasted long after the stars lit up, and the Seven Stars turned around in the north. Couples crept off to private places among the sand dunes, and returned, smiling, to rejoin the throng.

115

A sleepy horde responded to the sun-up drum. They mumbled their morning prayers, then pulled the mats over themselves again and went back to sleep. But Flyingbird was mindful of Sister Bear, who would expect her morning trip to the beach as usual. Yawning and stretching, she went to the bear cage, and taking the leash, led Sister Bear down the latrine path to the beach. It was full daylight, but the only sounds came from the waves and the seabirds.

Flyingbird played and tumbled with Sister Bear on the beach. They threw clumps of seaweed back and forth, and raced on the sandy shingle. Flyingbird sat on Sister Bear's back, and they ambled up the beach.

"We could just wander away from here, and never come back," whispered Flyingbird to the bear. "By the time everyone wakes up, we'll be far away."

Looking up, she saw me perched in a nearby tree, watching her.

"Spirit Bird," she began, "everyone is asleep. I could run away with Sister Bear, and take her far away in the forest where she could hide in a cave. But if I do, I will shame my village. Worse yet, I'll never see Bigbear again. Do I have to choose between Sister Bear and Bigbear? The Hearth Spirit promised me a plan, but I can't see a way out. Can you?"

In my anthropology classes I'd been taught that it's improper to interfere with the cultural practices of other people, so I hesitated. Then I thought of Sister Bear, with her flayed skin still attached to her head, being worshipped and eaten at the same time, and decided to help after all. I considered the options. The bear could be turned loose, but she wouldn't leave Flyingbird. They could run away as Flyingbird suggested, but I pictured the girl and the bear wandering lost in the forest. Both had been part of the village as long as they could remember. Could they find enough food? What about tigers? Flyingbird knew the sea, not the forest, but the sea wasn't a place for a bear. And Sister Bear had never had a chance to learn bear ways, or to find her way in the woods. With two people, they'd be more likely to survive. They couldn't be away too long, but if they could wait out the full moon, it would be too late for this year. A bear festival couldn't be held in the waning moon, and after that the sea would be too rough for the returning boats.

"Wait here," I tweeted, and flew off to look for Bigbear.

I almost woke the wrong visitor, wrapped in a mat with a wavy brown beard sticking out. Then I recognized Bigbear's song stick lying beside him, and flew down to land on his shoulder and prod him with my claws. He didn't move. I pulled at the mat with my beak, hoping he wouldn't wake up loud and grumpy. Bigbear opened an eye at last, and stared meditatively at me. Then he uncurled from his mat and sat up. I flew a few feet toward the latrine path, then stopped on the ground. Bigbear followed, and I led him to the beach.

"What are you doing here alone with Sister Bear? Why did the bird bring me here?"

"They're going to kill Sister Bear and eat her. But she isn't an ordinary bear. She's my sister. We're running away. Please don't tell." Tears brimmed in Flyingbird's eyes.

"I think the bird brought me so I could go with you. You'd have a hard time alone in the forest, and if you tried to come back, your clan might be angry enough to kill you. Please let me come."

"Of course, dear Bigbear, I want you to come. But are you sure? To leave all the people you love?"

"I've already left them for you," Bigbear reminded her. "I'll sneak back and get a few provisions."

They counted off on their fingers the things they would need: mats, gourd bowls, basic tools, song sticks, and fire from the hearth. Bigbear went back to the village to collect them quickly and quietly. When he brought them, Flyingbird wrapped everything in the mats, making solid bundles to carry on their backs.

"Do you know the paths through the forest?" asked Bigbear.

"I've never been far into the forest. We dare not cross the village again to get to the forest path, anyway. But there's a trail the hunters use that starts from the cove where we had our picnic. Do you think we could row the boat that far with Sister Bear in the boat? She's heavy." Bigbear decided he could. "The bear is no heavier than a boatload of fish. If Grandmother Wind breathes into the sail, we may get around the point before anyone else wakes up."

"They'll get the boat back later." Boats were too precious to waste.

The bear climbed into the boat as if she had been yachting all her life. They put her in the middle for stability, and each sat on one end. Bigbear rowed the boat from the front, while Flyingbird guided it with the stern oar. I flew alongside, not sure how I could help.

A breeze hastened the boat to the cove. They hauled the boat on shore and left it where it could be easily seen and retrieved. Flyingbird found the entrance to the path, and I followed them into the forest.

"There may be spring traps set by hunters," Flyingbird warned. "The hunters tie pieces of yellow-dyed bark-cloth to warn people, but they aren't always easy to see, and sometimes they fall off. Spirit Bird, you keep an eye out, too."

A deer had been caught in the first trap we came to. Flyingbird thanked the deer spirits and we stopped to have spit-roasted venison for breakfast. Bigbear skinned the deer and wrapped the choicest part of the leftover meat in the hide. It was heavy to carry, but it would provide food for several days. Trudging farther up the trail, a shady oak tree invited a rest. Bigbear started to gather the acorns scattered on the ground, but Flyingbird pointed out that they didn't have grinding stones to make flour, or bowls to leach the tannic acid out. Sister Bear, however, didn't need to worry about grinding and leaching. She was eating the acorns as fast as she could.

"This was the right thing to do. The Spirits are leaving us food."

The trail became steep, and Flyingbird and Bigbear looked for handholds, forgetting to watch for traps. But suddenly I saw one. I gave them a warning tweet, dropping an object from my claw. Flyingbird stopped abruptly to pick it up, and spied the yellow ribbon.

"Wait, Bigbear!" she called out.

"What is it?"

"Stop! An unsprung trap!"

Flyingbird stopped to consider the best way around the trap and idly examined the object I had dropped.

It was shiny dark amber, a teardrop shaped amber button, with a hole drilled in the narrow end. A fossil ant was visible which reminded me of the button I bought at the antique store. Flyingbird strung the amber on her cord with the crystal and the pearl. It seemed appropriate as a gold-colored treasure for the Golden clan. With the black knife and white needle, she had five amulets. When she had one more she would be ready to be the village leader. But I wondered if she would ever see the village again.

As darkness descended, the top of the mountain came in sight. Sister Bear stopped and sniffed the wind, rotating her head from side to side. Then she struck off on an overgrown branch path. "Wait," called Flyingbird, but Sister Bear didn't. So we followed the bear, twisting through a dense patch of oaks that neatly screened the mouth of a large cave. Sister Bear went straight in and disappeared into darkness. Flyingbird and Bigbear looked at each other. We waited outside.

When Sister Bear reappeared, she stood on her hind legs and gave us the welcome greeting with her paws. Flyingbird and Bigbear hesitated, but I went ahead. Some light filtered in through the oaks, and as my eyes adjusted, I could see the edges of a rock overhang. The floor of the cave was dry and sandy. Bears had denned in the back, and generations of hunters had made fires near the front. No living creatures were there except us. It looked like a safe place for the night. Bigbear began to arrange rocks in a square for the Hearth Spirit. Flyingbird went out to gather wood for the fire. I followed in case of trouble. She had collected an armful of sticks, and was ready to return to the cave when the clatter of falling rocks startled us. A scream, then a moaning sound, then silence. What nature of beast had fallen? It sounded human. I flew in the direction of the noise to investigate. A person lay still at the foot of a waterfall. One leg was bent and bleeding.

The clothes were strange--a leather cloak and trousers. Black straight hair was bound into a topknot that rose straight up from the forehead. Young. I thought, for the face had neither hair nor tattoos adorned it. Girl or boy? I wasn't sure. Another groan, and the eyes opened, startling me. I looked into a face resembling my own human face. The epicanthic folds made eyelids that turned the black eyes into shiny beads looking out of slits. What was she doing here?

Flyingbird caught up with me. "It's a girl! And she's hurt! Look, Spirit Bird, her leg might be broken. What should we do?"

By flying around as if I were pushing a seal toward her, I reminded her of the time Straight Pine broke his arm falling on the big rock beyond the tidepools.

"That's right! Birdwing straightened Straight Pine's arm out, and bound it together with a stick on each side of the arm. Let's do that, and then I'll find some wild garlic to chew, for more inspiration. First, though, we have to take the girl to shelter in the cave, and get her dry by the fire. I'll stay with her now. You fetch Bigbear."

Both Sister Bear and Bigbear came to see what they could do. Bigbear held the injured girl by the shoulders while Flyingbird put moss on the wound and straightened her leg. The girl bit her lip but didn't cry out. Bigbear took a granite axe out of his carrying basket and cut small branches for splints. The girl's eyes flicked open briefly as Flyingbird took off her inner robe and used it to keep the splints from rubbing the broken leg. Bigbear cut a piece of vine, and lashed the contraption together.

How could we get the girl to the cave? She was in shock, and too weak to hop on one leg. There was no way for two people to carry her on the narrow trail. Sister Bear showed us the solution by edging over and presented her back to be climbed on, as she always did for Flyingbird. Flyingbird and Bigbear lifted the girl across Sister Bear's back, and walked on either side to steady her until they reached the cave.

Bigbear made a bed of pine needles for our strange and unexpected guest, and covered the needles with his own sleeping mat. They stretched the girl out, and Flyingbird laid the other mat on top, to keep her warm. Flyingbird looked around for something else to do. It was fully dark, and she couldn't go looking for garlic. Bigbear and Flyingbird settled down in front of the fire and cooked their venison on sticks, softly talking about this turn of events. The girl awoke, and looked at them with both fear and curiosity in her eyes. They offered her water and meat, which she accepted, and seemed less afraid. Soon she went to sleep.

Without mats, Flyingbird and Bigbear huddled against Sister Bear for warmth. Outside, wind howled as a storm gathered strength. The sky lit up with lightning bolts, and it rained in sheets.

"I've never seen the Storm Spirit so angry," murmured Bigbear. "Angry at us, or helping us? Even if the bear were still there, they couldn't hold the festival in this storm. Maybe we should've relied on the spirits, instead of running away."

"You don't think we did the right thing?"

"I don't know, but it's done. We have to go on from here."

Hail began to ricochet off the rocks in front of the cave. Bigbear added more twigs to the fire, and thanked the Hearth Spirit for her warmth. Seeing that Sister Bear and their visitor were both sound asleep, Flyingbird and Bigbear warmed each other outside and inside by the light of the fire. I tucked my head under my wing.

At sun-up the next day, prayers were said with hand clapping instead of a drum in the cave at the top of the mountain. The trees dripped, and it was still cold, but the wild rain of the night before had ceased. The strange girl lay between the mats on her pine-needle bed, groaning now and then.

Sister Bear went out alone into the forest, while Bigbear went looking for some food to supplement the venison. Flyingbird went out to find wild garlic. She recognized the spiky tops, dug up the bulb, and cleaned it. Sitting on a rock with a view out to sea, she chewed the garlic bulb and pondered what to do. As she chewed, she noticed a grove of willows, and remembered that Birdwing used willow bark when Sister Bear scratched her arm, so she peeled a bit of the bark off, and carried it back to the cave.

Her preparations were simple. She put the willow bark in water in her gourd bowl, then raked a small rock from the fire and dropped it in the bowl to warm the concoction. After a moment, she fished out the rock and gave the bowl to the girl, pantomiming that she should drink. Flyingbird held up her head, and we both studied her.

The contrasts between the girl and the people of Bird Mountain Village were many. Her thick hair was black as obsidian and straight as pine needles. Nobody along the coast ever wore their hair in a topknot. Where did she get those eyes? She had very little hair on her arms and legs, and no tattoo around her mouth at all. Maybe she was too young for a tattoo, but she was a little taller than Flyingbird.

Flyingbird brooded beside our guest. I could imagine what she was thinking. This girl posed an impossible dilemma. She wouldn't be able to go anywhere for a long time. Weeks, at least. We couldn't go away and leave her here to starve. Could we manage, with winter coming on? We could go back to the village for help - but *would* the villagers help, considering what Flyingbird had done?

Flyingbird remembered Birdwing's instructions. She reached for her pouch, tied to her golden belt, and took out Birdwing's antique bone needle. The girl opened her eyes and stared at the belt with curiosity. Flyingbird looked uneasy.

"Do you think it's all right for a strange girl to see my belt?" she whispered to me.

Birdwing hadn't covered that. Probably so, I thought. The women weren't shy about exposing their belts to each other. Anyway, I hoped that was right. I nodded.

Flyingbird held the needle in both hands at the level of her eyes, and looked into it. She saw Birdwing on the beach near the borrowed boat, trying to comfort Sunflower and Father. The storm had blown the boat back to the village. Villagers and guests lined the shore, watching for the Sea Goddess to return the bodies as well. No one had discovered that the song sticks were missing, so no one had figured out that they ran away. I wondered how Flyingbird and Bigbear would be received if they came back from the forest instead of the sea.

The girl struggled up onto her elbows to see what Flyingbird was doing, and clenched her teeth at the jolt to her leg. A bunch of odd sounds came out of her mouth.

Flyingbird pointed to herself. "Flyingbird", she said, by way of introduction.

"Vying Buhd", said the girl, in a surprisingly deep voice. Pointing to herself, she produced a long string of syllables. Flyingbird tired to say the same thing, and the girl laughed, and shook her head.

She reached for a stick, and sketched in the sand the outline of a big animal with a long curling tail. Then she drew stripes on it.

"What kind of a creature is that?" Flyingbird wondered aloud.

Bigbear returned with more wood for the fire as well as some walnuts and a few apples the birds had left almost intact.

"Who drew the tiger?" he asked. "Have you seen one nearby?"

"No, the girl drew it. Maybe it's her name. So that's a tiger. She drew a long tail, so we should call her Tigertail."

"You haven't ever seen a tiger? You're lucky! Tigers prowled more than once near Dragon River Village. Last year a tiger pounced on one of my cousins, right in front of all of us, and took him away. Later my uncle found a piece of his robe. We buried it to keep his spirit from wandering."

Speaking of burials reminded Flyingbird of the vision in her needle, and she told Bigbear about it.

"Should I try my other amulets? That's what Birdwing taught me to do."

"You know the answer!"

Flyingbird brought out her deer's ear pouch again, once again attracting the eyes of Tigertail. She sat quietly by the fire, rubbing the smoky topaz crystal which Father found the day she was born. She felt Father and Sunflower calling her, "Return, return." Holding the pearl between her thumb and forefinger she saw its many colors, and thought of the intertwined lives of herself and her new sisters. They needed her. Which one would become the leader if she didn't go back? She'd been learning the village songs and lore for all her fourteen years, and they were newly arrived. The obsidian knife reminded Flyingbird of Bigbear's obligations to the Blue clan, and the polished bone needle told her that Birdwing still had lessons to teach her. Even the amber, her gift from me, was urging her to return.

She rewrapped the amulets with care and put them all away, while she considered what to say to Bigbear. He waited for her to speak.

"I've been kept alive for some purpose," she said, "and I have an obligation to the village. The amulets tell me we should go back."

"What about Tigertail?"

"She could ride on Sister Bear's back, now that she can sit up by herself. We can walk beside her side most of the way, if we take the trail directly to Bird Mountain Village. Where the path gets too steep and narrow, we'll have to walk in front and behind to help keep her steady on the bear."

We spent another night in the bears' cave, nested into the sandy floor and huddled together for warmth. The next day dawned clear. It didn't take long to tidy the cave and return the hearth rocks to a pile of stones near the front. Sister Bear was willing to carry Tigertail, and we set forth slowly down the mountain.

"Perhaps the Spirit Bird would go ahead, to prepare people for our return," suggested Bigbear, as we neared the village.

Flyingbird agreed, so I flew into the village as the advance party. I perched on the dance ground pole, turning around and around and swishing my tail to attract attention.

Sunflower saw me first.

"The Spirit Bird has come with a message!" she called out.

I tweeted and flew toward the forest path.

"We must follow. Hurry!" said Father, running ahead, with Sunflower and others not far behind.

Just where the path comes out of the forest, the two parties met. The village group stared at the stranger on Sister Bear's back, with Flyingbird and Bigbear looking weary and travel worn, holding her up.

"Are you a gift from the spirits? We thought the Sea Goddess had taken you," said Sunflower, with hugs for both Flyingbird and Bigbear, and even Sister Bear.

"What's this creature you've brought us?" asked Birdwing, inspecting the girl, who sat quite still looking back at them. "I guess it's a human, but it has funny eyes and hair as straight as nettles."

"She makes sounds, but she doesn't talk our language. She fell down a waterfall, and broke her leg. I've fixed it as well as I can, but she needs your help for the leg to heal right. We couldn't leave her on the mountain. There was no one else to help her."

Tigertail was put to bed in Birdwing's hut. The broken bone ached almost unbearably, but Birdwing's willow bark infusion helped. She soon fell asleep, worn out from riding the bear down the mountain.

Birdwing washed her with seawater, muttering to the Hearth Spirit, "We may have a problem here. Give me your wisdom to help solve it." She removed the bone bird from her hair and rubbed it with her fingers to think more deeply.

The villagers and their guests sat in the moonlight considering the fate of Sister Bear. They assumed that she had gone into the mountains to rescue Tigertail, and that Flyingbird and Bigbear had only followed.

"No . . .," began Flyingbird, but Birdwing gave her a silencing look. Birdwing had seen the truth in her needle, but there was no need to tell it.

Tomorrow it would be too late for a Bear Festival at the full moon. By the next moon it would be too dangerous out on the sea for the visitors to return home. The Spirits had helped Sister Bear escape, and she brought this strange creature from the woods. Should they sacrifice such a bear? They decided to have a feast the next day with everything but bear meat. They drank millet wine to seal their decision. One by one, people rolled into their sleeping mats.

"Soon we'll build a new house for you and Bigbear, but we may have a problem because of Tigertail," Birdwing whispered to Flyingbird as they extinguished the outdoor fire.

"Why can't she live with Sunflower in my sleeping place?" suggested Flyingbird.

"Did Tigertail ever see your golden belt?" asked Birdwing.

"Yes, at least twice, and maybe three times. I used my inner robe for her splint, and later I opened my pouch twice. I'm not sure about the first time I took off my inner robe to wrap on her leg, but I saw her staring at my belt later. What does that have to do with where she sleeps?"

"Tigertail may have to sleep with you and Bigbear. The problem is that Tigertail is not a girl. Although different from us in many ways, one thing is obvious. Tigertail is a man. You know what it means that he has seen your golden belt."

29

I finished my dance, untied the bow of my costume and caught my breath. How could Tigertail be a man? There wasn't a hair on his face! I shook it out of my mind with a toss of my head.

"You have the spiritual force to become a shaman," Yol-i's Mother told me after the *kut*. "Sometimes I feel spirits hovering near you. One of them takes the shape of a bird. I know you don't want to acknowledge it - nobody does - but you'll have terrible luck until you give in to your fate. Why don't you come study with me?"

"I don't have the calling," I refused her well-meant offer as politely as I could. "Archaeology is my career. That's what I'm studying."

"You need a Korean mother," Yol-i's Mother persisted. "And you'd be just the daughter I always wanted. But if you won't be my apprentice, at least come visit me more often."

I like the old shaman, so I promised more frequent visits, although I didn't know how I'd find the time.

"I'd like to have a Korean name," I suggested. "If you give me a name, wouldn't that be like being my mother?"

"She already gave you one," laughed Elaine. "She calls you `So-yong,' - Western Dragon - behind your back."

"Why dragon?" I asked. I didn't think I was very dragon-like, but the idea pleased me. It was a lot better than being a sheep.

"You have a secret life somewhere else. You appear and disappear the way dragons do. You think you're scientific and western, but that's just your surface. In your bones you're mystical and eastern. Your year is the Sheep, but you have a Dragon aspect. Your obedient side and your adventurous side are warring, and the spirits won't give you any peace until you make those parts of yourself come together and interact."

"Um," I said neutrally, not wanting to agree to such superstition, but also trying not to be impolite.

"Did you know that Elaine is a Sheep, too? She was born two Sheep cycles ahead of you. But her other aspect is the Tiger." She smiled at us fondly. "Neither dragons nor tigers are supposed to be good for girls - but you two are different. You're both independent spirits, each in your own way."

"If you were a painter or a poet, So-yong could be your signature," said Elaine. "It would make a handsome name stamp."

"It is poetic. Better than Jade Princess, which sounds so cold."

"We think of jade as warm, and highly precious," Yol-i's Mother objected. "But Jade Princess is more like a title than a name."

Elaine told her about the antique chest she chose, which reminded me of my amber pieces. I reached into my jeans pocket, but found only the one with the spider in it.

"Where's my other amber button? I was looking at them just before I danced," I remembered. "Let's look around on the floor in case I dropped it."

We looked on the floor and felt under the cushions, but didn't find it. "I'm sure you'll find the button," said Yol-i's Mother. "Amber has strange qualities. The button will come back when it has done its job, when the solution to your problem is near. It will be found where you least expect it."

I don't have a problem, I thought but didn't say.

30

Some artifacts were too infrequent in my pits for reliable statistics. I decided to ask Ki-dok if I could record the artifacts from his pits by the same system. I couldn't add them to the random sample, but they would enlarge the descriptive power of my study. He was agreeable, providing I would teach him my methods, which I was glad to do.

Lugging my laptop to the university, I located a three-prong outlet and set up my system up near it.

"Let's start with the pottery," I instructed in my best Graduate Teaching Assistant voice. "Not knowing what variables might prove useful, I've recorded everything I could think of. For each potsherd, I measure the thickness with my calipers. Then I record the color, in chroma, hue and value, according to the Munsell Soil Color Chart. I've given arbitrary numbers to the design techniques - 1 means incised, 2 for impressed, 3 for rocker-stamping, and so on. See, here's the list. I've also coded the designs. Rim sherds have more variables. First, I estimate the rim diameter according to the curvature of the rim, by matching the sherd against this chart. Then the rim shape gets a coded number - beveled, rounded, flat, and so forth. I match the rims to these drawings when in doubt. At first I was recording hardness on the Moh scale, but all the sherds are the same so I dropped that variable - it doesn't vary!

"When the data sheets are ready to enter the data into the computer, I retrieve the file called SHERD."

I jabbed the required keys.

"This program is set up to ask for the data in a certain order. Each sherd gets its own unique sequential identification number. I also include the field number for cross-checking. Then the exact location is recorded - the grid square number, the north-south coordinate, the east-west coordinate, and the depth. Next I include the values for the variables. It takes time, but the results are usually worth the effort. You can have a lot of fun playing with the data when it's all in the computer."

Ki-dok looked dubious about the fun.

For a demonstration I used my files on the sherds from the seven squares excavated so far. Merging the seven files, I produced a histogram that showed the distribution of sherd thickness. I admired the effect of blue bars on a yellow background, shorter and then taller to short again.

"Notice that there's a central tendency of around seven millimeters, ranging from just under five millimeters to just over nine. Also see how the highest bars are the ones in the middle. That suggests that the thickness of the vessel has a normal distribution. It's likely that it won't be important in the analysis. However, the rim diameter data tells us something else."

I typed the necessary commands into the keyboard. A new histogram with three distinct clusters appeared.

"These three separate peaks alert us to the possibility of three distinct classes of vessel. We don't know yet whether these data reflect only the mouth of the vessel, or the overall size. Until we can dig some more, adding your data will increase our understanding of the variability in the sherds, and what it might mean.

Ki-dok nodded, squinting at the screen.

"If I separate these again according to the square where they were found, an interesting pattern emerges. All of the sherds with large diameters are in two contiguous squares, while the smalls and mediums are evenly divided among the other squares. This makes me wonder whether there was a special area for storage, represented by the large vessels. For now this is a hypothesis to be tested with further data. Already I can see that there are several different design patterns among these sherds, so it's not a case of just one or two broken jars."

"We usually just look to see what other sites have similar pottery," said Ki-dok. "It's true that you're recording much more detail, but in the end, what will you know about the site that I don't know?"

"I'll know about people's behavior. For example, if there was considerable food storage, that implies something about their collecting strategies, or perhaps even the beginnings of plant domestication. It's a small but important piece in the understanding of the transition from foragers to plant and animal domesticators."

We began to examine each sherd and record its variables. Ki-dok caught on quickly, and we got a lot done in a couple of hours.

At lunch-time Ki-dok suggested that we go to the student cafeteria. It was crowded and noisy, but we found a corner where we could almost hear each other.

"Would you like to see the site of Amsadong?" he asked. "It's an important Chulmun site, not too far away. In fact, it's within the city boundaries of Seoul. We reconstructed several of the houses for a museum on the site. It's quite interesting."

"I'd love to see it," I answered eagerly. "Are there site reports? I'd like to read them before I see the site."

"I'll ask Professor Lee for permission to let you read our report. How well do you read Korean now?"

"Better than I speak it. Of course I can sound out the alphabetical writing, and I can recognize maybe a thousand characters, most of them related to archaeology. I know that isn't nearly enough, but I have a good dictionary, and I'd like to give it a try anyway."

I told Ki-dok about the antique store, and about losing one of the amber buttons I bought. That reminded me to ask about the things for sale that seemed to be from burials.

"Isn't there a law against tomb robbing, and selling the things from graves?"

"Yes, there are strict laws. But it's hard to enforce them. Nobody wants to crack down on their relatives, and in the countryside, everybody is related."

"It would be easy to patrol the antique stores."

"It's not their fault. They're just businessmen."

I disagreed, but there was no use pursuing it.

Ki-dok promised to call me when he could borrow a car to take me to Amsadong, and I went out to wait for a bus.

31 ⬏

At eight o'clock the next morning, Ki-dok appeared at International House with the site report from Amsadong.

"Oh, thank you," I mumbled, flabbergasted. "But I didn't mean for you to come so far out of your way to give it to me."

"I am at your service," said Ki-dok rather formally, with a slight bow. "Can you go tomorrow to Amsadong?"

"Tomorrow I have my Korean lesson. But perhaps I can change it."

Dong-su was still giving me Korean lessons irregularly, but he made no more suggestions for trysts. I was pretty sure he had a new girlfriend.

"We'll go in Dong-su's car. He'll come with us, so it will be all right. Could you meet us, though, at the end of the subway line? It's so far to drive here in the rush hour traffic."

Of course I agreed. The Seoul subway system is safe and easy and cheap.

When Ki-dok left, I took the report upstairs and arranged my big dictionary on my desk for a day of heavy translating. I wanted to be prepared for tomorrow, and I was glad Elaine was gone for the day so I could have peace and quiet to concentrate on the task.

The subway exit where I waited is at the southeast corner of the Seoul subway system. The subway is clean and convenient, but crowded. It's easy to ride, with its color-coded stops, and names in roman letters as well as *hangul*. I arrived early enough to have the site report copied at one of the underground shops

My escorts arrived at the appointed time, both of them in business suits, and I felt supremely underdressed in my jeans. It's funny how the wrong clothes can make you feel disadvantaged. A twelve-lane highway along the Han River went all the way to the site. It didn't gibe with the site report, so I couldn't get I oriented.

"The report describes a two lane road crossing a bridge over the Han River, and then a dirt road. Are you sure this is the same place?"

The two men laughed. "We call this road Olympic Folly," said Dong-su.

"The building boom for the Olympics was both a boon and a problem for archaeology," added Ki-dok. "We discovered a lot of new sites, but we weren't prepared to dig so much at once. We were all ve-e-ery busy."

Dong-su parked near a square glass building, which covered a large section of the site, preserved so that visitors could walk around in it and see the excavations. Ki-dok pointed out the house floors, the square

130

central hearths, and other features. Several house floors were cut into the one beneath it, showing rebuilding at the site. Outside, we walked around the rest of the park.

"A pavement feature was found about here," said Ki-dok, stopping in the road. "It has no depth, so it couldn't have been an oven, but it did have fire-cracked rocks. We called it an outdoor hearth. There's another one over there. Storage pits between the houses were found for the first time in South Korea."

Six reconstructed houses stood together. Straw thatch made a conical roof that came to the ground, covering a small entranceway. Inside, four large corner posts slanted inward to hold the roof beam. A partition had been made in one house, arranged in the pattern of the burned posts that had actually been found at the site.

"Is there a house god in the rafters?" I asked, getting a feeling of deja vu.

"How did you know about house gods?" asked Ki-dok in surprise. I shrugged my shoulders. "We held a *kut* to bless the house, and placed a bundle on the beam for the house god to dwell in. It was on television, with Professor Lee explaining the ceremony. He's quite photogenic, and the show got a very high rating."

Ki-dok reached along the rafter and brought down a dusty object. Unwrapped, the parcel revealed an archaeologist's trowel, accompanied by a large potsherd.

"We thought this would be a fitting abode for the house god."

"I've always liked whimsy," I smiled, but I studied the sherd carefully. It was a rim sherd, with five rows of short slanted lines making a band under the rim. Below the band were semicircles of punctates, and below the punctates, an incised zigzag pattern.

"Looks like you selected a ceremonial pot to leave for the house god," I observed. "This is fancier than most of the sherds I've seen."

"That's from one of the larger pots. It came from this very house," answered Ki-dok. "So of course the House God would feel at home."

They knew about other sites in the vicinity, so we spent the rest of the day climbing over ruins. A large fortress with earthen walls, dating from the Three Kingdoms period, was found when the Olympic stadium was built. It was made into a park, which we roamed around. We munched a lunch bought from a street vendor as we looked at the remains. Then we climbed a narrow path to a hill fort used by both Paekche and Silla of the Three Kingdoms, in the early centuries A.D. The view from the top was panoramic - it was easy to understand why a fort would occupy that spot. Finally we visited reconstructed pyramid-shaped stone tombs which were memorials of the early Paekche rulers. One was the largest stone tomb in Korea, Ki-dok said.

Dong-su insisted on driving me back to I-House, so I countered by inviting them to dinner. Dong-su regretfully couldn't stay, but Ki-dok accepted.

 I ran upstairs to wash up a bit, and change to a skirt since Ki-dok was dressed in a suit. Elaine was just popping out the door, looking quite glamorous in a red dress, and a little flushed.

"Have a good time, wherever you're going," I called to her fleeting back. A few seconds later I glanced out the window, and saw Elaine getting into Dong-su's car. No wonder he drove me back. So they both get their fling, I thought. Who needs it? Still, I felt betrayed by both of them.

Ki-dok and I decided to stroll up the street and try one of the appealing *bulgogi* restaurants that I had sniffed on my walks to the subway. The *bulgogi* tasted as delicious as it smelled. Strips of beef marinated with garlic, shallots, and soy sauce were cooked in sesame oil right at the table, accompanied by rice and *kimchi*. Something about *kimchi* made me nostalgic - and made me think of the lattice pattern in my dream, too. "I have something for you," said Ki-dok, when we laid down our chopsticks.

He handed me a package, using his right hand to give it to me, while the fingers of his left hand touched his sleeve respectfully.

"What's this?" I asked, discovering a gold chain in the package.

"It's for your amber button, to hang it around your neck, since you have lost one and can't make earrings."

"You're very sweet," I said, "but I can't accept a gift." Remembering about Korean gift giving, I wondered what string was attached. I didn't have to wait long to find out.

"Please, you must take it. You can do me a favor and meet my parents. Tell them I can't marry the girl they chose," he pleaded.

"It's none of my business," I sat back, horrified. "What would they think of me?"

"In Korea we often use a go-between to say difficult things. You will charm my father, and he will listen to you. I cannot ask him myself."

"I can't ask him either! You said Dong-su is too young to be a go-between, but I'm a lot younger."

After dinner Ki-dok and I wandered through the streets. The night streets were filled with vendors crowded together along the sidewalks. We stopped and watched a man with a giant slab of caramelized sugar. He scraped off bits with a knife and stuck them to a stick, creating a confection somewhere between a lollipop and cotton candy. We bought one to share. It made the chin sticky, but tasted delicious.

The next vendor had a huge crowd around her, so of course we had to elbow into the crowd to see what was going on. When we got close enough, I was amused to see a small computer. People gave the operator a few hundred-*won* notes and some information, and came away with a sheet of paper off the printer.

"What is it?" I asked. The papers were printed out in *hangul*, and I couldn't catch what was written.

"They're telling fortunes by computer. Shall we try?"

The needed information was the date of birth, the sex, and the first letter of the family name. The computer automatically changed the solar date to the lunar year, because proper fortunes are related to the moon. I found this combination of high-tech and ancient custom beguiling.

My fortune told me that I will always have good health, and usually will be lucky. However, unhappy events are coming in my 29th and 44th years. I will find something lost in an unexpected place. At birth I was blessed with good looks and cursed with high intelligence.

"That's why they ask your sex," I explained to Ki-dok. "High intelligence for a man would be a blessing, not a curse."

He smiled self-consciously. "I'm afraid you are right."

32

Elaine got home much later than I did, but I hadn't fallen asleep yet. She asked me about my evening, perhaps to forestall any questions from me about hers. I told her about the computer fortunes, and she laughed when she read mine.

"This is ridiculous. Half the people in Seoul probably got the same fortune. Would you like to visit to a real fortuneteller? I need to observe a fortune-telling session. Come with me and have your fortune told when I interview Mrs. Choe."

Elaine disappeared around the corner to brush her teeth, and I pretended to be asleep when she came back. I definitely didn't want to hear about her escapades with Dong-su.

The fortuneteller invited us into an old-style Korean house with sliding paper doors and a tile roof. Elaine and I entered a plain room with a polished paper floor. Several books were arranged on a low scholar's desk, and against the wall stood a graceful bookcase with irregular spaces for books and knickknacks and several chests. A cracked and yellowed scroll, covered with elegant calligraphy in vertical columns, hung beside the bookcase.

Mrs. Choe indicated that we should sit on the floor cushions in front of the scholar's desk, while she sat on the other side. Elaine took out her notebook and tape recorder.

"Clara has two questions," she explained in Korean. "She has lost an amber button. Perhaps you can tell her where to find it. That is her simple question. Her difficult question is, can she find a mate who will accept her as she is? She is Korean born but American raised, and this is causing many problems for her."

"Kara," the fortune-teller began, pronouncing my name as well as she could, "tell me your birth date, and the hour of your birth."

"I don't know the hour. The date is November 29, in a Sheep Year."

"You were born in a Sheep year - very good for boys, not so good for girls. Your life will be interesting, but not calm. I think you are quick to jump into new situations, and smart enough to handle them in the long run, but in the middle . . ." she let the sentence hang.

The fortuneteller consulted a large chart.

"I could be more precise if I knew the hour of your birth, but I can tell you this much. You must find a husband born in a Horse year. A Horse is best to live with a female Sheep. The horse is more stable, which is good for you."

There was a silence, while the fortune-teller examined my face.

"You have dreams. What did you dream recently?"

"I dreamed I was a bird," I told her, definitely the short version.

"Birds are message carriers. There is a message for you in your dream, but you are resisting it." She reminded me of Liesl, with her talk of repression.

Mrs. Choe took a bird carved from cream-colored, translucent stone from the bookcase and placed it on the scholar's desk.

"You must look into this jade bird, and see where your thoughts take you, while I make some further calculations."

It was very delicately carved - a bird in flight, carrying a small sphere in its claws. I turned it to admire its lines.

33

Looking down from atop the bird pole, I saw the inhabitants of Bird Mountain Village in their council circle, discussing what to do about Tigertail. His leg was healing nicely, and he had learned enough of the language of Bird Mountain Village to get along.

Tigertail listened while the villagers considered the problem. He had seen Flyingbird's golden belt, so he was her husband. There was no appeal from that. Bigbear was her husband, too, and she was pregnant with Bigbear's child. A woman having two husbands was not the problem. The founding ancestors of their own village included four women sharing two men, and the leader of Dragon River Village, Blue Squirrel's mother, had three husbands. The problem was that Flyingbird and Bigbear didn't want to share their house with Tigertail. Another difficulty was that it *was* unknown among Tigertail's people for a woman to have two husbands. He couldn't agree to share Flyingbird, but his eyes showed that he would gladly marry her if he could have her to himself.

Tigertail was staying in Birdwing's hut. He was beginning to get around pretty well by leaning on his singing stick, whittled for him by Father. On the singing stick Tigertail had carved a tiger with a curling tail, and under it three bears and a bird.

"I thought you were all bears when I first saw you," laughed Tigertail, when asked to explain the scene. "I thought I was being rescued by three bears."

"What about your earlier life?" asked Sunflower. That should come first."

"No, the person I used to be died in the mountains, and Tigertail's life began then. That was a new birth, with a new name and a new singing stick."

"Flyingbird and Bigbear found Tigertail, so they're responsible for him," said Birchleaf, to start the discussion. "We should build a house with two hearths, one for Tigertail and one for Bigbear."

"What about Flyingbird's children?" asked Sunflower. "How will they know which hearth is theirs?"

"Children often look like their fathers. Since these men look so different, maybe there won't be a problem," noted Third Uncle. "Anyway all that will matter is that they're Flyingbird's children. That's easy to know."

"Tigertail could go back over the mountain. He must have a home somewhere," said Father, who knew the belt sighting was accidental and not Flyingbird's fault, since she thought Tigertail was a girl.

Tigertail sat in the circle, squatting on his good leg with his bad leg stretched out in front. He didn't understand how these people could cross their legs like that. It looked very uncomfortable. He was trying to follow the conversation.

"I no go home," Tigertail explained when it was his turn. "Brother is village leader. Send me to kill tiger. I no go home without tiger skin. With tiger skin, I become leader. I like stay here, with kind people. Flyingbird, Bigbear, Spirit Bird save my life. Without them, I die on mountain. My life is theirs now. I not want to cause trouble."

"Can't you accept him in your house at another hearth, Flyingbird?" asked Pebble. "You wouldn't have to sleep with him. He doesn't look grown up yet anyway, with no beard."

"I am grown up," said Tigertail. "Men of Stone Tribe no have thick beards like yours, or hairy backs. But I not want to live at Flyingbird's hearth unless *she* wants."

"My mother Blue Tortoise had three husbands," Father reminded them again. "It worked out fine. The men weren't jealous of each other. They often went fishing in pairs, to leave the third husband alone with Mother. She has a good life, with plenty of fish and meat."

"I guess Tigertail could live with us at his own hearth," volunteered Bigbear reluctantly, remembering that his grandfather indeed had co-husbands, and mindful that there was no other way out. "What do you say, Flyingbird?"

"What can I say? I'm willing to try. I have no one but myself to blame for Tigertail's seeing my secret. If it doesn't work we can band together to hunt a tiger, and send Tigertail back with a tiger skin."

"In that case, it looks like a good day to start the house," said Birdwing. "Let's get busy."

Since Flyingbird would one day become the leader, the ground selected for the new house was to the south of Birdwing's. The men chopped down the trees growing on the spot and put the usable ones in a pile. After a request to the Hearth Spirit for blessing, Flyingbird drew the outline of the dwelling on the ground, making it long enough to surround two hearths. Using their shovels made of deer shoulder bones, the work party scooped out the ground to about a meter below the surface. Tigertail and Bigbear each selected rounded stones from the stream that ran into the freshwater lake. They made the square hearths about two meters apart, to allow some privacy between the hearths. The house was almost twice as big as an ordinary one, and they would have to find an extra-tall tree for the long roof beam.

Tigertail helped as much as he could, but with his leg in a splint he couldn't help fell the tree for the roof beam. Grandfather directed the men to a tree he had been watching for years. In the meantime, the women chopped smaller limbs to make the walls. Two pine trees with crotches at exactly the same height were selected for the end posts.

The hardest part was raising the roof beam. More millet wine was poured out for the hearth spirit. Holes were dug for the two crotched posts to rest in. Then they put the posts on the ground with the points at the holes, and the crotches toward the middle. The roof beam was set across the two crotched posts. A team on each end began to raise both end poles at the same time, while others steadied the roof beam, until the poles were straight up and the ridge beam spanned the two trees some eight feet off the ground. Soil was tamped firmly around the posts. Teams added the side logs from both sides at once, leaning them on the ridgepole but keeping it in balance. By the time six poles had been placed on each side, the ridgepole was quite steady, but they added six more side poles for extra stability.

Millet stalks from the harvest, tied together in bundles, were used to cover the logs and make the house weatherproof. The soil excavated from the floor was used to seal the edges from the outside. The house looked quite grand when it was finished.

The last step was to bring embers from Birdwing's hearth, and make new fires for the Hearth Spirit in the twin hearths. Flyingbird sprinkled millet wine on both hearths. The sleeping mats were placed beside the hearths, with Flyingbird's and Bigbear's at one hearth and Tigertail's at the other. The new occupants brought in their belongings, and placed them carefully and neatly. It seemed strange to Flyingbird to be making her house with two men, but exciting, too.

After supper, all the villagers came into the new house for a housewarming. Flyingbird poured millet wine into bowls and the villagers welcomed the new Hearth Spirits with libations from their sticks.

"Tell us about your people," Flyingbird requested of Tigertail. "You've heard our songs and stories several times now, but we don't know much about you."

"I not know where to begin. We not have story songs like yours. My grandparents went to Rock Shrine Village from far away, near Seven Stars. If you go up to mountain where you find me, over top, and down, down again you come to big river. River leads to my village. Rock Shrine Village built where salt from sea barely reaches with tides. River is wide, sand islands all along in it. Keep going down river you find another sea. That sea yellow and muddy, not clear and blue like your sea. When tide comes in, water rises like flood, and when goes out, leaves shiny brown mud. Mud all around.

"All along river live Stone Tribe, my people. At next big river going toward Seven Stars, Tree Tribe live. Farther in same direction is Water Tribe. Far, far away, sacred mountain has sacred lake. That is whole story about my ancestors."

"Do your people know the Hearth Spirit? And Grandmother Moon?"

"Moon shines on our village, just like here. I watched moon every day on walk up to mountaintop, so I know same moon. Rock Shrine Village have hearths, but no spirits live in them. Our spirits live in rocks and big trees. Family spirit stays on roof beam."

"One of ours does too! Our village spirit lives in the birth hut, on the roof beam!" exclaimed Cockleshell, proud of her knowledge of her new village.

"Did you say that your *brother* is the leader?" asked Birchleaf. "That is very strange. Among our people, we believe that only women should be leaders."

"Yes, brother is leader. But sometimes women can lead village. We choose leaders for wisdom. Man, woman, not matter. I sent away to get tiger skin because I too rash, too daring. Not wise. My brother think quest either kill me or teach me wisdom. Nearly killed me. Would have killed me, if Flyingbird, Bigbear, and Sister Bear not help."

"And don't forget the Spirit Bird," said Flyingbird. "Did you notice she came back this morning?"

"Yes, I see. On village pole, sitting. When you save me, I saw bird first. Eyes look human, like my eyes, not yours. I very afraid. But bird bring help."

"I noticed that your eyes look like the Spirit Bird's. That's one reason I thought it was right to help you," Bigbear said.

"Do your houses look like ours?" asked Sandcrab, remembering that the houses were different in Acorn Village.

"We not have spirit window, but we build houses same way as you. Our villages bigger, though. Rock Shrine Village has as many houses as two people's fingers and toes."

There were murmurs of amazement, marvelling at such a large village.

"Why do you wear such funny clothes?" Seaweed giggled.

"Maybe your clothes funny," replied Tigertail with good humor. "We no weave like you. We make clothes from animal skins, mostly deer. I think your robes more comfortable than our stiff capes and trousers. We paint designs, not embroider."

The villagers talked far into the night, making Tigertail feel welcome in his new home. Gradually people felt sleepy and went home to bed, until only the house inhabitants were left, to roll into their sleeping mats and spend the first night in their new home.

 "What did you see?" asked the fortuneteller.

"I saw a village by the sea," I replied, honestly but incompletely.

"That's where you'll find your amber," the fortuneteller promised me.

"And the man who will love me for what I am?"

"Don't depend so much on a man to give your life meaning. Only when you know yourself is love possible. But there is a man in your future. I told you he was born in a Horse Year. You will find him in the same place as your amber button."

34

The next day I had a phone call from Ki-dok. "Can you have dinner with my parents and me at the Chosun Hotel tonight? My father wants to meet you. You know what to tell him, don't you? He speaks English very well, so don't worry about having to speak Korean."

I was trapped by my own actions. I said no to Ki-dok's request, but I kept the gold chain. Elaine told me bluntly that in Korea, accepting a gift is a promise to do a favor for the gift giver, although the specific connection may not be stated.

"What time? What should I wear?" I asked with dread, my stomach telling me it couldn't possibly accept any food until the ordeal was over.

"The car will come for you at six o'clock. Wear whatever you like. Well, don't wear jeans. It's a fancy place. And my father and mother are quite traditional. They will dress up."

"Help!" I said, turning to Elaine for advice and comfort. "What can I wear? What can I say?"

I hadn't brought anything to Korea with me to dress up in, so what to wear was not an imaginary problem.

"Wear your black skirt. Let's see what you have to go with it," said Elaine, practical as ever. "Anything of mine would overwhelm you."

Eventually Elaine chose a black sweater, borrowed from Liesl. I added the amber button on its chain, as the only jewelry I had. I borrowed gold drop earrings from Elaine, and assessed myself as well as I could in the bathroom mirror.

"You look very elegant," said Elaine. "Now for the other question. Tell the old bastard to leave his son alone."

"Thanks for your help. I'm in big trouble and you make jokes. Some anthropologist you are! The poor old man's just trying to do his parental duty. Don't you feel sorry for him, caught in a changing world with a rebellious son?"

An elegant silver Hyundai came to pick me up. There was no one in it but the chauffeur, which I thought was odd, but I allowed myself to be handed into the back seat.

Arriving at the Chosun Hotel, I found the two Mr. Ohs standing at the front door to greet me. The elder Mr. Oh was straight and slender, his abundant silver hair combed back in a shining halo. He looked born to wealth and power. People always bowed to him, I guessed, and my insides gave another squeeze.

"I am Oh Ki-mun," he introduced himself gravely with a slight bow.

"Clara Alden," I said bowing in reply but automatically offering my hand at the same time. It was the wrong thing to do, but my hand was taken politely. The elder Mr. Oh was too suave to bash heads with a bow and a handshake at the same time.

Ki-dok's mother sat stiffly in the lobby, her back straight. She looked both kind and severe. Her face was perfectly round, accentuated by her dark hair which was drawn into a tight knot at the base of her neck. Her clothes were expensive and impeccable, western in style but made of the finest silk, imparting a subtle Korean flavor.

"I am Min Chun, Ki-dok's mother," she introduced herself. "First time I see you."

I knew by now that women didn't take their husband's name in Korea, but I didn't know whether to call her Mrs. Min or Mrs. Oh or what. I settled for not calling her anything. Instead, I gave my name and greeting in Korean, this time bowing properly, which won an approving smile. I relaxed a little, having passed the first test. This event at least was better than the dinner with Ed's parents, which was a disaster from the start.

The dinner was western style, sitting in chairs with knives and forks to eat with. I was disappointed in a way, remembering many feasts seated on cushions, but perhaps the awkward posture would have added one discomfort too many.

We chatted about this and that until the dinner came, and then the Ohs became silent. I searched for a topic of conversation. I brought up the *mudangs* and Elaine's research. No help from either man. I asked about the aftermath of the Olympics. Short answers. I tried archaeology, but ended up giving a monologue.

After dinner we sipped coffee, and once again talk flowed easily. I began to hope I could get out of my chore, but at last the topic arose.

"Ki-dok said you had something special to tell us," said his mother to me. "Would you like to tell us now?"

Ki-dok stood up and excused himself. "Tell them while I'm gone," he mouthed as he left.

"In America," I said, trying to work up to the subject as Dong-su taught me to do, "young men and women choose their own marriage partners. That way they know each other well when they marry. We believe couples are happier choosing each other than when someone else chooses for them. I read that this custom is becoming common here, too."

"Isn't there a lot of divorce in America?" objected Mr. Oh. "Why don't love marriages work better, if the couple are better suited to each other?"

"Although it's true that there's a high divorce rate, many marriages do work. My parents have been married for 32 years, and they still love each other."

"Ah, but your parents are Korean. Probably their parents made the match." The elder Mr. Oh invited me to sneer with him at the barbarian Americans.

"No, they're of English descent," I said quickly. "Most of their ancestors went to America before the revolution."

Seeing the blank faces of Ki-dok's parents, I added, "I'm adopted."

"Who were your real parents?" the elder Mr. Oh demanded to know. "They must have been Koreans."

"I consider Mom and Dad to be my real parents, and I've never tried to find out anything about my Korean birth mother," I said firmly. "I was adopted as a small child. I don't remember Korea at all, although I'm enjoying getting to know it now."

It was time to get to the point. Looking at Ki-dok's mother, I plunged in further. "Your son asked me to tell you something he can't tell you himself. It is not my business, and I'm embarrassed to tell you."

The silence at the table was total. Clicks from other knives and forks, and voices from other tables filled the void. I took a deep breath.

"Although your son appreciates your concern for him, he does not wish to marry the girl you've chosen for him."

"Thank you for telling us," said Mr. Oh with a stiff face. "I thought it must be something like that. Of course, we cannot go back on our word to the girl's parents."

"That is a lovely amber bead you are wearing," said Ki-dok's mother, moving to less difficult ground. "And quite a pretty chain."

I explained about the lost mate to the amber bead, and that Ki-dok had given me the chain.

Another chilly silence followed, broken this time by the elder Mr. Oh.

"So you have chosen my son, and tempted him to defy his father. Did you stay in a *yogwan* with my son?"

"No! Well, yes, but in different rooms. We are good friends, but not - " the sentence was unfinishable.

Ki-dok returned, and we all stood up to go. As we waited for the driver to bring the car, the elder Mr. Oh spoke to his son in Korean.

"She is quite unsuitable for you. Her manners are terrible, she even talks when people are eating. She looks men in the eyes in a very brazen way, and she smiles too much. She talked to your mother when she should have talked to me. She has friends who consort with *mudangs* and other lower class elements. She likes digging in the dirt. She knows nothing about her background. Probably she was born to a whore by an American soldier. The only thing to say for her is that she is quite pretty - not necessarily a good trait for a wife. You cannot marry her."

I found my understanding of Korean was all too good. Had Ki-dok said he wanted to marry me? How could I continue to work with him? And why did my life have to have *two* wretched evenings like this?

The car came at last, and took me home. I mustered a polite good-bye in Korean, and fled into I-House.

Elaine looked at my miserable face and demanded to know all. When she heard the whole tale, we tried to figure it out together.

"Ki-dok assumed you would marry him if his parents approved. So he thought up this scheme to get you together. But it backfired."

"Do you realize," I said slowly, "that I've been rejected by one lover's parents for my appearance, and by another would-be lover's parents for my upbringing. In the nurture-nature thing, I'm an impossible mismatch. I can't be myself, whoever that is, and please anyone."

"I would say that both Ed and Ki-dok were pleased with you. Not to mention Dong-su," she added wryly.

"Maybe I'm a girl to play with but not to marry."

"Sounds good to me, girl. Marriage isn't all it's cracked up to be, anyway. Get in all the playing time you can. And please remember that you had no intention of marrying Ki-dok in the first place. If you insist on finding Prince Charming, you just have to find that Year-of-the-Horse guy in your magic village by the sea.

35

It was one of those rare snowy days in Seoul, and danger lurked on the streets. Not because of the cold - it wasn't much under freezing - but because of the cars. Snow clearance and sanding appeared to be unknown, and the drivers didn't seem to have a clue about how to maneuver on the slippery stuff. Even from my room I could hear the crunch of cars sliding into each other out on the main street. Elaine had gone to a distant village for a week. It was a chance to study Korean without interruption, but I felt restless and couldn't concentrate on my work.

I found myself drumming on the desk with the flat of my hands. What was that Bird Mountain Village rhythm?

DONK daki daki, DONK daki daki . . . and I was there again, but not on the village pole. It took a moment for my eyes to adjust, and to realize I was on the roof beam of the birth hut. Birdwing was beating the drum, with Flyingbird's mother and her aunts assisting. It wasn't going as well as Flyingbird's own birth, though. There was too much blood on the floor, and on Sunflower's feet. Flyingbird was very pale.

"I can't push anymore," panted Flyingbird.

"Lie down," instructed Birdwing. "Let me feel the baby."

Birdwing's expert hands felt the contours of the infant in Flyingbird's belly. She shook her head.

"The baby is upside down. That's especially bad for a first-born. I'll have to turn it around. Sunflower and Magpie, hold Flyingbird's hands. Pebble and Birchleaf, hold her shoulders down. Flyingbird, I'll try to hurt you as little as possible. I'll have to do it between the next contractions."

As soon as Flyingbird's belly relaxed again, Birdwing thrust one hand inside and massaged with the other. The contour moved. After another spasm gripped Flyingbird, the baby was quickly flipped over all the way. Flyingbird gave several more pushes while Birdwing gently pulled, and finally the birth was accomplished.

Pebble and Birchleaf took care of the baby, while the others made Flyingbird comfortable and gave her a drink of water from a gourd dipper.

"It's a girl," said Pebble, but this time there was no rejoicing. If Flyingbird didn't live, the baby would die too, for there was no nursing mother in the village.

"Let me hold her," said Flyingbird weakly. "She's the image of Bigbear, don't you think?"

It was high noon, and the winter sun streamed in at an angle through the southern smoke hole.

"Let's call her Sunshine," Flyingbird suggested.

None of the older women answered her. I knew why. If she should die, it wasn't right to give the baby a name.

"It's all right," Flyingbird reassured them. "My Spirit Bird is here. Didn't you see her? Look up on the rafter. That's a sign I'll recover. Please go tell Bigbear."

"He can't come in until the bleeding has stopped. You must rest now."

Quietly they dedicated Golden Sunshine to the Hearth Spirit.

Flyingbird did recover, and Sunshine was a strong healthy baby from the first. Bigbear held her in his big hands, and marveled at the tiny fingernails, at the perfect little being who came into the world in such a difficult way.

It wasn't all happiness in the village, though. A breach birth means that someone has seriously disturbed the harmony of the village. Birchleaf was the first to remind them of it.

"I think it's Tigertail," she said to Pebble. "We shouldn't have let him stay. The Hearth Spirit is insulted to have such a funny looking creature at one of her hearths. He spoiled Flyingbird's pregnancy. We'll have to send him away."

"I don't know," answered Pebble. "He's a very helpful person. He fishes, and takes his turn grinding acorns, and helps to build boats. He even showed us how to make firmer nets, that the fish can't slip through so easily. Flyingbird told me he's never touched her. How can Tigertail be the problem?"

Birchleaf complained to Black Uncle as they gathered clams near the shore.

"The Hearth Spirit is angry, or she wouldn't have sent Sunshine to be born upside down. Don't you think it's Tigertail? He seems sneaky to me, with those funny narrow eyes."

"He is funny looking," agreed Black Uncle. "But is that enough to anger the Hearth Spirit? I don't think we have anything to worry about."

As Sunshine grew, and began to smile, she seemed to have been substituted for the sun itself. The rains came with a ferocity never known before at Bird Mountain Village, turning everything into a swamp. The millet rotted in the fields. Water got into the storehouse and spoiled the dried fish and acorn cakes. The seas boiled up, and it was impossible to go fishing. Mildew grew on their clothing.

For the first week, people were cheerful enough. They stayed inside and worked on various crafts, making things of wood, or cloth, or basketry. Flyingbird didn't mind having nothing to do but play with Sunshine, and Bigbear and Tigertail enjoyed the baby too.

By the second week a certain crabbiness was breaking out in the village. Edible food was dwindling, and the discomfort of all that wetness got on everyone's nerves. Birchleaf brought up the anger of the Hearth Spirit again. This time she got more response.

"Certainly the Hearth Spirit is angry," Pebble concurred. "We have to decide what to do."

"How could it be Tigertail?" asked Birdwing, when Birchleaf and Pebble brought the accusation to her. "He has adapted to our village very well. I think we'll just have to wait. The rains will be over soon."

The members of Flyingbird's household were unaware of the growing antagonism toward Tigertail, focused as they were on their new treasure.

The next calamity twisted the tension a notch higher. The village drumskin tore across the middle with a hiss, as Birdwing was beating it one morning for the sun-up ceremony. Even Birdwing had to believe that meant something was amiss.

"This drum was brought to Bird Mountain Village by my Grandmother's Grandmother," said Birdwing sadly. "The cover was made of the hide of a kind of deer that doesn't live here - a deer with very big antlers. It's the end of our connection with our distant relatives, who live near the Seven Stars. We can replace the drumskin with hide of our deer, but it will never have the same resonance. I'll make a new drum, and then dance to the Spirit World for instructions. We must find out what all these troubles mean."

Flyingbird helped Birdwing make the new drum cover. They chose a fawn's spotted skin which had been tanned the previous spring, and dedicated it to the Hearth Spirit. Taking the old skin carefully from the round wooden frame of the drum, Flyingbird used it as a pattern to cut a circle with her obsidian knife. Then Birdwing made holes in the edges, and strung deer gut through the holes in a star-like pattern, pulling the drumhead tight on all sides, while Flyingbird held the drum. The two ends of the gut were tied together, and then the drum was dunked in water to shrink the leather down tight as it dried.

Birdwing brought up the matter of the talk against Tigertail. Flyingbird was appalled.

"It could be true, Flyingbird. *Something* is surely wrong here. I'll have to ask the Spirits."

It took several days for the drum to dry, especially with the continuing rain. Birdwing hung the drum over the hearth for the Hearth Spirit's undivided attention.

Birchleaf by now had convinced nearly everyone that the problem was Tigertail. Even Sunflower and Father thought it was probably so. Straight Pine didn't believe it, though, and he said so to Tigertail.

"What? This is the first I know of such talk! Your customs are different from mine. Can you explain it to me?" Tigertail was upset.

"I thought you knew. When things go wrong, like Sunshine being born upside down, or too much rain, or the drum breaking, it means the village is out of harmony. Somebody is causing it, with bad actions or bad thoughts. It can be someone alive or someone who has died. Birchleaf thinks it's you, and she has most of the village believing it. Bigbear and Flyingbird don't blame you, of course. And I don't think Birdwing does either, although she won't say. I think it's probably a living villager, because it's been a long time since anyone died. Ghosts usually don't wait so long to make trouble."

"What shall I do? Should I just go away?"

"If you go, I'm going too. It's almost time for me to find a wife in another village, anyway. We could go to Three Rocks Village, where my cousin Oyster lives. Let's do it. If it makes the rains clear up, the village will be better off. If the rain continues, then they'll know it isn't you."

"Shall we go now?"

"I'll get a boat."

Neither stopped to say good-bye - they just picked up their song sticks and left. No one saw them leave, rowing the boat out into the storm.

Darkness fell. People began to wonder where Straight Pine and Tigertail were. Red Uncle counted the boats, and found one missing. Flyingbird and Magpie were both frantic when they realized the song sticks were gone. The two had left, on purpose.

"Why did Tigertail have to steal my son?" Red Uncle asked in a fury. "It was right for him to leave, but wrong to take Straight Pine. They'll both drown. Tigertail should just have drowned himself."

"Well, now the rains will stop," said Birchleaf smugly.

And sure enough the rains did stop. But the food supply was low, and new calamities occurred.

Pebble and White Uncle went out fishing, and the net tore just as they were hauling the fish into the boat. Most of the fish fell back into the sea. Sunflower turned over the soup pot while it was hot, and badly scalded her arm, besides losing a good pot of soup. A tree branch fell on Great

Uncle, and knocked him out. Saddest of all, Seaweed's baby was stillborn, and had to be buried in the cemetery in the placenta jar.

"We must have a ceremony to appease the spirits. It can't be delayed any longer," Birdwing decided. "Harmony has to be restored, or we will all die."

Just as the sun went down on the night of the next full moon, the villagers brought their mats and made a circle. Birdwing put on her best robe, and fastened her hair on top of her head with the bone bird pin. She put her six amulets on a string around her neck. Then she washed her face and hands in the sea. She came to the circle and stood in the middle of it.

Flyingbird beat the new drum, and the rest of the villagers clapped to the rhythm. Birdwing stared out to sea. An owl hooted in the stillness.

Just as the huge yellow moon rose out of the sea, Birdwing began to dance. She went full circle around the villagers six times, and then began to speak in a strange high voice.

"I am Golden Sunbird. I came here from the land of the Seven Stars with my three sisters and two husbands, to found a peaceful village. Now you have disturbed my sleep in the Spirit World. You have made disharmony."

"What is the root of the disharmony?" asked Birdwing in her normal voice.

"One person causes the trouble. A person with a jealous heart. A person who cannot bear to see others happy."

"I told you it was Tigertail," whispered Birchleaf.

"But Tigertail has gone, and still we have troubles," Birdwing was saying to Sunbird.

Suddenly Birdwing began to whirl around, faster than seemed humanly possible. Now her voice was an imitation of Birchleaf. "Tigertail is causing the trouble. Tigertail looks evil. Tigertail should never have come here. Tigertail should not be allowed to stay."

Birchleaf couldn't suppress a smile of triumph.

Sunbird's voice was heard again. "The trouble-maker is not Tigertail. The troublemaker is one of you-ou-ou-ou." The voice went off in a screech.

Birdwing spun around the circle again, stopping abruptly in front of Birchleaf. "Stand up!" she ordered, in Sunbird's voice.

Birchleaf stood.

"You are the one. You have slandered Tigertail. You drove him away, and Straight Pine with him. The village will not be in harmony until you find him, and say you are sorry."

Birchleaf's face went very pale, and she fell down in a faint.

Birdwing sat on her mat, and gradually recovered her own composure.

Flyingbird looked around at her fellow villagers. They knew that the spirit Sunbird had spoken truly, and most of them felt a little guilty themselves. Everyone sat silent, without any motion.

"We have to find Tigertail," Flyingbird pointed out, to get people moving again. "We only know that they went away in a boat. That could be anywhere. And we are out of food. We could starve while a search party looks for them. Who has a suggestion?"

But they sat silently. I was the only one who knew where to find Tigertail.

I flew down from my pole and picked up a pebble and put it in front of Flyingbird. Then I went for another, and another. I arranged the three stones in a triangle, and then flew back to my pole.

The villagers stared at the rocks.

"That's right!" said Magpie suddenly. "I think they would have gone to Three Rocks Village. Straight Pine adored Oyster, and missed him very much when he left to marry. Besides, it's the nearest village, and Straight Pine knows the way. If they're safe anywhere, it's likely to be there."

"Even with a full moon, we can't send a boat out tonight. It's a long day's journey each way. I guess we can last with nothing to eat for two days. I'll start early tomorrow. Who wants to go with me?" asked Flyingbird.

"Tweet!" I said.

Flyingbird looked up at me on the village pole.

"Do you know the way to Three Rocks Village?"

"Tweet, tweet," I affirmed. I had been in a cage when I was there before, but I thought I could find it. And I could fly by the light of the moon.

"Go now. May Grandmother Moon guide your journey."

I flew out over the sea, stretching my wings to catch the wind. I hoped that Tigertail and Straight Pine had arrived safely in Three Rocks Village. But, I reasoned, Sunbird would have known if they had drowned. I was sure I would find them there.

The rocky shore has several landmarks. I passed the rocks where Flyingbird and Straight Pine got trapped by the tide, and then the cove where Flyingbird and Bigbear first made love. Then I could see three large rocks out in the sea, the ones that give the village its name. Grandmother Moon guided me all the way, and having done her duty, she went to bed behind the mountains. The sun was already lighting up the sky on the far side of the sea.

150

The people of Three Rocks Village straggled out of their houses to the sound of the sun-up drum, and assembled in a circle. I perched on their white pole with a carved seal on top, and waited for someone to notice me.

Tigertail saw me first.

"Flyingbird's Spirit Bird! Look, Straight Pine! What do you think she wants to tell us?"

"She's come to take us back! It's all right now!"

I flew to the prow of the boat to show them that was true. Tigertail went to thank Oyster and the other villagers for letting them stay there.

Straight Pine whispered to a girl with big brown eyes and a tattooed mouth.

"I have to go back to my village now. Do you want me to come back and build a house with you, White Leopard?" he asked hopefully.

Leopard stretched, catlike. She liked to live up to her name.

"Golden Straight Pine, I hope you'll come back soon. We'll have a happy house, with lots of daughters."

Oyster gave Tigertail and Straight Pine some provisions to take back to Bird Mountain Village, for the rains had not lasted as long in Three Rocks Village. Leopard walked them to the boat, carrying their song sticks.

On the way back, Straight Pine threw out the fishnet, and soon it was filled. Riding the current, the boat reached Bird Mountain Village by sundown.

Birchleaf was the first one to spot the boat, and she was on shore to apologize even before Tigertail was out of the boat.

"It's all right," said Tigertail. "I'm glad I wasn't the cause of the troubles. And I'm glad to be back."

Bigbear and Flyingbird both hugged him. "We knew it wasn't you."

They feasted on the welcome fish and told Tigertail and Straight Pine about the full moon ceremony. Flyingbird and Tigertail sat very close together, while Bigbear held Sunshine.

"I think Sunshine and I will sleep in Birdwing's house tonight," Bigbear said. "It's time you two had a little privacy."

36

My parents were on their way to visit. I made reservations for them at the Chosun Hotel. Elaine and I tidied up our small spartan room at International House to avoid as much as possible the invidious comparison with the luxury hotel. The weather was still nippy, but the spring colors were coming out - the pinks and yellows of the early flowers. Korea would look pretty for Mom and Dad.

I was glad to have an excuse to take a week off from my research. The dig data was all processed, both mine and Ki-dok's. I had slogged through every site report on the neolithic in Korea that Ki-dok could dig up for me. My file of cards with Chinese characters, their Korean pronunciation, and their meaning in English, had outgrown the original file box and was in danger of spilling over into a third.

My spoken Korean was improving, although I still thought of it as "taxi-driver Korean" - I couldn't use it to discuss archaeology, for example, although I knew the words. A month or so earlier I had realized that Dong-su was teaching me only formal Korean, but I needed to know the other five forms, and when to use them, in order to be proficient. How do children learn this complex language? I wondered.

My parents had rented a car for a week, and I made an intensive sight-seeing plan, to make the best use of their time. We would make a quick swing around the peninsula, seeing Mt. Sorak on the east, Pusan and Kyongju the old Silla capital in the south, and the old Paekche capitals of Kongju and Puyo on the way back. The rest of the time we'd make day trips from Seoul. I wanted them to see the Folk Village, the Buddhist temple of Popjusa at Songnisan, and of course the archaeological sites as well as Seoul itself.

The first thing my parents wanted to see was my living arrangements. They feared the worst, but found I-House better than they expected. There were only two chairs, so Mom and I sat on my bed.

"This bed feels like a slab of concrete," Mom said. "How can you sleep on it?"

"It was worse before I bought the comforter," I answered, lifting the sheets and showing them the thick quilt between the bottom sheet and the mattress. They laughed, and Dad accused me of being the Princess-who-slept-on-a-pea.

"It's not so bad. It keeps my back straight."

"It's a tiny room, but we're both busy, so we're not here much. And we're not allowed to give parties in here," Elaine smiled.

Mom admired Elaine's wooden chest, and Elaine told her about the antique area. From Mom's enthusiastic interest, it was clear that antique hunting had to be added to the itinerary. Mom had also heard about other great shopping, at East Gate which was nearby, and near South Gate. This hadn't been in my plan either - although I should have known. She also wanted to visit museums and art galleries.

Over dinner at I-House, where my parents insisted on eating, we made a new plan for their time in Korea. It included more of seeing what I was doing and meeting my friends, and much less sightseeing. I'm still their little girl.

"You'll have to come to Korea again, then," I said, giving up my plans. "I wanted you to see the beautiful countryside, and the magnificent remains of the Three Kingdoms civilizations."

"We came to see you, you know, not to sight-see. Heidi was disappointed she couldn't come, too. We all miss you," said Dad, giving me a pat.

"Oh, Dad, I've missed you too! I'm so glad you came!"

Our trip to the Folk Village was a huge success. We spent all day wandering through the old houses from different parts of South Korea, and looking at the furniture, agricultural tools, spinning and weaving equipment, kitchens, and so forth from the past. Dad is a history buff, and Mom loves antiques, so they had a great time. None of this was strange to me any longer, and I felt I was sharing a piece of my own past that I had only recently come to know. I found myself looking at all the sliding lattice doors with their paper covers, seeking a familiar pattern, one like my dream. Because the angry voices were so persistent, the dream seemed like a key to my earliest memories. One house had a door that was close, but not exactly right.

Budding forsythia framed the group of *changsung*, "devil posts". The effect was delightful. We posed beside them for a passing stranger to take our picture with Dad's camera.

"These were village guardians," I explained about the *changsung*. "They were always carved in pairs, one male and one female. I think that means men and women were equally important in Korean villages, in spite of Confucianism that makes men dominant. Every three years a new pair of posts was carved and set up beside the old ones, so there was always a row of posts in various stages of decay. A colorful ceremony to bless the village, and to drive out evil spirits, was held each time new posts were carved."

"Do they still carve the devil posts?"

"Perhaps in some remote villages. But most places are too anxious to be `modern', and not to be seen as superstitious. That doesn't stop the *mudangs*, though," I added as an afterthought, and told them a bit about the women shamans and the *kuts* I've attended with Elaine.

For lunch we stopped to have Korean pancakes at a small restaurant.

"These are delicious," said Mom in surprise. "What are they made of?"

"Pea flour, with whole green onions mixed in. Last week, when we were looking for sites near the Han River, a village woman offered us some pancakes she had just made with wild greens. She used wild onion, wild garlic, and something that looked like spinach. They were so-o-o-o good."

"Isn't it dangerous to your health to eat things like that?" asked Mom. "How do you know they're clean? What about hepatitis?"

I brushed this aside. I hadn't so much as caught a cold.

"It's amazing how many wild plants are still eaten, especially in the spring. A woman showed us twenty-three edible plants growing wild on the hillside behind her house! She let me make a botanical collection. I recorded the Korean names of the plants and the part that's eaten. I'm hoping to find someone who can identify them by their Latin names. I didn't have the right equipment to press the plants properly, but I put them between newspapers and weighted them with books until they dried."

"Why is that important?" asked Dad.

"Maybe these are relatives of early cultivated plants."

"My little girl is always thinking," said Dad affectionately, patting my arm. "How's the work going?"

I told him with more technical vocabulary than was absolutely necessary, irked by the condescension implied in always being Daddy's little girl. My father seemed impressed, as I intended.

"And this Oh Ki-dok you're working with? How is he?"

"He was quite stiff and shy to start with, but now he's comfortable with me. He brings me every report I mention that I'd like to read, even though I tell him I'm coming to the university or the museum to read them. It's actually embarrassing. I've started to watch what I say."

"I read a book about Korean customs that said such `mentions' are interpreted as requests. Do you think that's it?" suggested my mother.

"Maybe I should read that book too. I've made several gaffes with Korea manners." I gave them an expurgated version of the dinner with the Ohs.

"Customs are very strong in all of us," pronounced Dad a bit pompously, trying to be comforting, I suppose.

The trip to the antique stores was a follow-up success. Even Dad was interested, since he'd just seen similar items in their living contexts.

As we wandered from store to store, Mom got more and more interested in the old chests. She asked endless questions about the wood they were made of, how old they were, the region they came from. I translated, using my pocket dictionary a lot, and found myself gradually drawn in.

Mom was attracted to a low table, with the same cloud pattern carvings that Elaine liked. The ends of the top curved upward like the eaves of a temple roof. We learned that these little tables are writing desks - the scholars who used them sat on the floor.

"Aren't these dragons great?" I said, getting into the spirit of the thing. Dragons were carved on either side, and the legs had a graceful S-shape.

Mom agreed, and insisted on buying it for me, along with a matching chest. I didn't resist. I'd just fallen in love with these pieces of furniture, and I knew my parents could afford the gift. Who could say when I'd be in Korea again?

For themselves, Mom and Dad picked out a chest of pear wood, with brass fittings, and arranged to have it shipped home. The beautiful grain of the wood had been polished by the centuries.

"I need to buy a small present to take to the *manshin* next time I go to visit her," I remembered, looking around at the clutter of objects. "I wonder what she'd like?"

"What's this?" asked Mom, holding up a cluster of brass bells attached to a handle.

"It's a shaman's rattle. They shake it in a certain kind of *kut*, to call the spirits. Maybe that would make a good present for Yol-i's Mother."

"Who is Yol-i?" Dad wanted to know.

"Just a boy. Actually, he's must be a man. I've never met him. He's the *mudang*'s son. Women are rarely called by their given names in Korea, but they're often called by the name of their oldest son. `Yol-i's Mother' is the name of the *mudang* Elaine works most closely with. I've been to several of her *kuts*, and we've become friends. She's sorry for Elaine and me being so far from our families, so she's a kind of stand-in mother."

"I'd like to meet her," said Mom. "She'll have to call me `Clara's Mother', since I don't have a son."

I bought the bronze bells, and we went to lunch. I talked my parents into ordering ginseng chicken, and told them it would make them live forever. I liked the flavor better than the ginseng tea.

I polished up the bronze bells before taking them to Yol-i's Mother, and was surprised to discover an etched pattern of a bird on the handle, and tigers on the bells. It was a nicer present than I realized when I bought it.

Elaine went with us to visit Yol-i's Mother, bringing a gift of a small bronze Buddha, which Yol-i's Mother's spirits had commanded her to bring. My parents took rice cakes.

"Your daughter is very talented," the shaman told Mom and Dad through Elaine's translation. "She dances enchantingly, and I think she sees spirits, although she won't say."

The *mudang* gave me a sly look.

"I told her she should give up this silly business of digging in the ground for spirits of long ago" - I had been unsuccessful in explaining archaeology - "and become a *manshin*. But her soul is too American. She will go her own way."

The *manshin* glanced at my parents to be sure they weren't insulted, since being a *mudang* is considered low class. They just looked mystified, but glad that I had some kind of talent that was being praised.

Yol-i's Mother warmed to my parents. She could feel that they were sincerely interested in her work, and didn't look down on her, so she showed them her altar, where various spirits lived. Her special spirit is the Mountain Spirit - the Old Man with the Tiger, which was represented by a painting of an old man riding on a tiger, like the one Dong-su showed me in the temple at Soraksan. She also had a special helper - her sister's daughter, who died of smallpox at the age of ten. The child's spirit lived in her colorful ceremonial dress, folded on the altar.

The bronze Buddha, brass bells, and rice cakes were added to the altar collection, with the rice cakes stacked to make a tower.

"I've seen the Mountain Spirit in Buddhist shrines, but I didn't expect to see the Buddha on a *mudang*'s altar," I said.

"There's no reason to exclude any kind of power, if you can control it," Yol-i's mother explained.

"You do have a knack," she said to me, pointing to the bells. "Recently I dreamed about bells with tigers on them."

"I didn't even know there was a design until I polished it," I confessed. "And my mother actually found it."

"Your mother has a knack," Yol-i's Mother amended.

Mom told Yol-i's Mother about the scholar's desk and chest that I chose.

"Clouds and dragons," mused the shaman. "Yes, that is right for you, So-yong Western Dragon. And I'm glad you'll have something old from Korea to take back over the sea with you when you go. I had

156

planned to give you the yellow robe before you left, but I think you should have it now. It should be the first thing to go into your dragon chest."

"I couldn't take it!"

"But you must not refuse this gift. The spirits would be offended. It will give you power, and you will surely return."

She looked at me with narrowed eyes.

"I can tell you have something on your mind, something to do with tigers. Perhaps we should show Mr. and Mrs. Alden what a *kut* dance is like. It won't be real, but the form is the same. Slip into the robe and dance for your parents."

"It's time to go now," I said, not liking this turn of events.

But I was persuaded to put on the robe and dance, while the *manshin* beat the drum.

37

This time I recognized the birth hut right away. The chant was the same. I heard it before my vision cleared. I had no sooner arrived than so did the baby boy, sliding out on a big "Ho!"

"This one is Tigertail's," said Magpie, smiling at the infant. "Look at his black straight hair. Will Tigertail be disappointed that his first-born is a boy?"

"I don't think so," Flyingbird answered. "It's unnatural, but boys are at least as important as girls in his home village."

The baby was bellowing his indignation at being abruptly squeezed out of his nice cozy place. Birdwing wrapped him in a rabbit skin blanket and cuddled him, and he soon settled down.

After he had been dedicated to the Hearth Spirit and the Birth Hut Spirit, Birdwing called to Bigbear and Tigertail, "It's a boy, with healthy lungs. We'll have to teach him to talk softly."

Both men came into the small hut. It was too crowded for everyone, so several of the women left. That's when I noticed that Seaweed was there, too. She must be a mother now, I realized. Women without children weren't allowed in the birth hut.

"Look at that," said Bigbear. "I think this one's yours, Tigertail. Look at that black hair! It sticks straight up! What do you want to call him?"

"In Rock Shrine Village we name boys for something about their appearance. The first thing everyone will notice about this boy is his hair. How does Straight Hair sound to you?"

"Nice," said Flyingbird. "Go tell Sunshine she has a brother named Straight Hair."

Sunshine was a bright and eager child, and she had prospered under the attention of three adults in the household. She was enchanted with Straight Hair, and wanted to mother him just like the adults. Bigbear showed her how to hold him with his head cradled. Sometimes they let her carry him in the sling on her back, just for a minute. She was very proud.

Cockleshell spent a lot of time with the three small children - Sunshine, Straight Hair, and Seaweed's son Rabbit. She taught Sunshine and Rabbit clapping games, and was the first to pick up and comfort any child who tripped and fell. Clearly she loved children, but the Hearth Spirit had not blessed the house she shared with Sandcrab.

"What am I doing wrong?" she asked Birdwing. "I followed all your instructions, but still no baby grows. What can I do?"

"The song of our ancestor Sunrise tells that she longed for a baby for several years, but no child came. Then she - - - but why don't I just sing you the song? You sing the refrain. It goes, `Send a girl, send a boy.' Let me fetch her song stick."

The song stick of Sunrise was unusually tall.

"Her father said she'd live a long life, so he carved her a long stick. She did, too. Long enough to know six great-grandchildren. See, they're on the bottom of the stick."

Birdwing stood with her hand on the stick, found the sign of the nest, and began to sing.

"I was born and grew up
in Bird Mountain Village,
where I did my embroidery
uneventfully."

"Send a girl, send a boy," sang Cockleshell.

"I courted a boy
from Three Rocks Village.
He rowed to our fishing grounds every day,
I went out fishing every chance that came."

"Send a girl, send a boy"

"We built our house together
and made love night and day.
But a year went by, no baby came.
After two years, no baby was sent."
"Send a girl, send a boy"

"There were no wise elders to mix me potions,
no wise elders to pray for me.
So I went to the mountain
the sharp-pointed mountain
and asked for a baby with bushy brown hair."

"Send a girl, send a boy"

"On top of the mountain
birds were nesting.
Even birds have babies,
why not I?
The mountain took pity,
and sent me a baby
it sent my darling Birdnest
with bushy brown hair.

Birdnest grew up happy,
and played with her cousins,
and we all embroidered
uneventfully."

"Do you mean," asked Cockleshell, "that I have to find the pointed mountain and ask for a child?"

"What do you think? Are you as brave as Sunrise?"

"Did Sunrise go alone?"

"The song doesn't say. But I think it would be all right to take a sister."

Cockleshell asked both Seaweed and Flyingbird if they would come.

Seaweed was always a little frail, and she thought she might be pregnant again.

"If you can wait until after this one is born . . . "

"I'll go in a few weeks," interrupted Flyingbird. "You know about my famous curiosity. I want to go everywhere. But you'll have to nurse Straight Hair for me, Seaweed. Except for the matter of milk my men can look after the children. Do you have enough milk for both babies, do you think? It'll only be a couple of days."

"That's one thing I have plenty of," Seaweed bragged. "I'll be glad to."

Flyingbird told Bigbear and Tigertail that she was going with Cockleshell to climb Pointed Mountain, so Cockleshell could ask for a baby.

"Do you know the way?" asked Bigbear, concerned.

"Shall we come, too?" asked Tigertail.

"I need you two to stay home and look after the children. We'll row a boat up to the cove. Pointed Mountain can be seen from there. It shouldn't take us more than two days. Seaweed will feed Straight Hair. You can't come anyway; this is women's business. Don't worry, my Spirit Bird will come along. She'll protect us."

Cockleshell and Flyingbird packed some acorn cakes, and strapped straw sandals on their feet. I perched in the prow of the boat while they rowed, saving my strength for the flight ahead.

It might have been a pilgrimage for Cockleshell, but for Flyingbird it was a merry outing. The two young women sang as they climbed the steep peak, following deer trails. Twisted pines grew where they could huddle out of the wind. Near the top, the bare granite stuck out like the bones of the earth. They scrambled up loose scree to a kind of saddle between two peaks.

"Which peak is the right one?" asked Cockleshell anxiously.

"The higher one," Flyingbird answered decisively. "We'll get the best view from there."

It wasn't far to the top, but it was more like rock climbing than hiking. It took quite a while for them to find the right hand and footholds to climb the last bit. At last they stood on the top, breathless from both the climb and the view. I was glad for my wings.

"It's like being a bird," said Cockleshell. "There's Bird Mountain Village - and look! - there's Three Rocks Village!"

"How big the sea is," Flyingbird added. "I wonder if there's land on the other side. I wonder if I'll ever know."

While Cockleshell said her prayer, Flyingbird explored the mountaintop. There was a huge bird nest, so this was probably the right place. She sat down beside it, and made a discovery. Scratched into the rock was a picture - a horizontal line with a half circle above it. A rising sun! Sunrise! Sunrise had left her signature, a good omen. Cockleshell drew her shell sign beside the sunrise, and they started down the mountain.

I flew up high over the mountain. The view was familiar. Was this the peak that I climbed with Dong-su? I wish I had known then to look for the rock pictures.

But maybe all the views looked alike, and I hadn't been on this very peak. Mom would like to come here and paint, I thought. I soared in the sky until Flyingbird and Cockleshell reached home safely.

 "That was a lovely dance, dear," my mother applauded.

"Hear, hear," added Dad. "How did you learn to do it?"

"I just watched the *manshin* and copied her. You should see her dance. She could enchant a stone."

But Yol-i's Mother declined to dance, saying she must save herself for tomorrow's *kut*.

"I must never dance for mere amusement," she said. "My guardian spirits would be offended and leave forever."

She sent us on our way back to Seoul with lucky papers covered with cryptic signs in red.

38

It was fun to have time to be a tourist. With Mom and Dad visiting, I had a chance to see a lot of places I hadn't been to before. On Mom's request, the three of us headed for Southgate Market in the rental car. Having never had a car in Seoul, I didn't know where it was possible to park. It turned out the answer was nowhere. The traffic is terrible, and Seoul is full of one-way streets. I wasn't very familiar with the area, even as a pedestrian. After driving around for half an hour, in desperation Dad returned the car to the Chosun Hotel, parked it in their garage, and we walked the eight blocks or so to the market.

Dad was grumpy over the terrible driving, so I looked for a way to soothe him. Right at the entrance to the market I saw a store with all kinds of camping gear, all terrific bargains, of course. This was just the ticket. He began examining everything, and, through me, asking the prices.

"I think I'll just walk along a few shops and see what's there," said Mom. "You'll find me browsing farther on."

Dad picked out a backpack and a sleeping bag, after undoing both and examining them minutely for defects. But negotiating a sale turned out to be complicated. The owner wouldn't come down on his price enough to suit Dad. Finally the owner suggested keeping the asking price, but throwing in a hat, a solution that made them both happy. The proprietor didn't have the right change, so he disappeared down the street to get it. When he came back, it took a while to wrap the purchases. Then Dad decided the hat wasn't the right size, and swapped it for another.

Finally we were out again in the alley, looking for Mom. We glanced in the stores on both sides, strolling in no particular hurry. Then we came to a fork.

"Which way?" Dad turned to me for advice.

I didn't know how to second-guess whether Mom would have gone right or left.

"You take the right and I'll take the left," I suggested.

"And then we'll all be lost! You and I have to stick together."

I asked a woman at a central clothing stall if she'd noticed a foreign woman in a red blouse, but she just shrugged. Hordes of people pushed by all the time.

"What kind of a shop will she be in?" I asked Dad. "The clothing stalls are all right in the street, so we'd see her if she were buying clothes. What else would she be looking for?"

Dad frowned, and then snapped his fingers.

"Rice paper. She mentioned paper to paint on, and brushes. Is there a store like that around here?"

I hadn't any idea, so we decided to circle the entire market, looking for a stall with paper or brushes. No luck.

"Now what?" Dad looked at his watch. "We've been here two hours. She's probably getting worried."

"Where would she go if she decided to look for us?"

"Probably to the store where she left us - if she could find it again in this maze."

This seemed as good a theory as any. Walking back in that direction, we noticed paint brushes sitting out on a table in front of a shop. On a chance, we went in, and sure enough, Mom was there, way in the back. Many kinds of paper were spread out in front of her, as she made her selection. She didn't even know she was lost.

"Mr. Kim is the nicest man!" said Mom when she saw us. "He's invited us to an art gallery tonight. There's a special show of water colors by a Buddhist monk. Here's the address. We didn't have any plans, did we, Clara?"

"I didn't realize you would have four people," said Mr. Kim. "Here's another ticket for your daughter."

"Four?" said Mom, as if she had been presented with a great mystery. "We're only three. One, two, three," she pointed, as if perhaps he didn't have his numbers down firmly.

"But you said your daughter was here . . ."

Dad got it.

"This *is* our daughter."

Somehow being their daughter in Korea was even stranger than being their daughter in America.

The gallery showing was a big social event, with well-dressed Koreans nibbling canapes. Most of the women wore chic western dresses, but one had on the prettiest *chima-chogori* I had ever seen, in pink, with a spray of pinker cherry blossoms embroidered on the skirt.

"You'd look stunning in one of those," Mom said to me. "You should buy a Korean dress before you leave."

"It'll have to be before *you* leave," I teased. "My grant doesn't cover an embroidered silk dress."

The paintings were appealing. I would have bought every single painting, if I had any money. There were cranes, painted with an effortless economy of line, and boys on buffaloes, and tigers. Each one included a poem, written in flowing calligraphy. Mr. Kim explained that the poem and the writing were both considered part of the painting, as well as the picture.

I fell in love with a painting of a peasant looking up at a sassy-tailed rooster on the roof of a traditional house. A kind of lattice window shone with light. The painting was silly, whimsical, profound. My eyes kept returning to it, searching for its meaning. I had found my lattice design at last.

Mr. Kim introduced us to the monk who was the artist, and several other monks as well. They were all dressed identically, in gray Korean-style robes, and white rubber shoes. Their heads were shaved, and at first they all looked alike to me. As they talked, though, they became individuals.

Mom fastened on the crane paintings, and she compared notes on technique with the artist-monk, as one painter to another. The monk demonstrated the motion of cranes, and then there he was, dancing a crane dance in the middle of the exhibition. The other monks spontaneously clapped for him. The familiar rhythm transported me to the world of Flyingbird.

39 ⌒

I was too familiar with the birth hut, and all its new-born rituals, but there I was again. Flyingbird's attendants included only Birdwing, Sunflower, and Seaweed. Birdwing had barely begun the chant when the baby appeared.

"Another boy!" Birdwing announced. "It's a good thing you got your girl first. Not a trace of Tigertail in this one."

"This baby almost couldn't wait for the Hearth Spirit's fire to be lit. If we'd had warning he would come today, everybody else wouldn't have gone out fishing."

"Since Sunshine's the one who's minding Rabbit and Straight Hair and Fawn, it's good it was quick. I'm glad we haven't had to leave Sunshine in charge for long," Seaweed said.

Flyingbird was examining her newborn.

"He's the image of Bigbear. I once said I'd have a boy named Littlebear. Does he look like a Littlebear?"

"It's a perfect name," said Birdwing. "Let's ask the Spirits for blessings for Littlebear."

What about Cockleshell, I wondered. Was her pilgrimage to Pointed Mountain in vain? Whose child was Fawn?

When the fishing boats came back, and family groups assembled, I could see that Fawn was the baby Seaweed had been carrying when Cockleshell and Flyingbird made the trek to the mountain.

Cockleshell welcomed Littlebear, but with a little sadness. I wondered how I could help her with her problem. Maybe there was a disturbance in her life somewhere that caused her barrenness.

While the villagers were roasting fish on the beach, I explored Cockleshell and Sandcrab's house. I didn't have anything special in mind, but I thought some clue might be there. I poked around in corners, looking here and there. The jar with pinched ridges that Cockleshell brought from Shell Island Village to hold her treasures sat on a ledge. I pushed off the gourd cover with my beak, and looked inside.

Something in that jar made me feel uneasy. I gave the jar a push, making it tumble over and spill the contents. Cockleshell's pearls and bracelets scattered on the floor. The jar looked empty, but something was stuck in the bottom. My uneasiness increased. I put in a claw, and tugged on something hard, with ridges.

A shell mask came out in my claw. I remembered that simple shell, with three holes punched in it for eyes and a mouth. Cockleshell had brought it from Shell Island Village, saying something about the spirits. Could this object be causing the problem?

Sandcrab came into the house.

"Who's in here?" he asked.

"Tweet."

"Flyingbird's Spirit Bird? What are you doing? You've made a mess with Cockleshell's ornaments."

"Who are you talking to?" asked Cockleshell, coming in too, and spotting me on the ledge.

On an impulse, I picked up the shell mask, and flew out the low door. I didn't know where I was going, except out of there. The spirit of the object might be jealous of Cockleshell's switch to the Golden clan. Still, it might be dangerous to try to throw it away. Where would its power be neutralized? The shell mask trembled between my claws.

Birdwing was still in the birth hut with Flyingbird and Littlebear, so I flew there. Birdwing would know what to do. I placed the shell mask at her feet. Cockleshell and Sandcrab came puffing up, followed by the rest of the curious villagers.

Birdwing looked at the mask, and then at me.

"Maybe the Spirit Bird is right. This may be the cause of Cockleshell's barrenness."

"The mask?" said Cockleshell. "It's not evil. It helped cure me of a sickness when I was small."

"Why don't we try leaving it in the birth hut?" said Birdwing. "The Spirit Bird brought it here, where it could help you, instead of hindering you in your house."

"I'll try it," Cockleshell agreed.

I flew around the village once, to get a glimpse of Sunshine and Straight Hair. They were sleeping like puppies, piled together. As I soared up toward the mountains, I hoped the new cure would work for Cockleshell and Sandcrab.

40

The clapping stopped, and the monk was no longer a crane. The foreigners who were there applauded in appreciation.

"How did you learn that?" asked Mom.

"Observing," said the monk. "It's just like painting. If I didn't know how to dance like a crane, how it feels to be a crane, I couldn't paint them. If you don't become what you are painting, the picture has no soul."

Mom bought her favorite crane painting, but it had to stay in the exhibit until the next day. The monks invited us to lunch at their temple when we came to pick up the painting. We were having all sorts of unplanned adventures.

Chogye-sa Buddhist temple is the center of one of the two Korean Buddhist sects. It's right in the city of Seoul, reached by a narrow alley from a main street. We read in the guidebook that it wasn't an ancient complex, and we weren't expecting much, but we were surprised.

"Look at that marvelous pine!" said Dad, pointing. I saw heads turn in disapproval of his pointing finger. The pine had a mottled trunk, as if it were painted. A sign identified it as a rare White Pine. It looked very old and dignified.

The main building may not be old, but it's colorful. We walked first around the outside of the building, which was covered with paintings of scenes from the Buddha's life. Mom's friend the crane painter joined us, and told us the stories portrayed by the paintings. My favorite was the scene where Prince Gautama, the future Buddha, discovers death, disease, and poverty in the world. Mom liked the one of the Buddha sitting under the bodhi tree, gaining enlightenment. Dad had no comment; he was examining the way the building was constructed.

Our host took us inside to meet the head of the sect.

The room we were ushered into was set with stiff furniture arranged in precise rectangular order. It reminded me of Professor Lee's office. We stood for a few minutes in silence, until the Head Monk, a dignified portly man, entered. He gestured for us to sit and offered us tea.

The tea was served in small handleless china cups, and it was just off the boil. The Head Monk picked his up and sipped it as if it were cold water. I almost dropped mine, but I sort of juggled the cup between my hands and managed to get it to my mouth, expecting it to burn my tongue. It seemed like some kind of a test that I had to pass.

To my surprise the liquid went down with ease, and didn't burn at all.

41

"Here comes your Spirit Bird, late for the birth of your second daughter," said Cockleshell to Flyingbird. "Shall we introduce her to Shining Eyes?"

Shining Eyes was a tiny baby, but alert, and her black eyes seemed to look around the birth hut, searching me out. I flew down next to her - a thing I had never done in the birth hut before.

"Maybe the yellow bird will be Shining Eyes' Spirit Bird, too," said Sunflower.

"I think she just likes this baby," Flyingbird smiled. "Have you ever noticed that the bird has the same eyes?"

The baby and I eyed each other, and came to an understanding. We both had cross-cultural problems.

I wasn't needed in the birth hut so I flew out, looking for the other children. Sunshine was big enough to look after the smaller ones now. I guessed she was eight or nine. Her brown hair bounced as she ran barefoot on the beach, chasing a toddler. The smaller girl screamed with delight, and laughed when she was caught.

It was easy to spot Straight Hair - he stood out from the others with his shock of black hair. The smaller boy had to be Littlebear, and Rabbit was in between in age. A girl a bit smaller than Littlebear was digging in the sand.

"Let's look for magic shells," proposed Straight Hair. "Come on, Fawn, let's walk down the beach."

So that one was Fawn. The unknown little girl was either Rabbit and Fawn's sister or Cockleshell's daughter. I hoped she was the answer to Cockleshell's prayer on Pointed Mountain, and that the shell mask would be a problem no longer.

Sandcrab and Tigertail pulled a boat up on shore.

"Look, there's the Spirit Bird! The baby must've come!" Tigertail sprinted away toward the birth hut.

Sandcrab ran along the beach and scooped up his daughter.

"Spirit Bird, this is Turtle. Thanks for helping us. She's such a joy."

42

We were invited to eat lunch in the monk's dining hall, where the fare was strictly vegetarian. We had my favorite seaweed soup, a bean dish, and several kinds of cooked greens. The food was surprisingly filling. Even Dad, Mr. Meat-and-Potatoes, enjoyed it.

Mom was curious about Buddhism, and asked a lot of questions about the rules, and the discipline the monks follow. The monks were very knowledgeable, not just about Buddhism, but about current events, Korean customs - almost any topic. After lunch the artist brought the painting Mom had bought.

"I brought two paintings," he said. "One is your crane painting, the other is a present for Clara. I saw her appreciating it, and I want her to have it."

We looked at the paintings. He had given me the watercolor with the lattice window. The lattice window from my dream. I didn't know what to say, except, "Thank you, I'll treasure it."

I wanted to ask about the cottage in the picture, but Dad was anxious to go. He took snapshots of the monks and the paintings, and then we headed for the Secret Garden.

There are three Yi Dynasty palaces in Seoul, and the Secret Garden belongs to one of them. Once the private preserve of the king and his consort, it's now a public park. It's especially pretty in the spring, with flowering trees reflected in the many ponds dotted around the grounds. Since Dad had such a bad first impression of Korea, I particularly wanted him to see it.

We didn't get there, though. On the way we ran into the granddaddy of a traffic jam. Cars just piled up and didn't move. Taxis turned around to get out of there. Dad followed their example, and once again, he drove back to park at the Chosun Hotel. I thought I heard Dad grinding his molars. He was definitely muttering bad things about Seoul traffic. Just when he was beginning to like Korea.

"Let's skip the Secret Garden for today," suggested Dad. "What do you say we go to the zoo, to look at the new baby tigers? The zoo is out of the city, according to this map, which might mean I'll be able to park the car."

At the zoo, two tiger kittens cuffed each other playfully. I looked into the mother tiger's eyes, and found myself transported to my other world.

43

Perching on the village pole, I saw that it was Birdwing beating the morning drum, though her hair had turned altogether white. Four naked children of various sizes came running up to Flyingbird, who had robes ready to slip over their heads so they could join the circle. Two of the children looked like the people of Flyingbird's village - they must be Sunshine and Littlebear, I thought - but the other two were a little different. The smallest was a girl with black shiny eyes. The boy had straight black hair like ravens' feathers, which didn't bush out at all. Shining Eyes and Straight Hair still were well named.

After the sun-up ceremony the villagers sat on their mats - all but Tigertail who squatted flat-footed in the way of his village. He could never learn to cross his legs properly. There were other new children in the village - another girl sat beside Clam, and Seaweed was suckling an infant. Cockleshell and Sandcrab had two girls and a boy of different sizes sitting between them. Straight Pine and four of the other boys were missing - married out, I suppose. And where was Grandfather? Was there a new commemorative pole in the cemetery?

"Today we must talk about the tiger that has come near the village," said Birdwing, opening the discussion. "Shining Eyes found the tiger's paw prints yesterday near the lake. We've never had a tiger prowl so near. What should we do?"

Both Tigertail and Bigbear had experience with tigers, but they waited for those born in the village to speak first.

"Perhaps if we catch a deer and leave it out, the tiger will go away," suggested Tall Sister. "It must be hungry to come so near the village."

"But if we feed the tiger it will keep coming back for more food. Then it will be very angry if we run out of things to feed it," objected Sunflower.

"What if we leave a deer far away up the trail?" Pebble mused. "Would the tiger still come back to the village?"

"Couldn't we ask the Hearth Spirit to send the tiger away?" asked Birchleaf.

"How about Flyingbird's Spirit Bird? I see she has come again. Can she help? Perhaps lead the tiger away?" suggested Magpie.

Everyone looked up at me, with my yellow tail hanging down over the village pole. I didn't have any help to offer. Their ideas all sounded reasonable to me.

"What do you think, Bigbear?" asked Birdwing. "You once told me about a tiger at Dragon River Village. How did your village deal with the problem?"

"They tried a lot of things to make the tiger go away, but finally they had to kill it. I was sorry that such a beautiful creature had to be killed, but the tiger was a killer, too. It ate one child before we set out to hunt it. I think we should kill this tiger before it strikes. Our children are too precious to risk any of them. What do you think, Tigertail?"

"I agree. But if we decide to hunt the tiger, we must have the spirits on our side. A tiger is strong and swift. It has slashing teeth and tearing claws. The only chance people have against a tiger is to outsmart it, and use its own strength against it."

Tigertail thought out a strategy to kill the tiger, which involved the help of Bigbear and Flyingbird. And me, too.

"It will be dangerous," Tigertail warned.

Tigertail sharpened a large and heavy axe on the sandstone whetstone for hours until it came to a thin, sharp edge. Then he made sure the axe was firmly bound to the wooden handle, rewrapping the sinew twice until he was sure it was so tight it couldn't slip.

Flyingbird searched for a poisonous plant with wide leaves and small yellow flowers. When she found it, she ground the root on a special grinding stone, marked with red ocher so that it wouldn't ever be used for food by mistake. She even buried the mixing stick when she was finished.

Bigbear rewrapped two double-curved bows, fixing the bone backing plates firmly in place. The extra curve gave them more power than simple bows. Then he chipped some new arrowheads, making them regular and symmetrical with pressure flaking on the edge, and attached them to willow shafts. I dropped yellow feathers from my tail, which he added for good luck. The arrows were ready to dip in the strong poison paste, and then wrapped in tough leaves so that no one would be cut accidentally.

That evening, Birdwing called a ceremony to ask the Hearth Spirit, as well as Grandmother Moon, to protect the hunters. The full moon was rising. The light would be right for stalking a night prowler. To make themselves less easily seen, the hunters smeared ashes from the fire on their faces and arms. Wearing only their underrobes, Tigertail, Bigbear, and Flyingbird walked silently, single file, toward the Looking Pool, where the tiger's large paw had left its imprint. Tigertail shouldered his sharpened axe, and Bigbear and Flyingbird each carried a bow, with a quiver of arrows on the shoulder, easy to reach. I flew behind them. The other villagers stayed at the fire, silently continuing to ask for the Hearth Spirit's aid.

After Looking Pool, Tigertail found the tiger tracks going up the mountain. Moving slowly and silently, we followed the tracks.

We hadn't gone far when I saw a dark shape, padding just as silently down the mountain, headed for the village. I flew quietly above it, to make certain it was the tiger, then gave a tweet of warning. Tigertail, Flyingbird, and Bigbear stopped, and looked up toward the sound.

On a rock, four meters above them, stood the tiger. Bigbear and Flyingbird moved off to the right and left, according to plan. Tigertail stood alone with his axe, just below the rock. Flyingbird and Bigbear nocked their arrows and drew back their bows, aiming just in front of Tigertail. Tigertail braced the axe in front of his chest, leaned against a boulder, with his legs apart and steady. The tiger switched its tail and crouched. It was a huge creature, six feet long. The black stripes on its tawny fur accentuated the powerful muscles, poised to spring.

The tiger roared just as he leapt directly at Tigertail. Blood coursed down Tigertail's chest. Flyingbird and Bigbear shot their poisoned arrows, and moved in closer, each loading another arrow as they came. But there was no need for more arrows. The tiger lay beneath the boulder, dying with a gasp and a shudder. Tigertail had studied how tigers leap, and directed the axe exactly to the tiger's throat as he pounced. The weight of the enormous beast did the rest. Even when Bigbear and Flyingbird shot their poison arrows, the tiger was already dying. Tigertail was covered with blood, but mostly it wasn't his. Only the tiger's sharp fang had caught his left shoulder, and left a gash.

When they were sure the tiger was dead, Tigertail skinned it, leaving the head and tail attached to the skin. It took all three to carry the heavy skin back to the village. As they reached the outskirts, they went single file, with Tigertail in the lead, holding the tiger's head above his own, the others following with the skin held high. Tigertail gave a perfect imitation of a tiger roar, and burst from the trees into the firelight.

The waiting villagers tensed to run, but quickly realized it was not a live tiger. Their fright lasted only a heartbeat. When they heard the reverberating roar of the pouncing tiger, they feared the worst, but kept their silence. Now they saw the three hunters triumphantly carrying the tiger skin smeared with blood.

The tiger's head was placed to face the Hearth Spirit, with the skin spread out behind. The tail pointed straight toward the forest. The three hunters gave brief thanks to the Hearth Spirit and to Grandmother Moon, and then went to rinse off the tiger's blood in the sea. The Uncles cut

173

fresh willow branches and began to carve new prayer sticks in honor of the tiger, shaving the ends down expertly into patterned curls. Flyingbird gathered willow bark to put on Tigertail's wound, which was deep, but not critically placed. Birdwing wrapped the willow bark in place and tied it around his shoulder and under his arm with a narrow hempen cord.

Then each person put on ceremonial robes, and reassembled at the hearth around the tiger skin. Birdwing led the prayers of thanks. She rubbed her hands in gratitude for being saved from the tiger, and for the lack of serious wounds. She also thanked the tiger for leaving them his beautiful pelt, which would make fine cushions and covers and trimming for robes. After the ceremony they brought out millet wine, drinking it and pouring libations all through the night. Tigertail was urged to tell the tale of the deed several times. Gradually the story turned into a song, to be remembered for generations. The villagers stayed up to greet the sun, and then rolled into their sleeping mats.

By noon, the village was stirring again. Shining Eyes and Straight Hair were especially proud that their father was the one who actually killed the tiger, but Sunshine and Littlebear got some reflected glory, too. The children were all wide-eyed over the tiger skin, and the head with its sharp fangs. The heroic deed of standing still to let the tiger jump, and using the tiger's own strength to kill him would become a legend.

The next day, at the after sun-up council, Tigertail gestured his wish to speak.

"I was sent away from my village to kill a tiger," he began. "Now I have killed a tiger."

Tigertail paused, to let the implications occur to the others.

"My children, Straight Hair and Shining Eyes, have never seen my kinfolk. The other children of the village have visited with their fathers' families. Would it be right for my children to meet their grandparents and lesser cousins in Rock Shrine Village?"

"Would you come back, or do you want to stay in Rock Shrine Village?" asked Birdwing. "How about the children? Certainly they should visit. But Shining Eyes, at least, belongs to this village, and should come back here. Straight Hair will have to marry elsewhere but he is still young. We would not like to have him leave so soon."

"I would come back, and bring Shining Eyes. If Straight Hair wanted to stay, the choice would be his. In my village it is usually the boys who stay, and the girls who marry out, so Straight Hair has a rightful place in Rock Shrine Village."

"It wouldn't be safe for you to travel with just the two children," Tall Sister pointed out. "You need a bigger traveling party."

174

"Flyingbird, Bigbear, and the other two children will come, too if you all agree. My relatives would never believe my story if I just brought my two children back! Anyway, I want to have the company of my house mates. Can the village allow Flyingbird to go away for a while? I don't know exactly how long we might be gone."

"How dangerous is the journey?" asked Birdwing.

"If we don't travel in the dark, the main danger is from bears and tigers. We know how to handle a tiger," he gestured significantly at the tiger skin. "And bears don't attack if you leave them alone."

"Will the children survive the trip? How long does it take?" put in Tall Sister.

"I walked for six sun-ups to get to the top of your mountain from my village. We can go slower with the children. But they can make the journey. They're the strongest ones of all."

"Are you sure you know the way back to your village? It's been a long time. Sunshine, the first born, has seen thirteen summers," worried Sunflower.

"When I came to your mountain, every day I looked back and sighted where I had been. There's a mountain with four peaks near my village that can be seen for a long way. We will watch for it, and when we spot it, it will help us find the river. I'm sure I can find the way."

It was decided that they could all go. The children were excited, and eager to help with the preparations. Sunshine was put in charge of getting her own things together, and also those of Shining Eyes, who was only five. Straight Hair and Littlebear packed their own baskets, and helped organize food for the journey.

Sunflower made new carrying baskets from thin flexible willow branches. Each person took her gourd bowl and libation stick, an extra set of ordinary clothes and ceremonial robes, sleeping mat and, of course, song stick. The adults carried all the tools they would need, except heavy tools like grinding stones that they would have to find along the way if they needed them.

Provisions were spread among the seven carrying baskets, according to the size of the carrier. Embers of the Hearth Spirit were carried in a small pottery bowl, exactly as they carried fire on boats. The travelers also brought gifts for Rock Shrine Village - some of Pebble's intricate yellow and white baskets, and a precious lump of obsidian from Whitehead Mountain.

When finally they were ready to leave, the village performed a special morning ceremony, asking Grandmother Moon to watch out for them.

"If you need me, send me a message by Grandmother Moon - she'll be able to see us. I'll respond right away," Flyingbird promised. She and her family said good-bye, leaving the village smaller and quieter.

The trek to the top of the mountain occupied a long day, with the heavy packs. The children were all good hikers, even little Shining Eyes. Sunshine wanted to lead the way, but spring traps were an ever-present danger, so the adults took turns going in front. Sunshine was always second. I flew over the treetops, watching out for trouble.

When we came to the fork that Sister Bear had taken so long ago, it was now a well-worn path. Following the trail to the cave, we watched for signs of bears. There were no recent dens in the back, and it seemed safe to camp in the cave. Flyingbird made a fire and gathered the ingredients for a soup of dried fish and berries, while Tigertail and Shining Eyes took the water jar to the waterfall before the velvet dark of the forest night obscured the trail.

"This is where I fell over the waterfall and broke my leg," Tigertail told his daughter. "The Spirit Bird found me, and your mother and Bigbear saved me. Sister Bear saved me, too - I rode on her back to the cave."

Shining Eyes looked around.

"Right here? In this very spot?"

"In this very spot," affirmed her father.

Taking the water jar on his shoulder, Tigertail stood to go back to the cave.

"Daddy, there's a bear. Right behind you," Shining Eyes whispered. She knew better than to scream.

Tigertail turned to look. The bear stood on its hind legs and gave the sign of welcome.

"Sister Bear!" shouted Tigertail. He put down the water jar and hugged her shaggy neck.

"Did you know we were coming? Flyingbird is here, too."

Shining Eyes petted Sister Bear shyly, and made friends. The bear got on all fours and turned around. Tigertail lifted Shining Eyes onto the bear's back.

"Look who's here," said Tigertail at the cave mouth. "Come out and see."

Flyingbird hugged her old friend, and scratched her nose. "So you learned how to manage in the forest. You're a pretty smart bear."

Sister Bear was introduced to all the children, and she let them romp around her. After a bit, she put back her head and made a combined growling and hooting sound. A rustling in the leaves came closer, and out of the woods trotted two small bear cubs. Sister Bear showed them off proudly. The children were delighted, and so were the cubs.

"So you stayed away because of your babies!" said Flyingbird with delight. "How many have you had?"

Sister Bear declined to answer.

It was getting too dark to be away from the Hearth Spirit, so they all went into the cave. That night Flyingbird once again slept curled up against Sister Bear's warm fur.

On the long trek, Tigertail made a game of teaching everyone some of the words of his language. At first they had a hard time with the sounds, but they copied Tigertail and soon got them close to right. The children learned faster than Flyingbird and Bigbear. They learned the counting names of their fingers, the polite words, and what to call their relatives. They learned the words for parts of the body - "nose, and neck, and knee," Shining Eyes liked to say, pointing to the right places.

Tigertail found the headwaters of the big river without any trouble, and the party of seven followed its banks. The next two nights they found caves to sleep in, but after that they had to make camp in the open.

The good weather held. Bigbear shot a deer with his bow, giving them plenty to eat. I kept up with them, but there were no more dangers to warn them of. I like to fly high and enjoy the rugged scenery. I was glad no one put me in a basket! I saw another wide river joining the one we were following, just around a bend, and flew down to learn which way to go next.

"We're almost there," Tigertail said, as eagerly as a child. "Let's wash in the river and change into our best robes."

Tigertail put on his old leather cape, and wound the tiger tail around his waist like a belt. The rest of the family wore their black and white ceremonial robes. Flyingbird wore her necklace of smoky topaz, pearl, and amber. In all their finery, they approached Rock Shrine Village.

I flew to perch in an immense oak tree that dominated the village. Beneath the tree a pile of rounded stones was heaped, and next to it was a cleared space, which brought to mind Bird Mountain Village's dance ground. About fifty houses were lined up in neat rows beyond the tree, each with the door facing away from the river.

A child saw us coming and ran screaming to its mother, "Strangers! Strangers!"

A huge crowd of people dressed in leather trousers and capes came down the river to meet us. Flyingbird hadn't seen so many people since Bird Mountain Village invited all their relatives to the Bear Festival.

Flyingbird, Bigbear, and the children all made their accustomed sign of greeting. But Tigertail held his two arms forward, his fingers together and his palms out. The local people responded in kind, and came closer.

"Who are you?" asked a middle-aged man in words the people of the Golden clan couldn't understand. "Who are these hairy people in strange clothing you have brought with you?"

"I am Tigertail, Brother Long Legs. Have you forgotten me? You sent me away to get a tiger, but it took a long time. I've brought you the tail for proof."

"Are you really Tigertail? Are you not his ghost? We thought you were killed in the mountains. Many snows have come and gone. Come, eat some food and tell me everything."

"This is my wife, Flyingbird, and my co-husband, Bigbear. And our children, Sunshine, Straight Hair, Little Bear, and Shining Eyes. I expect you can tell which children are mine and which are Bigbear's," he smiled.

The people of Rock Shrine Village made us welcome. Soon the children were romping and playing chase with the children of the village. I thought they were safe, now, and wouldn't need me to keep watch.

44

I took my parents to the university, to show them my computer output, and the artifacts my crew had excavated. When I introduced them to the distinguished Professor Lee, he brought them to his oversized office, gave them coffee, and praised my work, which made a big hit with them.

"She's too smart for a girl," he said, meaning it as a compliment. "You'll have a hard time finding her a husband."

"She'll have to make her own choice of a husband," laughed Dad. "But we're proud of her."

Some of the students who worked with me on the dig met my parents, too. I prodded them to explain the random sample, but they were too shy, so I explained it myself.

Ki-dok came in, and seeing my parents, tried to sneak out without being seen. But I called to him to come meet them.

"Your parents?" said Ki-dok in surprise. "I thought you had Korean parents."

I remembered that he hadn't heard me tell his father that I'm adopted.

"Lots of Korean babies were adopted in America," I explained.

"I'm Richard Alden," Dad said, extending his hand. "We adopted Clara when she was very small."

Ki-dok tried to shake hands and bow at the same time, and nearly bumped my father with his head. Now he was in complete confusion. He bowed to Mom and she bowed back.

"Oh Ki-dok," he said. "First time I meet you."

"How did you get into the archaeology business?" asked Dad, making conversation.

"Archaeology is not a business," replied Ki-dok stiffly "It's a profession."

"Just an expression, no offense meant," my father apologized. "How do you think the dig is going?"

"It's confusing, so far. We find ma-a-a-any unexpected things."

They chatted about the excavation a bit, and Ki-dok relaxed.

"I wish we had time to go see it," Mom said. "Do you let visitors come?"

"Not just anyone, but you would be welcome."

"We have to go back too soon, but I was wondering about Clara's friend Ed, who's coming to visit in two weeks."

"What?" I squeaked.

Dad looked at me blankly.

"Ed bought the ticket to visit you months ago - a non-refundable ticket for his spring break. Surely he wrote you."

"I haven't read his letters."

"No wonder he sounded so wistful about our seeing you. Does he always call you Jade Princess?"

"It's a name he made up when we first met."

On the way back to I-House, I told my parents about the dinner with the Howlands, and my break with Ed.

"So that's why you suddenly wanted to come to Korea! But why are you punishing Ed for what his parents did?" asked Mom. "Whatever their attitude is, he's the one that counts, isn't he?"

"I think I've learned the importance of family here in Korea," I answered. "Our American push toward individual independence isn't the whole story. I don't mean that I'm looking for a Korean family; that would be silly. I mean Ed. He'd be miserable if his parents rejected him, as well as his future children, because of me, because I have an Asian face. It just wouldn't work."

"Maybe you shouldn't take it on yourself to decide on his behalf," Mom suggested.

"Anyway, he's coming," said Dad. "You owe him a chance to talk it out. You can be very stubborn, you know, Clara. Not always an admirable trait."

Before they left, Mom bought me a Korean dress. We found one that was simply gorgeous - yellow-gold on the top gradually changing into deep brown at the bottom of the skirt. Good luck characters were embroidered in gold all around the bottom. I felt like a princess in the dress, but I couldn't imagine when I would ever wear it. It seemed like a terrible extravagance. But Mom insisted.

"You look like a Korean princess," she said. Maybe I was a Western Dragon in disguise.

45

I read Ed's letters to find out when to meet him at the airport. I felt guilty about not reading them before - he was very contrite and took the full blame. A little doubt was creeping into my hurt. Maybe I was wrong a bit, too?

"Hello, Jade Princess," Ed said awkwardly, as he emerged from customs. "Am I welcome?"

"I'm embarrassed to say it, but I'm terribly glad to see you. I'd even kiss you, but that would upset people - public displays of affection are frowned on. How long can you stay?"

"Two weeks. That's how long my spring vacation is. Which isn't long enough. We'll have to spend the whole time talking, to get caught up. Why didn't you answer my letters? I've felt terrible. I wasn't sure you'd even meet the plane."

"I'm sorry, Ed. I thought it was better to make a clean break. That's what made me think of applying for the scholarship and coming here. I didn't read your letters until last week, when Dad told me you were coming. But I guess I was only thinking of myself. Now you're here, and I *am* glad to see you."

Ed claimed he wasn't tired.

"I changed my watch, so I won't know what time it is in Boston. Let's go find some dinner."

I took him by subway to I-House and chattered about Seoul and the archaeology project.

Coming out of the subway, we were engulfed by the activities of the street. On spring and summer weekends, the wide major street near I-House is closed to traffic for several blocks. People pour into the street, using it like a park. Groups of teenagers gather around a guitar player to clap and sing. Younger kids form circles and play volleyball or badminton without a net. Adults sit in rings to chat. There's some individual activity, and some people in pairs, but most groups are circular, enclosed.

We stood on the sidewalk for a better vantage point to watch. On the far edge of the throng, streamers outlined a space like an open tent, with a tall pole in the middle, and four ribbons stretched from the pole to the ground. Strolling in that direction, we came upon a *kut* in progress right in the street. Within the ribboned-off space a group of people, mostly adults, sat on mats, dressed in their Sunday best, the men in business suits and ties and the women in *chima* and *chogori*. Their shoes were neatly arrayed in pairs at the edge of the mat.

"Is this a performance, or a ceremony?" asked Ed, when I explained the *kut*.

"I'm not sure. Let's watch and see if we can tell."

Uncharacteristically, a microphone was in use. One *mudang* chanted atop an *onggi* jar while another held the mike. Onlookers formed a ring outside the central square, gawking freely.

Suddenly I spotted Yol-i's Mother. As usual, she was in charge.

"I think it's real," I whispered. "Watch the woman in the red and green robe. I know her. She's a real shaman."

Yol-i's Mother had seen me, too. She beckoned for us to come over, and I introduced Ed.

"*Annyonghashimnikka*", said Ed, using his only Korean.

"He seems like a nice young man," said the shaman, approvingly.

Ed had used the most polite form of the greeting. I didn't translate the reply for him.

"You came along at just the right time. You will dance for us, won't you? I have a yellow robe with me."

"We can't stay. Ed hasn't had any dinner. Anyway I couldn't dance in the street in front of all these people. It was bad enough in the villages with an audience of just the village women."

Yol-i's Mother could always cajole me into dancing. Before long, I was wearing the yellow robe with my arms parallel to the ground, and looking into the distance.

46

Flying Bird and her family were hospitably received in Tigertail's village. They sang the songs of Bird Mountain Village to entertain their hosts, and pitched in with the daily chores. People were impressed with how well behaved the children were, and intrigued by their soft and gentle voices.

In spite of the general acceptance, not all the people of Rock Shrine Village were pleased with their visitors. A certain faction found them unsettling. For one thing, they looked funny. All that outrageous hair, bushing out instead of hanging down like proper hair. Their eyes weren't right, either, and they didn't know how to squat without putting their bottoms on the damp ground. Instead they sat cross-legged on mats. For another thing, they couldn't speak properly. Their soft voices sounded like sea waves, not like human talking. And then their behavior! Imagine Tigertail having a co-husband! What a scandal! What would the spirits think? How could Tigertail have married one of them?

The grumbling group was led by Long Legs' wife, Granite. She was delegated to get the leader's attention.

"He's your brother," Granite scolded Long Legs. "You sent him on the tiger quest, and you're responsible for what he brought back. Don't you think he should make amends?"

"Amends for what?" Long Legs smiled, not realizing Granite was serious. "He did kill a tiger, as he was sent out to do, and he brought us the tail to prove it. Just because it took him uncounted sun turnings to do it is no reason to punish him. Let's see, Jade wasn't born yet, and now she's almost full grown. How long was that?"

Granite was not diverted.

"But he brought those strange people. Do you think it's true they live by a far-away sea? I'd think he made it up, except that they're so hairy, they're like monkeys. They must come from the ends of the earth! And these odd children are our kin! Isn't that disgraceful?"

"They're quiet, and polite, and willing to learn our customs. I think they're all right. But you brought it up. What do you think I should do? Do you have a suggestion?"

"Send Tigertail on another quest," Granite suggested. "It's not clear that the first one counted, since he got help from these bear people and a magic bird. Test the Rock Spirits, and see if they meant for him to live."

Long Legs promised to consider the matter.

He spoke to Tigertail in privacy.

"A few people think you shouldn't have come back. They feel it's inauspicious or even dangerous to have these shaggy-bear-people here, and they're angry to be related to your children. Now they're just grumbling, but perhaps after a while they would do you or your children harm."

"Must we leave right away? We came so the children could get acquainted with their relatives. I hate to take Shining Eyes and Straight Hair away from their grandmother, when she's just begun to know them. Don't you think it would be cruel to take the children away from our mother so soon? Haven't you noticed how much she enjoys having them around?"

"Well, of course, that's true. Our mother has already learned to love your strange children. And Straight Hair is her only grandson."

Long Legs mused for a moment.

"It's been suggested that you should go on another quest. When you come back safely, there can be no further question that the Rock Spirits approve of you. What do you think of that?"

"A quest? Where? For what this time? You know I like adventures."

"Go to the sacred mountain of our forefathers, and bring back some of the shiny black stone. We've almost used up the sacred supply brought here by the first founders. The nodule you brought was welcome, but it won't last for more than another year."

"Isn't the mountain very far away? Do you know exactly how to get there?"

"I've never been there, but I know the way. Grandmother trusted me with the instructions, to pass on to some adventurous person when we ran out of black stone. You have to sail north along the shore of the Big Muddy Sea. You can stop and visit with our distant relatives in the Tree Tribe where the next large river adds its silt to the sea. They live on many small islands, as well as up the river, like us. The Water Tribe lives even farther north, near the mouth of the Great River, where our elder sister Moonbeam lives in Jade Village."

"Moonbeam! I'd love to see Moonbeam again. How is she?"

She's married to the village leader, whose name is Carver. Moonbeam would take good care of you."

"Of course I'll go. Flyingbird will want to go too. Her village teases her about her boundless curiosity, her wanderlust."

"Maybe Moonbeam knows directions to the sacred mountain from Jade Village. If not, here's what Grandmother said. You must find the Great River which begins a day's sail toward the sunrise from Jade Village. Then follow the river very far, until you come to a mountain at the top of the world. The top of that mountain is filled with a sacred lake, where our ancestors worshipped since the beginning of time. Nearby is the cliff of black shiny stone. Bring back a pack full of it. But that isn't enough. You must also find six other treasures. That will be enough proof that you are favored by the Rock Spirits. You and your family will always be welcome here."

"I understand about the black stone. But what do you mean, other treasures?"

"Whatever the Rock Spirits lead you to."

"How long would this journey take?"

"You might get there and back in two moons if you take the boat up the river as far as you can, and then climb. The moon of the first snow is the third moon from now. If necessary, you could spend the winter in Jade Village."

"The journey sounds too strenuous for the children, and maybe too dangerous. And who would take seriously a quest with four children in tow? Anyway Shining Eyes and Straight Hair should stay here with their grandmother, that was the main purpose of coming here. Can Sunshine and Littlebear stay, too? If they stay, will they be well treated?"

"I'll guarantee the fair treatment of all your children. You want to take your wife along. How about your, er, co-husband?"

"I think he'll want to come, anyway it will take three of us to handle the boat. I see that Flyingbird's Spirit Bird has come back. Now I know we'll be safe."

"Spirit Bird? Can you see it?"

"Look in the tree. The yellow bird. The people of Bird Mountain Village say she was present at Flying Bird's birth, and has been there whenever she is in danger. The bird knows to come when she's needed."

"How do you know it's *that* yellow bird?"

"Look at the crest on the top of her head, and her long tail. Especially look at her eyes. They're like ours. Have you ever seen another bird like that?"

Long Legs had to admit he had never seen a bird like me before.

"And you'll see, the bird will come with us. Do we have to make a boat, or is there one we can use?"

"Use my boat, it's new and seaworthy."

"I'll talk to Flyingbird and Bigbear."

185

47

"No wonder the *manshin* says you're a natural shaman," said Ed, affectionately patting my arm. "You dance entrancingly, and with your whole spirit. I hope you don't want to make a career of it, though. I want you to make a career of me."

"What? When I've invested so much time and energy in archaeology? You'll have to wait in line." I was teasing, but I meant it, too.

Elaine and Liesl joined Ed and me for dinner, which helped ease the continuing tension. Ed was curious about their work, and about Korea. The conversation flowed easily. I was glad to be with Ed again. He's a male I can relax with, unlike most Korean men I've met. Maybe I just understand the cultural clues better. Whatever it was, I was unwinding.

The talk turned to the *kut* in the middle of the street.

"You should've seen Clara dance," said Ed. "Her feet hardly touched the ground. She seemed to have gone to another world."

"Were you a yellow bird again?" Elaine turned to me. "Whatever happened to that baby girl you saw being born?"

"She has four children and two husbands," I smiled. "Now they're visiting a village that's probably on the Han River. My subconscious mind provided quite a soap opera, prehistoric style."

Ed looked curious, but I didn't elaborate. There was too much to tell, and not enough time.

Soon Ed started yawning, and couldn't stop. We made a plan to meet at Ed's hotel the next day around noon. I put him in a taxi, with directions to the taxi driver.

"He seems nice," commented Liesl. "Why did you want to get away from him?"

I thought back to the moment of my realization that I *am* Asian, a realization provided so disagreeably by Ed's mother. How could I explain it to Liesl?

"It was Ed's parents, especially his mother. They were so shocked to see my Korean face. I think they're biased against anybody who isn't 'white' - at least as far as being welcomed into their family."

"That's what his mother did. You told us before. But what did Ed do?"

"Nothing, I guess. That's the problem. He always accepted me, but he must have known his parents wouldn't. Why did he set up such a meeting?"

"Wasn't it his mother who planned the dinner?"

"Yes, but he could have told his parents beforehand, just the same. Anyway, once I knew how they felt, I had to get away from Ed. His family is close, I couldn't let him leave them for me, whether he wanted to or not. Parting was painful, but there are other girls out there."

"I see the problem," said Liesl. "My boyfriend is from the Italian-speaking part of Switzerland, and that was enough to send my parents into a swoon. But now that they know him, they don't mind so much. Maybe that would happen with Ed's parents."

"Clara's real problem is that she's looking for an identity, either Korean or American. It has nothing to do with Ed. His mother was just the precipitator of the crisis," Elaine cut in.

"My real problem is that I'm tired," I said, sounding crabbier than I meant to. I hate to be third-personed, and I hate pop psychology.

But, when I went to bed my mind was too busy to turn off. I found myself wondering if there were any people anywhere who didn't distrust others who looked different.

There was enough moonlight to outline the hill outside our window. As I looked at it, my room vanished, and I was perched on a rock pile, looking at a dark hill with the same outline.

48

The family from Bird Mountain Village had a sun-up ceremony the morning after Long Legs proposed the quest to Tigertail. I watched as they sat on their mats to discuss this new development. Flyingbird, of course, was anxious to go - she wanted to see all of the world, however far away, and however difficult it might be to get there. Bigbear thought he should go, too, to help get provisions and row the boat. Besides, he didn't want Flyingbird and Tigertail to go without him.

The children were glad to stay in Rock Shrine Village while the adults went on their quest. Straight Hair and Shining Eyes had never seen so many people with black hair and oval eyes, and they thought it was great. Sunshine and Littlebear had been teased and called "hairy bears" by the village children, but Sunshine told them about the real bear in the mountains, and how they rode on her back, which made them acceptable.

"How long will you be gone?" Sunshine asked Tigertail.

"We don't know. Uncle Long Legs thinks the trip will take about two moons, but if the ice comes early, we may have to wait in the north for the spring thaw. Don't worry about us. If we haven't returned in the spring, by the time all the new leaves are out, it will mean the spirits have kept us. In that case, Uncle Long Legs has promised to take you back to Bird Mountain Village," Tigertail told the children.

"Just in case, I've drawn Long Legs a map in the sand, and Sunshine, I know you remember the way. But we expect to be back before snowfall. We'll have the Spirit Bird to protect us, so we'll be safe."

The days were getting shorter, and it would have been dangerous to dally. The three travelers prepared to leave in two days. Tigertail brought fresh water in a jar, and nuts, and some dried apples. Fish caught along the way would round out their diet. I flew to the boat, perching on the prow as we left, with the adults gesturing fond farewells to those on shore.

We caught the ebbing tide, to take us rapidly out to the Muddy Sea. Tigertail remembered these treacherous mud banks, steering through the small channels with the stern oar, while Flyingbird and Bigbear rowed. At last we were out in the main channel of the sea, beyond the mud.

The sea was not so muddy away from shore, but it still had a yellowish hue. Along the way there were many islands, most of them populated with small villages. Our little boat stopped often, to visit and give and take messages for the Rock Shrine Villagers, and to learn about the local channels and tides. The inhabitants of these villages were Stone

People, related to Tigertail and others at Rock Shrine Village. Tigertail talked to them, but Bigbear and Flyingbird couldn't understand their dialect.

We stopped more briefly with the Tree People, who live where the next big river to the north pours out to the Muddy Sea. The Tree People were not so friendly, but they were curious enough about us to let us pull up our boat for the night. We stayed just long enough to exchange gifts and hear the latest gossip, to tell to those in Rock Shrine Village who had relatives here.

Twelve days of rowing, and sailing when the winds were right, took our small boat to the mouth of the Great River. Tigertail studied the river, and recalled the map that Long Legs had sketched for him in the sand.

"This has to be the river that leads to the sacred mountain. But our instructions are to go around the coast a little farther to find Jade Village, where Moonbeam lives."

"Tell me about Moonbeam," Flyingbird asked.

"She was a little mother to me when I was a child - she used to carry me around on her back, and find especially sweet berries to pop into my mouth. I'm sure she'll try to help us in our journey to the sacred mountain."

Continuing along the coast, we kept watch on the land. Soon plumes of smoke were visible, rising and merging into a white cloud

"That must be Jade Village!" said Bigbear.

After beaching our boat, Tigertail, Flyingbird and Bigbear walked toward the village, which was some distance back from the muddy coast. I flew ahead.

"Look at all the smoke plumes!" said Flyingbird. "This must be a huge village, even bigger than Rock Shrine Village. As many houses as trees in a forest! I wonder how the sea can feed so many people at once."

"I wonder if the forest helps feed them, too," suggested Tigertail. "It is a lot of people, but we collect nuts and apples and deer at Rock Shrine Village, just as you do."

As we approached the village, loud howling and barking increased furiously, and two furry creatures ran out at us.

"Careful of the wolves!" said Bigbear, ready to fend them off with his song stick.

"Wait! I've never seen wolves with curly tails held over their backs like that," answered Flyingbird. "I think they're not wolves - I don't know what, but something else."

A woman came out to silence the dogs, and to greet the visitors. Her long black hair was caught at her neck with a jade ring. As wife of the village leader, she was in charge of checking credentials. Opening her mouth to ask who they were, she suddenly recognized Tigertail.

"Ah, little brother!" Moonbeam beamed her pleasure. "Are you a spirit? You disappeared on your tiger quest, and I never expected to see you again. Who are these shaggy people you've brought with you?"

Tigertail introduced Flyingbird and Bigbear, explaining their relationship, which didn't faze Moonbeam. She quieted the dogs, explaining that they were tame.

Moonbeam invited us into her house. Rugs on the floor and hangings on the walls made the one-room dwelling feel cozy. They had nice geometric patterns, but I couldn't tell what the thick weavings were made of. Moonbeam offered millet wine for refreshment, and Flyingbird presented Moonbeam with the baskets they'd brought, to be distributed in the village.

After they talked and rested a while, Moonbeam presented Tigertail and Bigbear with small jade heads, pierced to be worn on a cord. The heads, exquisitely carved out of light green jade, were human-like, but with grotesque, distorted faces.

"Show the jade head anywhere in this region, all the way to the grasslands in the direction of sundown and to the high mountains in the direction of sunup, and you'll be given safe passage through that land," Moonbeam explained. "Everyone recognizes them. The heads represent the village guardians. Having one in your possession is a sign that you're a relative or a friend. In the old days it wouldn't have been necessary, but in recent years robbers have come, stealing grain and animals. We have so many distant relatives that we don't recognize them all, but still we want to be hospitable. This way we can tell friends from enemies."

Moonbeam gave Flyingbird a small flat yellowish jade, carved in the shape of a bird with a crest and long tail.

"Welcome, my brother's wife," she said.

"How did you know that a bird is my familiar spirit?"

"The bird is the sign of a village leader," replied Moonbeam. "My husband wears one, too. People of second rank wear jade turtles. Strangers need to know who is important."

Flyingbird added it to her necklace with the topaz, pearl, and amber. I realized it was her sixth treasure, including the obsidian knife and the bone needle. Birdwing told her she would receive six amulets, and that the last one would be the most important. It meant that she was ready to be the leader of Bird Mountain Village. But she was so far from home!

"Did this pretty yellow bird come with you?" asked Moonbeam. "I've never seen a bird like that. It must be a messenger birds from the spirits.

"She's Flyingbird's familiar spirit, who saved her life three times. She saved me, too, when I broke my leg."

"Your familiar spirit must be one of these dogs," said Tigertail, but Moonbeam only smiled. They strolled through the village, with its neatly arrayed houses. Each house was covered with thatch from the roof down to the ground, just like houses in other villages they knew. Naked children were watched by women holding sticks which they twirled rapidly.

"Is that some kind of game, with the sticks?" asked Tigertail.

"They're making yarn," answered Moonbeam. "It was strange to me, too, when I first came, but I've gotten so used to it, I forgot you wouldn't know. I learned to do it too."

Moonbeam asked one of the women to demonstrate the spindle whorl. We watched as she took some fluffy stuff out of a basket, drew it into an elongated mass, and attached it to the stick. She slipped a ceramic weight with a hole in the middle over the stick. Whirling this contraption around turned the fuzzy pile into yarn.

"What on earth do you do with so much yarn?" Bigbear wanted to know.

"We make it into cloth. It's more time-consuming than tanning hide, but more comfortable. But your clothes," she said to Flyingbird and Bigbear, "are woven, so you know about looms." Moonbeam took them into a house with looms.

"They do weave at Bird Mountain Village," Tigertail explained. "They use bark cut into strips and nettle fiber. I've never seen anything like that fluffy stuff you use to make such soft cloth."

"It comes from the dogs. In winter they grow thick double coats of fur to keep themselves warm. In the spring when they shed the soft inner coat, we collect it to spin. The rugs and wall hangings you saw in my house are made from dog hair. They make the houses cozy in winter. Our winter clothes are woven from it, too."

They explored the village further. Millet plants waved in the fields, and other plants unknown to the visitors grew in rows, too. Gourd vines stretched from the ground to the roof tops, dotting the thatch with bright yellow blobs. Here and there black piglets trotted after large sows.

"Aren't those big pigs dangerous?" asked Flyingbird.

"Not at all; they're quite tame. We eat most of the males before they grow up, so most of the adults are not boars, but sows. The piglets are quite delicious, and a large pig feeds many people at a feast."

There were also birds with orange and black feathers, scratching the soil.

"Why do the birds stay near?" asked Tigertail. "You can catch them and eat them so easily!"

"We do catch them and eat them," laughed Moonbeam. "They stay here because we feed them, and because they can't get away. We raise them from eggs, and when they're small chicks, we clip their wings. The eggs are good to eat, too. It's much more convenient than hunting, and we need them to feed all the people who live here. We can have some for supper, and you'll see how tasty they are."

The chicken stuffed with wild mushrooms was delicious, and so was the pig meat, cut into cubes and cooked with millet. After dinner, the people of Jade Village were curious about these hairy people who lived far away on the Sunrise Sea. They had only heard legends of this faraway place, so Tigertail and his crew stayed three nights, feasting and telling stories. Then it was time to ask the way to the sacred mountain.

49

"How about a morning at Kyongbok Palace," I suggested the next day, after a satisfying reunion romp at Ed's hotel. It seemed just like old times, and I was feeling happy. But my mood was shattered as we went through the lobby. People were averting their eyes and saying things that distressed me. I picked up that they assumed that Ed was a G.I., and I his prostitute. I hurried Ed out, and even though he couldn't understand what was said, my ears burned.

At Kyongbok, Ed and I strolled out to a water pavilion. He took my hand, oblivious to the frowns from passing Koreans. I saw them, though and took my hand away. The cherry blossoms were in full bloom. Reflected in the pond, they doubled their glory.

We sat in the sunshine, talking about our lives. I still didn't want to talk about his parents' attitude toward me.

"You do love archaeology, don't you?" observed Ed. I wondered if he was envious of my new independence.

"Are you jealous?" I asked.

"Maybe. But I know that's unfair. I'm putting a lot of effort into becoming a lawyer, too. I wouldn't want to give it up."

"Wives are sometimes jealous of their husbands' work, I think. The difference is that men don't have to choose between a personal life and a profession to feel accepted by society. Sometimes women do."

"I wouldn't make you choose. We could work it out."

"But you and I have to live in our culture. We can't wrap ourselves up in a cocoon as if no one else existed. There are forces outside us that insist on choices. And there are other cultural forces, too," I said, thinking of the problem of slant-eyed grandchildren for WASPs. I was intrigued, though, that my WASP parents were happy to raise two Asian daughters. Different people, different values.

"My mother sent you a letter," said Ed, pulling an envelope out of his jacket pocket, and perhaps reading my mind. "I haven't read it, but I know how she feels now. I think you should read it in private."

I took the cream-colored envelope with scrolly initials and put it in my purse to read later.

For lunch, we walked to a famous Buddhist restaurant recommended by Liesl. It's in a section of Seoul that still has old-style one-story houses with tile roofs. The restaurant is down a side street, and then through a tiny orderly garden. At the entrance to the restaurant, rows of shoes lined up on the steps showed that this was a traditional place. We arranged ours neatly at the end of a row, and stepped up in our socks to the polished wood floor.

A grey-robed monk signaled for silence, and led us to a low table for two. We sat side by side on cushions. Some kind of entertainment was in progress on a small stage, and everybody in the restaurant watched quietly.

The stage was simple - a slightly raised wooden floor, with plants along the back, and a cardboard moon hanging from the ceiling. A singer chanted traditional songs, and a percussionist beat the drum.

€ 50

"Your boat isn't right for a river journey," said Carver, Moonbeam's husband. "The current in the river is too swift to sail against, so you have to row instead of sail. You'd better take one of our boats. But they need five rowers, for two pairs of oars and the stern oar, to pull against the river current. You'll have to take Moonbeam and me, too."

Tigertail and his mates were glad for the company. Carver had been to the sacred mountain once, and remembered the way. Moonbeam, like Flyingbird, enjoyed seeing new places, and she had strong arms for rowing.

When they came an area of rapids, Carver explained, they'd have to leave the boat and climb, but they'd be glad to have it to ride back with the river flow.

We set out early in the morning, with provisions for ten days. The boat was light, made of birch bark over a frame of pine wood, and could be carried around some of the lower rapids. Without a pole to provide a perch for me, I had to fly alongside. Still, flying was easier than rowing. The river was wide, and swift currents changed sides now and then. Although this was the time of low water, when the current was at its gentlest, they had to keep the boat close to the edge of the broad river, keeping out of the powerful main stream.

The people who lived in the villages on the riverbanks knew Moonbeam and Carver, so we didn't need the jade heads for safe passage. Each night we stopped in a friendly village to chat and feast and sing; the next morning we continued on. I loved the melancholy and haunting songs in this region.

After making five camps, the river began to narrow, and we came upon fewer villages. Finally the boat could go no farther. Tigertail and Carver pulled the boat up on the bank, turned it upside down, covered it with brush, and left it.

They bounced up the trail, glad for the chance to walk and exercise different muscles. Now aching arms could rest, and their legs get a good stretching. I had to just keep flying, but the winds carried me aloft, and I could play with the air currents. Carver guided us along the stream, following a trail that steepened and narrowed. The top of the world seemed to be close, but around each turn a peak yet higher came into view.

Without any warning, a high waterfall appeared ahead of us, spilling down the mountain. It pulled us forward like a magnet. As we got closer, we saw that the waterfall splashed into hot, bubbling pools.

"This mountain looks just like Whitehead Mountain," whispered Flyingbird to Bigbear.

"It *is* Whitehead Mountain," said Bigbear, who had made the trip from Dragon River twice. He pointed with his chin.

"See, up there is the peak we first saw from the other side. And if we go behind the waterfall, we can climb up above the lake. Farther still is the cliff of black stone."

Tigertail was astonished that Flyingbird and Bigbear knew the mountain.

"Are you sure? This is our sacred mountain and your sacred mountain? How can that be?"

"Strange, isn't it? But no one lives up here, and it's far from any settlements. Maybe it's not so surprising that our people haven't seen each other," replied Flyingbird. "I think it's proof that the spirits *do* live here, if such different people have both found them here."

"Haven't your people ever found our prayer sticks?" asked Bigbear. "We always leave them at the hot pools, at the lake and at the black cliff."

The people of Jade Village couldn't understand the Bird Mountain Villagers, because they were speaking their own language.

Tigertail asked his sister in the Stone language, and she conferred with Carver.

"No, Carver hasn't ever seen or heard of the prayer sticks. Maybe this isn't the same mountain after all."

Before dipping in the warm pools, Bigbear and Tigertail cut nearby willows and made prayer sticks to leave for the spirits. They carefully made shavings from the top, until there was a curly bush around each stick.

"Is that what you mean?" asked Carver. "Are those the prayer sticks? We thought they were made by the spirits themselves. So the hairy people are the spirits!"

"Oh, no!" said Flyingbird. "You mustn't say that, or the real spirits might become jealous and harm us. But we *are* the children of the spirits. And so are you."

"Why don't we pay a call on your people, if we're so close?" suggested Carver.

Bigbear had thought of this, too, but reluctantly decided against it.

"It's not close, it's quite far. I'd guess it's half as far as we came from Jade Village, and the path is steeper. If we went there the snows might come, and then we wouldn't be able to get back to Rock Shrine Village. The children would worry."

Single file they took the path up to the lake, and marveled once again at its size and beauty. Then they trekked down to camp by the black cliff. Around the campfire, Bigbear told the story of how the Spirit Bird had saved Flyingbird and the rest of the party from falling over the cliff in the mist.

Beyond the fire, I thought I saw the yellow eyes of a tiger, so I flew over to investigate. There *was* a tiger, lying with her head on crossed paws and seeming to listen to the talk around the fire. Tail curling around her side, she didn't even twitch.

Perhaps the tiger's lonesome, I thought. She certainly doesn't seem to mean us any harm. She looked very peaceful lying there. It would be a shame to kill this elegant creature.

The fearsome beast lay without stirring. I kept quiet.

In the morning Flyingbird saw the tiger tracks.

"There was a tiger here last night. Look how close it was, just beyond the fire. I wonder why the Spirit Bird didn't warn us," she mused.

"I wonder why the tiger didn't bother us," added Bigbear, "when it was so near."

"Maybe it was the Mountain Spirit's tiger," suggested Tigertail. "It might have been protecting us."

We went to the rim of the lake once more for a last look. Golden larches and dark green pines reflected in the sparkling water. With final glances, they left reluctantly, to go to the cliff and fill their pack baskets with chunks of obsidian. Then it was time to start back toward the boat.

Riding the river current down the Great River wasn't fast, but it was easy. They took turns steering with the stern oar, while I flew above. We only had to make two camps before we were back at Jade Village.

51

When the performance was over at the Buddhist restaurant, Ed and I had to decide what to eat. The easiest thing was to order the whole vegetarian meal, and see what came.

The grey-robed waiter took our order, and returned shortly with hand-carved wooden bowls. The "plate" was a wooden tray on a pedestal. For utensils, we had wooden chopsticks and spoons, carved from the same glowing wood. It was a pleasure to hold them.

We didn't know exactly what we were eating, but it was all delicious. There was a savory soup, a tofu dish, a spinach-like vegetable flavored with sesame seeds, and too many other dishes to count.

As we were chatting, replete with the delicious meal, Ed said something that made me laugh. I giggled and leaned my head toward his shoulder. Four men sitting at a nearby table made a rude remark in Korean, and they all guffawed knowingly. I didn't understand all the words, but I caught the drift.

I'd had about enough of Korean assumptions about a Korean girl and an American man. I swiveled around and snapped at them, "*Miguk saram imnida*," - I'm an American.

"Married your meal-ticket, did you?" said one of them in Korean, less abashed by my un-female-Korean behavior than the others.

I couldn't find the words to answer him, and I burst into tears in frustration. Ed, of course, didn't know what was going on, but he had the presence of mind to pick up the check and go pay it, while I went to the restroom to recover my dignity. It was quite a while before I could stop sobbing.

We slipped into our shoes in silence.

"What did those men say? Do you want to tell me about it?"

"Not yet. Let's poke around in the antique stores. Usually only foreigners are there."

There's a big, fancy store not far away, with stone grave carvings of Yi Dynasty officials out front. It looked like a safe place to me, away from the taunting Korean men.

I calmed down as we looked at the gorgeous old chests, individual tables and lacquered hatboxes. I picked up a sewing kit, and looked at the array of needles. One was made of bone.

52

"We have the black stone now," observed Tigertail, "but we don't have six other treasures to take back. Moonbeam, where should we go to get the six other treasures? What should we look for?"

"I can give you six treasures," said Moonbeam with an impish look, "but they'll take up a lot of room in your boat, and you have to return as fast as you can."

"It won't take us long to get back," replied Tigertail, "but we can't accept six treasures from you. You've already fed us, and lent us your boat, and given us your strong arms to help row to the sacred mountain. You've given us beautiful jades of a value well beyond that of the baskets we brought. Just tell us which direction we should go. Maybe we could collect jadestone."

"The jadestone comes from far away in the mountains," said Carver, "and you can't make the journey at this time of year. The snows will come too soon."

"Look at what I have in mind before you decide," Moonbeam insisted.

She collected a rooster and a hen, two piglets male and female, and two puppies.

"If you get these treasures back to Rock Shrine Village alive, they will reproduce their kind. Don't eat these animals, for they will be the founding ancestors of their lines. But their descendants will be edible and delicious."

Tigertail was delighted with this solution to the six treasures problem. It was so simple. The tame animals were definitely treasures, and the villagers would be astounded. The three travelers would have to hurry back with their live cargo, but the current would help them until they came to Forked River, where they would turn in toward Rock Shrine Village. And the tide would take them most of the way up the river, if they caught it just right.

"There's one other thing I'd like to ask of you, if I could," Flyingbird said, as we prepared to leave. "Is there a big deer that lives near here, with giant antlers? I wanted to replace Birdwing's torn drumskin, if I can get exactly the same kind. You see, those deer don't live in our forest. The drum was brought down from the north."

"Is this the right sort of leather?" Carver brought out a tanned hide with a purplish cast.

"That looks just the same! I'll trade you one of my amulets for it. Birdwing will be so pleased."

"You'll need all your amulets for your return journey. We get these hides from our neighbors to the north, and give them woven blankets. There are plenty of hides - please take it."

I dropped a few yellow feathers, to leave as a memento for Moonbeam and Carver.

"Thanks, Sprit Bird. I'll add your feathers to a wall weaving."

Moonbeam provided food for the animals - millet grains for the chickens, and acorns for the pigs. The puppies could share the fish the humans would catch for their own food. Each pair of animals was in its own basket, securely placed in the bottom of the boat as Tigertail pushed off from shore.

The puppies got seasick on the journey, and their basket had to be rinsed out several times. The piglets were happy as long as they were fed, but the chicks fluffed themselves up in the bottom of their basket and looked miserable.

We had just missed the incoming tide on the last part of the journey, and all three humans had to row hard up Forked River. Tigertail was too eager to wait. His second quest had produced such unexpected treasures!

Long Legs had seen the boat from the top of a nearby hill. He came to greet us, along with Granite and the children, and was followed by most of the villagers.

"So the spirits did send you back! Well done! What treasures did you find?"

"Something you never heard of. Something so extraordinary you won't believe it's possible. Help us bring our things up on the bank, and you'll see."

Tigertail put the three baskets in a row, while the villagers gathered around. Granite was right there in front, eager to see the treasures first.

Tigertail took the chickens out of their basket and let them run around, throwing a few millet grains near them, which they stopped to peck.

"Orange birds? Are they a treasure? What are they good for?" Granite was disappointed.

"To eat, of course. But you mustn't eat these birds. When they grow up, the female will lay eggs. The eggs will hatch, and then there will be many more birds. You'll have birds to eat without having to hunt them. And you can eat the eggs, too, when there are enough birds."

"But won't they fly away? What good is that?"

"Their wings are clipped, as you must clip the wings of all the chicks. Moonbeam showed us how to do it, and we'll teach you."

Bigbear put the piglets on the ground. They ran around screaming, until Bigbear gave them acorns.

"These animals are good to eat, too," Tigertail explained. "But you must let them grow up and have piglets of their own. They're very succulent, much better than the strong-tasting stringy meat of wild boar. We had a fabulous feast of them at Jade Village."

Finally Flyingbird took out the puppies. Their small tails curled up in a ring over their fluffy backs. Glad to be on land again, they began to chase each other.

"Are these good to eat, too?" asked Tigertail's mother. "They look like wolves, and wolves are *not* good to eat."

"No, we didn't bring them for food, although Carver says they're tasty when they're young. But they're useful in many ways. If you treat them well, they're eager to learn whatever you teach them. They'll bark loudly to warn you when strangers are coming. They'll help you hunt if you train them. They can protect the children. And their inner fur coat can be spun into warm cloth. Bigbear and Flyingbird will teach you to spin and weave, if you like."

Bigbear distributed obsidian to each household. It was gratefully received, although it didn't have the impact of the live treasures. Flyingbird saved the reindeer hide for Birdwing's new drum.

After supper the villagers gathered in the clearing under the big tree, and Tigertail told about their travels. He had to tell every detail about Moonbeam and her family and about Jade Village, as well as all the gossip he had picked up along the way. To be sure he had it right, and remembered it all, he had sketched pictures on the sail with a piece of charcoal.

"You wouldn't believe how many pigs and dogs and chickens there were in Jade Village. There were more than one person's fingers and toes together. I couldn't count them."

Another surprise was the sacred mountain.

"And then it turned out," finished Tigertail, "that Flyingbird and Bigbear had been there before and it's also *their* sacred mountain. So we must be related, even though we look so different. We're children of the same spirits."

Long Legs looked very worried, and Granite was downright alarmed. Tigertail was truly blessed by the spirits. Would the spirits take revenge on her?

"Twice I've sent you on quests, and twice you've come back with the object I sent you for as well as something unexpected. I think you are blessed and beloved by the Rock Spirit. You must stay here, we need you as the village leader."

Tigertail protested. "I can't stay here. I married into the Golden clan of Bird Mountain Village, and my home is there now. I thank you for the offer, though. And I thank you for the quests. I quite enjoyed them," Tigertail added with a grin. "They've brought me much pleasure and unexpected adventures. But could I leave Straight Hair in my place, not as leader, but perhaps as a possible leader some day. Would you treat him as your son, since you have only daughters?"

"Of course."

53

"I wish you wouldn't tune me out like that," Ed was saying. "It's creepy. Is Korea getting on your nerves, or is it me?"

I wasn't sure how to answer. It's the combination, I thought.

"People see us together, and they make assumptions I don't like," I answered carefully.

"How do you know? Can you read their minds?"

I felt a quarrel hovering.

"No, but I can understand most of what they *say*. It bothers me. A lot. I never thought I'd be embarrassed to take you around Korea. Come back with me to I-House and we can sit in the lobby and talk. No one will harass us there."

The students at I-House weren't allowed to have visitors of the opposite sex in our rooms, so Ed and I sat in the lobby next to a giant fish tank.

"Tell me about your excavation," said Ed, looking for neutral conversation. "Who else is on the dig?"

I told him about the students helping in my area, and Ki-dok and the other students in his locality. The two groups had a kind of friendly rivalry, and whichever team uncovered the most interesting find that day got to drink beer bought by the other team.

"Tell me about Ki-dok," he said.

So I related the tale of our first meeting, when Ki-dok was so bashful.

"He's better, now. Enough so that he conned me into telling his parents that he didn't want an arranged marriage. That was pretty terrible."

"Who did he want to marry? You?"

"Elaine thinks so, but he certainly never mentioned it to me if that was what he thought. The first time he asked me to speak to his parents, when we were in Kyongju, he just talked about Dong-su."

"Dong-su? And who is Dong-su?"

"My tutor. He's been teaching me to speak and write Korean all year."

I tried to speak evenly, but I was tired, and shaken by this long day with Ed, and I didn't want to discuss Dong-su now.

Ed's jealousy burst into the open.

"Which one have you been sleeping with? Or both of them? Or both at once?"

Oh, lord, I thought. He knows there was someone else. But how? It must have been the "Buddhist poses" I learned from Dong-su. I shared them with Ed without thinking, and he *knows* there's been someone else.

"All the men in Korea," I said, starting to cry. "I've slept with every one. Everyone in Korea thinks I'm a whore, and now you do too!"

The students in the lobby stared, embarrassed or just interested, according to their own cultural habits.

Liesl appeared in the doorway, and I was grateful to see her.

"Join me for dinner?" she invited us.

"Let me run upstairs a minute and freshen up."

Ed went back to his hotel early. I was upset and so was he. He'd been boiling all day about our love-making - and probably thought it was guilt that was bothering me.

I didn't feel guilty. I wondered if I should. I wondered if some of Elaine's attitudes had rubbed off on me. I could taste the garlic from the *kimchi*, which I deliberately ate too much of. It gave me indigestion.

54

The travelers arrived at Rock Shrine Village just before an early wet snow covered the houses and the fields, and the mountain paths were slippery and treacherous. The return to Bird Mountain Village was postponed until spring, so we settled in.

With many helpers, the family of the Golden clan built a house. Flyingbird insisted on a spirit window, although it wasn't the local custom, but they decided to manage with just one hearth. The baby animals could live inside with the family in the winter, and stay reasonably warm.

When the weather was cold, people tended to stay by their warm fires making tools, containers, or clothing. The weather was cyclic, with warmer, sunny days between bouts of bad weather, so the villagers were rarely cooped up inside for many days.

One sunshiny crisp day Granite invited Flyingbird to help her make pottery. The local clay was excellent, all full of glittering mica bits.

"Show me how to make a conical base like that," asked Flyingbird. "In our village we always start with a flat slab of clay pressed onto a large leaf."

"Just flatten out your coil a little, and twist it around, smoothing the edges together. Like this," Granite demonstrated. Flyingbird tried it several times until she got it right.

When the conical pots were tall enough, Granite and Flyingbird decorated them with rows of fingernail impressions around the top. Granite was left-handed, so her rows curved in the opposite direction from Flyingbird's. All over the conical body they drew herring-bone designs with sharpened sticks.

"This designs stands for stalks of grain," Granite explained. "We keep grain in these vessels."

Granite made one especially large pot with decorations more elaborate than usual. First she drew seven rows of short oblique lines around the rim of the vessel. Then she switched to a bird bone tool, making round impressions in sequences of dotted lines, that swagged around the band.

Finally, the body of the pot was decorated with nested zigzags in the usual way.

"This is a ceremonial pot," Granite explained, "to hold millet wine for celebrating the day the sun turns back. The sun rises farther south every day this time of year, but one day it comes back. We have a feast dedicated to the Sacred Stones, especially the stone that marks the spot of the sun-turning."

A pavement made of river stones with flat sides was spread on the outskirts of the village. On this pavement Granite built a fire to harden the pots. The rocks held the heat well for a continuous firing. There wasn't any ritual, but Flyingbird said a prayer to the Hearth Spirit, according to her own custom.

The feast of the sun-turning required days of preparation. The houses had to be all cleaned out, and the fires extinguished, to be relit later the same day. Special feast foods were prepared, and new clothing laid out.

Early in the morning of the feast day, everyone gathered at the big tree, and looked across the fields to see the sun come up exactly behind the Sacred Sun Stone, as Grandmother predicted. In celebration, and in gratitude, everyone ate, and danced, and sang, all day and all night.

Gradually the days grew longer. Flyingbird passed the time teaching Granite and the other women how to spin the puppies' hair into yarn. She made simple spindle whorls out of broken pieces of pottery, and slipped them over straight sturdy sticks. The puppies didn't have a lot of undercoat to shed, but there was enough to teach the women the principle of spinning, so they could see what the yarn should look like. Bigbear constructed a simple loom, tying small stones to the warp strings to keep them in place. Tigertail collected elm bark to demonstrate the plain weaving of Bird Mountain Village. Flyingbird made appliques with a small piece of cloth, teaching the stitches that would attach them firmly to the robe.

The animals survived the winter, and were active and healthy. Tigertail gave lessons in clipping the birds' wings, as the chickens produced several further generations. Flyingbird's family learned new games to play, and a different way of tanning leather, and the days passed.

Finally, the yellow and pink flowers began to bloom. It was time to think of leaving. Straight Hair came to his father with sad eyes.

"I don't want to leave," he began, looking at the ground. "I can't live all my life in Bird Mountain Village, anyway. I want to stay here and live with Grandmother. When I'm old enough I'll build a house with Cousin Jade. I can come and visit over the mountain sometimes, and bring Jade. What do you think?"

"I think we should have a meeting after sun-up in the morning. In the meantime I'll consult your Grandmother."

Straight Hair smiled, because Grandmother had suggested it in the first place.

After they greeted the sun, the family from Bird Mountain Village sat cross-legged on their mats, and considered Straight Hair's petition.

"I'll miss you very much," said Flyingbird, ruffling her older son's hair affectionately. "But I always knew you'd have to leave us. That's the way it is with sons. Grandmother wants you to stay. You've learned the language pretty well. If you'll be happy with Jade, then you should stay. But promise you'll come visit soon."

Sunshine signaled her wish to speak.

"Could I bring someone back with me to Bird Mountain Village? Can Big Ears come back with us? I explained to him that I have to go back, especially since I'm the oldest girl in the village. He says he doesn't care, that if Tigertail can live with a woman leader, so can he. Please? I've seen fifteen summers now - I'm as old as you were when you built a house with Father and Tigertail." The adults sighed. They grow up so fast. "You can teach me the secrets and give me my first tattoo at the next full moon. It will be all the more reason to keep visiting back and forth over the mountain."

They agreed to both the children's requests, and prepared to leave. Before the return journey, Grandmother insisted on a ceremony for a safe trip. At dusk on the day before their departure, Grandmother led the whole family from Bird Mountain Village, and Big Ears as well, to the sun-turning stone. They stood around the stone in a circle.

Grandmother reached into her deerskin bag, and brought out a belt with overlapping shells hanging loosely from it. She hung the belt loosely around her waist, then put on a cap with antlers attached. She sprinkled millet wine in each direction, and finally on the stone itself. Taking up her skin drum, Grandmother beat a rhythm on it with her hand while she danced around the fire. The shells rattled loudly. It was easy to believe she had called up the spirits.

"Safe journey back, safe journey back," she chanted, beating the drum with her hand.

Flyingbird and her family stopped for the last night of the trip in the cave near the waterfall. They could see the sea far below, but it was dark and too far to go. Tigertail made a square hearth for the Hearth Spirit, and Big Ears went with Sunshine to collect wood. Flyingbird and I sat outside the cave, thinking about Bird Mountain Village.

The full yellow moon rose into the night sky. As Flyingbird watched it, a shadow began to stretch across, partly dimming the light of Grandmother Moon.

"Is this a message?" Flyingbird asked me. "Birdwing said she'd send a message by Grandmother Moon if she needed me."

"Tweet," I said, meaning I had no idea.

"I'm going down the mountain right now," she called to Bigbear. "Birdwing needs me."

"We'll be there tomorrow," said Bigbear, preparing deer chunks to roast on their fire. "It can't be that urgent. Besides, it's dangerous to descend the mountain at night. You might miss a spring trap, or drop down a waterfall."

"I think I should go now," Flyingbird worried. "Birdwing sent a message." She thought a moment. "You don't need to come with me. But can you bring my things when you come? I can travel faster without my pack."

"I'll come with you, and carry both packs."

"You can't leave Tigertail with four children. Spirit Bird will go with me. We'll be all right.

I couldn't see very well at night, so I agreed with Bigbear that we should wait for morning. I tried to tell Flyingbird, but she paid no attention to my tweeting. She started down the mountain, carrying only a small parcel. I had to fly along.

Around the first bend we found an old friend - Sister Bear!

"How's your night vision, my old playmate?" Flyingbird asked her.

Sister Bear answered by inviting Flyingbird to climb on her back. I perched on the bear's head to watch for the yellow strips of elm bark that warn of spring traps, and we three negotiated the steep trail down the mountain.

We expected to find everyone asleep, but the villagers sat in a quiet circle around a fire in the dance ground. Birdwing lay with her head on Sunflower's lap, breathing raspily.

Flyingbird slipped softly down from Sister Bear's back and ran to Birdwing.

"I saw the message on the moon, and I came to help however I can," she said to Sunflower.

Birdwing opened her eyes, and smiled to see Flyingbird. She held out her wrinkled hand and drew Flyingbird near. "I'm glad you're back safely. Now that you have your six amulets, you're ready to be the leader of Bird Mountain Village. Tomorrow you will begin."

"I brought you something." Flyingbird opened her parcel. "A new reindeer skin for your drum. I hope it's the same kind of skin as the old one."

Birdwing rubbed the soft skin on her bony fingers.

"It's exactly right. Just like the original that Sunbird brought with her from the far north. Sunflower will help you make the new drum. But it won't be my drum. It's yours."

Flyingbird beat the drum for the sun-up ceremony. By the time Bigbear and Tigertail and the children got down the mountain, Birdwing had gone to the Spirit World.

55

Ed wanted to see the DMZ - the demilitarized zone, created after the stalemate that ended the Korean War. I wasn't thrilled about it - (I like old things better), but to please Ed I agreed to go. It turned out that Michiko, Liesl's roommate, was interested in the trip, too, so we included her. We planned a day-long tour to Panmunjon, the truce village, as well as one of the tunnels cut through the mountains into the South by North Koreans, and a small Buddhist temple. At the last minute Liesl decided to come too.

Michiko did speak a little English, learned in school, but she did better in Korean. We conversed in a mixture of the two that Liesl called "Korenglish."

It wasn't far to Panmunjon, but we had to go through several military checkpoints. I began to feel like I was in "*M.A.S.H.*" This was a different world from the civilian Korea I knew.

To get to the truce village, we got off the bus and were driven in an armored jeep through a gate in the barbed wire fence and out into "no-man's land," the DMZ itself. A sergeant showed us the various ways that the fence was made difficult to cross - extra rolls of barbed wire on top, and spikes pounded well into the ground to prevent tunneling. Panmunjon village is manned (an accurate word here) by troops from four U.N. countries, as well as North and South Koreans and U.S. military, but it's more like an institution than a proper village.

We were allowed to walk around the table that sits half in the north and half in the south. That was as much of an incursion into North Korea as was permitted. We were amused that the guards assumed that Ed and Liesl were together and that Michiko and I were their guides. They were pretty surprised when neither of us could banter fluently with them in Korean. We were a kind of mini-United Nations, just the four of us.

I was glad to get back on the safe side of the fence. But the tunnel at our next stop made me feel less safe. We had to wear heavy, clumsy army helmets, perhaps to emphasize the danger. The tunnel had been blasted by the North Koreans almost all the way through the DMZ before it was discovered, we were told. It's wide enough for four armed soldiers to run abreast. When the North Koreans realized that the tunnel had been discovered, they blocked it up, leaving booby traps behind. Several men were killed clearing it out.

I hated the vibes I got from these places. Why, in such a beautiful country, were relatives forever at odds? It wasn't even Korean ideas that divided them, but competing ideologies imported from the West and imposed by Western powers.

"I think my uncle was killed near here," said Ed. "Right near the end of the war. He's buried somewhere not far from the DMZ."

"An uncle of mine died here too," Michiko unexpectedly chimed in. "My family fled south, all the way to Pusan, and then across to Japan. My uncle came back to fight. Maybe our uncles buried near each other."

"Did you grow up in Japan?" Ed asked, surprised.

"I was born there, and this is my first trip to Korea. Japanese look down on Koreans, and my boyfriend's parents not like him be friendly with me. My parents not like it either, so they sent me here."

"Are you glad you came?" I asked.

"I thought I would be happier here, away from the discrimination. But you know, it's just as hard. I don't know exactly how to be Korean. I try, but I make mistakes. How about you," Michiko asked me. "Are you more Korean or more American?"

"I could never be a real Korean. There are so many things I don't understand. But I love earning about Korean culture."

The third stop, a peaceful Buddhist temple, restored our spirits. It hadn't been well cared for - there were no resident monks because it's so close to the truce line - but its mossy overgrown serenity was a welcome antidote to all the remembrances of hostilities.

When we got back to I-House, some of the Overseas Koreans were practicing the Farmer's Dance. It's very lively, with high skipping kicks, and I stopped to watch.

"Come learn it too," Michiko invited me.

I joined in the circle. It was a lot like the *mudang*'s dance.

56

When she discovered that we had cultural confusion in common, Michiko warmed up to me, and regularly joined our group. She began to sit with Elaine, Liesl and me for meals, and made a determined effort to speak English and to follow the conversation. One day when she had no classes, I invited Michiko to come with us to the Buddhist temple in Seoul. We chose the temple for our destination because Ed was curious about Buddhism, and Liesl volunteered to explain its many variations to him. Michiko confessed she knew little about Buddhism, but wanted to learn.

I told Michiko about the artist monk, and showed her my watercolor with the peasant house and the lattice door. She asked what made it so meaningful to me. I told her about my repeated nightmare with unseen people having a screaming argument somewhere beyond the lattice screen. She listened thoughtfully.

"Koreans do yell at each other sometimes, but what can your dream mean?"

Ed met us in the subway station, and we all walked together to the temple. The alley is easy to miss, but once you find it, the temple pops right up at you, incongruous in the midst of skyscrapers. We admired the ancient lacebark pine with its mottled trunk, and then began circling the building while Liesl told us the stories depicted in the colorful paintings on the outside walls.

"How could anyone be so shielded from life that he wouldn't have heard of poverty, old age, illness, and death?" wondered Ed, looking at the painting of young Gautama discovering these things.

"The Buddha came from a regal family - he was a prince. His mother was distressed by a prophecy at his birth that he would serve mankind, so she never let him go outside the palace grounds."

"I wasn't royalty, but I sure had a protected childhood," I said. "So I believe the story. I wasn't allowed to see evil places like bowling alleys and skating rinks where the hoipolloi gather!"

Ed and Elaine laughed, but Michiko and Liesl asked what was wrong with them?

"My father thought that because people *drank beer* in those places, they were a terrible influence I had to be shielded from."

We looked at the painted Buddha under the bodhi tree.

"Why did it take him so long to find enlightenment? How many years could you sit under a bodhi tree?" Michiko asked as we admired the depiction of the Buddha meditating.

"Oh, you're so literal-minded," Liesl sighed. "I look at Buddhist painting as art, not religion," Liesl sighed. "It doesn't have to make sense to me. I just appreciate it."

The main door to the temple was open, inviting us to take off our shoes to step inside. Bright and festive paper lanterns of many colors and shapes jostled for space on the rafters. Korean women dressed in *chima-chogori* brought in more lanterns in a steady stream, presented them to be hung, then bowed toward the altar and clapped their hands. My friend the crane-painter stood on a ladder, helping to hang the lanterns. While we watched the swirling people and admired the varicolored lanterns, the artist monk spotted me and came over to say hello. I was glad to see him and flattered that he remembered me.

He herded us outside, and I introduced the group to him.

"But I don't know your name," I said in embarrassment.

"My name is not important, but you can call me Bul-ja."

Michiko spoke to him in Japanese, and he replied in the same language. They chatted for a bit, and then he apologized to the rest of us for leaving us out.

"You are much too young to have been forced to use Japanese in school during the occupation," Liesl said to Bul-ja. "Did you study in Japan?"

"I spent three years there, studying art history. But I didn't agree with Japanese interpretations of Korean art, so I came home, and made this my vocation." He waved his hand around, indicating the temple grounds.

"Michiko tells me you showed her the painting I gave to you, and that the lattice door is one you have seen in a dream," Bul-ja said to me. "That's strange. Was it the lattice that drew you to that painting?"

"Yes, it was. There must be many lattices like it," I guessed, "but I've looked everywhere I've been in Korea and have never seen that pattern except in your painting. But that one is exactly right. I feel I could step inside that cottage and be home."

"You have American parents. I thought you must be their guide, when I saw you at the gallery. Are you adopted, then?"

"Yes. I knew very little about Korea before I came here to study."

"Do you know your year sign?"

"I was born in a Year of the Sheep."

"May I ask what is the month and day of your birth?"

"November 29."

"It *is* a strange coincidence. Or perhaps not. Do you want to find your Korean family?"

"I didn't come to Korea looking for a lost family, but if I should find them I would be - what? Interested, but shy and afraid, perhaps." But I couldn't resist asking, "What do you know?"

"Let me tell you a story. You might be in it and you might not - probably we will never know, but you can decide if you want it to be a story about you. Let's go sit in the shade, though, shall we?"

We found an empty bench near the lacebark pine. My friends listened as attentively as I, as if fearing to break the spell. Bul-ja began his story.

"In a Year of the Sheep, a middle-class family with two boys of six and seven and a baby girl, lived in the southern port city of Pusan. The ancestral village, where they went for family festivals and to clean the ancestors' graves, was in the countryside not far away. A grandmother and grandfather lived in one thatched cottage in the village, an uncle and aunt lived in another at right angles to the first, making an ell.

One day, a tragedy occurred. A ferryboat overturned in the sea, and all on board drowned, including the parents of the three children. The two boys didn't know what to do when the parents didn't come back. They tried to take care of their baby sister, but the neighbors sent a message to the uncle in the ancestral village. The aunt came to Pusan, and took all three children back to the village in an ox-cart. We all stayed in the uncle's cottage - the one in your painting, I recreated from memory, because it is no longer there. Replaced by a western-type house with a plastic roof! But that's not part of the story.

"After a short time, Uncle said they couldn't afford to keep the baby girl. Boys were useful, but girls were a burden, needing a dowry when they married, and worse yet they would leave home to raise sons for another family. So Uncle decided to give the infant to the orphanage. Aunt cried and begged and quarreled, but none of it did any good. Uncle took the baby away, and we never saw her again. She was born in a Year of the Sheep, on November 29."

This story fit with my nightmare, or perhaps my memory, but I couldn't believe it related to me. How many girls would have been born in Korea on the same day? Hundreds? Thousands? Sheer coincidence! But I found myself thinking, if my birth mother is dead, I will never have to confront her. But I will also never get to know her. It also meant I didn't have an American soldier for a father, and the implications of that which the elder Mr. Oh had spelled out so painfully.

"Who were the boys?" I asked. "Are they still alive?"

"The elder brother is me. Second Brother died of cholera in a dreadful epidemic a few years later. My aunt and uncle raised me in the village, along with their children. They helped me go to college. They were very kind - you have to understand their point of view, their situation. I don't want you to think badly of them. They just couldn't afford to raise a girl."

"What was your sister's name?"

"That's odd too. Her name was Ka-ra."

"Similarities in the names are definitely coincidental, because I was named for my mother's mother, Gramma Clara. But I'd be happy to claim you for an elder brother. I don't have a brother at home."

"Then let us believe we are brother and sister. Come see me again before you go back to America, Little Sister."

That same evening the lantern festival for the Buddha's birthday took place. We bought lanterns, lit the candles inside, and joined in the parade. It was especially joyful for me with my perhaps-brother, Bul-ja, who knew how to dance like a crane. The lights glittered in the bouncing lanterns.

C.57

The first thing I noticed as I swooped into Bird Mountain Village was the new alignment of houses. I was disoriented at first until I sorted out the changes. I perched on the bird pole to get a better perspective on the changed shape of the village. Birdwing's house was gone, and had been replaced by another a bit farther from the dance ground. Tall Sister's house was missing, too, but two new houses had sprung up in the second row beside those of Cockleshell and Seaweed.

A handsome woman with long bushy hair ducked out of one doorway. A girl with black wavy hair followed her, and the two of them spread their mats and sat in the dance ground. Another young woman came to join them, carrying an infant on her hip. I wasn't sure who any of them were. How long had it been since I visited? I'd been absorbed with Ed.

When the child went down to the shore to play, the women took out their embroidery, and chattered softly.

"I don't know what to do, Sunshine," said the woman with the baby. "Birchleaf is determined that neither your daughter Yellowbird nor my daughter Whitepine will be trained to be the next leader. I heard her tell Pebble that *her* granddaughter, Pebble's son's daughter, should be the leader."

"The village would never approve, Shining Eyes. That's an outrage! The leadership is passed down only through women. Why does Birchleaf disapprove of our daughters?"

"She says our daughters are foreigners. They `look funny' she says, so neither could be a proper leader. I've passed on to Whitepine the narrow eyes of my father Tigertail, and Yellowbird has Big Ears' black hair."

"Calling our children foreigners is the silliest thing I ever heard! Our children were born here. Since when did the color of hair and the shape of eyes matter? Mother told me that the whole village voted to accept Tigertail, as they later did for Big Ears. It's ridiculous!"

"You know how Birchleaf can stir things up. She keeps on talking until people believe her. Pebble already agrees with her. She'd like to bring her granddaughter back from Shell Island Village. But of course that child is Red clan, not Golden clan, and special permission from our village is needed for her to settle here, as well as from the Red clan. I wonder what Birchleaf and Pebble will do."

"What can they do? Mother Flyingbird is the leader here. She's well-liked and powerful. Birchleaf and Pebble don't have a chance."

215

"I wish I could agree. Birchleaf will make trouble for our children, you can be sure. She might use magic against them. She's been grouchy and difficult since Black Uncle died."

"Let's tell Mother when she returns from Dragon River Village. She'll know what to do."

Magpie brought her embroidery and laid out her mat to join them, and the sisters talked about other things. You could never tell what side Magpie would take. She'd rather have peace than wrangle, so she goes with the majority, whatever they want.

I looked everywhere for Flyingbird, but she wasn't in the village. I'd never been to the village when she wasn't there. I must be needed for something right here, I thought, instead of wherever Flyingbird is.

I caught movement in a clearing in the midst of a circle of trees, so I flew off to investigate. Birchleaf and Pebble carried baskets which they were filling with walnuts.

"It's Yellowbird we have to take care of most urgently," said Birchleaf. "She'll soon be old enough for Flyingbird to start teaching her the songs. Whitepine can be dealt with later, but once Yellowbird's lessons begin, it will be too late, for she'll be protected by the Hearth Spirit. It's urgent to do something now, before Flyingbird gets back from Dragon River Village."

"'Take care' of Yellowbird? You don't mean to harm her? Birchleaf, that's going too far! We'd be found out, and banished from the village! Our houses would be burned and our names forgotten. We'd be wandering spirits. I'll have no part of that!"

"We won't do it ourselves. We'll ask the spirits to do it," Birchleaf whispered. "It's safer that way. No one will ever know."

"How? Will the spirits do evil? They are responsible to Flyingbird!"

"It is not evil to do away with a child who would become an imposter leader. The spirits won't want to be invoked by a funny-looking stranger. They'll be on our side."

"You're on your own," said Pebble with a shudder. "I won't help you this time. It's far too dangerous." Pebble picked up her nut basket, only half full, and left the clearing.

Birchleaf sat on a rock and looked at the ground, idly pushing leaves around with her left foot. I wished I could read her mind. After a while she got up and went to the beach where Yellowbird was absorbed in arranging shells in patterns. Yellowbird looked up when Birchleaf's shadow fell across the shells.

"Do you want a pretty shell?" Yellowbird asked. "Do you like this pink one?"

"Thanks," said Birchleaf, accepting it with a close-lipped smile. "Would you let me have a lock of your pretty black hair, too? I need some black thread for sewing."

Yellowbird let Birchleaf cut off a bit of hair with her obsidian knife. I followed her to her hut. Before long she came out again carrying a workbasket, and I thought she would join the women embroidering in the dance ground. Instead she returned to the clearing, and laid out her work. As I watched, she constructed a doll out of cloth. First she wrapped Yellowbird's hair in a leaf, and wrapped cloth around it as the body of the doll. She inserted sticks for arms and legs, and the pink seashell became the doll's face.

When the crude doll was finished, Birchleaf put it in the basket, and circling far around to avoid the dance ground, went down to the shore.

"Sea Spirit, Sea Spirit," she called six times. A huge wave rolled in and crashed at her feet, and Birchleaf threw the doll into the wave.

"This is Golden Yellowbird. Take her to your kingdom under the sea."

The doll swirled onto the sand once, then was pulled back and disappeared. Birchleaf looked satisfied, and walked away. I flew over the foamy waves, looking intently, but couldn't find the doll. It simply wasn't floating on the sea. I wondered how it could sink so fast. What to do? It might take weeks to find Flyingbird and tell her, because she had gone far away to Dragon River Village. But Birchleaf's power might work any time - Yellowbird played along the shore every day, where the Sea Spirit could snatch her. She wasn't safe. Perhaps I could tell Sunshine to watch out for her. But how?

I flew down right beside Yellowbird, making sure she saw me. Then I swooped at her head and pulled out several hairs with my beak. She screamed and ran to her mother, crying.

"What on earth is the matter, Yellowbird?" said Sunshine, hugging her.

"A yellow bird with a long tail pulled my hair," she sobbed. "It has eyes like Daddy's. The bird stood on my shells, and then pulled my hair."

"That's strange," Shining Eyes frowned. "That sounds like Mother's Spirit Bird, but she's never done anything mean before. Besides, Mother's far away, collecting obsidian from Whitehead Mountain. Why would the bird be here?"

"That's the bird!" shrieked Yellowbird, covering her head with her arms and throwing herself into Sunshine's lap.

I stalked over to Sunshine with stiff legs, and dropped the beakful of hair. Then I flew to a birch tree and plucked a leaf, which I brought back and lay beside the hair.

"It's a message, but I don't understand it," said Sunshine. "Shining Eyes, what is there that connects hair and a birch leaf?"

"Birchleaf took a piece of my hair, too. She said she needed some black thread," Yellowbird answered.

Sunshine and Shining Eyes saw the significance at the same time, and they touched their amulets.

"Birchleaf has made a fetish of Yellowbird, and means to harm her," whispered Sunshine.

"Keep Yellowbird in sight at all times until our mother returns," answered Shining Eyes.

They had been warned, which was all I could do in the village. I had to get Flyingbird to come home as soon as possible. I flew north along the shore. It would take days to fly to Dragon River Village, and nearly a week for them to row back, but even a day saved might make the difference. Time might be short for Yellowbird.

A few boats bobbed on the sea, and I investigated each one, but they were only people fishing. As I neared Three Rocks Village, I saw many people on the shore, doing the dance that asks for safe journey for departing visitors. It would be great good luck if it was Flyingbird's party, already heading home. I landed on the seal pole to look the situation over.

Oyster was helping Flyingbird, Bigbear, and Tigertail load their boat, and added carved wooden netting needles as a parting gift. They were about to leave anyway, but farewells could take hours. I wondered if I could get them to hurry. I tried to think of a way to give Flyingbird a clue. To start with, I plucked a birch leaf and dropped it by Flyingbird.

"Why, hello, Spirit Bird. You usually turn up for ceremonies and travel, but we missed you on this trip. What are you trying to tell me about Birchleaf?"

Good, she understood that much. I wanted to tell her about Yellowbird, but the only yellow bird around was me. I fell over and stuck my legs in the air.

"Sleeping? Dead? Is Birchleaf dead?"

I tried to indicate myself by running around in circles.

"Birchleaf is dancing?"

I pointed a claw at my chest.

"Birchleaf has pneumonia?"

I perched on the boat. She understood that.

"Yes, it's urgent, whatever it is. We're ready to go. We're coming now."

At the sun-up ceremony the next morning, Flyingbird beat the reindeer-leather drum, and the villagers greeted the sun with their dance

218

as usual. But Yellowbird was not her usual cheerful self. She danced listlessly, and afterwards clung to Sunshine. Instead of playing on the beach she lay down in the shade with dull eyes.

Flyingbird felt Yellowbird's burning cheeks and then looked for a garlic bulb to chew. Using the wisdom passed down by Birdwing, Flyingbird made a tea of herbs, flavored with flowers, but Yellowbird couldn't keep it down.

The next day Yellowbird was worse, lying limply on her bed. Flyingbird consulted her amulets. This illness seemed unnatural, so she decided to call upon the spirits and as the cause of Yellowbird's illness. The moon would be full that very night, an appropriate time to contact the spirits. A fire was built for the Hearth Spirit. Everyone put on ceremonial robes, and brought out their mats.

Yellowbird lay near the fire, motionless. She didn't stir even when the fire was lit. The rest of the villagers made a circle around her, and sat with crossed legs, their hands in their laps. Just as the round moon climbed out of the sea, Flyingbird began to chant and sway.

"Hearth Spirit, Grandmother Moon
Come to us now.
Hearth Spirit, Grandmother Moon
Come to us now."

The circle of villagers began to sway with her, but Yellowbird still didn't move. Then Sunshine and Shining Eyes added their voices to the chant.

"Hearth Spirit, Grandmother Moon,
Come to us now."

Soon everyone was chanting, even Pebble and Birchleaf. Flyingbird rose, raised her arms, and shuffled around the fire and Yellowbird. Around and around she went, faster and faster. Then she began to mumble.

"Yellowbird's soul has been stolen and thrown into the waves. Sea Spirit, Sea Spirit, return the child's spirit. She is too young, she is needed here."

From my perch on the bird pole I could see the incoming tide. Something floating in the water glinted in the moonlight, catching my attention. I spread my wings and glided to it. A pink sea-shell reflected the moonlight, attached to a water-logged cloth bundle. Scooping up the object with a talon, I returned to the circle. I wasn't sure what to do with my find, but before I could decide, it slipped out of my claws, and landed on Yellowbird.

Yellowbird opened her eyes and sat up. She reached for the soggy doll and threw it onto the sand with a shudder.

219

Flyingbird came out of her trance, and Yellowbird ran to her and hugged her. "I'm better now, Grandmother Flyingbird." Then Yellowbird went around the circle hugging all her relatives, except Birchleaf, who looked away.

"Who knows anything about this fetish doll?" asked Flyingbird, staring around the circle. She opened the bundle and found the black hair inside.

"Your Spirit Bird pulled out some of Yellowbird's hair and dropped it by Sunshine," said Pebble, trying to protect Birchleaf. "I saw her."

"Is this true?" Flyingbird asked Sunshine.

"Yes, but she also dropped a birch leaf. Then Yellowbird told us that Birchleaf cut off a piece of her hair, and took a pink shell she was playing with. Shining Eyes and I were afraid something might happen. We watched Yellowbird constantly, but we were too late."

"Why would you do this, Birchleaf? You have always had a jealous heart, but to harm a child - -"

"Yellowbird should not be taught the songs of our ancestors. She should not become the leader," Birchleaf screamed. "She is not one of us! Can't you see how different she looks! She would bring evil upon us! I did it to save the whole village." Birchleaf crossed her arms defiantly.

"Tomorrow morning we will have a council to decide what to do about Birchleaf. Now we must thank the Hearth Spirit and Grandmother Moon for persuading the Sea Spirit to give back Yellowbird's spirit, and go to bed."

In the morning, Birchleaf was gone. Her tracks led down to the sea. The villagers burned her house and belongings, according to custom.

58

"There's a tour to Songnisan on Saturday," Elaine pointed out, helping me keep Ed entertained. "Liesl and I are going, and there's still room on the bus for you and Ed. It's a chance for him to see some of the beautiful countryside, and learn more about Buddhism. The tour visits Popjusa temple, and then goes to a village blessing *kut*. We'll have a private tour of the folk art museum, too."

Ed agreed to go, so I made us reservations. I was eager to see the *kut* - it was the one where the *mudang* dances on sharp knives without cutting her feet - and I was glad to have a whole day with other people around, to put off dealing with Ed's suspicions. I didn't want to tell him anything about Dong-su. I thought that episode was irrelevant and meaningless, and it would only make Ed unhappy to know.

On the bus, someone gave a lecture on *mudangs*. The speaker began by saying that this was a religion called *mu gyo*, which had been around for 20,000 years.

"How does he know that?" whispered Ed.

"Maybe there's an Upper Paleolithic site with a fossilized *kut*," I responded facetiously.

The "expert" went on to say that *mu gyo* changed from a male-dominated religion to a female dominated one, as it is at present. In the old days, he said, one leader had both political and religious functions. But when Buddhism made shamanism irrelevant, women became shamans.

"He is certainly stuck in his own attitudes about gender roles," I said under my breath. "There's no reason to believe the *mudangs* were ever mostly male. To look for ancient male shamans is nothing but Confucian prejudice, in my opinion."

"Cool it, Clara. I just like to know what the evidence is. You know how lawyers are. What do they base their claim on?"

"A couple of historic documents. But they mention both men and women shamans, both portrayed as powerful people. If you assume that women were unequal, it doesn't make any sense. So to say it was only, or even mostly, men who were shamans is simply to air a prejudice about women in the past."

This is a subject that irks me, and I probably sounded pretty fierce. Ed looked out the window, not prepared to take the other side.

The S-turns snaked up a steep mountainside. Looking back, we could see ridge after ridge, the near ones green, the distant ones increasingly pale blues. Spring colored the woods with various shades of wild azaleas lighting up in patches of purple, pink, and salmon.

Turned loose at last at Popjusa temple, our busload of sightseers straggled up a broad path. The uncut forest was lush, with low herbs growing under the gnarly pines. Liesl provided the rest of us with vignettes about this temple, and about temple architecture.

"Popjusa was founded during the Silla kingdom," Liesl told us. "It's been renovated several times, but the original style has been kept. In Buddhist temples, even if there aren't any surrounding walls there's usually at least one gate, with four fierce guardians to keep evil spirits out," she explained, as we came to the entrance.

We paused to admire the guardians, bigger than life, with their grimacing faces. Their clothes, and even their bodies were painted in bright colors. A small gatehouse protected the wooden statues from the elements.

"Why these fierce gatekeepers, Liesl?"

"The guardians represent the Four Heavenly Kings," she explained. "That's the King of the East with the lute. You can tell the King of the West because he holds a crystal ball and a dragon. The King of the South has the sword, and the one carrying the pagoda and the yellow bird is the King of the North."

I looked curiously at the yellow bird, so accurately carved it seemed almost alive. I felt a kinship with it, and I wondered what meaning a yellow bird might express in Buddhism. Liesl said it was a messenger between the other world and this one.

The temple buildings were strung out along a central axis, or formed symmetrical pairs on either side. Our group of sightseers peered into these and other structures, while Liesl gave dates and descriptions to anyone who asked. I was drawn to ordinary things, like the huge metal pots the monks used for cooking their meals, and the squid hanging on a line to dry outside the kitchen. Apparently this group of monks was not vegetarian.

"That's a graceful pagoda," observed Ed, pointing to a five-tiered wooden building.

"It was first built in 553 AD," Liesl was happy to be prompted, "and renovated in the 17th century - and then again not too long ago. Another small pagoda is said to contain the jewels left when a famous monk was cremated. Do you know that Buddhists believe that the bodies of holy people leave jewels behind when they're burned?"

"That's a little gem of wisdom," said Elaine.

Liesl made a face at her.

We four went to inspect a standing cement Buddha, one of the tallest in Asia.

"Why does the Buddha wear a flat hat?" asked Ed. "It looks like a mortarboard, to wear at graduation."

"That kind of headgear is uniquely Korean, I think," answered Liesl. She thought a moment. "But flat hats are depicted in Chinese paintings that represent the mythical emperors. I don't know if there's any connection. There are some odd statues with hats like this from the old Paekche kingdom, conquered in the seventh century, so they're at least that old."

"Where did the hats come from, then?"

"The ancient Koreans worshipped rocks, and it wouldn't have taken much work to chisel features and add a stone hat to a natural rock that already had a roughly human shape. Some say these standing statues represent the Matreiya, the Buddha of the Future." A bas relief of another Buddha, not far removed from its Indian origins in its details, caught our attention next. Then we all took each other's pictures in front of various monuments.

At the foot of the hill stood the Folk Art Museum. Its famous founder was in residence and ready to discuss his collection. Just as there are many Korean folk tales about tigers, they are a favorite of folk paintings as well. Tiger paintings adorned the walls, often looking more comical than fearsome. Large magpies, known in folklore to be in cahoots with tigers, perched on trees in some of the paintings. Tiger cubs appeared, too.

"Look, there's a cross-breed. That striped tiger has a spotted leopard baby among her other cubs," Elaine pointed out. Just like Flyingbird's children, I thought.

Outside again, I bought Korean vegetable pancakes at a stand, while Elaine got drinks for our group. We found a place to eat our lunch at a good vantage point to watch the *kut*, near the edge of the dance ground. Liesl spread the blanket she'd had the foresight to bring, and each of us assumed the posture we adopted for ground sitting - Liesl with her legs straight out in front, Elaine on one hip with her legs bent, and Ed and I cross-legged.

The ceremonial area was mostly a dance ground. A central pole, covered with long streamers, stood in the center, marking the space as sacred. In the back, a small temporary building contained a shrine and altar. Above the fruit-laden altar, paintings of spirits overlapped on all three walls, as if the spirits were quarrelling over such a small space. The upper row of paintings featured men with mustaches and beards, representing martial spirits, and the lower row contained paintings of women, including one centered over the altar, with two *mudangs* dressed entirely in white with peaked caps, on either side of a woman with a halo.

"The halo comes from Buddhist art," explained Liesl. "In Asia, religions aren't exclusive. The symbolism is thoroughly mixed on this altar. But don't you love that tiger?" A tiger painting on the far right side dominated the representations near it, seeming to look back at us with its glittering eyes.

Along the side of the dance ground, the orchestra assembled. Two of the large red hour-glass-shaped drums, a long stringed instrument called a *kayagum*, and two sets of brass gongs were arrayed on a large mat. The musicians wore traditional clothing, even the men, for unlike the women's ceremonies I'd seen before, this orchestra was mixed.

As the percussionists began the beat, a trumpet call was heard from behind the shrine. The player, a man dressed in traditional farmer's clothing, his white coat tied over white baggy pants, came to the front of the dance ground and began to play a shrill tune. He gave the long, thin instrument his all - his eyes bulged and his face turned red. We westerners winced at the harsh sound, but the Korean audience loved it, cheering and clapping and demanding an encore.

Finally the serious business of the day began. The presiding *manshin* appeared, wearing a red robe with multi-striped sleeves topped by a sleeveless green robe. Her hat was adorned with a string of green and red beads hanging under her chin and a yellow plume which cascaded down in back. Holding several sets of bells in her right hand, and a pair of butcher knives in her left, she began a lengthy chant in an ancient form of Korean, of which I couldn't understand a single word. At the end of each line she rang the bells vigorously.

When she finished this invocation, the *mudang* handed the bells to a blue-robed apprentice, and began to dance, slashing the knives through the air. Her dance was slow at first, and almost courtly, but soon worked into a frenzy, quicker than the eye. Suddenly she whirled herself behind the shrine, and reappeared in a trice on the other side wearing a red robe and a different hat, this one covered with multi-colored ribbons.

Assistants in blue dragged three large *onggi* pots into the clearing as the *mudang* continued to leap and prance. Two jars were placed beside each other and a third was balanced on top, making a tower. Another assistant brought the two large knives, perhaps four inches broad, now bound firmly together with white cloth with the blades parallel and a few inches apart.

The *mudang* slowed her dance and reached for the pair of knives. With perspiration making droplets on her face and her eyes looking nowhere, she pressed the knives to her ears, lips, and tongue, and then against her legs, drawing a little blood to show that the knives were sharp. Picking up a trident, she cavorted around the stage again, while the drums beat and the helpers chanted. The large knives were placed on top of the tower of pots with the sharp edges upward, and the *mudang* took off her shoes and socks. The blue-robed acolytes helped her ascend the tower to stand on the knife blades.

Barefooted, the *manshin* danced on the knife blades, while the audience held its collective breath. Even the drums became silent as she sang her final chant, giving divinations for the village, still standing on the knives.

With a crash of cymbals, the *mudang* was helped down from her pottery tower and gulped *makkolli* from a brass bowl. She showed her uncut feet to the astounded crowd.

"That was quite a performance," said Ed. "I wonder how it's done. Do you think they switched sharp knives for dull ones?"

"Cynic," I said. "Don't you believe the spirits protected her?"

"Do you?" asked Ed in surprise.

"Let's say I just get caught up in the event. But I'm not sure it's trickery. Unexplained things do happen."

It was audience participation time, and the orchestra began again. I had noticed a little old Korean woman staring at me across the way. She now came over and beckoned for me to dance. Taking both my hands, the crone whirled me around, urging me to dance faster and faster.

59

Flyingbird sat on a mat outside her double-hearthed house, her ancient gnarled hands folded in her lap. Wisps of white hair escaped from the jade bird pin that held her bushy waves on the nape of her neck.

"What was it you wished for as you rubbed your amber pendant, Great-grandmother Flyingbird?" asked a little girl with wavy black hair and small shining eyes.

"I wished to see my Spirit Bird again before I go to the spirit world forever. Look up at our village pole and see if she has arrived."

"There's a yellow bird with a crest on its head, and a tail with long feathers," replied the child.

"That's the right bird, Sunbeam. Beckon her here."

I felt sad that Flyingbird was losing her sight, and couldn't see as far away as the top of the pole. I flew down and perched beside Flyingbird's song stick. The song stick was completely covered with pictures and signs to remind the singer of the many special events in Flyingbird's life.

"Tweet," I said to call attention to myself.

"Ah, my Spirit Bird," said Flyingbird, her dark eyes lighting up. She looked me over critically. "You're the same as ever. Your plumage is as yellow and your voice as sweet. You don't age a bit. You don't belong to time. You haven't met Sunbeam, my great-grand-daughter, Sunshine's granddaughter and Yellowbird's daughter."

"Sunbeam is in line to be leader," Flyingbird told me. "She's learning the songs. She has memorized the songs of the first founders, and she knows the song about stealing the girls from other villages. She knows the song of the boat trip to find wives for Sandcrab and Clam, and the songs about expeditions to Whitehead Mountain. She can sing the song about saving the bear, one about killing the tiger, and another about bringing pigs, dogs, and chickens to Rock Shrine Village and from there to Bird Mountain Village. Flyingbird looked at the stick, reminded of her eventful life.

"You've had such an exciting life, Great-grandmother. Hardly anybody gets to travel as much as you have. Which was your favorite adventure?" pestered Sunbeam.

"I don't know. I've had a good life. The Hearth Spirit blessed me, and my Spirit Bird protected me from harm. Two loving husbands and four lively children were given to me. It hurt my heart to lose your grandmother Sunshine to the Sea Goddess, when your mother Yellowbird was not yet grown. The Sea Goddess gave back Yellowbird, when her spirit was thrown into the sea, but she took Sunshine later. My precious

Shining Eyes is still with me, reminding me of Tigertail. Your mother and Shining Eyes' five daughters have been such a comfort to me. And you are a delight to me too." Flyingbird gave Sunbeam a hug, and Sunbeam rubbed her nose on Flyingbird's age-thinned cheek.

"Littlebear and Straight Hair have made the long trip from Rock Shrine Village to see me one last time. And they're not so young themselves! I treasure all my dear ones, and all my adventures. How could I choose?"

"I know my favorite. It's in the song about Sister Bear."

"Why don't you sing it now, to show me you have it all exactly memorized."

Sunbeam picked up the song stick and ran her fingers down it until she came to the carving of a bear. The bear stood on its hind legs and waved its hands like a person. Standing beside the stick, Sunbeam began to sing.

"I was just a child
in Bird Mountain Village
playing on the sands,
looking in the tide pools,
racing my cousin along the beach."

"Happy the child, happy the bear," sang Flyingbird.

"And then one day
My grandfather came out of the forest
with White Uncle and Clam,
carrying a small she-bear."

"Happy the child, happy the bear."

"The bear was my sister.
We tumbled together-
on the sands, in the water, and
in the house.
We loved each other.

"Sister Bear copied everything I did
and had the best manners
in Bird Mountain Village.

"She slept her first winter
in her bear way,

and I went on a boat trip
with some of the villagers.

"Our first destination
was Shell Island Village.
I watched the villagers
kill a bear, and eat it.
I worried for Sister Bear.

"The next year, it was our village's turn
to host the Bear Festival.
I could not let my village
kill Sister Bear.
We ran away, Sister Bear and I.
Bigbear came too,
so did the Spirit Bird.

"The Spirit Bird
found Tigertail,
and Sister Bear helped
take him to the village.

"Sister Bear was allowed
to go back to the mountain,
back to her cave,
but we have seen her
many times.
Sometimes she brings
her cubs
to play with our children.

"The spirit of Sister Bear
will be one of the village ancestors
The love of that bear
will always be with me."

"Happy the child, happy the bear," Flyingbird finished the refrain.

A crowd had gathered around to enjoy the song, which was the
favorite of the village children. They all had stories of how and when
they had seen Sister Bear and her offspring.

"Is this your Spirit Bird?" asked one of the small boys, noticing me
beside the song stick.

"She came for my final ceremony," said Flyingbird.

Her words squeezed my heart, and I felt tears in my eyes.

"What's the best thing your Spirit Bird did?" asked a brown-haired child.

"She was always there when I needed her, but most important was the way this bird helped me make the right decisions. She showed me how to look beyond surface differences, and to respond to people's hearts. And she gave me this amber, which has protected me even when she couldn't be here herself."

Flyingbird let the children see the three treasures she wore on a cord - the smoky topaz crystal her father found the day she was born, the pearl from Cockleshell, and the amber teardrop. The jade from her sister-in-law Moonbeam held her hair on the back of her neck, and her other treasures - the bone needle and obsidian knife, making six amulets altogether - were still kept in her private pouch. One of the village puppies nosed over to lick the amulet. Flyingbird picked him up and stroked his curly tail.

"This is about the twentieth descendant of the dogs that Straight Hair and Littlebear brought us from Rock Shrine Village. That village was so amazed at the six treasures we brought back from our quest to Whitehead Mountain! And the chickens and pigs are doing well, too. Nobody has counted their generations!"

The next morning at sun-up, Flyingbird could barely walk. Sunbeam helped her out of her house for the morning ceremony.

"It's time to say good-bye," she said, in a trembly voice but with a firm spirit. "It's sad to leave you all, but there are many people I love who are already in the spirit world. You must each come by and tell me your messages for them. Then I will be prepared to go. Sunbeam will come first."

Flyingbird gestured for Sunbeam to sit beside her.

"Don't go, Great-grandmother!" Sunbeam pleaded. "I love you!"

"You already know most of the songs. Shining Eyes is the leader, now that she has found her sixth amulet, and you will learn more from her. When the time comes, Shining Eyes will tattoo your mouth for you, and make it a beautiful blue. And someday, you will have daughters and granddaughters. Remember to tell them of me."

After everyone had come by, Flyingbird sat with Shining Eyes, Littlebear, and Straight Hair.

"Don't be sad, children of Tigertail and Bigbear. We will meet again in the Spirit World. You all have brought me joy, and so have your children and grandchildren. Not many people live as many seasons as I have. I only wish I could say good-bye to Sister Bear. But I suppose she's gone to the Spirit World ahead of me."

Boats with twelve sticks were sent out to all the villages along the Sunrise Sea to tell them the day of the coming burial. Two grandsons went over the mountain to tell Flyingbird's descendants in Rock Shrine Village to come, too.

Shining Eyes washed her mother's body with seawater, and Sunshine's daughter Yellowbird helped dress Flyingbird for her last trip to the spirit world. Flyingbird's best black and white embroidered robe was wrapped around her, and the two women lay all her possessions beside her. The small yellow and white basket that Pebble had made so many autumns ago held bracelets and earrings made of various kinds of rocks and shells collected on the beach. One of Flyingbird's favorites had been made for her by Sunbeam, with pretty pebbles of various colors rubbed to roundness by the Sea Goddess.

Under her robe, they put Flyingbird's woven golden belt that told the story of her ancestry, and the deer-ears pouch with a polished bone needle and a sharp obsidian knife. Around her neck were her other treasures - quartz, pearl, and amber. The jade bird held her hair at her neck. Her gourd bowl was laid out, with its carved dipping stick. Only the song stick would remain in the village, so that her descendants would remember her life.

When the twelve days had passed, and the mourners were assembled in Bird Mountain Village, Straight Hair, Littlebear and the younger sons of the village dug a long narrow pit in the cemetery, in a space between Bigbear and Tigertail. Before the sun was up, Flyingbird's body and all her belongings were wrapped in her sleeping mat, and placed on the bottom of the pit.

Sunbeam, Yellowbird, and Shining Eyes sang the songs of Flyingbird's life at the sun-up ceremony. Then a long line formed, from the oldest to the youngest person. As each of them walked by the open grave to say good-bye, each dropped a small tribute to Flyingbird. The men brought fishhooks, arrowheads, or knives, and the women brought pieces of cloth, baskets, and small pots. Sunbeam left a tiny jar with loop handles that Flyingbird had helped her make. It contained some of her tears for her great-grandmother.

While the procession went by, Shining Eyes beat the drum in the usual rhythm, her eyes shiny this time with tears.

A brown she-bear watched from the edge of the woods, and at the end of the procession, waved its paws in a gesture of farewell.

I dropped a yellow feather into the grave.

60

The old woman I danced with led me back to my place beside Ed.

"I enjoyed the dance," she said to me. "I like a girl with spirit."

I felt dazed and bereaved, my mind still at Flyingbird's funeral, but I managed to thank her with a smile. I couldn't talk as we picked up our things to leave.

On the bus going back, Ed asked me about my dancing. He wondered if that was related to the changes he saw in me.

"You seem to go into real trances. What was that you said before, about a prehistoric bird? Was that a joke?"

"I don't know if it's trancing. I feel like I'm in another time as well as another place. I've seen the whole life of a prehistoric woman. She was named Flyingbird, for the yellow bird I became when I was there. I was her spirit protector. I was there when she was born, and I've just attended her funeral. So I suppose this is the end of these visits - unless one of her descendants draws me back." I smiled. "No, I don't mean that. It was just a long techni-color dream."

Ed wanted to hear more about my "visions," so I told him, and Elaine and Liesl, about Flyingbird's life on the long ride back to Seoul. As I told her life story, I began to realize that Flyingbird was *my* protector, rather than I hers. She was free-spirited while I was inhibited, independent while I was dependent. She was generous with her love, while I imposed conditions. The person I now wanted to be was neither Clara the American nor Clara the Korean, but Flyingbird, with the wind in her hair.

At last the weather was warm enough to reopen the dig. Ed still had a few days of vacation left, and he was eager to see the dig in progress. I think he wanted to keep an eye on Ki-dok, too, in case he had been my lover.

My crew and I began excavating the last two-meter square in our random sample. I hoped we would make one more important find to justify random sampling to Ki-dok and Professor Lee. As before, the dry sand slumped into the square annoyingly, with only a few finds to break the tedium.

The first artifact we found was a tiny jar, with small loop handles on the shoulders. I brushed it off and passed it around for the crew to admire. It looked like a child's toy.

"It must have gotten lost in the sand," guessed one of the students.

Digging farther, a whole cache of objects came to light - small pots of several kinds, arrowheads, fishhooks, knives. The edges of the cache were unclear in two directions, but sharply defined on the shorter sides.

"It looks like a long, narrow pit," observed Ki-dok, "with these objects mounded in the middle."

The students troweled the sand away slowly. After the heap of stone and bone tools and small pottery pieces had been removed, they reached a rounded bone, like a skull. Was it a burial? I took over, brushing the sand off slowly. Gradually the forehead was revealed, and then the eye sockets.

"This *is* a burial!"

I called to Ki-dok to come and see. Burials are very rare in the Korean neolithic. Work stopped everywhere else so that the whole crew could watch the unearthing of the grave. Only a few of the largest bones were left, but it was clear that the body had been interred in an extended position in a long narrow grave, with the objects deposited on top. There was no trace of a coffin.

As we slowly cleared away the dirt, more objects appeared. On the skeleton's chest lay a crystal of smoky topaz, a pearl, and a teardrop-shaped amber piece. The amber was cloudy with age, but it gave me the shivers to see it there. At the waist we found a tiny obsidian knife, and a highly polished bone needle. After drawing and photographing this level, the crew removed the bones and put them into a labeled box. The best find of all was under the skull - a delicately carved jade bird.

"This looks like a Chinese-style carving, not Korean," said Ki-dok. "And jade of this pale yellowish color is only found in Manchuria. There must have been long distance trade!"

"We've found the grave of the village leader," said Hwang-ok. "He had a rich burial."

"Nothing like this has ever been found before," added Ki-dok. "We'll always use random sampling after this!"

"You can't always count on such spectacular results," I warned, but I felt rather smugly that the method was vindicated. I tried to keep Flyingbird out of my thoughts, but she crowded me insistently. What about the amber? Was she then real? Impossible. Just coincidence. The amber in the grave was cloudy, showing its great age. I couldn't tell if it held an insect.

As the crew washed and catalogued the artifacts that evening, Ki-dok remarked on the similarity of the shape of the amber bead from the grave and my remaining one, which I still wore on the gold chain he gave me.

"This man had the twin of your amber bead, except that it has an ant in it, and yours has a spider. Amber must have belonged to men in

232

neolithic times. It is found on men's clothing in the Yi dynasty, so why not in the neolithic?"

"What makes you think the skeleton is male?" asked Ed. "Was enough of the pelvis left to be sure?"

"I'm not a specialist in human bones. We won't know until they've been studied. But it must have been a man, because he had such a rich burial. He was surely a great chief."

I smiled, thinking of the blue-mouthed women of Bird Mountain Village.

"Couldn't there have been women leaders?" I asked.

"That would be unnatural," replied Ki-dok. "If this burial is a woman, she must be the wife of the leader."

I raised my eyebrows. That wasn't logic, it was a statement of belief! But for once I didn't argue. How could I explain about Flyingbird and Bird Mountain Village?

Ed and I walked on the beach, leaving a long row of tracks in the sand.

"You have many amazing talents," he said, looking at me out of the corner of his eye. "Do you think you could have traversed time? Did Flyingbird exist?"

"I could explain everything but the amber as coincidence, or informed guessing. It's so strange that a piece like my lost amber button should turn up here, aged by seven thousand years, or so. It can't be! Still, it's hard to believe that Flyingbird came completely from my imagination. I learned a lot from her, things I couldn't have known on my own. She was entirely accepting of people the way they were. I was taught to sit in judgment - not for people's looks, or their ethnicity, but for more subtle things: their manners, their clothes, their way of speaking. It was inclusive of me, this teaching, but I was taught to recognize 'our kind of people'. Although 'our kind' was an intellectual construct, not an ethnic one, it's none the less exclusive for that. I'd like to believe Flyingbird existed and that I had a part in her life."

"I want to be part of your life. Marry me, Clara, and never run off again. I missed you every single day."

"What you see is what you get," I told him. "I'm going to be an archaeologist. You aren't planning to change me, if I agree to be trapped in your bird cage called marriage?" I didn't want to be sweet-talked into a bad decision.

"We can manage both our careers."

"Two careers are only part of the problem. You once said to me - do you remember? - 'Clara, you have a mirror. You know you have an Asian face.' The funny thing is, I *didn't* know. That wasn't what I saw in the mirror. I saw instead an almost-white-girl, with wavy walnut hair, only a little different around the eyes. It never occurred to me that you called me 'Jade Princess' because you *focused* on the Asian eyes. Now I know that I'll always look Asian. And, like Tigertail's, so will my children."

"It's my favorite look, Jade Princess."

"But what about your family? Your mother's letter was charming and friendly. She says she hadn't thought it through, and that character is what's important. I don't know if she's truly reconciled though. I wouldn't want her to take her uncertainty out on my children."

"Mother wants to get to know you better. I've told her you're very special. But you've changed in Korea."

"In what ways?"

"You're more sure of yourself. Less dependent. In a way your self-assurance makes me feel left out."

"If you love the 'fraidy cat that I used to be, I'm sorry. She's gone. I came here as a coward, running away from you, running away from my Asianness, running away from conflict of any kind. But this year in Korea turned out to be a quest instead of an escape. I searched for the neolithic and found not just a whole village, complete with house floors, refuse, and a burial, but a living people; I searched for my Koreanness and found an American with a Korean face. I searched for independence - and learned that it must be coupled with love, and adventure with security - things I wished for Flyingbird at her birth, without realizing I wished them for myself. It is not enough to be 'strong and swift and wise and beautiful' or even enough to be courageous and persistent. You have to have people to share your life with. I know that much, but I still have a lot to learn, and you may find me difficult. I'm not through trying my wings."

"My mother didn't know what she was stirring up," Ed teased.

"Please take me seriously. Your mother deserves a round of applause for propelling me out of my middle-class nest. I was protected like a China doll, wrapped in layers of silk and stored in a closet."

"You're so easily hurt, Clara. It makes everyone want to protect you."

"I'm getting tougher. I don't want you to protect me from life. When I first came to Korea, I was overprotected here, too. Elaine, and Liesl, Professor Lee, Dong-su and Ki-dok all shielded me from the culture one way or another. But by the time my parents came, I was strong enough, and knowledgeable enough to shield *them*. That felt great. I want to *use* the knowledge I've gained, not get stifled in silk again. I need to make my own mistakes."

"The new Clara is even better than the old one. I hope you haven't outgrown *me*."

"You seem to be holding your own. But please don't press me for a decision."

"Okay, let's see how things work out."

"One more thing I have to know, now that an amber button has turned up. Do you know what your year sign is?"

"The Year of the Horse. Elaine tipped me off that that would be in my favor. Looks like in the Asian scheme of things we're just a pair of domesticated animals. Good thing I've always liked lambs."

My hair was blowing in the breeze, and Ed tucked a stray strand behind my ear.

"Oh, I almost forgot, I brought you a present," said Ed, producing a bulky parcel wrapped in newspaper from his bulging jacket pocket.

"Elaine says that when you're asking a favor, you should bring a gift. Do you like the gift-wrapping?"

"Yesterday's *Hanguk Ilbo*. So thoughtful."

I began tearing off the newspaper carelessly. A yellow wing was revealed, and talons wrapped around a sun disk. I looked at Ed in surprise.

"Maybe you do know how much Flyingbird meant to me. Do you also understand how mixed it is to be Asian-American? Flyingbird taught me that I have to be both, not choose one or the other."

I peeled off the rest of the paper slowly, tantalizing myself until the elegant shape of the whole carving was revealed. Holding my gift with both hands, I turned it to admire from all sides. The golden bird was as glorious as I'd remembered.

"Ed. . . I don't know what to say! It's perfect. It's . . . it's me as the Spirit Bird. How did you find it? How did you know?"

He gave me a peck on the nose. "If you could forgive the cliché, I guess you could say - a little bird told me."

Author's Notes

I am an archaeologist who studies both Korea and China, hence the prehistoric story is based on the actual archaeological discovers of Korea and northeastern China. However, there are a few exceptions.

No such burial as Flyingbird's has ever been found. Neolithic burials are very scarce in Korea, possibly because the acidic soil consumes bones relatively rapidly. Nor has any amber been found in Neolithic contexts. The amber and the burial were necessary for the story.

The jade bird on the cover is from China some 3000 years later than the events in the book. It was just too beautiful a depiction of the Sprit Bird for me to pass up. Most other material evidence described is factual.

One way to read about the real archaeology is through my books, *The Archaeology of Korea* (1993, Cambridge University Press), and *The Archaeology of Northeast China* (1995, Routledge). Particular sites you will recognize in the novel are Osanni, Tongsamdong, Sopohang, and Amsadong in Korea, and Houwa in China. These sites have been excavated by Korean and Chinese archaeologists, who are not to blame for my interpretations, or the way I have peopled the sites. I leave the fun of ferreting out the details of the sites to you, the avid archaeological reader.

The East Coast people are modeled after the Ainu, variously called "Caucasian" (surely a misnomer) and PaleoAsiatic. They are not Mongoloid. The Ainu have lived in northern Japan since the beginning of written records. I have used the ethnographic record to describe the prehistoric people. There is no reason they couldn't have lived on the east coast of Korea, but there is no evidence that they did, especially since burial data are scarce. The people of "Rock Shrine Village" are described as Mongoloids, partly because the pottery of the early Neolithic in Korea suggests a divide between the peoples of eastern Korea and Japan on the one hand, and inhabitants of western Korea and China on the other, and partly because for the story I needed physical differences in prehistoric times as well as in the present.

As for the descriptions of 20th Century Korea, they are based on my own observations during many years of fieldwork and visiting in Korea, and on reading the work of my colleagues in anthropology. I particularly want to thank Laurel Kendall for her lively descriptions of mudangs, and for letting me use her evocative onomatopeia of the way the drums sound. I hope it is obvious that, like Clara, I love Korea but sometimes find it mysterious. The best that I could wish for you is that you will be able to go and visit yourself.

Quick Order Form

✉ ***Postal orders:***

RKLOG Press
5878 S. Dry Creek Court
Littleton, CO 80121-1709

Name: _____

Address: _____

City: _____ **State:** _____ **Zip:** _____

Telephone: _____

e-mail: _____

____ Book(s) at $15.95 each $ _____

    Plus shipping ($4.00 for first book,
    $2.00 for each additional book) $ _____

                           TOTAL $ _____

Make check or money order payable to **RKLOG Press**

Quick Order Form

📧   *Postal orders*:

     RKLOG Press
5878 S. Dry Creek Court
Littleton, CO 80121-1709

Name: _____

Address: _____

City: _____ **State:** _____ **Zip:** _____

Telephone: _____

e-mail: _____

_____ Book(s) at $15.95 each $ _____

     Plus shipping ($4.00 for first book,
     $2.00 for each additional book) $ _____

                TOTAL $ _____

Make check or money order payable to **RKLOG Press**

Quick Order Form

✉   *Postal orders*:

RKLOG Press
5878 S. Dry Creek Court
Littleton, CO 80121-1709

Name: _____

Address: _____

City: _____ State: _____ Zip: _____

Telephone: _____

e-mail: _____

_____ Book(s) at $15.95 each $ _____

     Plus shipping ($4.00 for first book,
     $2.00 for each additional book) $ _____

                 TOTAL $ _____

Make check or money order payable to **RKLOG Press**

Quick Order Form

☑ *Postal orders*:

◤RKLOG Press, LLC
5878 S. Dry Creek Court
Littleton, CO 80121-1709

Name: _____

Address: _____

City: _____ **State:** _____ **Zip:** _____

Telephone: _____

e-mail: _____

_____ Book(s) at $15.95 each $ _____

Plus shipping ($4.00 for first book,
$2.00 for each additional book) $ _____

TOTAL $ _____

Make check or money order payable to **RKLOG Press, LLC**

Quick Order Form

 **Postal orders:**

RKLOG Press
5878 S. Dry Creek Court
Littleton, CO 80121-1709

Name: _____

Address: _____

City: _____ **State:** ____ **Zip:** _____

Telephone: _____

e-mail: _____

____ Book(s) at \$15.95 each $ _____

Plus shipping (\$4.00 for first book,
\$2.00 for each additional book) $ _____

                                    TOTAL $ _____

*Make check or money order payable to **RKLOG Press***